TOP NOTCH

A MIA MURPHY MYSTERY

STEPHANIE ROWE

COPYRIGHT

coincidental and not intended by the author or the artist. There are excerpts from other books by the author in the back of the book.

READER BUZZ

companion that I've ever read! I absolutely cannot wait until we get the third book!" Five-star Goodreads Review (Danielle B.)

"I love this book, this series and this author!" Five-star Goodreads Review (Riding Reviewer)

CHAPTER 1

FRIDAY NIGHT WAS the kind of dark that was every assassin's dream, which meant that it wasn't exactly the perfect weekend-starter for me.

The rain was hammering so loudly on the metal roof of my marina that even an entire army of drug dealers firing assault weapons could have snuck up on me without me hearing them.

I'd been outside checking for assassins for almost twenty minutes, which was more than enough time to get absolutely drenched, thoroughly chilled, a little freaked out, and up to my ankles in mud and puddles.

And yet, I couldn't remember the last time I'd been so happy. If ever.

Because freedom, friends, and a home will do that for a girl.

Whistling cheerfully, I sloshed through the flooded parking lot behind the marina, finishing up my nightly pre-bedtime property check for assassins. As had been the case for the prior four nights since I'd arrived in Bass Derby, Maine, there were no professional killers lying in wait to pop me.

Witness protection? Who needs witness protection? Hah. No one would bother to follow me to this small, lakeside town.

Sure, I'd had a couple amateur murderers pointing guns at my face this week, but I was alive and they were in jail, so yay for me. More importantly, they'd had nothing to do with my ex-husband's drug empire, the one I'd spied on for two years and then testified against, in a move that had made me all sorts of popular with his slightly bitter and vengeful family. My former in-laws hadn't followed me to Bass Derby (so far), so I was calling my decision to move here a win.

Equally delighted to be traipsing around in a cold downpour was King Tut, my massive rescued/purloined Maine Coon cat. He was trotting happily beside me, his ears nearly flattened to the side of his head from the rain. His black coat was dripping, his gray mane was soaked, and he looked thrilled with life.

I grinned down at him as we rounded the corner on the south end of the deck that stretched across the entire front of the marina. "Pretty great, right?"

He didn't answer me.

Instead, he froze in place, one paw raised mid-step. His body went stiff. His tail went still, except for a tiny flick at the end, and the fur on his back went up, his gaze fixed on the latticework lining the backside of the deck.

I shined my flashlight in the direction he was looking, and I saw a hole in the latticework that I hadn't noticed before. A gap big enough for a human.

Alarm shot through me, and the hair on the back of my neck stood up. Had that been there since I'd moved in? Or had someone made that hole tonight?

Fear started slithering down my spine, and I scowled. I was so over being scared. "I'm sure it's fine," I said aloud. "What are the odds that someone came here to kill me?"

Low. The odds were super low.

But not zero.

Which meant I needed to check it out. Discovering an assassin while I was awake and only a few feet from my car gave me marginally better survival odds than being asleep in my bed when the assassin came to visit.

When it came to death, I needed any additional edge I could squeeze out. "King Tut, if someone explodes out of there with a gun, you kill him."

My kitty cat ignored me. In fact, he still hadn't moved from his stiff-legged, puffed-out-fur stance, which was really unnerving. Was he in predator or defender mode? I really hoped there was some creepy crawly under there that King Tut was going to have for dinner, and not an assassin who was going to dump my precious body in the beautiful lake I now lived on.

I took a breath. An assassin hired to kill me wouldn't bother to lie in wait. I had no skills. They'd just walk up, pop me in the head, and collect their paycheck. So it was probably fine. If it wasn't, I'd be dead already.

But I still had to check. Because, you know, in case I was wrong.

"It'll be fine. I'm very good at evading death." My voice sounded confident, but my heart started pounding as I unwound the hairdryer that I'd had draped across my chest like a Miss America sash.

Luck had taught me that I was very skilled at defending myself with corded projectiles, so I'd decided to lean into that discovery, instead of being embarrassed by it.

Self-defense was important, right?

I wound the cord around my hand, and swung the hairdryer to test the balance.

Yep, good.

Although I'd also used a nail gun and an electric pencil sharpener as weapons, my first choice was the hairdryer. It was just the right weight for the perfect tradeoff of maneuverability and impact potential. Plus, it was innocent-looking, so surprise was always on my side.

Gripping the cord tightly, I crouched down and shined my light under the deck, keeping my weight balanced so I could leap up and bolt for my car if I needed to. I might be good with a hairdryer, but flight was still my favorite option.

Me? Non-confrontational when it came to violence? Heck, yeah!

The beam illuminated an old wooden barrel on its side, tucked up close to the entrance, blocking my view under the rest of the deck. It was wet from the rain, making the beam of the flashlight reflect back at me.

I grimaced and bent lower, angling my light to the sides to try to see around the barrel. There were several cement blocks, old boards, a couple canoe paddles, a half-buried keg, and other abandoned junk that was impossible to identify in the dark night.

What I could tell, however, was that there was plenty of space for a hit man to squeeze past the barrel and retreat into the shadowy recesses of the 100-ish-foot-long deck. The puddles obscured any possible footprints, leaving me with no way to tell if someone had recently crawled under there.

I tried to listen for movement, but all I could hear was the hammering of the rain on the wooden deck slats, against the metal roof of the marina maintenance building, and into the puddles surrounding me.

Short of crawling through the mud to the back of the deck, I had no way of knowing if a professional killer was hiding under there in waterproof pants, waiting for me to nod off to sleep.

Crawling under there didn't feel like the best choice at this time.

Or any time, for that matter.

King Tut crept past me and slithered past the keg. His feet disappeared into the puddles, but he didn't make so much as a ripple, despite his snowshoe-sized paws. He suddenly lifted his head, his body tense as he stared into the dark underbelly of the deck. He went utterly still again, except for the twitching of the tip of his tail.

I knew that stance. He was about to launch. Fear shot through me. "Wait, don't—"

He hissed and shot under the deck and out of sight. I could

hear scuffling and yowling. And…was that a curse? Had someone just *cursed?* The hair on my arms stood up—

A hand came down on my shoulder. "Mia."

I screamed and leapt up, cracking the back of my head on the underside of the deck. I tried to swing the hairdryer, but it caught on the keg and nearly ripped my arm out of my shoulder.

Crap!

Being the quick-thinking pivoter that I am, I hurled the flash-light at my assailant and ran for my car as I tried to get my keys out of my pocket—

"Mia! It's me!"

"Hattie?" I stumbled to a stop and whirled around.

The silhouette of Hattie Lawless, the seventy-something race car driver who leased space in the marina for her local eatery, Hattie's Café, loomed in the darkness. She held up her hands. "It's just me. Relax."

"Relax? I've had four people try to kill me recently." I put my hands on my knees, bending over as I tried to catch my breath. "I thought we decided you weren't going to surprise me like that anymore."

King Tut shot out from under the deck and sprinted past me into the marina store, carrying something in his mouth. A dead animal? Crud. I hoped he didn't put it in my bed. But yay for a dead animal and not a murderer. Unless it was my potential murderer's hand. King Tut could definitely take off an unsuspecting appendage.

He was handy like that.

"We didn't agree I wouldn't surprise you." Hattie sloshed through the puddles as she headed toward me. "We agreed you wouldn't try to kill me if I did. There's a difference, and I'm pretty sure that hurling a metal flashlight and a hairdryer at my head violates our pact."

"I don't think that's what our agreement was, and you're well aware that I'm a little jumpy when people sneak up on me." I'd kept my pickpocketing, con-artist childhood hidden from Hattie, but she'd recognized me from the news as the ex-wife of Stanley Herrera, drug kingpin.

I'd spent two very stressful years as a spy for the FBI gathering evidence on him, and now that he was in prison, I was trying to pretend I had a chance at a normal life. I was on day five as the new owner of the Eagle's Nest Marina in Bass Derby, Maine, seizing my chance for the friends, home, and the life I'd never had.

So far, Hattie and my mail carrier, Lucy Grande, had helped with the friend goal. The law-abiding life? Not so much. Murder will do that. But I was hoping day five would be the charm. Or I had been, until Hattie had snuck up on me, mostly because I couldn't think of a single innocuous reason for her to be in my parking lot at midnight in the middle of a storm.

She held out my flashlight. "Either way, you have terrible aim. My head thanks you."

"I have great aim when it counts." Like when an assassin, or a hot police officer (oops), was sneaking up on me. I tucked the flashlight in my pocket, no longer needed now that we were under the floodlights from the marina. "What's up?" My hairdryer was still caught in the keg, which made me feel a little naked, and not in a good way.

"We have a situation," Hattie stated.

"We do?" I tensed. We'd had a lot of situations in the last few days, but I'd thought they were over. "What happened?"

"I'll tell you on the way. Hop in." She pointed at her truck, which was idling, headlights on, in my parking lot. Attached to her truck was a boat trailer, which was half-submerged in the lake. Lucy was strapping a small, worn-out motorboat to the metal struts.

Apparently, they'd been busy while I'd been sneaking around my property checking for professional killers. Good to know that the rain on my metal roof could drown out that much noise. That made me feel safe.

Lucy waved enthusiastically. I narrowed my eyes in suspicion, but waved back, because that's what newbie friends did.

In another month, when our friendships were secure, I'd probably glare at them suspiciously.

But for now, she got a wave, but I was still suspicious.

They were both way too cheerful for being in my parking lot in a storm in the middle of the night. Something was definitely up. "Is that my boat on your trailer?"

"Yes. Mine is currently unavailable. Let's go." Hattie started heading toward the truck.

"Unavailable? What does that mean?"

"It was there one night when I went to bed, and gone in the morning."

I stared at her. "Stolen? Who would steal a little boat?"

She raised her brows. "It's an extremely cool boat. Worth stealing. However, I imagine it just got free and drifted away. I'm still searching the coves on Diamond Lake. I'm sure it'll turn up."

I put my hands on my hips and made no attempt to move. "My boat has a leak. It's been sinking all week."

Hattie sighed and turned to face me. It was raining so hard that her jacket was glistening, and her cheeks looked like they were coated in glass. "The boat's not sinking. It just has a month's worth of rain in it, because you haven't bailed it out. It'll be fine."

I folded my arms over my chest. "Fine for what, exactly?" I might have known Hattie for less than a week, but I already knew better than to blindly trust any of her plans.

Hattie set her hands on her hips, looking impatient. "A little trip to Dead Man's Pond."

Going to a place called Dead Man's Pond at night during a storm in a sinking boat sounded like a fantastic idea. "Why would we be doing that?"

Her eyelashes fluttered as the rain hammered them. "We're going to rescue some old ladies."

"Seriously?" I wasn't sure I believed her. Hattie knew there was no chance I'd refuse to help rescue some senior citizens from a storm. "Who needs rescuing?"

"You remember Bootsy Jones and Shirley Kincaid?"

"Of course I remember them." Bootsy and Shirley were part of a group of senior quilters-for-hire called the Seam Rippers. Last I'd seen them, they were dressed up in leather, blasting rap music, and drinking margaritas. They were absolute spitfires, and there was no way I could snuggle down and sleep while they were stranded somewhere. *If* they really were stranded. "Why are they out on the lake? Were they camping?"

Maybe they weren't really in trouble. Maybe this was a guise for going out drinking with the girls…or something more nefarious that Hattie was hiding from me.

She sighed. "They were hunting a ghost."

I stared at her. "Ghost? Did you just say *ghost?*"

Hattie nodded. "The ghost of the man that Dead Man's Pond was named after a hundred years ago. His name was Jack Brown, but the locals affectionately called him Jack the Ripper."

Jack the Ripper? Because that was a charming, innocuous nickname. "Was he a serial killer?"

"It's possible, but never proven."

I looked over at Lucy as she jogged up. "Is she serious?"

"Totally. It was never proven." She grinned. "According to Hattie, the Seam Rippers got hired to make a fundraiser quilt for the Halloween Fest in October, so a few of them decided they needed to get in the spirit. It's difficult to channel proper Halloween mojo when it's Memorial Day."

Ohh… I could see where this was heading. "They decided to commune with a serial killer's ghost?"

"It's for Halloween," Lucy said, with just a wee bit of sarcasm that my highly tuned senses were able to pick up. "What good are *friendly* ghosts?"

"No good," I agreed, with equally subtle sarcasm. "Deep, debilitating terror is the only way to channel Halloween. Or even just everyday living. Fear is such a great motivator."

"Right?" Hattie nodded. "See, Lucy? Mia gets it."

Lucy raised her brows at me. "Does she?"

I grinned at her wise skepticism. "Of course. I love fear. It's super fun."

"You young'uns are such wimps. You're lucky to have me around to toughen you up." Hattie gestured impatiently. "They hired a ghost whisperer from Portland to take them out tonight. Bootsy texted that they're stranded. They've been out there for hours, but they're running out of tequila, so Bootsy called for a rescue."

Lucy and I exchanged knowing glances.

"So, basically, they waited until midnight to call for help because they were having too much fun until now." It wasn't surprising. I'd met the Seam Rippers. Why abandon fun if you don't need to?

"Pretty much." Hattie grinned. "When that alcohol wears off, there's going to be a boatload of very cold, very wet, close-to-death old ladies on that pond, unless we go save them."

I believed her now. Given what I knew about the Seam Rippers, it made sense. But… "You want to rescue them in a sinking, old boat? Why not call Devlin?" Devlin Hunt was a local police officer who also carried the honor of being Lake Police. He was capable, charming, and distractingly attractive. "Saving people on lakes is literally what he's paid to do."

"Why delegate when we can do it ourselves?" Hattie asked.

"A lot of reasons, actually."

Lucy tucked her hand around my elbow and leaned on my shoulder. "Come with us, Mia. It'll be fun."

"You'll be the hero that you long to be," Hattie said.

I eyed the blue-haired senior. "I don't long to be a hero." Been there. Done that. Still paying the price. Heroism was extremely overrated.

"Yeah, me either, but sometimes we get what we get." She started toward her truck, sloshing through the puddles that were getting deeper by the moment. "Let's do this. The girls are waiting."

I glanced at Lucy. "You realize there's no way this little adventure is going to turn out fine, right?"

She grinned, despite the rain dripping off her hood onto her cheeks. "It involves Hattie. What could possibly go wrong?"

Hattie started honking her horn at us and flashing her high beams.

I sighed. "A lot. Definitely, a lot."

Lucy raised her brows. "And you'd want to miss that?"

"Yes. Absolutely." But as I said it, I started walking toward Hattie's truck. Because who was I kidding? I totally wanted to go. Lucy and Hattie were already becoming friends, and, although I was committed to a law-abiding life, I'd never been able to shake the need for adventure that had been trained into me by my infamous, con-artist mom, Tatum Murphy.

Lucy laughed. "Me, too." She slung her arm over my shoulder. "Have I told you how happy I am that you moved to Bass Derby?"

I pulled open the door as Hattie yelled at us to hurry up. "I am, too." I paused before climbing into the truck. "One promise, though."

Hattie raised her brows as Lucy squeezed into the back seat. "What's that?"

"No murder. No dead bodies. Nothing illegal." That last one was critical. I was desperate to leave the world of crime far behind me.

Hattie grinned. "That's an easy one. Nothing fun like that is on the agenda. A murder would be great though, right?"

"No!" Lucy and I spoke at the same time.

I shook my head as I climbed in. "What's wrong with you, Hattie? Seriously."

"Nothing. I'm flawlessly fantastic. As always."

Before I got the door closed, a furry black shape shot through the open door and into the cab, landing with bared claws and twenty-five pounds of soaking wet fur in my lap.

Hattie grinned. "See? Even King Tut wants to go."

I grimaced as his claws dug into my thighs. "Well, he can't come. It'll be too dangerous." I went to pick him up, but he let out a low, terrifying growl as he fixed his yellow eyes on me.

I decided not to pick him up.

I'd seen what the fifteen-inch daggers hidden in his fluffy paws could do to a bare hand. Would he do it to me, too? He might. That was the kind of love we had.

"Don't make him mad," Lucy whispered. "No one move."

See? Lucy also respected his claws. Probably because he'd almost decided she was dinner when they first met. The trauma was real for Lucy, apparently.

I eyed my cat. "You can't come with us."

He stared at me and growled again, daring me to force him out of the truck.

Um… He was my cat, and I loved him, but we were still sorting some things out in our relationship. One of which was apparently who was in charge.

"The animal can swim better than I can," Hattie said. "Let him come."

"What if he falls in?"

She reached over the back seat and put an orange life jacket in my hand. "It's for dogs, but it'll fit him."

"A dog life jacket?" I'd never even heard of that, but it made sense.

"Yeah. I got it as a housewarming present for you. As soon as I met King Tut, I figured he would wind up on the lake at some point, and no responsible owner takes their pet out without a life jacket. I was going to wrap it up for you, but hey, no time like the present. Welcome to Bass Derby."

My heart got a little mushy. "Aww…that is so sweet."

"It's not sweet. I just really appreciated how he terrorized the chief of police, and I want to make sure he has a lot more opportunities to do it. The more he's with us, the more chances he'll have to bring that kind of beauty into the world."

I grinned. "I do like that kind of beauty." Okay, fine, so I had a little bit of a bias against cops, even the hot ones like Devlin who were playing bodyguard for me.

"Hattie, we all know you're sweet, so give up the pretense," Lucy teased. "Mia, I was going to give you a sledgehammer as my housewarming present, but I forgot to bring it tonight. I know how you like swinging things that can kill people."

"Really?" I grinned. "You guys are the best." A life jacket for King Tut and a sledgehammer for me? They'd both nailed it. I was on day five of my new life in Bass Derby, and I already had real friends? Yay, me.

"All right, are we good, then?" Hattie asked as she revved the engine. "Off to save some old ladies from a serial killer's ghost?"

Who could turn that down? "I'm in."

Lucy grinned. "Me, too."

"King Tut?"

He flicked his tail and purred.

"Let's go, then." Hattie hit the gas as I reached for the door to close it, leaving me dangling out of the truck for a terrifying moment before I got the door yanked shut.

Yep, this was definitely going to go well. I had a good feeling about it. Really, I did. I mean, yeah, my hairdryer was stuck in the keg under my deck, leaving me unarmed and defenseless, but I doubted any assassins would strike when I was with Hattie.

So, what could possibly go wrong?

A lot.

A lot could go wrong. I was with Hattie and Lucy, after all.

But at least my cat would float, right?

So it would be fine.

CHAPTER 2

DEAD MAN'S Pond was very, very dark.

I'd thought it was dark in the trunk of a car when I was a kid, hiding out to help my mom with her next con. But *this* was the true meaning of darkness, and I wasn't sure I was delighted to have found it.

Hattie's headlights lit up the shoreline in front of her truck, and I could see the ruts of other trucks that had been there, but when I looked out across the pond, it was pitch black. Not a single house. Not even a twinkling star or a helpful moon.

Just rain.

Darkness.

And us.

"You're sure they're out there?" The same darkness that made me wish I hadn't come also made me glad I had. I could never leave Bootsy and the others out there.

"Bootsy's truck is over there." Hattie pointed to the left as she and Lucy began to walk my boat off the trailer, each of them on opposite sides. King Tut was already perched on a bench, like he was an ancient Roman king being escorted in his chariot.

As he ignored his minions, I turned and saw a beat-up pickup truck with a trailer attached to it parked by the edge of the clearing. It looked abandoned and alone, as if it had been there for years.

Hattie waded into the water. "If they took her truck, that means they probably took her boat. It's old, but it's got the shallowest hull."

"Is that good?"

"Dead Man's Pond has a lot of rocks just below the surface." Lucy was up to her knees in the water now. "It's broken so many propellers and sunk so many boats that Bass Derby banned all boats except canoes and kayaks from the lake."

I set my hands on my hips. "So, motorboats aren't allowed?"

"Correct." As she acknowledged the illegality of motorboats, Hattie gripped the edge of my motorboat and hoisted herself up over the edge, landing in the boat with impressive ease, while Lucy held it steady.

King Tut's orange life vest was the only bright thing in the night. He'd lifted his face to the rain, clearly basking in the storm while his tail switched with delight.

Weirdly, I totally got his joy.

It was ridiculous to be out here in this weather, which was exactly why it was exciting. I'd been raised to do things I wasn't supposed to do, and I hadn't been able to change how good it felt to tread outside the lines. "You guys are no good for me," I announced as I slogged through the water to the boat, sucking in my breath as the cold water surged into my boots.

"We're perfect for you," Hattie said with a grin.

I grinned. "You are, actually." I gripped the edge of the boat across from Lucy, braced my hands, bent my knees, and then tried to launch myself over the edge of the boat. I made it just far enough to impale my stomach on the rim of the boat. "Oomph."

"Oh, come on." Hattie grabbed the waist of my jeans and pulled, dragging me right over the edge so my stomach scraped the entire way across until I landed in the well of water in the bottom of the boat.

King Tut gave a look of complete disdain as I sat up, spitting out the stale water. Behind me Lucy vaulted up easily onto the boat almost as easily as King Tut had, because she was handy like that.

"Let's do this, ladies." Hattie pulled the rip cord on the little engine, and the boat started right up. She let out a whoop, and then opened up the throttle.

It was a small boat with a tiny motor, but I still wasn't prepared for the sudden movement. I fell backwards, landing in the soggy boat bottom again, while Lucy and Hattie grinned at me. King Tut ignored me and turned to face the wind and rain whipping in his face.

Lucy grinned at me. "You're so agile around boats. It never ceases to amaze me."

"I'm getting better, so back off." I made a face at her, then sat down on the middle bench as Hattie headed out into the lake. My eyes were beginning to adjust, and I could see the faint reflection of the water as the rain hammered into it. The trees were pitch black along the shore, and the water stretched farther than I would have thought. "How big is this pond?"

"It's more like a small lake," Hattie shouted. "It's a couple miles long, and there are a bunch of coves and streams that run off it."

The pond widened as she drove, and it was only a minute or two until I couldn't see the shore at all. The glistening of dark water stretched as far as I could see. The raindrops shooting through the beam of Lucy's light looked like icicles knifing into the water. I felt like we were the only people alive.

It was pretty incredible.

I leaned over the edge of the boat and stuck my hand out, letting it skim through the cold water. The droplets felt like they were dancing as they hit my skin. I took a deep breath, inhaling the air that was so fresh that it felt like I was the first person to breathe it. "This is amazing out here," I shouted over the roar of the engine and the rain.

"Isn't it?" Lucy shouted back. "Being on the lake at night in the rain is incredible."

We rode in the darkness for another minute or two, then Hattie slowed down. "We're at the reef."

Lucy handed me the light she'd been holding. "You scan up ahead for Bootsy and the others. I'll watch for rocks."

"You got it." I took the spotlight, moved up beside King Tut, and pointed the light across the lake. I was startled by the sight ahead, hundreds of rocks poking their destructive little peaks out of the water. "We're going through *there*?" Now I understood the broken propeller issue.

"Yep. Jack the Ripper's ghost is said to haunt Crossbone Cove, which is on the other side of this reef. That's where the gals are," Hattie said.

"Naturally, that's where they are." I shined the spotlight ahead, but all I could see were rocks and water. No boat of stranded women.

Hattie cut the engine to a slow crawl as Lucy moved to the front of the boat. She leaned over the bow, shining her light directly into the water. "Go right," she said. "It's a little to the right."

"What's a little to the right?" I kept scanning up ahead.

"There's a channel through here that's deep enough for a small engine," Hattie said. "If you can't find it, then you have to row through. I have a good sense of where it is, but sometimes it just seems to vanish."

Because that wasn't creepy.

King Tut moved over to sit on my lap, and I scratched his head. "Don't worry," I told him. "I'm sure you could take on a serial killer and win."

"You already did," Lucy said. "Plus, this one's dead, so I think you're good."

See? We were good. *Nothing to see here, folks.* I looked ahead, trying to find some sign of the stranded women. "Hello!" I shouted. "Bootsy! Shirley!"

My voice echoed across the pond, but there was no answer.

"We're definitely in the channel." Lucy was leaning over the bow now. "You can go a little faster."

Hattie sped up slightly, but it still took us an eternity to get through. By the time we were through, I was so cold my hands were shaking. The adrenaline was gone, replaced by an ache in my butt from the hard, cold bench. At least King Tut's soggy fanny was keeping my thighs warm, so that was good.

Cats were so handy.

"We're getting close," Hattie said. "You should see them soon."

I scanned with the spotlight again, and this time, I saw something flash in the distance, as if my light had reflected off something metal. "Bootsy!" I shouted. "Shirley!"

There was silence, and then I heard a strange ca-caw, ca-caw, ca-caw sound echoing repeatedly across the water. I grinned, relaxing. If they were being silly, they were probably all right. "Ca-caw? They're ca-cawing us? Do they think they're spies, trying to give us a secret code?"

"It's illegal to be out here in a motorboat," Hattie said. "There have been complaints of boaters recently, so Devlin has been patrolling the pond."

Devlin, the pesky, ridiculously hot cop with whom I'd almost had an intimate moment with the other day. "You think he's around?" Not that I cared if he was around. Really. I didn't.

"If he is, we can't take the chance of him finding any of us. Who wants to get arrested?"

Another round of "ca-caws" echoed across the lake.

"Answer them," Hattie said. "They're not going to admit they're out there unless they know it's us."

Who was I to argue against avoiding the cops? It was literally my childhood mantra, and the first lesson my mom ever taught me. I cupped my hands around my mouth. "Ca-caw! Ca-caw! Ca-caw!"

There was silence, and then a bunch of lights came on up ahead. White, blinking Christmas lights, to be precise. And then rap music boomed across the lake, and I heard women's voices hooting and hollering.

I grinned. "I think we found them."

"It sounds like the alcohol hasn't worn off yet," Lucy observed. "That's good."

"Sure is." Hattie turned up the engine, and we picked up speed as we headed for them.

As we neared them, the Christmas lights gave off enough light that I could see four women stretched out in a boat about as small as ours. I saw Bootsy and Shirley, plus two women I didn't recognize. One looked to be the golden-years age of the Seam Rippers, but the woman lounging in the bow of the boat was closer to my age.

As we pulled up beside them, Bootsy held out a margarita glass. "Hattie! Lucy! Mia! Welcome to the party!" Her coat was shiny from the rain, and droplets were glistening on her brown cheeks, but she looked to be in a fine mood.

Lucy caught the edge of their boat as Hattie cut the engine. A few ropes were flipped back and forth, and then we were tied up beside them. They had coolers packed with food, and there was a mini, portable generator that a blender was plugged into. All of them were holding pink margaritas, and they were stretched out on what looked like outdoor couch cushions.

"Welcome, ladies!" Bootsy picked up a pitcher and started filling glasses with pink, crushed-ice slushy drinks. "Lucy, so great to see you. And Hattie, as always, a pleasure." She finished filling the glasses and held them out. "Come join us!"

As Lucy and Hattie accepted drinks, King Tut and I observed them with cagey suspicion. "You guys don't look very stranded."

Bootsy held out a glass to me. "Oh, we're definitely stranded. Our anchor is caught on something. Have a strawberry delight, Mia."

"No thanks." As King Tut kneaded his claws into my thighs, I looked around at the women all sitting back, laughing, and drinking. I'd briefly suspected that this was simply a ruse to get me out drinking with the girls. Clearly, I should have held onto that thought for a little longer. "It's pouring rain, freezing, in the middle of the night."

"It sure is." Bootsy raised her glass. "All the more reason to embrace the blessings we have."

"Right?" Shirley toasted with hers. "Friends, tequila, and waterproof gear. Thank heavens for all of that."

Bootsy shoved a margarita into my hand. "It's my special recipe," she said. "This is the last of our supplies. Let's enjoy it while we can."

The drink sloshed, and King Tut immediately poked his paw in the overflow and licked his claw. When he went back for seconds, I moved it away, because a King Tut without inhibitions was a scary thought.

A part of me was pretty dumbfounded that no one was in a rush to get back to shore, but I had to admit that the Christmas lights were pretty spectacular the way they lit up the sheets of rain. All the women were dressed in heavy gear, and they'd even erected a shelter with a tarp and metal posts. The cushions looked thick and soft, and the women's laughter was infectious.

I felt the warmth of their friendship even through the cold gripping me, and suddenly, I was very grateful Hattie and Lucy had brought me along. My mom had always been working on her next con, always looking ahead to how we could skate through to our next success.

She never sat and basked. We never stayed in one place long enough to put down roots or make connections.

But right now? With these women? I felt like I'd been given the chance to experience something I'd always wanted. Well, maybe not the uncontrollable shivering and being stranded in a storm on a lake, but these women? Yes. A thousand times, yes.

"Mia, I don't think you've met Esther Neeley." Bootsy pointed to a woman in a black jacket, black pants, and black boots. "She's one of the Seam Rippers."

I recognized the logo on her jacket and the brand of her boots from my days helping my mom freeload off of celebrities in the Hamptons. I was pretty sure Esther's outdoor gear cost significantly more than my mortgage payment. I could see the glitter of massive diamond studs in her ears, reflecting the twinkling Christmas lights.

My time with my mom had taught me how to analyze people in a split second. Esther wasn't just rich for Bass Derby. She had *money*, and she didn't hesitate to spend it on nice things for herself. The amount of money Esther was wearing would have made her a target of my mom in a hurry.

She was on her right hip and was doing side leg lifts, not spilling even a drop of her drink. "Call me Rogue. No one calls me Esther. Esther's an old lady name."

"You are old," Bootsy pointed out.

"And fighting it every step of the way." Esther, aka Rogue, shifted to her left hip and began to do leg lifts with her other leg.

"What are you doing?" Hattie asked.

"YouTube exercise videos are the best. Seven days a week, two hours a day. I'm a machine."

Esther might be wealthy, but she definitely hadn't decided to sit around and get stale while her money got bigger in the stock market. "I'm impressed," I said. "Can I hire you to train me?"

"Nope. YouTube is free. Train yourself. I don't do anything for money." She winked at me. "If you have enough money, sweetheart, the world is your playground."

"I know." I'd seen it from the inside, outside, and downside over my lifetime.

"Do you?" She paused, her leg suspended near her ear. "What do you know?"

"Mia's husband was a drug kingpin, and she took him down," Hattie said. "She gave up all that money to do the right thing."

"Damn." Esther gazed at me speculatively. "I wouldn't give up my money to do the right thing. I might pay someone else to do the right thing for me, but I wouldn't give up my own payload. I love my money."

I couldn't tell if Esther was kidding or not, but I had a feeling she wasn't. Which I kind of admired. My mom had drilled "save yourself first" into me as a kid, which had served me well more than once in my life.

Bootsy gestured to the other Seam Ripper in the boat. "And you remember Shirley Kincaid?"

The last time I'd seen her, Shirley had been wearing black leather pants, stilettos, and enough gold chains to anchor her solidly during a tornado, but she'd traded the heels for boots and the leather for light-blue rain gear. "Hi," I said as I ran my hands through King Tut's soggy fur. "It's great to see you again."

"Back at ya." Shirley beamed at me. "We were so impressed how you were willing to die to catch a killer."

I cleared my throat. I hadn't been willing to die at all. I'd just gotten sucked into a risky situation that had required creative thinking and a swan dive onto pavement to escape. But they were all looking at me with such admiration, I couldn't quite bring myself to admit the truth. "Thanks," I said. "It was no big deal." Another lie. Almost dying was still a big deal to me.

"What?" Esther raised her brows. "You risked death to catch a killer? Why on earth would you do something asinine like that?"

"To save me," Lucy said. "I appreciated it."

Esther snorted. "I'll bet you did." She eyed me, her eyes gleaming with curiosity now.

I shifted restlessly under her stare. "It just happened," I muttered.

"Did it really?" Her eyes widened. "Wait a sec. You're her. You're the one they were talking about."

"They?" I frowned. "Who is they?"

"The Founder's Society ladies. They were at Dutch's Salon getting their nails done, and boy oh boy, are they pissed at you for running over the Welcome to Bass Derby sign."

Right. The sign that I hadn't run over, but that everyone blamed me for. So glad to know that was still happening. "Who are the Founder's Society ladies?"

Hattie grinned, a hint of wickedness gleaming in her eyes. "My best friends. Oh, wait, no, scratch that. They don't actually like me. It's hard to keep track sometimes."

"They have no taste," Esther snorted. "Bunch of uptight pansies, if you ask me."

Bootsy was the only one who gave me an actual answer. "Any town resident who can trace their ancestry back to one of the gravestones in the town's original cemetery is eligible for membership in the Founder's Society." She gestured to the gang in the boat. "Except for Hattie, none of us qualify."

"Which is why they don't like Hattie," Rogue said. "She turned them down. That never goes over well with people like that."

Hattie snorted. "Why waste our energy on them when we have drinks, girls, and ghosts to enjoy? Did you summon Jack's ghost yet?"

Ooh… I'd forgotten about that. I didn't believe in ghosts, but if they said yes, that would be so good.

The only woman I hadn't met yet shook her head. "He wasn't very communicative tonight," she said. "Usually, he likes to visit during storms, but not tonight."

"Men," Hattie scoffed. "They're always on their own schedule." She leaned back against the side of our boat and stretched her legs out across the bench, facing the Seam Rippers. She looked like she belonged in a lounge chair on a Florida beach, not in a sinking boat during a middle-of-the-night storm.

Hattie was so chill. My mom would love her. And probably recruit her.

Bootsy pointed her glass in the direction of the woman who was speaking. "This is Glory Starr. She's a ghost whisperer. Her family used to have a camp on Diamond Lake back in the day."

Glory had flaming red hair, in drenched ringlets that went almost all the way down her back. She had big gold hoop earrings, a beaded, feathered rope in her hair, and pink hiking boots. Her rain pants were purple and black tie-dye that matched her coat, but her rain hat was bright yellow, like a lobsterman during a storm. She looked like she was in her late twenties, but it was difficult to be sure.

"Glory." Hattie sounded friendly. "Great to see you again. I think the whole ghost thing is a scam, but I heartily admire female entrepreneurs and believe the world needs more of them, so great job on making your business a success." She raised her glass. "Cheers to women power everywhere."

Glory looked slightly taken aback, but everyone else clinked glasses and offered assorted sentiments about strong women, assimilating massive amounts of personal net worth, free love, and heavy drinking, which I think pretty much covered all the basic values in life.

Even King Tut meowed and went for my drink again, clearly offering his support to women everywhere. I was pretty sure he'd be a feminist, if he wasn't a massive, terrifying, arrogant cat-beast, who I adored with all my heart.

After everyone had finished the toast with heavy imbibing, Hattie settled back. "Glory, didn't you get yourself an invite to perform at the Callahan New Year's Eve party this year? That is some good marketing right there. If you could become the preferred party performer for all those high-brow events, that'll buy you diamonds like Esther's in a hurry."

"My diamonds are worth a lot more than being an upper crust party trick," Esther said. "It takes years of personal sacrifice, risk, and reward to get these babies."

Would it be rude to ask Esther how she'd earned all her money? I was so curious.

"I don't *perform*," Glory snapped. "I'm a spiritual guide. I connect. It's an art. Spirits don't visit just anyone, you know."

I sat back and studied Glory while she explained the art of ghost summoning to the other ladies. She spoke with authority. Made eye contact. Provided details.

Either she was a very, very good liar, or she was telling the truth.

Since I didn't believe in ghosts, I was going with the liar option.

Having grown up with a con artist mom and spent most of my formative years working one con or the other, I was well aware of the opportunities to con people. Like, for example, getting people to pay money to summon ghosts and then not actually producing any spiritual entities.

I admired Glory. She was very good at spinning her tale. I knew that took a lot of practice. And honestly, if people were willing to give her money for a chance at chatting with a ghost, why not?

Wait. Had I just thought that? She was a fraud, right? So, never mind. Bad Glory.

Dammit. I had to remember that I wasn't a criminal anymore, and therefore, had no bond with people who reminded me of my mom, who I'd missed every day since I'd left her and our con artist life behind.

"Wow," Hattie said, when Glory finished her explanation. "That's an excellent description. I'd be willing to pay you to summon my dead mom after hearing that."

Glory looked delighted by the praise, which I totally got. A compliment from Hattie was rare and glorious. "Thanks, Hattie. I—"

The sky suddenly flashed white.

Conversation stopped, and Bootsy turned off the music. "Everyone quiet."

A few seconds later, we heard the low rumble of thunder. King Tut dug his claws into my thighs, and I slid my hand around the handle of his life jacket.

"Thunderstorm," Hattie said. "Still far enough away, but we don't want to be out here if that gets close."

"Time to go." Bootsy chugged her drink and stood up.

The women started packing up with impressive speed, handing their items over into our tiny, leaking boat at an alarming rate. Their gear would sink my boat before any of us even got into it. I needed to stop that in a hurry. "Lucy? You think maybe we could get Bootsy's anchor free?"

I wasn't a boat person (yet), but Lucy was.

She followed my gaze to the rapidly increasing pile of gear in our boat. "Yeah, let's try that. Good call."

While the women continued to offload into our boat, Lucy, King Tut, and I climbed into their boat. Lucy and I shined our spotlights into the water. The chain for their anchor disappeared from sight into the darkness.

"I can't see what it's hooked on," Lucy said.

"Maybe you can swim down there and find the end of it," I suggested.

She raised her brows. "Maybe you can do that. You're the one with a marina full of used wet suits."

"There's nothing I'd love more than to dive into freezing, pitch-black water to free an anchor, but I didn't bring my wetsuit."

She grinned. "Bummer."

"Yeah, totally." I glanced over my shoulder, grimacing when I noticed that my boat was sitting visibly lower in the water than it had been when we arrived. I looked back at Lucy. "Any chance you can muscle the anchor free?"

"I'll try." She braced herself, gripped the chain, and leaned back. The boat tipped precariously and slid across the water toward the chain. King Tut yowled in protest and leapt back into our boat.

"Help me," Lucy ordered.

She was about a hundred times stronger than I was, but maybe another one percent would make a difference, right? "Okay." I moved beside her and gripped the chain lower down. "On three. One. Two. Three."

We both pulled, but the anchor didn't move.

"Harder," Lucy said. "Lean into it."

I braced my foot on the boat and leaned back. My fingers were aching from the effort of holding onto the wet chain, but I grimaced and leaned harder, Lucy grunting beside me.

I felt something slide, and excitement leapt through me. "Did you feel that?"

"I did. Hattie! Come help!"

Hattie climbed over and squeezed in beside me. She grabbed the chain, braced her feet, and leaned back with a grunt.

I felt the chain move again. "It's coming!"

"Keep pulling!" Lucy shouted.

Bootsy squeezed in next to me, her fingers wrapping around just below mine. "Come on, girls! Let's do this! On three! One. Two. Three!"

The four of us threw our weight backward, and the anchor popped free. We all fell back, crashing into the bottom of the boat. "Get it before it sinks back down!" Hattie shouted.

I scrambled to my feet, lunging for the chain. I started to haul it in, but it was still heavy. Lucy recovered next, and she grabbed the chain.

We started dragging it in, but it was slow work. "How heavy is this anchor?"

"Eight pounds." Bootsy untangled herself from Hattie as Shirley and Glory tossed cushions from their boat to mine. Esther was sitting in the bow of Bootsy's boat, feet up, sipping her drink while everyone else did the work.

I admired that kind of attitude. I kind of wanted to feel that worthy.

"This anchor weighs more than eight pounds," Lucy said.

"Something must still be hooked on it," I added, my arms aching from dragging the anchor in. "Hattie, can you see what it is?"

She leaned over the edge of the boat and shined her light in the water. "You guys are pulling something up. It's big."

"Really? Is it something good?" Bootsy and Shirley climbed over the chaos and braced on the edge of the boat to peer into the water.

"I can't see anything," Shirley said. "It's too dark."

"You just have old eyes," Esther said, her feet still propped up on the rim of the boat. "Use your flashlight."

"You use a flashlight," Shirley snapped. "Get off your bony butt and come help."

"Fine." Holding her drink carefully in her left hand, Esther untangled her legs, and rose to her feet, moving across the boat with more grace than I would have expected, given the rain, the wind, the clutter, and the fact that Esther probably had a good eight decades in her. She peered over the edge as Lucy and I continued to reel in the chain. "It is rather dark down there, but it looks a lot like—" She went silent.

"It sure does," Bootsy said.

"Oh, man," Shirley chimed in.

King Tut put his paws up on the rim of my boat, peered into the water, and then growled.

Um...uh, oh.

"Um, guys?" I asked. "What is it?"

No one answered me as they continued to peer into the water while Lucy and I pulled the chain in.

"What is it?" Glory squeezed in next to them, tipping the boat just far enough to make me a little nervous.

I backed up a few steps and nudged Lucy to do the same, trying to counterbalance the others.

"Oh...no." Hattie sounded alarmed.

At that moment, something popped to the surface. Something surprisingly large. Hattie's light illuminated it, and I forgot to keep pulling the chain. "Is that a *person*?"

"A person?" Lucy dropped the chain, and the anchor shot back down to the bottom of the lake, taking the item with it. "Ack!" She lunged for the chain, and everyone helped pull it back up.

This time, when it popped up to the surface, there was no mistaking what it was.

A man with longish dark hair, a few wrinkles, and a watch that cost more than most small nations could afford. He was wearing jeans with a logo I recognized, beautiful leather boots, and a Canada Goose parka.

And he was, quite clearly, dead.

CHAPTER 3

"Holy cow." Hattie stared at the dead guy. "It's Rutherford Callahan!"

I blinked. I'd heard that name before. "The portrait artist who paints celebrities?" I'd seen his work on some of my childhood adventures with my mom.

"Yes. His family owns a lot of property on Diamond Lake." Esther looked thrilled. "I bet there's a scandal behind this. Rutherford was notorious for all sorts of escapades with his clients. Bass Derby will definitely get lots of press for this."

"Not good press," Shirley said. "We don't need some decadent celebrity getting drunk and falling overboard in some notorious fail."

"All press is good press," Esther said. "It's fun when things like this happen to famous people, right?"

"Not when we're supposed to be a sweet, charming New England town," Shirley sighed. "Murder doesn't match that."

Bootsy had pulled out her phone and was taking a picture of him. "Honestly, it's not surprising. If anyone in this town was to have a dramatic death, it would definitely be him."

"Totally predictable he'd meet his demise tangled in an anchor in Dead Man's Pond," Esther agreed, sounding thoroughly amused by the idea.

Glory, on the other hand, looked like she was about to pass out. Her face was ashen, and she was gripping the edge of the boat as if her life depended on it.

I felt her, because I was on the same train. Dead people weren't my favorite thing. But I had to admit, Glory's apparent horror might be considered a surprising reaction from a woman who specialized in ghosts, right? Seeing as how they came from dead people and all.

Oh, wait. Was that cynical? It might be cynical.

Either way, no one seemed to be making any effort to drag the dead guy into the boat, which I didn't exactly blame them for. I wasn't an expert on dead people, and even I could tell there was no chance of saving him. So, floating was fine for Rutherford.

"I'll bet some woman knows exactly where he is right now," mused Esther. "He paints nudes and sleeps with all his models."

My hands were starting to cramp from holding onto the chain. "What are we going to do with him?"

"I don't want him in my boat," Bootsy said. "That's seriously creepy."

"Cut him loose and let him sink back down," Esther said. "I'm sure he'd love to keep everyone guessing as to what happened to him."

"Oh…good call," Bootsy said. "He did like to mess with people." She looked over at our resident ghost whisperer. "Glory? What does he want?"

Glory still looked like she was going to throw up. "He's not talking to me right now," she rasped out.

Surprising, that.

"Really? He's not hanging around his body? That's weird. I totally saw him as the type to hang around and haunt people," Bootsy said. "Well, I vote for sinking him. I'm sure that's what he'd want."

Hattie frowned. "We can't sink him. Let's tie him to the boat, and we'll tow him in."

"I'm with Hattie," Esther said. "I'm sure he'd get a kick out of his corpse causing all sorts of drama and headlines. He'd definitely prefer that."

"Fine." Bootsy leaned over and shined the light on him. "His boot seems to be stuck on the anchor. Someone should untangle him and tie him to the boat."

"Yes, someone should definitely take care of that," Hattie said, as the sky flashed with lightning again and thunder rumbled in the distance, this time a little closer.

No one moved to tie him to the boat.

Lucy looked over at me. "You do it."

"Me? Why me?" I didn't like that idea at all.

She sighed. "Because you have experience. Obviously."

"Spying on my ex-husband, not dealing with dead guys!"

"It's closer than any of us," Hattie said. "All in favor of Mia getting Rutherford untangled from the anchor, raise your hand."

Six hands went up.

I stared at them. "No. Absolutely not. He's not my problem. I barely even count as a resident of this town yet."

"You're outvoted," Hattie said. Thunder rumbled again, louder this time. "But hurry up, because we don't want to be on a lake during a thunderstorm."

"Let's get our stuff back into our boat since Lucy and Mia got the anchor up," Bootsy said.

Everyone immediately moved away from our end of the boat, leaving Lucy and me holding onto the chain that was keeping Rutherford from being sucked back to the bottom of the lake by Bootsy's anchor. Even King Tut was over in my boat, licking the rain off his left hip, pretending not to notice the rapidly approaching lightning bolts.

I looked at Lucy. "You untangle him."

She raised her brows. "Can you hold the chain yourself?"

"Of course."

31

"Fine." She dropped the chain.

It shot back over the edge of the boat, dragging me face-first into the side of the boat. Lucy grabbed the chain as it slid out of my fingers, bracing herself as Rutherford disappeared from sight again. She grinned at me. "I'm sorry. I thought you said you could hold the chain yourself. My mistake."

I dragged myself to my knees, aware of the fact that no one was even trying to pretend they weren't laughing at my failure.

Rutherford chose that moment to pop back to the surface of the water. "Untangle his ankle from the anchor," Lucy said. "I'll hold him up."

The sky flashed again, and this time, the thunder rumbled sooner. "The storm's getting closer," Hattie said. "I personally don't want to get incinerated out here. Mia, stop wasting time."

I sighed. What was I going to do, make one of the senior citizens dangle over the water to untangle him? Glory could do it, but she was now leaning over the far side of the boat, and I was kinda sure she'd lost the battle not to throw up. "Fine. But just so you know, this is not one of the things on my bucket list."

"I'll pull him in." Lucy dragged the anchor in with impressive swiftness until Rutherford's soggy boot bumped against the boat. "Go for it."

"Fine, but I'm doing this under protest." I leaned over the edge of the boat as King Tut wriggled up beside me, peering over the edge of the boat.

He meowed once, but when Dead Rutherford didn't reply, he hissed and sat back down to resume his grooming.

Rutherford stared up at me, as if daring me to touch him. I grimaced and leaned over, gingerly touching his ankle. His boot felt like a boot, and his jeans felt like jeans, so I relaxed. "It's not that creepy," I announced. "This is fine."

I felt my way around his leg, and I found the chain from the anchor.

It wasn't caught in his boot, though.

It was caught on something else. I felt my way along the metal loops, and I frowned. "There's a second chain here. That's what our anchor is caught on. The second chain is the one caught around his ankle—"

My fingers touched something familiar, from the days of my youth.

My mouth went dry.

Lucy leaned over. "What's that look on your face?" she whispered.

"It's a padlock. Another chain is padlocked around his ankle," I whispered back.

Her eyes widened. "He was *padlocked* to a chain? You think he was—" She dragged her index finger across her throat in the universal sign for murder.

"I don't know. I hope not." I *really* hoped not.

I leaned over, following the second chain with my fingers. It hung straight down, so I grabbed it and started pulling. "The second chain is caught on something else. Can you shine a light?"

"You bet." A floodlight appeared over my shoulder, and I peered into the water as I pulled, watching as a second anchor came into sight. The chain was much shorter, and the anchor was bright pink. I looked at Lucy. "It's an anchor," I whispered.

Her eyes widened. "His ankle is padlocked to an *anchor*?"

I nodded. It didn't take a genius to realize that Rutherford hadn't fallen overboard in drunken delight after catching a big fish.

He'd been murdered.

CHAPTER 4

I'D HAD enough murder to last me a lifetime.

And from the look of horror on Lucy's face, she felt the same way.

"Maybe we just release the chain and let him sink back down?" Lucy whispered. "We never saw anything—"

"What's that pink thing? An anchor?" Bootsy peered over Lucy's shoulder before we could decide that none of it had ever happened. "Hattie? Is that yours?"

Lucy and I looked at each other in alarm. Hattie's anchor was padlocked to a dead guy's ankle?

"Is what mine?" Hattie asked.

I pulled the anchor into the boat and let it thud on the seat. "This."

Hattie raised her brows. "Yeah, that's mine. Where'd you find it?"

Oh, *man.* I exchanged worried looks with Lucy as I answered. "Rutherford," I said slowly, "has it padlocked to his ankle."

"Seriously? Why would he do that?" I saw the moment Hattie realized what was happening. She took a step back. "You've got to be kidding."

Esther let out a low whistle of admiration. "You go, girl. I had no idea you had that in you!"

"Holy spiked lemonade," Bootsy exclaimed. "Hattie!"

"What's going on over there?" Shirley was in my boat, up to her knees in cushions.

"Hattie killed Rutherford," Esther shouted back.

Hattie put her hands on her hips. "I didn't kill him!"

"Quick! Destroy the evidence!" Bootsy grabbed the pink anchor. "Sink him before the police get here!"

"No!" I shouted. "That might show us who really did it!" I tackled her as she went to hurl the anchor overboard.

Well, I tried to tackle her. What I did was knock the anchor out of her hand, flatten her to the boat, and then flip myself over the rail and into the pond.

I landed headfirst, and the water closed around me like the ice bath that no one wants to have. I gasped as I shot to the surface, sucking in air. My jeans and boots were heavy, and my coat was taking on water much too fast.

"Here! Grab the life jacket!" Lucy shouted as someone turned the floodlight on me, blinding me.

I scrunched my eyes shut as I lunged for the life jacket. "Turn the light off! I can't see!" I grabbed the life preserver and leaned on it, but it started to sink under me. I scrambled for a better grip. "It's not floating!"

The light turned aside enough that I could see, and I saw six women and one cat staring at me, varying degrees of amusement and horror on their faces. I fumbled for a better grip, pulling my upper body further onto the life jacket. "What?"

Lucy pointed. "The life jacket is over there."

I saw an orange buoyant vest floating a few feet to my right. "Then what?" I turned my head to see what I was holding onto, and I saw Rutherford's face inches from mine.

I was leaning on his chest.

"Oh, crap!" I let go quickly, but the zipper on my coat caught on his jacket, keeping me attached to him.

I tried to yank it free, but it didn't come. "This is so gross!" I yanked harder, which dragged Rutherford's face right up to mine.

Lucy leaned over. "Come closer. I'll help!" She was trying not to laugh, but the squeaking noises emanating from her weren't exactly subtle.

The others weren't even trying to hide it. Granted, it was a sort of horrified laughter, but I didn't really feel like laughing with them right now.

I tried to swim toward Lucy, but my breasts were literally stuck to a dead man's chest, leaving me face to face with his bright blue eyes. "I'm going to have nightmares about this," I shouted as I kicked, trying to at least get closer to the boat.

"Hang on. I want to take a video of this," Esther said. "Let me get my phone out."

"Oh, yes," Bootsy said. "This is pretty classic stuff right here."

"We could label it something about how Mia's breasts are his reward in the Afterlife," Shirley said. "It would totally lighten up the funeral. Everyone knows he was a manwhore anyway, right? It would be perfect."

"Oh my God," I shouted. "You people are insane! Seriously! Help me!"

"I got you." Lucy dragged Rutherford's chain in, giving me a ride on his chest back to the boat. His boot and mine hit the boat at the same time, with matching clunks. "Okay, try to get free again," she said.

I grabbed the edge of the boat and tried to use that to leverage myself off of him, but when I jerked backward, he came with me, rising out of the lake like a zombie monster on Xanax.

"Oh dear heavens," Shirley said. "Tell me you got that on video."

"I got it on slow-mo," Esther said. "This is fantastic. It's like *Jaws*, only better."

"Duh nuh. Duh nuh." Bootsy started chanting those two ominous notes.

I glared at her. "I can't even express how not helpful that is for me right now." The water I was floating in was pitch black, and deep enough that we hadn't been able to see the bottom. I knew that murderous great white sharks didn't live in this lake, but logic wasn't taking a front row seat right now.

I didn't want to wind up like Rutherford. "I need to get out of here. Now."

At that moment, lightning lit up the sky, and thunder cracked almost immediately afterward. Holy crap! "We're going to die! I don't want to die out here!"

"Oh, calm down," Esther said. "You're so dramatic for a drug dealer."

"I'm not a drug dealer!"

"Scissors," Lucy shouted. "Does anyone have scissors?"

There was a pause that was too long for comfort, and then Bootsy shouted. "I brought some. Hang on!"

While I hung on, Esther leaned over the edge of the boat, holding out a margarita. "While you're waiting."

I stared at her as my chin bumped my dead floatie's chest. "I don't want a drink right now."

"You're sure? You look like you could use one. I mean, you're tied to a dead guy, and all."

She had a point. If ever a situation called for a drink, it was probably this one. Before I could accept it, though, Hattie leaned over, flashing some scissors at me. "I'll try not to stab you."

"I appreciate that. Please hurry."

"Drag them in, Lucy!" Hattie shouted as she held up the scissors.

I gripped Rutherford as we bumped into the boat again, then Bootsy and Shirley helped me roll onto my side so that Hattie could reach us. "Cut his jacket, not mine."

"On it." She started to cut, and I gripped the lifejacket, grimacing as the blades flashed precariously close to my girls.

"Almost there. Hells bells, his jacket is thick!"

Lightning flashed again, followed by a loud crack that made all of us jump.

"Hurry up, Hattie!" Lucy said.

"Don't rush me!" Hattie kept sawing. "His coat's like seven layers thick."

"Oh for hell's sake. Don't you know how to use scissors?" Bootsy shoved Hattie aside, grabbed the scissors, and leaned in. She winked at me. "It takes a Seam Ripper to know how to use scissors." Three second later, the grip on my jacket released and I fell off Rutherford, sinking under the water.

"Oh, no, no! Don't you dare!" Lucy grabbed my jacket and dragged me back to the surface. "Onto the boat!"

I grabbed the edge of the boat, and tried to pull myself up, but I was so cold that my arms had no chance of dragging me out. Because we were going to blame it on the cold, not my lack of upper body strength.

"Let's get her in, ladies!" Hattie and Lucy leaned over, and together, they dragged me up. As soon as my shoulders were over the edge, the other ladies grabbed assorted body parts, dragging me across the edge of the boat until I landed on the bottom of it.

I groaned as I lay there, my cheek smashed against the cold, wet metal of the boat. King Tut hopped off the seat and crouched next to me, ankle deep in the water as he licked my forehead.

Would he eat me if I died? I moved slightly, just so he would know I wasn't dinner yet. He purred and sat on my arm, which was basically a cat hug. "I love you, too, kitty cat."

Hattie crouched next to me. "You all right?"

I nodded. "Fantastic," I said honestly. I mean, how could I not be fantastic? I was in a boat, not in lightning and shark-infested waters attached to a corpse.

Hattie winked at me. "Great!" She stood up. "Strap Rutherford in," she yelled. "Let's get out of here!"

The wind was whipping now, and the little boats were bouncing on the waves as the rain poured down and lightning flashed. "Mia?" Lucy leaned down close to me, bracing herself as the boat rocked violently. "Could you pick that lock and get

Hattie's anchor off his ankle?" Her voice was low, and she was eyeing King Tut warily.

I sat up. "Of course. Padlocks are easy."

"Do you think that might be a good idea?" She picked up the anchor, but didn't put it into my boat for the ride to shore.

I paused. "Tamper with a murder scene?"

She nodded.

"That's illegal." But as I said it, I looked past her at Hattie, who was helping transfer the Seam Rippers' gear back to their boat. "Devlin and Chief Stone will never believe Hattie murdered him."

She raised her brows. "But what if you're wrong?"

Oh, man. Hattie was a spitfire, but prison could break even the most resilient person.

Hattie looked over at us and frowned. "What are you two talking about? You look suspicious."

Lucy gestured her to come over, and Hattie made her way across the boat. "What's up?"

Lucy lifted the anchor. "Mia said she could pick the lock and get your anchor off his leg. We could make it disappear."

"Oh, my God. Yes!" Bootsy leaned over Hattie's shoulder. "Definitely, yes. Esther! Mia's going to get the padlock off his leg. Hattie's going to be fine."

"What? I didn't say that." Alarm rushed through me. Just because I was capable of it didn't mean it was the right thing to do.

Shirley put her hands on her hips. "No way. We'd get in so much trouble if we got caught!"

"You want Hattie to go to prison?" Bootsy glared at her. "What kind of friend are you?"

"A friend who wants all of us to stay out of prison," Shirley said. "If we let Mia do it, then we're accessories to hiding the body to protect Hattie from a murder rap!"

Bootsy gave us all a hard glare. "No one in this boat is going to say anything about Hattie's anchor being around his ankle, right?"

She paused especially long on Glory, who still looked ashen and pale. "No one will rat Hattie and Mia out, right?"

Everyone nodded, but Hattie snorted. "I didn't kill him."

Bootsy winked at her. "Of course you didn't. There's a totally innocent reason for your anchor to be around his ankle."

Hattie narrowed her eyes. "Do you think I'm stupid enough to use my own anchor?"

"No, not stupid, but maybe opportunistic." Bootsy turned to me. "Get her anchor off him."

I didn't know what to do. "This is murder, guys. What if the anchor shows who did it?"

"Yeah, it'll show who did it. Hattie!"

"I didn't kill him!"

Everyone ignored Hattie completely, and a rising argument ensued about hiding the body, disposing of the anchor, and assorted moral codes, until suddenly there was a flash of lightning and a crack so loud that everyone dropped to the bottom of the boat and covered their heads.

"Holy corpses," yelled Esther. "No one's going to prison if we all get electrocuted. We'll do this on shore!'"

"Amen, sistah!" Bootsy gestured to us. "Get on your boat. We'll meet you guys there!"

With the boats rocking, and the wind hammering us, we managed to get Rutherford tied to my boat and all of us into the correct boats. King Tut seemed completely undaunted by the storm, parking himself in the bow of my boat, his tail twitching with delight as the wind and rain whipped his long fur around.

For the less agile humans, it was pretty precarious trying to go between the boats with the wind tossing them around, but somehow, we all made it where we were supposed to be without anyone (else) falling into the cold, churning water.

I gripped the edge of my boat, my feet ankle-deep in water as Lucy untied the last rope holding us to Bootsy's boat. I'd tied a rope to King Tut's life jacket and wound it around my wrist, just in case he wasn't as adept at storm-riding as he thought he was.

"Let's do it!" Bootsy let out a whoop and hit the gas. The Christmas lights sparkled as she peeled out of the cove, heading toward the reef. Esther was in the bow, with a spotlight aimed down at the water.

"You watch Rutherford," Hattie shouted at me. "Lucy, keep an eye out for rocks!" She opened up the engine, and the boat leapt forward, but this time, I was prepared for it and grabbed the edge of the boat before I could fall.

As the tiny boat bounced and struggled against the waves, I made my way to the back of the boat, keeping King Tut's rope around my wrist.

Rutherford was bouncing along behind the boat. As I watched him disappear beneath the surface and pop back up again, I realized that whatever evidence of murder that had survived his submersion probably wouldn't last the drive back to shore.

The only evidence we had was Hattie's pink anchor, padlocked to his ankle and currently sitting on the rear bench of my boat. I looked over at Hattie as she squinted against the rain, shouting directions at Lucy, and skillfully navigating the rocks and the fierce waves.

Hattie was so bold. So vibrant. So alive. Everything I was burning to unleash in my own life. There was no way she could go to prison.

Lucy looked back at me, and I met her gaze.

I saw the worry in her eyes, and I felt the same way.

Crud. I was going to have to take that anchor off, wasn't I?

But what if one of the other ladies told the police I did it? Esther and Bootsy wouldn't, but I didn't know about Glory and Shirley. I would be in so much trouble if I got caught. Like, prison for sure.

I'd been taught from childhood that the number one priority was to never get caught, which meant sometimes walking away from a good opportunity.

If you weren't in prison, you always had another chance.

But if Hattie was in prison, she wouldn't have another chance.

I bit my lip and looked out across the dark lake. How far did friendship go? The only thing I wanted in life, that I'd given up literally *everything* for, was a life where I didn't have to worry about going to prison. A normal life. Friends. Community. I'd found it in Bass Derby. Did keeping it require me to become the person I'd spent the last decade walking away from?

"Mia."

I looked over at Hattie. "What?"

"Don't do it. Leave the anchor on him."

"But—"

"It's not worth it. I'll be fine, I swear."

I said nothing, and she grabbed my wrist. "Listen to me, Mia. If you do it, I will rat you out so fast you'll be in jail before you know what hit you. Got it? Because you know I will."

I narrowed my eyes. "You would turn me in for helping you?"

"After that speech? Yeah, I'd have to. Otherwise I lose all credibility, and you know I'm all about my reputation."

"But you love illegal things."

"Not the ones that will get my friends in serious trouble. Whatever happens, we'll handle it. We're scrappy like that. Okay?"

I let out a breath. "Okay."

She winked at me then let out a holler. "Hang on, ladies! We're past the reef!" Hattie hit the gas and unleashed the fury of our woefully inadequate dingy against the torrents of Dead Man's Pond.

Bootsy's boat wasn't much bigger, and it was weighed down by four women and a picnic, so their progress was equally slow. Our little boats crashed into the white caps, slamming us as the water raged.

Then Hattie turned the boat, so we were no longer being buffeted by the wind and the current. The moment we lined up with the current instead of against it, the boat leapt forward, and the bottom-dropping crashes smoothed out as she unleashed the full force of my little boat.

The water sloshed around my ankles as we roared across the

pond. King Tut stood with his paws on the edge of the boat, lifting his face to the wind, so I tightened my grip on his rope, just in case he suddenly catapulted through the air.

Up ahead, Bootsy had picked up speed as well. Behind us, Rutherford practiced his body surfing. Then there was another flash of lightning and instant thunder so loud that we all ducked and covered our heads.

"Get down," Hattie yelled.

I grabbed King Tut and yanked the protesting feline to the floor of the boat while Lucy slid off the seat beside me. Hattie crouched low, barely staying high enough to see where she was going. Not that there was anything to see. When there wasn't lightning, it was pitch black. "How do you know where shore is?"

"Instinct!" Hattie shouted over the roar of the boat and the storm.

More lightning, and the boat lit up. "This is insane," I yelled at Lucy.

"Totally. Isn't it great?"

I couldn't lie. It was pretty awesome being out on the water in the middle of the storm. Dangerous, yes. But also, incredible. The wind was fierce. The rain was still hammering. And the little pond was churning, like it was battling to keep us from stealing Rutherford from its watery clutches.

After a few moments, Hattie cut the engine, and I realized we'd reached shore. Relief rushed through me at the sight of Hattie's truck with the trailer in the lake, exactly where we'd left it. She drove the boat up onto her trailer. "Everyone out!"

Bootsy drove her boat onto the shore as well, and the women were piling out as fast as they could. Bootsy ran for her truck and trailer while the others climbed out, holding the boat in place.

The lightning and thunder were still in full force, and I was as fast as Lucy and Hattie to get out of our boat. I put King Tut in the cab of the truck, while Lucy and Hattie had the boat secured onto the trailer within seconds. Hattie hurried to the driver's door to pull the boat out of the lake. "We'll drag Rutherford out of the water, and then we can—"

At that moment, an SUV with flashing blue lights and a siren pulled into the clearing. *Devlin.* Its floodlights lit up the area, nearly blinding us.

Esther swore. "Hide the body," she shouted. "Don't let the cops see Rutherford until Mia gets the anchor off him!"

Hide the body. Seriously? Was that really the best thing to yell *after* the police had arrived? Devlin was mid-thirties, muscular, fit, and definitely still had the ability to hear.

As one might have guessed, the next thing that happened was Devlin's loudspeaker blasting into the night. "Everyone freeze."

CHAPTER 5

I FROZE.

No one else did. In fact, everyone else seemed to go into a frenzy. Hattie hit the gas, dragging the trailer, the boat, and Rutherford out of the lake. Bootsy shifted into reverse and her truck flew backward toward the lake, narrowly missing Devlin's front bumper as she backed the trailer into the water.

Esther drove the party boat up onto the trailer as Devlin got out of his truck. "I said freeze," he shouted over the storm, clearly annoyed to be so blatantly disregarded.

"You want us to get electrocuted?" Esther leapt off the boat, and she and Shirley quickly secured it to the trailer. To prove her point, the lightning flashed and the thunder boomed, and even Devlin ducked instinctively.

"All right, get the boats out!" he yelled.

"Wow. Great idea!" Bootsy hit the gas and pulled her boat out of the water. The moment her boat was out of his way, Devlin's spotlights lit up Rutherford, who was now on the beach, with a drag mark behind him.

Devlin's jaw dropped open. "What's that?"

"A dead guy. Probably murdered. God, don't you know anything?" Esther set her hands on her hips, glaring at him as

Bootsy parked her truck next to Hattie. "Are you really qualified for your job?"

"Murdered?" He pulled out his gun and aimed it at me, because I was standing right next to Rutherford. "Everyone out on the sand, hands up. And this time I mean it!"

I put my hands up, my heart hammering. In retrospect, it might have been a good idea to call the police *before* removing the body from the lake. Hindsight and all that, right?

Lucy put her hands up as well.

No one else did. In fact, Esther and Shirley were yelling at Devlin for not realizing it was a dead body. Bootsy was checking her boat to make sure it was secure.

Hattie was walking toward us. "Don't point that thing at Mia and Lucy. That's how accidents happen. Ladies, put your hands down. This is ridiculous."

Devlin looked over at her. "Hattie, I'm serious."

"So am I." She glared at him. "Look around, Devlin. Honest to God, do you need to draw a gun on any of us?"

To my surprise, Devlin stared at her, looked around, and then lowered his gun and holstered it. "Habit."

Lucy and I dropped our hands, slowly, carefully. But he didn't try to shoot us, so yay for that.

"You're in the habit of pulling guns on old ladies?" Hattie snorted. "That's reassuring."

He raised his brows at her. "I'm in the habit of reacting when I stumble upon a possible murder while the body is apparently being dragged out of a lake." He looked closer at Rutherford. "What happened?"

"Our anchor was caught on something," Bootsy said "Hattie, Mia, and Lucy came out to rescue us, and they pulled up the anchor. He was attached."

She kept it simple. Nicely done. Never offer the police any more information than is absolutely necessary.

"Attached? Who is it?" Devlin walked over and shined his

light on Rutherford's face, and swore when he saw how definitely dead Rutherford was.

"Rutherford Callahan," Bootsy said.

"The artist?" Devlin swore again, which made sense. What other appropriate response was there to discovering a dead body? Other than, "Hattie killed him," of course. But since we'd already done that, the profanity was probably the next best option. "Everyone stay put. I'm calling this in."

"Can we at least get in our trucks?" Esther asked. "Or are you going to make a bunch of old ladies stand in the rain?"

He sighed. "You can get in the trucks. But no one leave." He gave us all a warning glare, then walked back to his SUV to make the call.

"Let's go." We all dispersed to the trucks, and I climbed in the front as Lucy got in the back seat and Hattie slid into the driver's seat. King Tut was curled up on the center console, cheerfully licking the storm off his fur.

"No murder," I said to Hattie as I ran my fingers through King Tut's fur. "I specifically asked you if murder was going to be involved, and you said no."

"You summoned it to us with that question." Hattie turned the engine on and cranked the heat as I unbuckled King Tut's life jacket. "You get full credit for that one, putting it out there to the universe like that."

As if to agree with Hattie, the lightning flashed and the thunder shook the cab again. It felt much safer being inside the truck, but I couldn't help but turn around and look out the window. Rutherford was still on the beach with Hattie's anchor padlocked to his ankle. "I have a bad feeling about this."

"It might actually be a little more of a situation than you realize," Hattie said.

Lucy and I looked at Hattie in alarm. "Why? Did you kill him?" I asked. The minute I asked, I regretted it. What if she said yes? I didn't want to know that. I didn't want my fledging new

47

start to be ripped apart by the discovery that one of my new friends was actually a murderer.

To my relief, Hattie shook her head. "No, but—" Her phone rang, and she answered it on speaker. "What's up, Bootsy?"

No, but? What the heck was *no, but*?

"Is Glory in your truck?" Bootsy's voice echoed over the rain thundering on the metal roof of the truck.

Hattie frowned. "No. She was with you."

"She's not in here. I don't see her outside. Do you?"

We all twisted around in our seats, peering out the fogged-up windows. "I don't see her," I said. "Do you guys?"

Hattie and Lucy both reported negative.

Alarm suddenly shot through me. "Did you guys lose her in the lake?"

"No, she definitely got off on the beach," Bootsy said. "But I don't see her anywhere. I'll try to call her. By the way, we're not telling him it's Hattie's anchor, so don't worry, he'll never hear it from us that you killed him, Hattie."

"I didn't kill him!"

But Bootsy had already hung up. I didn't entirely blame Glory for bailing. It was the prudent thing to do when finding a possible murder victim. I was actually surprised that I forgot to do that, too.

I blamed Hattie and Lucy. Friends. They made you forget all best practices for staying out of prison. The thought made me smile. I had friends! "Why is Bootsy so convinced you killed him?" I asked Hattie. "Does she know something about you that I don't?"

Hattie shrugged. "She knows a lot about me that you don't."

"Well, of course. I was specifically asking about your proclivity for murder."

"Ah, that. It's not so much murder in general. It's Rutherford, specifically."

Lucy and I stared at Hattie, worry creeping down my spine. "Do you have a past with him?" I asked.

Hattie looked back and forth between us. "This is just between us, right?"

We both nodded, but I couldn't keep the grimace off my face. How ugly was this going to get?

"Here's the thing." She paused. "It's possible that the police might conclude I had motive to kill him."

Lucy groaned, and I felt like banging my head on the dashboard.

"What did you do, Hattie?" Lucy asked.

"I posed for him for a portrait."

I frowned. "Didn't he paint nudes?"

"And sleep with all his models?" Lucy added.

Hattie grinned. "Yes, and yes. Most of his work is life-sized, by the way." She glanced back at Devlin's truck. "The anchor is one thing. A torrid affair? That's a smoking gun right there, ladies."

Either Dead Man's Pond had been good for Rutherford's complexion, or Rutherford had been in his fifties. "Wasn't he at least twenty-five years younger than you?"

She eyed me. "Are you insulting my good looks?"

"No, I just, well, I mean…" I swallowed. "Go you, girl," I said awkwardly. "And…torrid?"

"Damn straight. I'm a cauldron of passion." Hattie grinned. "But being a sexual siren might not be helpful in this particular scenario, you know, given the little situation with my anchor, which incidentally was the anchor I was using with the boat that I lost. Find the boat, find the killer."

Maybe. If only it could be that easy, right. "How did you lose your boat?" I asked.

She shrugged. "It was tied to my dock and then it wasn't."

"Stolen?" By a murderer?

"Or it came loose during a storm. I don't know. But clearly, someone found it and misappropriated the anchor."

I grimaced. "Did you report it stolen?"

"No. Of course not. I figured it would turn up. I was right of course, so, there we go."

I sighed. "Next time, maybe report it."

"Next time, I'll expect a murderer to use it to kill someone, so I'll handle it differently, of course." Hattie's voice was dripping with sarcasm.

Because, right. Who would predict this little situation?

Lucy leaned over the seat. "Back to Rutherford. Is the affair with him really something to worry about? How would the cops find out that you posed for him? It's not like he's alive to tell anyone, and who would ever suspect it?"

"My portrait is hanging on display in his studio," Hattie said. "I agreed to let him keep it for a few months to ease the pain of when I dumped him. He didn't take it well, hence the smoking gun situation."

I started laughing. "Wait a sec. You're telling me that there's a life-sized portrait of you, naked, hanging in Rutherford's studio?"

"Yep. It's a little bigger than life-sized. Maybe eight by ten."

"Oh, dear heavens." Lucy sounded like she was struggling not to laugh. "I love you, Hattie, but there's nothing else I want to see less than a ten-foot painting of you naked."

"Why not? I look great. It'll give you two some life goals for your golden years." She looked back at Devlin's truck again. "After we finish here, we need to go get it before the cops investigate."

"Wait a sec." I held up my hand. "You want to steal a ten-foot portrait?"

"Sure do. Yep. Okay, Devlin's coming. We make this quick and then we're out of here." She looked at me. "You can break into Rutherford's studio, right, Mia?"

My skills were decent, but not unstoppable. But I didn't dare admit it when Hattie had such a hopeful look on her face. "There's nothing I want more than to break into a dead guy's art studio to steal a ten-foot painting of you, naked," I lied.

"Perfect." A hint of vulnerability flashed over her face. "I appreciate your help. This could get sticky."

It was that vulnerability that got me. Hattie was my friend. I couldn't let her go to prison. "Naked portrait stealing it is, then, right, Lucy?"

Lucy rolled her eyes, but nodded. "I'll probably need therapy after this, but for you, Hattie? I'm in."

There was a knock at the window, and we all jumped. Hattie quickly rolled it down, and Devlin leaned in. He looked at the three of us and sighed. "You three, again."

We all gave him innocent smiles. "Plus, King Tut," I said. "He's very sensitive about being overlooked." The cat in question ignored all of us in favor of ridding the lake from his fur.

Devlin ignored the cat, and leaned on the door frame. "Tell me what happened." His gaze landed on me. "You first."

"Me? Why me?" I felt my cheeks heat up as he leveled his gaze on me. Probably because I'd spent a lifetime evading the law. Nothing to do with the fact that we'd had an almost intimate moment less than twenty-four hours ago, and I still hadn't managed to completely forget about it.

Especially when he was looking all rugged and delicious leaning in the window like he was. Devlin was tall, muscular, and tempting. And he'd assigned himself my personal bodyguard, at the request of my most (and least) favorite FBI agent/handler, who I affectionately called Griselda, mostly to irritate him.

Devlin had given me his personal cell number so I could call him if someone tried to assassinate me.

So, he was my protector, and he'd also loved on my cat, sat with me in the moonlight, and come back to save me from a possible murderer. Things like that were irritatingly attractive. Irritating because I was absolutely, unequivocally, eternally burned out on men, dating, and relationships, thanks to my moderately-to-extremely traumatic experience with my drug-kingpin ex-husband.

Raindrops ran in rivulets down Devlin's mocha-brown skin, and I had a sudden and alarming urge to lick them off. *Yikes.*

Devlin didn't seem to notice my inappropriate fantasizing about him. Instead, he answered my question. "Because you're the only one in these two trucks who hasn't been in town long enough to have a history with the victim."

Hattie snorted. "I don't know about that. Mia gets around."

I rolled my eyes at Hattie as Devlin shot a quelling look at Hattie and Lucy, ignoring her remark. "You're my best shot at a straight answer," he added.

I almost started laughing. I'd literally been trained in the art of lying since I was born, especially to the police. If there was anyone least trustworthy in the two trucks, it was me.

Or, rather, the old me.

And I'd buried the old me, so Devlin was right. I was an angel, or at least working on it.

"It was like Bootsy said," I said. "Hattie and Lucy came and picked me up at my place, and we came out here to rescue them. Their anchor was caught on something, so Lucy and I pulled it free. Rutherford came with it. He was tangled in Bootsy's anchor, but padlocked to a different one. We were going to call you, but decided it was better not to get struck by lightning, so we brought him to shore. We were going to call you as soon as we got to the beach." I smiled innocently.

It really was a pretty basic story. Thankfully. Except for Hattie's anchor situation, but since I had no personal knowledge of whether it was Hattie's anchor or not, I figured I had a pass on sharing the info.

"That's it?" Devlin looked skeptical, which was incredibly astute of him.

We all nodded. "That's it," Hattie said.

"What else could there be?" I asked.

"I don't know." He studied me. "I suspect there's a lot more."

I thought of falling into the lake and getting attached to a corpse. "Nothing interesting." This was feeling far too attacky. I decided to go on the offensive. "The question is, why were *you* here?"

He raised his brows, a flash of amusement in his eyes. "I got a call that someone was on the lake in a motorboat. Being that I'm lake police, I decided to come check it out." He narrowed his eyes. "I'm going to give you guys a pass on being on the lake in a motorboat because you were rescuing Bootsy and the gang, but next time, leave it to me. It's my job."

"We didn't realize they were in a motorboat," Hattie said, with impressive innocence. "Or we would definitely have called you so you could arrest them for it after rescuing them."

"I'm not going to arrest them. They get a warning this time, but all of you, stay off the pond. This is the third complaint of boaters this week."

Oh…that was interesting. "Well, since one of them was probably the one where Rutherford was sunk, it might be good to check those timelines," I said, helpfully.

He raised his brows. "You do realize I'm trained to make those kind of basic assumptions, right?"

I shrugged. "I don't know. You were pretty slow on the uptake earlier this week when you were pointing the feather of justice at Lucy."

A smile quirked the corner of Devlin's mouth. "The feather of justice?"

"Yes. It's a pickpocket term. You wouldn't understand."

"You'd be surprised at what I understand. I did tell you about my past, didn't I?"

In a recent bonding moment, he'd told me about growing up in a gang in New York City, trying to bond over our shared criminal youth. I was incapable of developing close bonds with anyone who wore a badge for a living, so it was mostly a fail. But not as completely as I would have preferred. "You did."

He studied me for a second, as if waiting for me to declare him trustworthy and my bestie, but I didn't. I couldn't. The mere fact I found him attractive made me trust him even less.

Women did stupid things around attractive men. Like marry them without making sure they weren't drug kingpins. I'd not only been burned, but I was pretty sure I was actually still on fire, and always would be. "When were those complaints of boaters on the lake? Just in case I need an alibi or something." The "some-thing" being the fact that Hattie might need an alibi.

Devlin narrowed his eyes at me, then tapped the door impa-tiently. "I need to chat with the other ladies and secure the body. I'll try to get you guys cleared to leave as soon as possible so you can get dry, but I'll need to follow up tomorrow. Good?"

It wasn't good. If we waited around there for long, the police would beat us to Rutherford's studio. We had to leave now, before they finished processing this crime scene. "Actually," I said, as he began to turn away. "That doesn't work for us."

He raised his eyebrow at me. "Which part?"

"Waiting around for you."

His eyebrows went even higher. "Is that so? Why not?"

"Because when I was trying to help rescue Rutherford, before we realized he was dead, I fell in the lake. I need to get home and change into dry clothes. I'm freezing." The moment I said it, I real-ized that I was actually shivering. The drama of the moment had distracted me, but as soon as I thought about it, I realized it was true. My entire body was shivering, and my hands felt numb.

"She's in danger of hypothermia," Lucy added. "She was in the lake for quite a while."

"I was," I agreed. "And that water is cold."

His gaze scanned my wet hair. "You fell overboard?"

Hattie leaned forward. "It's true. She even got stuck on Ruther-ford." She held up her phone. "Look." To my horror, she started playing the video of me stuck to him, when his face came up out of the water.

Devlin's eyes widened, as we watched Bootsy cut me free and then I promptly sank out of sight under the churning water. His gaze shot to me. "Are you all right?"

"I'm a little traumatized, and slowly freezing to death, but other than that, fantastic." But dammit, it was sweet of him to ask. I hated it when he was concerned about my well-being.

He swore under his breath. "All right, let me get Rutherford untied from your boat, and then you guys can hit the road. I'll need more details later, but go get warm."

Victory was ours. "Thanks," I said, meaning it. His response also meant that he didn't think it was even remotely possible that we were involved in anything illegal, which also warmed the cockles of my formerly thieving heart. I wanted to be trusted. It was important to me. The fact Devlin did felt good.

"You bet." He paused. "I'll need a copy of that video in case there's a significant detail on the body that got washed off when you towed him in."

"Sure," Hattie said. "What's your cell number?"

Devlin rattled it off, then patted the door frame. "Drive safely, ladies. I'll be in touch." His gaze lingered on me for a fraction of a second longer than it needed to before he turned away and headed toward Rutherford's body.

I let out my breath, and rolled up the window.

"Holy cow, girl," Hattie said, staring at me. "That is some smoking heat when he looks at you. I'm not the only sexual siren working her magic in this town, apparently."

I grimaced. "It's nothing." But I couldn't help but watch him in the rearview mirror as he walked around the back of the trailer to deal with Rutherford. The spotlight from his SUV made the rain on his jacket glisten, and he moved with an athleticism that was much too tempting.

"It's definitely something." Lucy leaned over the seat. "He looks at you like he wants nothing more than to ferret out every single secret you have."

Dear heaven. I couldn't even imagine the damage that could be caused if all my secrets got out. Mostly to me. And my mom. And a few other prominent people. Celebrities.

"Like he's obsessed with you, but in a good way," Hattie added.

"He just saw me almost drown. That's all." I let out my breath, waiting for him to reappear. "He'll find out about the portrait and the anchor," I said, changing the subject. "It won't take him long. He's smart."

"I know." Hattie looked grim. "Great job getting us sprung." She paused. "Are you really freezing?"

"Yeah, but I'm fine. The heat's helping." Devlin reappeared and waved us off. "We're good. Let's go."

Hattie didn't hesitate. "Let's get out of here before he realizes that you preyed upon his protective instincts and decides that he shouldn't have let us go." She shifted into drive and eased the truck and trailer forward. "Mia, I keep a spare set of clothes in the back. Help yourself. I think there's a jacket in there."

"Here." Lucy handed a bag over into the front seat. "This is it."

"Great!" I unzipped it and inspected the contents. The jeans would be too big, but the Hattie's Café tee shirt and sweatshirt were perfect. The dry socks would be heaven. I stripped out of my wet clothes, my teeth chattering. Nothing could be done about my jeans, but the heavy rain jacket was glorious as I zipped it up and pulled the hood up.

I buried my face in the collar and shoved my hands in the pockets as I rested my feet over the heaters. "You're amazing, Hattie."

"Of course I am."

We had just reached the main road when flashing blue lights and a siren came streaking toward us.

"Chief Stone," Lucy said. "He never would have let us leave."

"No one answer your phone," Hattie said as she picked up speed on the main road. "The Chief will probably tell Devlin we have to come back."

My phone rang less than a minute later. I looked down and saw Devlin's name on the screen.

The race was on.

CHAPTER 6

LESS THAN TWENTY MINUTES LATER, Hattie pulled into the garage of a gorgeous log cabin on the edge of the lake. I frowned as she put the truck into park. "Isn't it a little obvious to park in his garage?"

"It's my garage. We're taking my pontoon boat."

"Your *boat*? Where's his studio?"

"Church Island. His dad bought the island a few years back because he didn't like the crowds of people going to church on the lake. It was too many people too close to his property. Rutherford took it over for his studio and inherited it when his dad died." She flung open the door. "Let's go."

"His dad? Who is his dad?" I asked.

"Famous movie producer. Dusty Callahan." Hattie leapt out and slammed the door shut. She was hurrying across the pine needles to the lake before she'd even finished explaining to us just how elitist the Callahan clan was.

Oh...I knew that name. "He won an Oscar, didn't he?" I asked Lucy.

"Six. He was one of our most famous residents," Lucy said as she and I climbed out of the truck. "It's really quite a scandalous story."

Oh...I loved scandal. "Tell me." My boots squished, soaking

the dry socks Hattie had given to me, but at least my feet weren't numb with cold anymore.

"Well, Dusty was married to a famous actress," Lucy said. "They had a daughter, Kate, the woman getting married this weekend at the Yacht Club. Then Dusty had an affair with his makeup artist. She got pregnant with Rutherford, and he fell in love with Rutherford."

"He ditched his wife and daughter for them," Hattie shouted from the dock. "Rutherford was his pride and joy. Spoiled him rotten."

"Think she'll cancel the wedding?" Jake Nash, the flashy owner of the Diamond Lake Yacht Club, had backed out on a fundraiser scheduled to be at the Yacht Club so he could host the wedding. I'd lucked out into being the backup location, and I was counting on that fundraiser to start to build my relationship with the town. If she cancelled the wedding, then Jake might be willing to take the fundraiser back.

Was it bad that my first worry was that Gladys and Wanda might move their fundraiser back to the Yacht Club? Probably. I hated it whenever I proved to myself that I wasn't as awesome of a person as I wanted to be. Sigh.

"Normal people would cancel, but that family isn't normal," Lucy said as she and I jogged toward the dock. "Kate and Rutherford never really got along."

Hattie snorted. "Kate would have the wedding just to spite him."

I frowned. "So, maybe she killed him?"

"No chance," Hattie shouted. "Kate was broke. Rutherford's been supporting her for years, because he inherited almost all of their dad's estate. If he dies, then her money is cut off. She needs him alive."

"Yeah, I heard that, too," Lucy said. "Now she'll have to make sure the wedding happens, because she'll need her new hubs to support her."

"Sounds like a great wedding, then." I didn't want to ever get stuck relying on anyone to support me, like Kate was apparently having to do. My mom might have had a lot of issues, but she was a successful female business entrepreneur, and she taught me that I was capable of taking care of myself. She'd taught me to be resourceful, no matter what I was facing.

I'd married Stanley for love, not need, which was why I'd been able to walk away when I'd realized it was a mistake.

"Thanks, Mom," I whispered as I followed Lucy and Hattie toward the dock. I'd be forever grateful to my mom for teaching me to be independent, no matter what I encountered.

Speaking of independent women, as I hurried past Hattie's cabin, I stole a quick glance at it. It was even bigger than I'd initially thought, with a gorgeous deck that stretched across the entire lake side of the cabin. On the near end was a big screen porch. The cabin was two stories high with a gorgeous stone chimney up on the back side. It was beautiful, cozy, and charming.

I didn't know where I'd expected Hattie to live, but the home had a feeling of luxury that I wouldn't have expected from her. Did she have money that I didn't know about? Not that I'd ask, but curious? For sure.

"Let's go!" Hattie shouted at me from the boat, and I hurried down, my boots sliding on the pine needles as I ran down the slight slope toward the shore. She was at the wheel of a massive pontoon boat. It had to be at least twenty-five feet long, maybe ten feet wide, with the gray metal pontoons that seemed almost as big as my car.

Hattie's dock was shaped like a U. The pontoon boat was in the middle, but there was a ski boat on one side, a kayak on the shore, and an empty slip on the right, which was where the missing boat probably lived.

"Get the bowlines," Lucy said, as she worked on the ropes.

"On it." Impressed with the fact I knew what she was talking about, I hurried out onto the dock and quickly untied the boat. I finished the second one and climbed on a split second before Hattie put the boat into reverse.

I settled down on one of the reclining seats. The boat felt like a living room. The seats were more like couches, vast, luxurious, and beautiful. The console was beautiful wood. The floor was pristine carpet. "You could host a party on this thing."

Hattie winked at me as she shifted into forward. "Oh, you have no idea."

Before I could decide whether I actually wanted to know more, she hit the gas. The boat leapt forward, the huge engine drowning out any chance of conversation unless I got closer to her and yelled.

Lucy came and sat down beside me, her hair whipping in the wind and the rain. "At least the lightning seems to have stopped," she yelled.

"For now," Hattie shouted. "There are more storms rolling in all night. Let's hope we make it back before the next one."

Diamond Lake was much rougher than Dead Man's Pond had been, but Hattie's boat handled it so much better than my little dingy. It was still bumpy, but I didn't feel like we might sink at any time. It gave me a chance to look around.

Unlike Dead Man's Pond, there were lights dotting the shore. I could definitely see some houses. I hadn't had a chance to go out on the lake yet, so this was my first trip. "This is pretty glorious," I shouted. "I need to get a boat."

"Why would the owner of a marina need a boat?" Lucy yelled back.

"Shut up." But I laughed as I raised my face to the wind. Two in the morning on the lake in a boat. A year ago, who would have thought this would be my life? It felt like the home I'd never had. I opened my eyes and looked at Hattie and Lucy.

They felt more like friends than anyone I'd ever met in my life.

I wanted to keep them. As friends. And out of prison. It was time to focus. "What's the plan?"

"We dock. We get the painting. We leave," Hattie shouted.

I grinned at the reminder that these women knew nothing about engaging in nefarious activities. "What's our exit strategy if we get caught?"

"Don't get caught," Hattie yelled.

"That's not a strategy," I shouted back over the roar of the engine.

"It's an island," Hattie shouted. "There aren't a lot of options." She pointed. "There it is."

Lucy and I turned around, but I couldn't see anything. The night was too dark. "Where?"

Hattie shook her head and waved me off, so I knelt on the seat and gripped the rail, watching the approach. It wasn't until Hattie slowed the engine that I suddenly saw the island, looming out of the stormy darkness almost right in front of us. She cruised around it, and then turned on a spotlight on the front of her boat, illuminating a reef of rocks like the one from Dead Man's Pond.

"Hattie," Lucy shouted. "The rocks!"

"I know. This is his private dock." Hattie slowed even more, gliding between the rocks, in a channel that I couldn't discern. "Sometimes his models don't want anyone to know they're here, so he built a dock that wasn't visible from the lake. Only his inner circle knows about it. The rest of the world thinks the dock out front is the only way to land."

As she cruised forward, the island seemed to swallow us up. The land closed around on either side of us. Trees loomed over the boat, stretching up tall. The water was quiet and still, blocked from the storm by all the trees. It was as if we'd drifted into a secret, magical world. The channel was barely wide enough for the boat. I reached out, and my hand brushed over a branch from one of the trees on the shore. "Did he build the channel?"

"It was here. Someone must have built it long ago. It's definitely designed for boats. He cleaned it out and built the dock, though."

"This is crazy," Lucy leaned on the railing, watching the island. "I had no idea this was here."

"Right? It's pretty amazing what he did with it," Hattie said.

She cut the engine, and I saw that we were drifting up beside a narrow dock. Lucy and I hurried to the dock side, and we caught the pilings as the boat eased up to it. We quickly tied the boat as Hattie opened a cabinet in the boat and rifled around.

As soon as we secured the boat, Hattie turned off the spotlight, and the pitch black of the night descended upon us. She turned on a small flashlight and handed it to me. She gave another to Lucy, and she kept a third. "Watch your step. The wood's slippery."

She hurried up the dock, and we followed her. My boot slipped once, but Lucy caught my arm. Hattie stepped off the dock into thick underbrush. I couldn't see a trail through the bushes, but she didn't hesitate.

We fell into single file, with me last. I shined the light upward as we followed the meandering, rocky trail. The pine trees were insanely high, but it was mostly deciduous on the island, the leaves new and fresh for spring.

The rain was pounding on the leaves and my hood, drowning out all other noise. It was so dark and quiet I felt like we were in the middle of nowhere, not a few hundred yards from shore.

The dirt became hard, and I shined my light down to see that we were now walking on a stone path. The stones were covered in moss, but it was definitely a path. "How big is the island?"

"It's about five acres. This way." Hattie angled off to the right, and we followed her up a small hill.

I stopped in surprise when our flashlights landed on an open clearing full of old, wooden pews. At the far end of the clearing was a stone altar, with a birch tree cross. Everything looked like it had been there for centuries. "This is incredible."

Lucy let out her breath. "I remember coming here as a kid until Dusty Callahan bought it. I forgot how pretty it is."

"It sure is," Hattie agreed. "Rutherford liked to paint in natural light, so a lot of modeling is out here. Wait until you see the church." Hattie pointed her flashlight to the right, and I saw a beautiful stone chapel. The windows were stained glass, and the doors were old wood, like barn doors. "It's in here."

I wished I could see the island in the light. I was willing to bet it was incredible. "That's such a bummer that they closed it to the public."

"Dusty was like that. People were hoping Rutherford might open it back up, but he loved his studio so much, he never would have given it up," Hattie said as she tried the door handle. "Locked. Mia?"

I grabbed my lockpicks out of my back pocket. We'd stopped by my marina to get them and drop off a sleepy King Tut, but I hadn't taken time to change into dry clothes. "Is there an alarm?"

"No, there's no electricity on the island. Just a generator for when he's painting in the cold or dark."

"Perfect. That means no alarm." I shined the light on the lock, studying it. The door handle was old, almost ancient, but there was a deadbolt that was from this century. Excitement raced through me. This would be trickier than the padlock I'd opened for Lucy earlier in the week. I'd missed this!

I put my flashlight between my teeth and aimed it at the lock as I kneeled down and went to work.

Fifteen minutes later, I was still working and not feeling quite as confident.

"What's taking you so long?" Hattie asked. "The police aren't going to waste time coming here."

"It's been ten years since I've done this kind of lock." I sat back and frowned, trying not to feel frustrated. "I used to be really good at it. I can do this."

Lucy leaned up against the doorframe. "Which are you better at? Pickpocketing or lock picking?"

"Pickpocketing. I'm a genius at it. I can get anything from anyone—" I stopped suddenly, staring at her in surprise. "How did you know I can pickpocket?"

She was grinning now. "You mentioned it to Devlin."

I grimaced. I hadn't meant to let that slip.

Hattie shined the light on my face, blinding me. "Who are you, Mia? Like, really, who are you?"

I bit my lip as I went back to working on the lock. "I don't like to talk about it." I felt something move in the lock. "Hang on. I think I have it." I leaned in, feeling the lock. I made another readjustment, and then there was a click. "Got it!" I tried the door, and it opened.

"We're in."

Hattie patted my shoulder as she moved past me into the church. "Nice work, my thieving friend."

"I'm not a thief." I quickly put my picks away and tucked them in my pocket. I shined my light into the chapel. The pews were gone, and it was a big open space filled with stuff. Clutter.

Lucy raised her brows. "You can pick locks and are an expert pickpocket. I think thief fits."

Their line of questioning was making me nervous. I didn't want to lose them as friends. It was too soon for them to know who I really was. I headed inside. "I'm not a criminal."

"Well, that's disappointing," Hattie said as she shined the light around the church. "It would have been really fun if you were." She pointed. "There."

Lucy and I turned to look at what she'd found, and both our jaws dropped. As promised, hanging on the interior stone wall of the chapel was a massive painting of Hattie. She was on a rock by the lake on her side, one knee cocked, with a gauzy white scarf draped around her neck. The rest of her? Stark naked.

"Oh, my," Lucy said. "That's a really big painting."

"I know. My breasts are practically the size of watermelons."

Of course, Hattie's comment made my gaze involuntarily shoot directly toward that part of the painting. "Oh. Wow."

"Right?"

"I guess."

Hattie's light lit up her portrait. "I love the way the sunset gives a golden hue to my skin. It's really a masterpiece."

"Were you really that close to the water?" Lucy asked.

"Yep. That rock is on the west end of the island. We needed to be there for the sunset. He wanted to do sunrise, but I obviously can't miss breakfast at the café. So, he agreed to sunsets. It really came out great."

I had a sudden vision of people boating by and seeing Hattie's naked backside stretched across the rock by the shoreline. "Isn't that kind of public? Surely someone saw you."

"Oh, they did, but who's going to be looking at my face, when they get a view of this gorgeousness, right?" She patted her butt and gave it a hearty squeeze. "Okay, let's wrap her up. Don't want this beauty to get rained on." She shined her light at a cabinet in the corner. "He keeps tarps and duct tape in there so people can take their portraits when he's done."

While she hurried off to get her rainproofing gear, I shined my light around the studio. I couldn't contain my curiosity. The man had been murdered. Were we standing in the middle of the reason why?

My light landed on another portrait leaning against another wall. I frowned at all the red, curly hair. "Is that the ghost whisperer?"

Lucy turned around and shined her light. "Holy cow. I think it is. Hattie? You think that's Glory?"

Hattie shined her beam, then whistled under her breath. "It sure is. I look better than she does, don't you think? Her skin is way too smooth and pale. No character. I got the tarp. Let's get this puppy wrapped up."

Lucy hurried over, but I stood there contemplating Glory for a moment. "She freaked out when we found him," I said, remembering. "And then she took off when we hit the beach. This portrait shows she clearly knew him."

Hattie and Lucy were moving fast with the tarp. "You think she killed him?" Hattie asked.

"Well, the odds are she was sleeping with him, right? What if she was a jilted lover?"

"Jealous over the passion he clearly put into my portrait,"

Hattie said. "I get that. Rutherford was very compelling. Most of his models fell in love with him. It was a trial for him. He never could understand why I didn't."

"Why didn't you?" Lucy dragged the duct tape along the end of the painting, strapping the tarp in place.

"I'm an independent woman. I'm not letting some guy dim my light." Hattie shined her light on Glory again. "But I can't speak for our friendly ghost whisperer."

"Huh." I wondered who else our artist friend may have messed with enough to get himself murdered. I wandered down the chapel, shining my light.

It landed on an easel in the corner that was covered with a tarp. I immediately walked over to it and flipped the cover off it.

I sucked in my breath when I saw it.

It was stunning. Literally, stunning. There was a softness, an emotion to it, that I'd never seen in any of his paintings. I could practically feel the brush drifting across the canvas, breathing life into this woman.

He loved her.

That was my first thought, and I was absolutely certain. Rutherford had loved the woman in the painting. Truly loved her.

She was sitting on the same rock as Hattie, naked of course, but Rutherford had been painting her from the back.

Her head was angled slightly, hiding her face from me. Her hair was beautiful brush strokes of light brown. The sunrise was vibrant orange and pink, the lake a glorious miasma of blues and greens, the foliage blurs of green.

She was like a vision in his mind, brought to life by his heart and his hands.

It was impossible to tell who she was. It was as if he'd painted it to ensure no one would ever know who had won his heart. The only identifying characteristic was a butterfly tattoo on her left butt cheek. I leaned in, shining my light on it. It was a beautiful, detailed design, intricate and complicated, the work of a true artist. The tattoo, not the butt cheek.

The wings were dotted with blue and pink, and Rutherford had painted every little line with great care. "Hey, guys," I called out. "Do you guys know who this woman is?"

Hattie and Lucy looked over. "No," Hattie said. "I can't see her face."

"What about the tattoo?" I asked.

"Don't recognize it," Hattie said. "But it's kinda cool."

"I don't recognize her either," Lucy agreed.

I could almost feel him whispering her name under his breath while he painted. I felt like I was invading a private moment by witnessing the painting.

I quickly covered it, then paused, my hand on the drop cloth.

Anyone who had been naked with Rutherford was a possible suspect, even this woman, or maybe, especially this woman.

I pulled out my phone, uncovered the painting again, and took a few pictures of the portrait, including a closeup of the tattoo, then retraced my steps to take a picture of Glory's painting. Now we had two suspects besides Hattie, so that was progress. When the police showed up to search Rutherford's studio, they would have other people to check out besides Hattie.

Things like that made me happy.

It also made me very interested to see what else I could find.

While Hattie and Lucy worked on wrapping up Hattie's painting, I continued to wander around. There were lots of paint jars, assorted fabrics that could have been used for strategic draping of models, some terry cloth robes, and a stash of hard alcohol in the corner.

I didn't find any other paintings. I did, however, find a locked metal filing cabinet. Curious, I pulled out my lockpicks. "I'm going to check this out—"

"You can check that later, if we have time." Hattie held up a large envelope. "I got my sketches and photographs, so let's get my portrait out of here before the police show up." She grabbed two small wooden platforms with off-roading wheels on them. "Come on."

I really wanted to check the filing cabinet, but I didn't want to get caught by the police, so I hurried over and helped Lucy lift the portrait while Hattie slid a wheeled platform under each corner. "Let's go."

Once the portrait was set on the wheels, Lucy and I rolled the massive painting toward the front door while Hattie grabbed a long board. "I'll go make a ramp over the steps outside so you can roll it down." She pushed the door open, then cursed and yanked it shut. "Someone's coming," she hissed.

Alarm shot through me. "Is there a back door?" See? This is why we needed a plan! I couldn't believe I'd let myself get distracted from basic thieving best practices. Being rusty wasn't an excuse. My mom would be so disappointed in me.

"Yes, but we won't make it. Push it against the wall!" Hattie shoved the painting back toward the corner, so it was diagonally across it. "Everyone behind."

"Behind?" I stared at her. "We're not hiding behind proof of motive for a murder—"

"I'm not leaving my painting!" She grabbed Lucy's arm and dragged her behind the gargantuan portrait. I spun around to look for a back door. I saw it in the back right corner, but before I could head toward it, I heard the front door handle turn. I dove for the painting, ducking behind it a split second before the door opened.

I squeezed next to Lucy and Hattie, holding my breath as footsteps whispered into the chapel. If it were the police, we were in such trouble. But when the lights didn't come on, I realized it wasn't the cops. They would have been loud and bright.

Curious, I inched my way to the corner of the painting and peeked around it carefully. Tiny beams of lights were darting around the far side of the chapel. I could see two people, wearing all black, including black ski masks.

For a split second, I had a flash of PTSD from the ski-mask-wearing assassin who had tried to murder me a couple weeks ago and I froze.

Hattie tugged my arm. "What's going on?" she whispered.

"Yeah, who is it?" Lucy whispered.

Their questions jerked me back to the present, and I gestured at them to stay quiet. Honestly, who talked when there were people running around in ski masks? I felt like total silence was the way to go. My partners in crime were clearly not professionals.

Some off-duty training was going to have to happen before we did another run.

But for the moment…I made a slicing motion across my throat to tell them to keep it down, then I edged one eye around the corner of the portrait again.

It was so dark in the chapel that it was difficult to see more than a silhouette, but one person was definitely a lot shorter than the other. Smaller in stature. A woman, I was pretty sure. The other had the broad shoulders of a man.

The intruders were moving quickly, and I could hear plastic rattling. I could also hear them whispering. It sounded like they were arguing with each other.

I leaned forward, trying to hear what they were saying, but at that moment, they split up. One of them ran over to wrap up Glory's painting, and the other one ran over to the painting of the Tattoo Lady. I realized suddenly that they were wrapping up the paintings. They were faster than we'd been, and clearly stronger, because they were carrying the paintings out the door within moments.

But as they hit the top step, the painting banged against the door, and the woman nearly dropped it, letting out a little yelp.

I froze in shock. I recognized that voice.

I'd met her earlier that night.

CHAPTER 7

I COULDN'T WAIT to tell Hattie and Lucy that I knew who had been there.

As soon as the door closed behind them, I whispered, "They're gone—" I cut myself off as someone slipped in the door as they hurried out. This man was taller and leaner, definitely not one of the two that had just left. A third person, for sure. "Wait. Someone else just came in."

"This place is like Grand Central Station," Hattie muttered. "Who is it?"

I shook my head, indicating that I didn't know and we needed to stay quiet. But my mind was whirling with what I'd just found out. I couldn't wait for this guy to leave so I could tell Hattie and Lucy.

He was quick, rattling cans and moving things around.

"Maybe I'll recognize him." Hattie squeezed her head next to my knee and peered out. "Where is he? It's so dark."

I tapped her head. "Shut up," I whispered. "You want him to come kill us?"

She poked me in the back of the thigh, nearly making my leg collapse. So, I pushed my knee into her shoulder, trying to crowd her back before she got us killed. They might not have seen murderers in action, but I had, and I had no interest in shining that light of fun and delight onto us.

"I want to see," Lucy whispered, leaning over my shoulder.

"Seriously." I shoved her back. "You guys—"

A sudden flash of light caught my eye, and I jerked my gaze back to the chapel as he sprinted out the door. I scanned the chapel, trying to figure out what light had caught my eye. It took me only a split second to find the flames licking at a pile of rags. "He set the chapel on fire!" I shoved the painting aside and ran across the studio.

The pile of fabric was already burning, and the way the flames were licking up the side of it made it clear that some sort of accelerant had been used. Or maybe he'd taken advantage of all the oils already around. I spun around, searching the chaos. "Hattie! Where's a fire extinguisher?"

She had her flashlight on now, shining it right into my face. "I have no idea!"

I held up my hand to block the glare. "You guys get the painting out of here. I'm going to look for something to stop it." I shined my light around as smoke started to burn my eyes, but all I could see now were cans and cans of paint and turpentine, and rags that had paint and grease stains. The place was a firestorm waiting to happen, and I was stuck in the middle of it.

Then I saw a fire extinguisher in the corner. I sprinted over to it, grabbed it, and yanked the pin. I started spraying foam on the fire—

"Get out, Mia," Hattie shouted, as she and Lucy wheeled the portrait out the front door. "Come on!"

Before I could answer, there was a sudden explosion from the front of the chapel. I yelped and dove behind the filing cabinet, shielding my head as paintbrushes rained down on me.

The fire was thick and bright, creating a barrier between me and the front door of the chapel.

I sprayed foam in front of me, to clear a path, but the fire was too strong now. I'd have to run through it to get out, but I'd get seriously burned in the process. That sounded fun…Oh! The back door! I sprinted for the back of the chapel, coughing as I ran.

I reached the door and tried the handle, but it was locked. Seriously?

I dug out my lockpicks, frantically trying to focus. I used to be great under pressure, but this was kind of extreme, and I was rusty. I went down on one knee, at least able to see because of the raging inferno behind me, so bonus points right there. I dropped the picks, swearing as I tried to find them in the shadows of the stone floor. I could feel the heat on the back of my neck, which was incredibly distracting.

Focus, Mia.

I imagined my mom standing behind me with a stopwatch, silently judging me for every second that I took. The minute I pictured my mom, I felt a sense of focus and familiarity settle over me. *I had this.*

This time, my fingers were sure and confident as I tried again. The lock clicked almost immediately, and I shoved it open. Relief rushed through me when I saw the outdoors. Yay for not discovering a windowless, doorless room that would be my casket as I burned to death!

Gratefully sucking in fresh air, I quickly packed up my picks and sprinted outside. The cold, damp air hit my face, breathing relief across my smoky, hot skin. I inhaled deeply, then coughed, the smoke still in my lungs.

Never again with the fire thing. It was much too terrifying for me. Across the clearing, flashlights were moving rapidly toward the trees. My friends or the arsonists?

Feeling like an idiot, I cupped my hands around my mouth. "Ca-caw. Ca-caw."

The lights stopped moving, and I heard an answering "ca-caw."

Yay!

"Mia!" Lucy scrambled across the rocks and flung her arms

around me. "We thought you were dead when we heard the explosion."

My heart tightened at her hug. "Glad you guys are okay, too."

"We don't have time for getting all weepy," Hattie said, but her voice was gruff with emotion. "We need to keep going. This island is going to be swarming with people soon."

"Right." I gestured at Hattie to go ahead. "I'll help Lucy."

"Perfect. I'll get the boat ready." Hattie squeezed past her portrait, and hurried up ahead, while I leaned my shoulder against the edge of the painting to stabilize it.

Lucy hurried back to the other end of it and got into position. As quickly as we could, we wheeled the albatross along the trail, using the light from Hattie's flashlight as a guide. We were just rolling it along the wooden planks on the dock when a fire engine siren rang out.

"That's the fire boat," Hattie said. "The police will be right behind them. Come on!"

Lucy and I wheeled the painting directly onto the pontoon. "Lay it down as much as possible," Hattie said as she quickly pulled up the ramp and locked the gate.

Lucy and I quickly moved to the side of the painting. We walked our hands down the sides of the frame and backed to the couches. We both sat down at the same time, the frame resting on our inside shoulder, as the boat emerged from under the cover of the trees.

The rain hit us like a deluge the moment we were out in the open, and I ducked my head against the onslaught, looking over my shoulder as we backed through the rocky minefield. It was so dark, I could barely see the outlines of the rocks, let alone a pathway through them. "Do you want me to turn on a light?"

"Shh. I'm concentrating." Hattie was looking backward as she drove the boat in reverse, and I held my breath as I heard the pontoon scrape over a rock.

We were silent as she navigated the reef. Each time I heard the metal pontoon thud against a stone, I thought we were done, but somehow, Hattie kept the propeller away from the rocks.

We emerged from behind the island, and suddenly the night was filled with flashing lights.

I turned to look as three boats with red and white whirling lights approached the island from the far side, only a hundred yards away. And behind them were flashing blue and white lights. Lake police. Devlin. They were all so close. How did they not see us?

Their sirens were making so much noise, combined with the rain, that our engine was being drowned out. And they were looking at the fire, not for a boat in the water.

My heart started hammering as Hattie continued to back up. All our lights were off, but the flashing lights were reflecting off our boat.

There was another loud bang, and I looked back at the island as a fireball seemed to explode up toward the sky. All the paint supplies were the perfect storm for the inferno.

I felt the clunk as Hattie shifted, and our boat began to inch forward. We held our breath as we watched the police and fire boats gathering at the main dock. All they had to do was look over and they'd see us, but the fire was taking all their focus.

My mom had taught me how easy it was to make people blind to what you want hidden simply by giving them something else to focus on, but sometimes it still amazed me. We were literally only yards from them, in a twenty-five-foot pontoon boat with a giant painting.

But they never looked over.

Driving with agonizing slowness, Hattie slowly eased our boat around the back side of the island, dipping us into momentary darkness. None of us said anything as she rounded the island, still going so slowly that I couldn't hear the engine over the pounding rain.

She continued to drive at that pace, gliding almost silently through the stormy darkness, until finally we were away from the island. "We need to get off the lake fast. Brace yourself, ladies."

I barely had time to shift my weight before she hit the gas. The engine roared, and the boat leapt forward. I gripped the painting, trying to keep it from bouncing as the boat lurched over the waves. I kept watching behind me, waiting for someone to come after us, but no one did.

Gradually, the flashing lights faded, and I couldn't hear the sirens anymore.

I looked over at Lucy and she grinned.

I smiled back. It felt good to win. It always did. Which is why a life of crime was addicting. All sorts of chances to have little victories that felt good.

There was just something so fun about crossing a line and getting away with it... Ack. No. Never mind. There wasn't.

I really needed to do better remembering that I was no longer a criminal.

Hattie didn't slow down until we reached her dock. She cruised into the slip and killed the engine. She grinned as she looked over at us. "Nice job, ladies. That was well done."

"We almost died," Lucy pointed out. "Especially Mia. Seriously. I need to stop hanging out with you guys."

"But we didn't die." I stood up, pushing the painting to an upright position. "That's really the point." That was always the point. If you survived and weren't in prison, all was good. "I saw one of the people in the chapel. I mean, I know who it was."

Lucy squawked and hit me on the arm. "What? And you're just telling us now? Who was it?"

Hattie was still watching me, her face thoughtful. "Mia hasn't been in town long enough to recognize many people in a split second in the dark," she said. "The list is short."

I nodded. "That is true."

Hattie winced. "You know a lot of Seam Rippers, so I'm really hoping it's not one of them."

"It was Glory."

Lucy let out a low whistle. "No wonder she took off when we got back to shore."

Hattie grinned. "A legitimate suspect for the police. That's fantastic."

"It doesn't mean she killed Rutherford," Lucy said. "Hattie reclaimed her painting as well."

I raised my brows. "Glory nearly freaked out when she saw Rutherford's body. I think she was throwing up over the side of the boat. I thought it was because it was a dead person, but what if it was more? That she loved him? That she killed him? That she was afraid of getting caught?"

Lucy leaned the painting against her shoulder as we rolled it down the dock. "You're right. Her reaction was a little extreme. I mean, the woman hangs out with dead people all the time, right? That's literally her job."

"Right? Plus, her little trio torched the chapel to hide any and all evidence."

"To be fair," Lucy said, "it might just mean they're smarter than we are. That would have been a good thing for us to do, just to make sure there's no evidence of Hattie. Who wants naked photographs of Hattie running around?"

"The world would be a better place," Hattie said. "Sunshine everywhere for all to enjoy."

"No one wants to enjoy that, Hattie," I said. "But the point is that we wouldn't have torched the building because we're not actually evil. It takes a desperate and callous mindset to burn a building. We wouldn't have done it, no matter how much it would have helped Hattie."

Hattie looked over at me. "You're right."

Lucy sighed. "That's a good point. We're going to have to up our game, apparently."

I grinned. "You're a little bloodthirsty, aren't you?"

"I'm working on it," she said cheerfully. "Obviously, we can't tell Devlin that we saw her there, because then he'll know we were there, too. So, what next?"

I rubbed my jaw against the painting to clear an itch, my mind already plotting. "You still think they won't cancel the wedding?"

"No chance." Hattie said as she finished tying the boat up. "Kate and Rutherford didn't get along. She won't care."

"Plus, I heard rumors that her new hubs is going to develop a Netflix series with her as the star," Lucy said. "It's her comeback chance. She's not going to mess that up. She's got to trap him while she can."

"The pre-wedding party will go on tomorrow," Hattie agreed. "The event planner running it is Abigail Dogent who is an elite wedding planner. They even flew in Olympia Reese to perform. There's no way they'll cancel it."

I couldn't keep my jaw from dropping. "Olympia Reese? The seven-time Grammy winner?" I was a little fangirl over Olympia. She'd grown up in Detroit, poor, broke, the daughter of an absentee dad and a mom who had been in and out of jail. Her grandma had raised her, and Olympia had gone on to become one of the hugest stars of our generation. Rich, successful, female power. She was my inspiration that I could overcome my childhood.

I'd met her at a party in the Hamptons when I was a kid. She'd been brand-new to her label, barely older than I was, being show-cased for the future star that she was on her way to becoming. It was meeting her that had made me decide I could change my life, too.

She'd gone from messed up childhood to Grammy-winning superstar with a net worth of almost three hundred million dollars. I'd gone from a messed-up childhood to a drug-kingpin ex, a decrepit marina, and three murders in the last three weeks. We were practically twins.

I wondered if she dreamed about our brief encounter the way I did. I bet she did. I was pretty spectacular, even back in the day.

I tried to clear my head from the idea that Olympia was coming to the party. I'd been around enough celebrities as a kid that I should be able to stay focused.

But this was *Olympia.*

No. It didn't matter. I had to stay focused. "Well," I said, "you guys know what we need to do tomorrow, don't you?"

Hattie grinned. "I do."

"I don't." Lucy also stood up, still holding her end of the painting. "What are you guys talking about?"

"We have to crash the party at the Yacht Club." Hattie opened the gate and set up the ramp to get off the boat. "Glory told us she'll be performing. We need to check her out."

Lucy brightened as we started wheeling the painting onto the shore. "I've always wanted to go to one of the Callahan events!"

Hattie gestured toward the garage. "We'll put the portrait in the back for now. I need to figure out how to get it into my house. Once this is over and I'm exonerated, I'm going to put it on display."

I gripped the painting more tightly when the wheels bumped over the terrain. "Do you have a wall big enough for it?"

"Sure. I'll figure it out."

"The party is invite-only," Lucy continued. "How are we going to get in?"

I was already thinking of a way in. Cons were my specialty. "We could dress as security," I said as we wheeled the painting into the garage. "Or the catering staff. Or—"

"We'll be plus ones." Hattie moved a seven-foot-high mirror to the side to get it out of our way.

I didn't want to know what the massive mirror was for.

Lucy and I turned the painting so it was sideways along the back wall of the garage. "Plus ones?" It had never occurred to me to try to get in legally. That didn't sound like nearly as much fun, honestly.

Which was good. That wasn't the kind of fun I wanted in my life anymore.

"All guests will get an invite for a plus one. Esther will definitely be invited," Hattie said. "Kate will hit her up to fund the Netflix series. Esther will be happy to bring me as her date. Lucy, you have some nice houses on your route. Any chance one of them will be invited but need a date?"

Lucy chewed her lips as she lifted the end of the portrait and used her foot to slide the wheeled platform out from under her end. "Let me think on it."

Hattie looked over at me. "Do you know anyone yet?"

I knew one person. "Would Beau get an invite?" Beau Hammerly was an astoundingly wealthy and successful, albeit reclusive and cranky, mystery writer who lived on the lake. I'd met him a couple times at Hattie's café. He had a crush on my mother, the infamous Tatum Murphy, after seeing a low-budget documentary on her criminal mastermind life.

Beau and I had formed an instant bond, despite his attempt to deny it.

Hattie grinned. "Of course Beau got an invite. Kate idolizes his success and money, while her fiancé, Victor Ramos, is desperate to get his hands on the movie rights to Beau's new book. But Beau would never go to something like that."

"I can make him go."

Hattie's smile widened. "I can't wait to hear that conversation."

I tried to lift my end of the portrait off the dolly, but Lucy waved me off. "I got it." She made quick work of the dolly and then we carefully leaned the painting up against the wall.

Together, we draped several blankets over the painting, then we stacked assorted debris in front of it. Two ladders. An ATV. A boat trailer. And even a spare fridge. By the time we were finished, the garage looked like a hoarder's dream. The painting was visible only if you knew what you were looking for, and it was difficult to get to it.

"All right then." Hattie wiped her hands. "Time to get everyone home—"

We all heard it at the same time.

The sound of a boat engine passing close by the dock.

"Lake police," Hattie whispered. "I bet it's Devlin." She swore. "My engine will still be warm if he checks it."

"I'll go see." I hurried out of the garage, skirted the driveway, and ran through the bushes down to the edge of the lake. The boat was already past, but I could see enough of the outline to know it wasn't Devlin's boat. It was a pontoon boat like Hattie's, big enough to fit Glory's painting if they wanted to.

Was it the arsonists, checking to see if it was Hattie's boat that had been at the island?

We hadn't seen their boat. I'd assumed they'd docked at the public dock, but they could have docked behind Hattie's. They might know we'd been there.

They might know we'd seen them.

Oh…that probably wasn't good for us to be targeted by a murderer and an arsonist.

It was a risk that they'd see me, but I stepped out into the water, trying to get a good look at the boat. But it was dark. I had no chance. They were already too far away, chugging around a bend in the lake.

But if that had been them, they knew exactly who we were.

I sloshed through the water and hurried back to the garage. "It was a pontoon," I told Hattie and Lucy. "Not Devlin. Big enough to carry Glory's painting. I think they were checking your boat."

Hattie frowned. "You think it's the folks from the island?"

"Glory might know about that other dock as well. They might have docked there behind our boat."

Hattie let out her breath. "They know we were there, then."

"Most likely, yeah." I looked at the painting, which wasn't quite completely hidden. "Maybe you should come stay at my place tonight."

"Hah! No one chases me from my own home." Hattie wiped her hands on her jeans. "Come on. I'll drive you guys home."

I looked at Lucy, who was chewing her lower lip. "Hattie, someone *murdered* Rutherford and tried to set you up for it. Then they burned down the chapel. If that was Glory, then she and two others know you were there tonight. If they think you can identify them, it's not a stretch to kill a second time—"

"Good. Let them come." She walked over to a lockbox on the wall, which wasn't locked, and pulled out two rifles. "I hope they try."

While I was being slightly alarmed by the number of guns I'd seen in the lockbox before Hattie closed it, Lucy let out a sigh of admiration. "Oh...I like those. You have so many. I only have four."

Four? She had *four*? I mean, I knew she had two, because she'd put one of them in my hand and expected me to use it a few days ago, but four? "You guys frighten me."

"Well, then, you need to toughen up." Hattie set the rifle on her shoulder. "Come on. I'm kicking you guys out. This gorgeous skin doesn't keep its sparkle without getting at least two hours of sleep per night. I gotta be at the café by four-thirty to prep."

I glanced at Lucy and gave her a look.

Lucy cleared her throat as we followed Hattie to her truck. "I really think you should stay with Mia or me, probably me, since I actually have furniture and I'm not sleeping on an inflatable raft in the marina store, but either way—"

"Get in." Hattie opened the door of her truck. "I hope they come for me. Rutherford was all sorts of a lot of things, but he didn't deserve to die. I'd be honored to do justice to his life by finding out who killed him."

I put my hands on my hips. "Do you want to do justice to his life by being murdered?"

Hattie leaned out her window. "That's an asinine question. No one's going to kill me. I always win."

"Rutherford didn't win."

"Rutherford wasn't me." Hattie jerked her chin at the truck. "Either you get in, or you're walking home. Which is it?"

Lucy sighed and climbed into the truck. "When she gets like this, there's no way to win, Mia. You might as well give in."

I still didn't move. "I don't want to come out here tomorrow and find you dead," I said. "I don't have a lot of friends. You matter."

"Aww…" Lucy leaned over the back seat. "That's so sweet."

Hattie grinned. "It *is* sweet. I appreciate it. But I'll be fine, I promise. Now get in or I'll shoot you."

"Hattie—"

"Mia." Her face softened. "Don't treat me like an old lady. I don't like it." There was an edge of steel to her tone that made me realize Lucy was right.

Hattie wasn't going to budge. I sighed. "Don't you dare die tonight."

"I won't. I promise. Now get in."

I took one last look at the lake, but there were no boats in sight. No one sitting there with a jar of kerosene and a lighter to burn down her house. It didn't mean there wasn't one anchored around the bend, but there was nothing I could do. "All right." Reluctantly, I got in her truck.

Hattie grinned at me as she hit the gas. "Don't look so worried. This is going to be fun. We get to go after another murderer."

I raised my brows. "And that's fun?"

"It sure beats me going to prison, right?"

"That doesn't mean it's *fun*." Pickpocketing was fun. Crashing a party at the Hamptons was fun. Hunting a murderer? Not fun. I'd thought my standards of fun were pretty flexible, honestly, but clearly, I wasn't in the same league as Hattie. "Seriously. We're talking about *murder* here."

"Semantics," Hattie said, waving her hand dismissively as she pulled out onto the main road. "We get to have quality girl time, cause trouble, expose a murderer, and crash a party that none of us were invited to. How is that not fun?"

"I'm really excited about the party tomorrow. We get to meet Olympia!" Lucy said.

Hattie nodded. "The food will be fantastic. I'm going to take notes."

I looked back and forth between them. "You guys do realize that this is about a murder, not food and celebrities, right?"

"They're all inextricably intertwined," Hattie said. "Just be grateful the murder isn't intertwined with flesh-eating zombies."

I stared at her. "Zombies."

"Right? Those would be bad. This, however, will be fun. Right, ladies?"

"Right!" Lucy leaned over the seat. "This time, though, I think we should make a pact."

I looked back at her. "What's that?"

"No one gets as close to being killed as Mia did last time."

"Deal," I said quickly. "I agree with that." I'd had enough quality time with guns aimed at my face lately. I was good. I didn't need anymore.

Hattie didn't answer, and Lucy and I both looked over at her.

"Hattie?" I prompted. "Deal?"

She paused the truck at a stop sign, then looked over at us. "Justice is at stake, both for my life and Rutherford's. I vote that we do whatever it takes. No playing it safe." She grinned. "Playing it safe is for wusses, and we aren't wusses."

"Wusses?" Lucy said. "No one has used that word in about forty years."

"They should. It's a great word." Hattie held up her pinkie. "I say, we agree that none of us actually get killed. Other than that, green light. What do you say, ladies?"

Lucy and I looked at each other.

My mom had always said as long as you didn't die or wind up in prison, it was a win. That was literally the motto I'd grown up with. And...hello? Time with Lucy, Hattie, and Olympia "Fine." I hooked my pinkie around Hattie's. "I'm in."

Lucy squealed and hooked her pinkie around ours. "This is going to be so fun. I can't wait."

Hattie grinned. "Me either."

"I can wait." I tried to be grumpy, but it was a challenge. I'd been raised on crashing fancy parties that I wasn't invited to. I had to admit, I was kind of looking forward to it.

Aside from the part that involved hunting a murderer, of course.

Because murder was...well...kind of a permanent thing if it didn't go well for us.

I didn't like that kind of permanent.

CHAPTER 8

IT WAS DAWN the next morning, when a heavy weight thudded on my chest, jerking me awake only a few hours later.

Panic shot through me. I yelped and dove off my makeshift bed as an irritated yowl insulted my quick reflexes.

I paused on my knees, and found myself eyeball to eyeball with a cranky King Tut.

Right. A cat. Not someone trying to kill me.

His fur was puffed out and his tail was stiff as he glared at me. Irritated, because I'd scared him.

Because that was what cats did: blame humans for their problems.

"You literally started it," I told him.

He glared at me. Unapologetic. Offended even.

"I love you, but you need to own that one," I told him, as I tried to get myself grounded. I'd been dreaming of a ghost with wild red hair chasing me with a flaming paintbrush while a bunch of people in black-tie attire cheered her on and Devlin waved handcuffs at me.

I groaned at the memory.

In one night, we'd found a dead body, broken into a murder victim's studio, stolen his property, and been witnesses to a massive arson incident. If someone had seen Hattie's boat there, she looked ten times as guilty as she had when it was just the anchor. "Why do I listen to her?"

King Tut turned his back on me and hopped up on the store counter and sat down next to his food bowl. I climbed to my feet, relief rushing through me at the smell of freshly baked muffins. If Hattie was baking, she wasn't dead or in prison.

After my fiftieth text to her last night to make sure she was still alive, Hattie had threatened me with an untimely demise and cut me off from further communication.

But she'd made it through the night, so everything was fine. Maybe not fine. Fine-ish. Sort of fine-ish.

No. It was fine. No prison. Everyone was alive. It was fantastic.

Perspective was everything.

"It's all good," I told King Tut as I cracked open a can of gourmet salmon blend for him. He'd suffered before I'd purloined him for his own good, so I figured he deserved the good stuff. I filled his bowl, then heard a truck engine outside.

Fear trickled down my spine, and I hurried to the door to look out.

It wasn't an assassin. Or an arsonist. Or the police.

It was a big landscaping truck. For a moment, I stared blankly at it, wondering why there was a landscaping truck backing up toward my store.

Then I remembered that I was hosting a fundraiser tomorrow to repair the tarnished reputation of the marina and secure the goodwill of the community I was trying to become a part of. I'd hired a landscaper, a junk removal team, and a carpenter/painter to get the marina into shape so that I could win over some local love before my attempt at the life I'd always dreamed of crashed and burned. Behind the landscaping truck, pulling into the marina were JunkBGone and I Love to Fish Painting. Yay!

I quickly got dressed, ran a brush through my hair, and had

just finished putting on my sneakers when I heard footsteps outside my door.

A rapid-fire knock at my front door made me jump, but a quick glance revealed it was a woman in her mid-fifties standing at my door. She was wearing a navy hooded sweatshirt that said Founder's Society, a matching hat, and she was carrying a little stack of papers.

Oh...the Founder's Society. The Seam Rippers had mentioned that they might not be happy with me.

I hurried over and opened the door. "Hello. May I help you?"

She smiled at me and waved a flyer in my direction. "My name is Agnes Higgleston, President of the Founder's Society. I wanted to stop by and welcome you to Bass Derby."

Whew. She wasn't going to yell at me for the sign. I smiled as I took the flyer. "Thanks. I'm so happy to be here."

"The Founder's Society is open to membership to anyone who has ancestors buried in the Bass Derby town cemetery." She studied me, clearly judging my response. "Our mission is to protect and preserve the integrity of our town, and to honor the town founders and their vision for a community that's beautiful, at one with nature, and economically viable."

That sounded like a decent idea to me. "That's great."

"It is," she agreed. "Do you happen to know if you're related to a family buried in our town cemetery?"

"I'm not aware of anyone in my family ever living around here," I said. I couldn't be more specific than that, because I had no idea who my biological father was. For all I knew, he could be the biggest crypt in the cemetery.

"Too bad. We're always looking for young members." She looked past me into the marina store, and her nose wrinkled in distaste. I didn't blame her, but her response flooded me with resolve. I was going to make the marina a place that people loved. I *was*.

Right now, I was living in the marina store, because the apartment upstairs smelled like rotting fish. But I had Smell-B-Gone cleaners scheduled this weekend and furniture arriving Tuesday. Once I wasn't sleeping on a pile of life jackets in the store, I'd have it in awesome shape.

Agnes eyed me. "I heard you had a little situation with our Welcome to Bass Derby sign."

Ah…and here it came. "I was present when it got destroyed, but I didn't do it." I met her gaze, kept my tone perfectly modulated, and smiled benignly, all perfectly designed to convey my absolute innocence.

In a moment of perfect timing, her gaze drifted to the wooden loon I'd nailed up above my front door. The loon that had once sat atop that very sign and then been lodged in my windshield. I'd hung it in a moment of rebellion, but now I could see that that might not have been the greatest idea I'd ever had.

She looked at me. "I'd heard that you stole the loon and hung it as a trophy, but I couldn't believe you actually had."

Um…yeah…I'd definitely blown that one. I cleared my throat. "It came home with me after the accident, so I gave it a home." I felt something brush against my ankle, so I immediately bent down and scooped up King Tut, the world's cutest massive cat. "Like King Tut. I also gave him a home." Actually, I'd stolen him from a terrible man, so maybe not the best example. "Would you like the loon back?"

She narrowed her eyes at King Tut, and he immediately growled at her in response.

I patted him on his head. *Nice kitty.*

"How are you going to fix this?" she asked.

I frowned. "Fix what?"

"The sign. The fact that you destroyed the sign, refused to acknowledge it, and are going to be single-handedly responsible for us losing the title of Best Lake Town."

Well, that was a lot to dump on an innocent newcomer to town, wasn't it? I wanted to deny it, shut her up with proof, and restart my arrival in Bass Derby. However, I couldn't tell the truth about what had happened to the sign, because it would get someone I loved in trouble. But running around denying it wasn't helping me either. Honestly, to be fair, the winners for this year's Best Lake Town hadn't been announced yet, but if Bass Derby didn't win for the twelfth consecutive time, then it probably had more to do with the recent murder spree than a destroyed town sign.

I needed to fix this, and there was only one way I could think of doing it.

I didn't want to do it. I didn't want to so much. I wanted to walk into this new life with a clean reputation. But I'd lost that the moment I'd been caught standing in the middle of sign carnage by the police chief.

What did I want?

I wanted a life in this town. From what I'd heard, Agnes and her Society carried a lot of weight in Bass Derby.

Which meant I had to do whatever it took, including take the blame for something I didn't do.

So, I took a deep breath, and did what I'd spent my life doing, and I lied. "Look, Agnes, here's the deal. I did break the sign." *Sob. Tears. Poor me.* "I feel absolutely terrible about it. But I'm going to take care of it."

"Really?" She looked very skeptical, which wasn't entirely uncalled for.

"Yep." I held up my phone. "I have a photograph of it. I'm going to have it rebuilt, better than before, and reinstalled. All at my own expense." At her stoic face, I added. "And…I'm going to have beautiful landscaping planted around it. Some pretty flowers." I'd promise to have it lined with fourteen-carat-gold leaf if that would get her on my side.

Calculated delight flashed in her eyes. "And a stone pillar with a flowerbed on top? I always thought that would look nice there. Are you going to do that, too?"

Wow. I was impressed. She was actually negotiating with me in return for not hating on me. I managed a smile. "Would that make you happy?"

She smiled. "It would."

"Then I'll do a stone pillar as well."

"Great. I'll drop by my design sketches and the name of the stone mason later today." She gave me a smile that was definitely warmer now. "Accidents happen. But good people own up to those accidents and make it right. I appreciate that."

Relief rushed through me. It had been the right choice. "Thanks. I'm really happy to be here. This town is beautiful, and I want to make it my forever home."

Her smile widened. "It is lovely, isn't it?" She nodded at the landscapers who were already pulling up weeds. "You're doing some upgrading?"

"I am. This marina is going to be special." I paused as sudden inspiration hit me. What better person to ask about how to make this marina matter to the town than the woman whose sole mission in life was to love the town? "Is there anything you'd like to see me do here? Any additions? Services? Things like that? What does the town need?"

Her face lit up. "Well! That sounds wonderful. As a matter of fact, I do have some ideas." She pointed to the tattoo parlor that was the third storefront on my property. I'd been told it had an active tenant, but it looked abandoned. I needed to ask Hattie about it.

"Change that into a store that showcases local artisans, especially Bass Derby artists. Support local," Agnes said.

I loved that concept! "Do you know anyone who would want to run a store like that?"

"You know, I probably do." She was positively bubbling over with excitement now. "I'll make some phone calls and get back to you. The Founder's Society has so many great ideas for this town. This property has so much potential. We could do so much! We have so many fantastic ideas but haven't had a place to do them! I'll definitely be in touch!" She whirled around and practically sprinted down the stairs, already pulling out her phone.

"Awesome! I can't wait." I waved good-bye as she hurried back to her car, feeling almost as excited as she was. Why hadn't I thought about leveraging local expertise to figure out how to rehab the marina? This was fantastic! Totally worth lying about the sign and footing the bill for a stone pillar. I knew exactly who I wanted to build the sign—

A car pulled up in front of the deck stairs, nearly running over Agnes. She yelped and jumped back as two women I recognized leapt out of the car. Wanda Barnett and Gladys Donovan, the two women running the fundraiser for the Diamond Lakes Conservation Association. Jake's Yacht Club, my very polished and upscale competitor, had given away their reservation in favor of paying customers who wanted to host a wedding there. Yes, the same marina we were going to be visiting without invitation in a few hours. And yep, that same wedding.

Small town life: inextricably intertwined.

Jake had been a bit of an arrogant toad about their reservation when he'd told them he'd given it away. The ladies had been mad but powerless to change his mind. And I'd been lucky enough to hear the conversation and offer my place for free.

I waved at them as they came up the steps. "Hey, ladies—"

"Drug dealer?" Wanda had her hands on her hips, glaring at me through her scarlet rhinestone glasses. "You're a *drug dealer?*"

Dread slammed into my gut as I saw Agnes whirl around and stare at us, listening. "No, no, you heard wrong—"

"Did I? Because I heard that you said you were a drug dealer, along with Hattie and Lucy, and you were going to be dealing out of the marina!" Wanda looked both horrified and delighted.

I winced, aware of Agnes inching back over to us, her phone clutched by her ear. "I *did* say that, but it was to keep a serial killer from murdering me." I felt like all lies were justified when told to escape serial killers. Seemed pretty logical to me.

Gladys, however, wasn't impressed at all with my serial killer survival skills. She actually ignored them completely. "So, you're not the ex-wife of Stanley Herrera, the drug kingpin who just got convicted based on evidence that included the testimony of his ex-wife?" Gladys was wearing a blue silk blouse, flowing white pants, and white heels. Her pearls were laid perfectly, and her sapphire and diamond studs sparkled as if she'd just polished them. While Wanda was the epitome of spitfire, Gladys was pure class.

Gladys might not find the humor in the situation. Or believe me.

And Agnes's mouth was hanging open now. Dang it! I was not going to let this cascade. I had this!

"Well, I am," I admitted carefully, "but I wasn't involved with his business. As soon as I found out about it, I reported him to the FBI and helped catch him." All facts. All truth. I was amazed at how liberating it felt to have the truth finally out. I'd been hiding who I was since I arrived, and it actually felt like a huge relief not to hide it anymore.

I let out a breath and smiled at everyone. The truth shall set you free!

Agnes turned away and headed back to her car, talking quietly into her phone. I couldn't get a read on her reaction. Had she believed me? I hoped so. I *really* hoped so.

Wanda, however, wasn't satisfied. "I heard you made a deal with the FBI, and *that's* why you didn't go to prison."

"Yes, not because you were innocent," Gladys added.

I grimaced. I *had* made a deal, but it wasn't because I had been guilty. It was because I was handy, and they'd wanted to use me. There was a big difference.

I could lie to them and downplay my involvement. I was a great liar. But these were the people I wanted to be my friends, the town I wanted to believe in me. The truth was, Griselda *had* forced me to spy on Stanley. He'd agreed not to put me in prison as a drug-kingpin accomplice if I helped. The fact that I hadn't actually been in on the drug thing hadn't mattered to him.

And it wouldn't matter to a lot of people. Making a deal with the cops spoke for itself.

But I didn't want to lie to them. That wasn't the life I wanted. It wasn't the kind of relationships I wanted.

"She's not answering. That means she did cut a deal." Gladys let out a curse that didn't match her fashion perfection. "I knew this marina was tainted. Who else but a criminal would buy it? What are we going to do now?"

"Jake said he could get us the middle school." Wanda pulled out her phone. "I'll call him—"

"Wait!" I used to be so much better at controlling conversations. It was so much more complicated when I had to consider the long-term, moral implications of my words. I hurried after them as they turned away. "I promise you, I'm not a drug dealer. I'm not bringing his business to town. I didn't know who he was. I swear it. Run your fundraiser here." I paused. "Please. I need it. I need to show the town that they can believe in me."

As I spoke, Agnes drove past me, giving me a long look before she sped up and left the lot. What did that mean?

"We can't take the risk. Our reputation is everything." Gladys narrowed her eyes. "I honestly feel like a little disclosure would have been appropriate. It's going to be incredibly difficult to move locations in a week for a second time."

"Yes. Disclosure would have been helpful." Wanda pulled out her phone. "Gladys, you call the caterers. I'll call Jake. We'll make this happen."

I followed them to their car. "What would you need to make you trust me?"

Wanda hesitated. "Honestly, I would do it. I love Hattie and I trust her. But we have a situation."

"What kind of situation?"

Gladys glanced at the landscapers who were unloading bushes at that very moment. "The mayor is on our Board. She said we couldn't hold it here. She doesn't want the Association tainted by association with you." She sighed. "We were hoping you would tell us the rumors were a lie, but since they're not…" She shrugged.

"The mayor?" Mayor Stone was Lucy's aunt and the mother of

the police chief, neither of which had helped Lucy from being accused of murder. The mayor was all about the squeaky-clean reputation of Bass Derby, and apparently, she'd decided I was a blight on her precious town. "Give me a few hours to change her mind."

Wanda glanced at the painter who was already on a ladder, scraping the old paint off. "I always loved this place, until Rusty bought it."

"We're excited that you bought it." Gladys nodded at the landscaping truck. "I can't wait to see what you do with it."

"I'm going to do great things, and all of it legal," I said quickly. "Agnes suggested that I turn the tattoo parlor into a store for local artisans and craftspeople, specializing in Bass Derby residents. What do you think of that?"

"Agnes said that?" Wanda frowned. "I hate to admit it, but it's actually a good idea. I hate it when she's right."

I grinned. *Yes.* I was on the right path. "Agnes is giving the marina her blessing," I said. "She's going to help me figure out how to best serve Bass Derby. It's going to be really great, and you guys will be in on the front end of it."

The ladies looked at each other, then Gladys sighed in capitulation. "Okay, here's what we can do. We need to keep working on finding an alternate site, but if the mayor calls us before we commit to another location, then we'll stay. Otherwise, we have to move it."

I was already reaching for my phone. "No problem. I can take care of this."

"I don't know." Gladys looked skeptical. "She was pretty adamant when she woke me up at five o'clock this morning to berate me for tainting the organization by associating it with you."

I was morally offended by that kind of assault to my reputation. "I'm lovely. She'll see that. Don't worry."

Wanda gave me a fist pump. "Good luck! You got this!" They hurried away, both of them pulling out their phones to start making calls.

I needed this fundraiser big time. It was time to play big. There was one person I knew who had the clout to clear my name in this situation, and that was the FBI agent who had roped me into the situation in the first place.

I hit send as I hurried across the front deck, but the phone went right into voicemail. "It's Mia. Call me back as soon as you can. It's urgent." Griselda always answered my calls right away. Or, he used to, when he was still relying on me as his big chance for the arrest that would make his career.

Apparently, now that I wasn't in constant danger of being murdered, he was free to shut off his phone. That made me actually feel good, because it meant that the risk of me being murdered had gone down. He'd never once turned his phone off in the entire time I'd been working with him, and he'd always taken my calls.

He'd made me a priority. Granted, it was for his career, but still.

But now, I did need him, so he was going to have to step up. Since the mess I was in was his fault, he had to fix it.

He'd call back soon. "Urgent" would get his attention. He'd probably think I was cornered by one of Stanley's assassins. He wanted me to stay alive to testify when Stanley appealed his conviction.

I paused to text him before I went inside Hattie's cafe. *Call me. Urgent.*

That should do it. Me, take advantage of Griselda's career hopes and dreams for my own personal needs? You bet.

And now...I needed to get myself an invite to the fancy wedding festivities across the lake. I knew exactly the angle I was going to take...if he were there.

I yanked the door open to Hattie's café. The place was absolutely packed, with people crowded into the booths and sharing chairs. The place went silent when I walked in. A few people glanced over at me, and then everyone turned away, and whispers filled the room.

I clearly heard the last name of my ex-husband whispered repeatedly. *Hererra. Hererra. Hererra.* I grimaced.

My mom had taught me to be anonymous. We'd lived in a world where we tried to be invisible and forgettable, so no one would realize that we'd been in their lives and taken from them. In and out, ghosts who no one could track.

After seventeen years of living life on the outside, I'd burned to belong to a community. To walk down the middle of the street and have people know my name. Friends.

But this wasn't how it was supposed to be. Whispers about my past by people who wouldn't look at me. It was the worst of each of the worlds, coming together.

I bunched my fists and forced myself to smile. "Good morning," I said. "I hope everyone is doing well today."

No one answered. Just the oppressive silence that nicely showcased the murmur of whispers.

Fun, fun, fun.

"Good morning, Mia."

Sitting at his usual table against the wall was Beau Hammerly, a local resident who liked to pretend he wasn't one of the most successful mystery writers in the world. With his uncombed gray hair, he looked like a ragtag charity case, but he was smart and sharp, and I liked him.

I grinned with relief. Beau was still talking to me, and he was who mattered at the moment. "Good morning, Beau."

He leaned back in his chair and clasped his hands behind his head, surveying me with his clear blue eyes. "I heard you stumbled across another body last night. That's two this week. Seems to be a habit."

"No habit." *Please, no habit.* I gestured toward the empty chair at his table. "Mind if I join you? I'll tell you all about it."

Beau looked affronted by my suggestion. "I prefer to dine alone."

"You've said that before, but my mom always told me that

people underestimate how much they need human connection. Most people are starving for it."

Was I above using my mom for my own advancement? Nope. Not at all.

He folded his arms over his chest and gave me an unimpressed look.

"You want to talk murder? I'm your girl." I pushed past him, bumping him slightly, then slid into the empty chair at his table. "Want to see a video of Rutherford when we found him?"

His eyes lit up. "Really? You guys recorded a murder victim?"

"Those old ladies are a hardy group. Honestly, no one seemed that upset." I pulled out my phone and pulled up the video that Hattie had sent me. "Check it out."

I set my phone on the table in front of him and pressed play.

Beau leaned forward, his eyes narrowing as he watched it. At first he looked alarmed, and then I saw the corners of his mouth start to quirk. "I need to watch that again."

I hit play again. "I'm fine, thanks."

"I can see you're fine." He picked up my phone and watched a third time. "This is brilliant. You have to send it to me."

I took my phone back. "What are you going to do with it?"

"Edit it so it looks like you murdered him and send it to the police. Obviously." He stabbed his omelet and shoved a piece in his mouth. "Research, Mia. Everything is research. That's a really clear shot of his face. The way he rose up out of the water like that? Brilliant."

I honestly wasn't sure I trusted Beau with it. I had a feeling Beau had a very nefarious side to him. "Are you going to the Ramos-Callahan pre-wedding day today at the Yacht Club?"

"No. Are you going to send me the video or not?"

"Were you invited?"

He narrowed his eyes and studied me.

I smiled at him.

"Why are you asking me?" He took another bite, but this time, he was chewing more slowly, watching me suspiciously.

"I need to crash it. I want to be your plus one."

"Why do you need to crash it?"

I wasn't about to tell him about the anchor. "I want to know who killed Rutherford."

"Why?"

"You have a lot of questions."

"Because I have more than the lowest baseline of human intellect. Why do you care who murdered a man you'd never met before last night?" He pointed a fork at me. "Truth or the conversation is over."

"Because Hattie's anchor was padlocked around his ankle."

He blinked. "Damn."

"Exactly." I pulled his wallet out of my pocket and set it on the table.

He looked down at his wallet, then flicked it open with one finger. His driver's license stared up at us, a stoic representation of reserve. "When did you get that?"

"When I bumped into you before I sat down." I was using it as proof of my skills. Of who I was. "I took it from your back pocket."

"Huh." He flipped the wallet closed, wrapped his fingers around it, and slid it back across the table toward him. "I could have you arrested."

"You could. Or you could listen to an offer I have for you."

He raised his brows. "I get offers all the time."

"I'm sure you do, but have you ever gotten an offer from a professional pickpocket, petty thief, and con artist?"

He picked up his coffee cup and took a leisurely sip before responding. "Former pickpocket, as I understand."

"Not actively practicing," I clarified, even though I'd used "former" to describe myself for the last ten years, ever since I'd ditched my mom. "But the soul is always what it is."

As I said the last sentence, I grimaced. I'd meant to sound intriguing, but as soon as I uttered the words, it resonated with truth. The few little forays I'd taken into my old way of life while helping keep Lucy out of prison had been fun. Too fun. Too tempting. Over the last couple days, I'd been increasingly wary that the Mia I'd tried to bury for a decade might be very much alive and well, and eager to be resurrected.

Interest sparked in Beau's pale blue eyes. "She speaks the truth," he said softly. "Now, *that*, I find interesting. What's the offer?"

"Go to the party today and take me as your plus one. You can leave as soon as we're in."

"The video's not that good."

"The video is a gift between friends. The party invite gets you access to me."

His eyebrows shot up. "You? That's abhorrent. You're young enough to be my daughter."

The shock in his eyes made me realize he'd completely misinterpreted my bold announcement. Dammit. I used to be so good at this. "No," I said quickly, waving my hands. "I didn't mean I'd sleep with you. God, that's horrible. You have a dirty mind."

"I don't have a dirty mind. You literally announced that you were my payment for getting you into the party."

"Ew. Gross. That makes me sound like a hooker."

He still looked wary. "Then what were you offering?"

"An interview. God, just an interview. Stories about my mom or my childhood. Lessons on how to pickpocket or run a con. The inside scoop on spying on Stanley. What drug lords eat for breakfast. Whatever you want. I probably have a lot of good fuel for one of your stories."

"Huh." He leaned back in his seat. "Interesting offer. Not nearly as horrifying as your initial one."

"I didn't make an initial offer. You put on your dirty old man hat and interpreted it incorrectly." I rested my forearms on his table. "I'm unlike anyone you've ever met, and you know it."

He raised his brows. "If I could interview your mother—"

"She's not around. I'm all you've got." I paused. "This is a one-time offer. Your only chance for the inside scoop you know you want to hear about."

He narrowed his eyes.

I met his gaze. "Please."

"You can't get in without an invite?"

"I could, but I don't want to live that life anymore. This is my home, Beau. I want to respect it."

His brows shot up. "Good answer, Mia." He paused. "I want six hours of interviews."

"Done."

"I want to meet your mother if she ever comes to town."

"Done."

"I want the video."

I grinned. "Of course."

"All right then. I'll pick you up at one. Be waiting on the dock. If you're not there, I'm going home, and you'll still owe me the interview, the video, and an intro to your mom."

I grinned. "I'll be there." I stood up. "Thank you so much. You can leave as soon as I'm in."

"Oh, I have no intention of leaving."

"Really?"

"No chance." He leaned back in his seat. "I'm not doing this for the interviews. I'm doing this because I suspect it's going to be interesting. I'm going to stay for the show. I can't even imagine what you're going to do."

"It's not a show, Beau. It's my life."

He grinned. "It may be to you, but it's a show to everyone else." He pointed to my phone. "A dead guy rising up out of a lake is definitely going into my next book." He waved me off. "Now go away while I finish my breakfast."

I laughed and stood up. "Thank you again. I'll see you—" Movement on the lake caught my eye, and I saw Devlin pull up to the dock with his blue lights flashing.

Was he here about the anchor? The arson? The theft? Or was he there to arrest Hattie? "Tell Hattie Devlin's here." I was already moving toward the door. "I'm going to go see what he wants."

I really hoped it wasn't Hattie.

CHAPTER 9

I HURRIED down the dock as Devlin pulled up to the main slip. He was wearing a navy jacket and jeans in the cool morning, making him look intoxicatingly rugged, which I didn't appreciate at all. "Hi."

"What's wrong?" His voice was urgent as he drifted in toward the dock.

"Wrong?" I caught a bowline and pulled his boat forward, as if I were an old pro at the lake thing. "What do you mean?" Other than the arson thing? The anchor thing? Floating Rutherford? The fundraiser situation? Hattie's watermelon-sized breasts? Other than those things, what could he possibly be referring to?

"Hawk texted that you were in trouble. What's up?" He was out of the boat before the boat had fully stopped, had that line wrapped around the piling and secured almost instantly.

I stared at him. "Hawk?" Hawk was Griselda's "team" name, but Devlin had never told me what team they'd been on together. A black ops assassination team? A pickleball team? Men were so uncommunicative. My guess was black ops pickleball.

"Yeah. Hawk said you texted that something was urgent. He's unavailable so he asked me to check it out. I was on the lake, so it was faster to come by boat." Devlin's gaze swept over my body. "You don't look dead."

Well, how about that? My urgent matter had been delegated. I was pretty sure that I was offended by that. "It was personal."

His eyebrows shot up. "I thought it wasn't personal between the two of you."

"Not personal like that. Just a situation." I paused, contemplating the gift that the universe had just dropped into my lap. I could pivot on this. "Maybe you could help."

He nodded. "What's up?"

"Can you call the mayor and tell her that I'm not actually a drug dealer? That I didn't have anything to do with Stanley's business, and I'm not running a drug ring in town."

He stared at me. "That's it? That's what's urgent?"

"Yep. The mayor apparently told Wanda and Gladys not to have their fundraiser at my marina due to my drug lord activities. They're trying to find another place, but if the mayor calls them first, then they'll have it here. I need this fundraiser to rehab my reputation."

His jaw tightened. "In the last eight hours, I've had a murder, a catastrophic fire, and the entire Callahan clan plus the mayor harassing me to fix everything yesterday. I haven't slept. And you want me to make a phone call about the fundraiser?"

I refused to feel bad for having needs. I set my hands on my hips. "No. I wanted Griselda to make a phone call about the fundraiser. It's not my fault the two of you like to trade off babysitting me."

He stared at me, and then finally inclined his chin. "Point taken." He swore and ran his hand over his head. "Next time, maybe be a little more specific."

"Next time, if I'm about to be murdered, I will contact you directly, seeing as how you're much more geographically desirable when it comes to in-person needs. If it's a favor that will annoy and inconvenience you that Griselda can take care of more easily..." I paused, thinking about it. "Maybe I'll contact you anyway just to irritate you."

The corner of his mouth quirked. "You'd do that, would you?"

"I might have to. My moral obligation after being unfairly attacked and judged."

He raised his brows. "I didn't attack you."

I raised my brows right back at him.

After a moment, he sighed. "All right, maybe a little. But in my defense, I thought you were in actual danger."

That was sweet. "Don't be sweet."

This time, he actually grinned. "I'm never sweet."

"That was sweet. I don't have time for sweet." I put my hands on my hips again, trying to change the subject to something less scary than a man who was attractive, charming, protective, and carried a gun. Oh! Like the gap in my latticework. "I did find a hole under my deck last night. It's big enough for an assassin to hide under." Seeing as how I'd made it through the night without being killed, I was pretty sure no one was hiding under there. "Maybe you could check that out?"

He narrowed his eyes. "Are you making that up just so I have to crawl through the mud?"

"No, but now that you mention it, that would be a fun bonus."

"Mia—"

"Never mind." I suddenly realized it was probably better to keep him away from the building. He might decide to arrest Hattie while he was up there. "What fire are you talking about?"

He started walking up the dock toward the parking lot, clearly oblivious to my deft attempt to distract him from the lattice hole. "Church Island. I'm surprised you haven't heard about it. It's a small town."

I grimaced and hurried after him. "What's on Church Island?"

He looked over at me. "A church."

Well, wasn't he going to be helpful? "The church was on fire?"

We reached the parking lot. "Which side is the gap on?"

"The right side. At the end of the building. Why would someone burn down a church?"

He spun around to face me. "How did you know it looks like arson?"

Whoops. He'd totally sidetracked me with his muscled quads and gotten me off my game. "You literally just said that," I lied.

He frowned. "I didn't mention arson."

"You did. You said you hadn't slept, that you'd been dealing with a murder, a catastrophic arson incident, and the entire Sullivan clan and—"

"Callahan clan," he corrected, still frowning at me.

I knew he was replaying his comment to me, trying to decide if he'd really said arson or not. The power was in the details. I'd remembered enough of them, then focused his attention on the wrong family name, and now he wasn't sure.

Classic con artist skills. I was glad I still had them after all the years of trying to be completely honest and angelic. Not that I wasn't still honest and angelic. But sometimes skills were needed, like to cover up that I'd been at the site of the fire engaged in activities that he might consider illegal and suspicious. No need for that, right? "Callahan," I agreed. "Right. I forgot. Any leads on who killed Rutherford or why?"

He looked at me suspiciously, and then resumed heading toward the deck. "Don't get involved, Mia."

"I'm not involved. I just spent the night dreaming of a killer ghost coming out of the lake and trying to drown me. It was a little traumatic. I figure information is power and all that."

He crouched down in front of the gap and pulled out his flashlight. "Don't get involved."

"You just said that."

"I sensed that it needed to be repeated."

His thighs were seriously corded. Why was he crouching? He was probably trying to distract me. It wouldn't work. I was immune to men for the rest of my life. "I'm offended by your lack of faith in my non-meddling character. Why would I get involved?"

He shined his light under the deck. "You got involved with the last one."

"Because you were going to arrest the wrong person, someone I cared about." I paused. Wow. What a perfect lead-in so I could ask questions without appearing as if I'd pinkie-sworn with Hattie and Lucy to get heavily and irrevocably involved. "Are you going to arrest the wrong person again? Someone I care about?"

He peered under the wood. "Who do you care about? Maybe you could give me a list of names of folks you would prefer I don't arrest."

I didn't like that answer. It was sassy and evasive. I did respect it, though. And okay, who was I kidding? I liked it, too. Sassy and evasive was kind of my thing. "So, who killed him, and why? Any suspects?" I asked, completely and obviously ignoring his question. Because I was also sassy and evasive.

"I don't see any footprints." He touched the broken lattice. "The break is new, though. Not more than a day or two at most."

Alarm shot through me. "Really?" I leaned over him and saw that the broken wood was still bright and clean, not aged at all. Fear trickled down my spine. "Should I be worried?"

"I don't know yet." Devlin walked along the side of the deck, stopping every few feet to shine his light through the lattice and inspect.

"See anything?" I crouched down to peer through the lattice with him, but there was so much junk under there that it was impossible to see very far, even in the daylight. I was going to have to have the junk removal people clear it out. Why make it easy for assassins to lie in wait?

Devlin put his hand on my shoulder and gently pulled me back from the deck. "On the chance there is someone hiding in there ready to kill you, I'd prefer you to stay out of range."

"Okay." A second round of fear shot through me, and I immediately scooted backward, letting him insert his heroic body between me and any incoming bullets.

It was easy to forget that my ex's mom had sent an assassin after me just before I moved to Bass Derby. Boston felt like a million miles away, but it was only a few hours. I wasn't safe if someone from my old life decided to come after me.

Something moved out of the corner of my eyes, and I jumped back instinctively as King Tut landed on the edge of the deck. He sat down, his fluffy tail twitching as he blinked at me. He'd save me, right? Maybe.

I let out my breath and clasped my hands on my head as some customers came out of the café. Instinctively, my gaze shot to them, and I quickly scanned them for guns, shifty eyes, or other assassin-like traits, but they looked like locals. Harmless. I would know, right?

"I'm going under to see what I can find." Devlin stood up and looked at me, then his face softened at my expression. "It's all right, Mia. It's safe."

"Right now it is." I let out my breath. "I'm sure it's fine. If someone was coming after me, Griselda would know and he'd warn us. Like before." Of course, last time, his warning had come about three seconds before the assassin had shot out my front door, but hey, I'd survived, so it was good, right?

"Hawk would warn us," he agreed, too easily, as if he didn't necessarily have full faith that Griselda would keep us safe. "Stay there. I'll be right back." Devlin raised his hand as if he were going to pat my shoulder, but he dropped it without touching me. Then he went down on his knees and crawled under the deck, right into the mud. King Tut leapt off and trotted after him, following Devlin into the darkness.

King Tut had a crush on Devlin, which I could totally understand. The man was crawling around in mud to make sure I wasn't going to be murdered. Granted it was because his bestie asked him for the favor, but since it was my life at stake, I appreciated it. A lot.

He and King Tut reappeared a few moments later. Both were caked with mud. King Tut trotted down to the lake to wash off, but there wasn't anything Devlin could do about the mud caked on his pants, his shirt, and his face. He was filthy, a mess, and completely attractive. "Can you stay with Hattie or Lucy tonight?"

I blinked. "What? Why?"

"I think it would be a good idea."

My heart started pounding. "What did you find?"

"Maybe nothing. I'm going to check with Hawk."

"*Maybe* nothing? So, maybe something, right?"

"There's no one there right now, so you're fine."

I put my hands on my hips. "*What did you find?*"

"I don't want to freak you out."

Men. They were so stupid sometimes. "It's a little late for that. Spill."

He sighed. "I found a listening device. It looks like it's been there for only a day or two. No dust or dirt."

Fear gripped me. "Why would someone put that under the deck? Nothing happens on the deck."

"I don't know, but I'm going to have someone sweep the rest of the marina and your car. Watch what you say on your phone until I can check it."

Holy crap. "You mean like not announcing that I'm taking over Stanley's drug empire and running it up here?" Like I'd claimed a few days ago to stave off a serial killer.

"Like that, yeah."

I closed my eyes. My hands were suddenly clammy. "I thought this was over."

He raised his brows. "You were one of the main witnesses against a major drug heavyweight who is going to be appealing his sentence. It won't be over for a long time. Years." He paused. "Have you had any more thoughts on witness relocation?"

"And give up Bass Derby? No. I'm not doing that." I'd been unwilling to go into Witness Relocation when I had nothing else to hold onto. But now that I had a home? There was no chance I was giving it up just to make it more difficult for the bad guys to find me. I took a breath. "It's fine. It probably has nothing to do with Stanley. Besides, if they knew I'm here, they could have killed me already. They didn't so, it's fine."

Devlin didn't look like he thought it would be fine. "Be careful."

"I am careful." I put my hands on my hips and tried to focus on something else. "Can you please call the mayor? It would be really helpful."

"The mayor." He didn't look all that amused that I was back on the fundraiser thing when there were much more police-y things to focus on.

"If I'm going to be murdered, I want to make the most of the time I have. I need that fundraiser. Please?"

He sighed. "I don't know what I'm at liberty to share with the mayor. You'll have to ask Hawk."

"I did ask Hawk, and you took over." God. Men. They were like trying to herd carts. Cats. Carts or cats. It didn't matter. Both were equally impossible to corral. "Call him now. He'll answer your call."

"I'm not calling him. He's not available. The fact he broke cover long enough to text me about you is enough."

Griselda broke cover to make sure I was safe? That was pretty adorable. He got a few brownie points back for that. But just a few.

Devlin put his flashlight in his pocket. "Is Hattie here?"

I blinked innocently. "Hattie?"

He raised his brows. "The woman who runs the café in your marina?"

"I don't know. I haven't been in the café today. Why?" Of course she was there. The café was open, and food was being served.

He rubbed his jaw. "You know anything about the anchor that was on Rutherford's ankle?"

Ah…we were already to that. "Well, I saw it was padlocked to him. I notice locks. It's my thing." I wasn't going to talk about the fact the anchor was pink. "The padlock was new. It hadn't been under the water long. Maybe a day at most."

He studied me.

I smiled.

"You happen to know whose anchor it was?"

"One of them was Bootsy's. From her boat. That's why they were stuck out there. Because their anchor was caught on him."

"What about the other one?" He was watching me carefully.

I could tell he knew it was Hattie's anchor, so I changed tactics, took advantage of my perceptiveness, and redirected my answer. "I don't know, but I doubt it belonged to the murderer. Who would be stupid enough to padlock a murder victim to their own anchor? If anything, they would choose someone else's anchor to send the cops off after an innocent person."

He sighed. "You know it's Hattie's anchor."

"Hattie's?" I blinked. "What are you talking about?"

"Give it up, Mia. I'm not an idiot."

"And neither is Hattie. She'd never murder someone with her own anchor. She's too smart for that. She'd definitely use someone else's anchor."

His eyebrows shot up and the corner of his mouth quirked. "I'm not sure that's helping her case."

"I don't need to help her case. Anyone who knows her knows she didn't kill him."

"I still need to speak with her." He looked up at the café. "Can you ask her to come out? I don't want to cause a scene for her."

Well, that was considerate for her at least. "Why don't you go around back? She can meet you at the kitchen entrance."

"Sounds good." He paused. "Mia, seriously. Be careful. Call me if you notice anything at all. It matters that you're safe."

"Because of the case, I know." Griselda had made it very clear that I was a lynchpin of their case against Stanley. I was tired of being nothing more than a tool for him. I turned away and started toward the deck steps.

"That's not the only reason," he muttered.

Devlin's words stopped me in my tracks. I turned to look at him, but he was already walking away, striding around the deck toward the back of the marina. Had I misheard him?

Not that it mattered. The last thing I needed was to start obsessing over the cop who liked to arrest my friends and was a pal of the FBI agent who had stolen my life from me.

I had to focus.

I had a high-class party to crash in just a few hours, a fundraiser to host, and a murderer to find before the scales of justice pointed its middle finger at my friend.

CHAPTER 10

I VAULTED up the steps and hurried into the café. Beau was already gone, and some of the crowd had left. I waved at Nico Stefanopoulos, one of the Greek twin football players who worked for Hattie, and headed straight for the kitchen.

I flung the door open and headed inside. Cris Stefanopoulos, the twin with culinary talents, was at the grill. Hattie was up to her elbows in flour, apparently in the midst of baking the fresh bread that she was a master at. "Hey, Hattie."

She grinned at me. "I'm Esther's plus one for the party today. Lucy said she got a date. You get Beau?"

"I did."

"Really?" Her face fell. "I was really looking forward to seeing you fake your way in."

I had to admit, a part of me felt the same way, but a bigger part of me was very happy I wasn't going to have to tap into old skills any more than I already had. "Devlin's here. He's coming around back." I paused. "He knows it's your anchor."

She grimaced and wiped her hand on her apron. "No problem. He has nothing on me."

I didn't say anything. Because we both knew that wasn't entirely true.

"Cris, I'll be right back. You're in charge."

Cris gave her a thumbs up as Hattie and I hurried outside. Devlin was already back there. My soggy cat was sitting at his feet, gazing up at him with hero worship.

I was the one who'd rescued the cat. Seriously.

Devlin looked over at us as we walked out. "Good morning, ladies."

Hattie put her hands on her hips. "Did you want takeout? Because you have to text it like everyone else."

He didn't smile. "Did you recognize the anchor locked around Rutherford's ankle?"

She stood taller. "It looked familiar."

"Was it yours?"

She shrugged. "It looks like one of mine, but I didn't look at it closely enough to make a definite call on it."

He held out his phone. "Here's a picture."

She took the phone and looked at it. I peered over her shoulder. I could see her initials etched on the side of it. "Yep, that looks like mine," she said. "My boat disappeared from my dock earlier this week, and that's the anchor that was on it."

Devlin took his phone back. "Why didn't you tell me last night that it was your anchor?"

"You didn't ask." She put her hands on her hips again.

He cocked an eyebrow. "Hattie."

"Fine." She waved her hands. "Because you would have done the same thing you're doing now, and running around wasting time looking at me, when I didn't do it. Plus, Mia was freezing and I wanted to get her home, not spend hours trying to convince you that I'm not stupid enough to use my own anchor if I were to kill someone."

I grinned. "See? I told you. Hattie would be a much better murderer."

"Exactly."

Devlin sighed. "Can you tell me how your anchor got padlocked to Rutherford?"

Wow. Right to the point.

Hattie raised her chin. "No. I have no idea."

He raised his brows. "But it's your anchor."

She threw up her hand in evident exasperation. "Are you even listening?"

"He's testing your story," I said. "He'll keep asking in a bunch of different ways to see if your answer changes. Cops are annoying like that."

The annoying cop in question shot an unamused look in my direction, so I smiled at him.

"My boat went missing, and now I'm wondering if it was actually stolen," Hattie said, drawing both of our gazes back to her. "Find my boat, and maybe you'll figure out who took my anchor."

Awareness suddenly dawned on me. "If it was stolen for the purpose of taking Rutherford out on the lake, then you have to wonder if they chose you specifically to take the fall." As I said it, Hattie looked over at me, and I saw that she'd just realized the same thing. Neither of us had thought about *why* the murderer had chosen to use Hattie's anchor.

She and I stared at each other as the thought sank in.

"Who would want you to go to jail, Hattie?" I asked.

"No one. I'm lovely."

I grinned. "I know, but it's your anchor—"

"Right, it is." She looked over at Devlin. "Find my boat."

Devlin had his little notebook out now. I thought he was making a note of Hattie's wise command, but as soon as he looked up, he didn't ask for a description of her boat. Instead, he said, "Where were you on Monday morning between two and five?"

Wow. He wasn't nearly as charming when he was in work mode. I didn't like how focused he was. It didn't bode well for Hattie.

"In bed," she said.

"Any witnesses?"

"To me being alone in bed? No. And my boat is a ten-foot hot pink fiberglass beauty with a twenty-horsepower motor. It's called Fierce Woman. You might want to write that down."

Of course that was her boat. How could she have anything less? Hattie was like a shining beacon of empowerment to every woman.

Devlin inclined his head. "I'll make a note. What about Tuesday evening between eleven and three?"

This wasn't going in a good direction at all. "Why?" I interrupted. "Is that when Rutherford was killed?" I asked, both to distract Devlin and because the more info I had, the better. "Or was he dumped that day? Was he killed before being padlocked, or was he drowned?" All questions I never thought I'd be asking.

Devlin looked at me. "Where were you on Monday?"

Seriously? Now that was just annoying. "Same as Hattie, but not with Hattie."

"No," she agreed. "We don't have that kind of relationship."

"Not that you're not attractive," I said. "If I was into older women, you'd definitely be my first pick."

She smiled. "Sweetheart, I'm everyone's first pick."

Devlin cleared his throat. "What about Tuesday night?"

"Tuesday night was busy. Wasn't that the night we were shot at?" Hattie said.

"Right. We were shot at by the man who was *actually* a serial killer, instead of Lucy, who the police were planning to arrest," I agreed.

"Between eleven and three in the morning," Devlin continued, clearly trying to regain control of the discussion, which really was a hopeless task.

Hattie and I were both really good at this sort of thing. She could have been my mother, except that she wasn't nearly as bad an influence on me. Or maybe she was, but in a different way. Hattie sucked me into things because it was fun, not because I was a helpless child. Not that my mom ever let me be helpless.

"Don't you have in your log what time all that went down?" Hattie asked Devlin. "Mia did call you, didn't she?"

"I did call," I agreed, "and you showed up. You're Hattie's witness for that little escapade," I concurred. "And after that, Hattie, you went home with Lucy, right? To give her an alibi so the cops couldn't blame her for more murders." I wasn't sure that the events happened during that time window, though. I'd have to look at my phone and see what time I called Devlin. It would be so fantastic if it was that easy to alibi Hattie out.

"I did go home with Lucy for that exact reason," she agreed.

"Funny that keeping Lucy out of prison actually gives you an alibi for a crime you didn't commit, right?"

"Also funny that the police keep coming after innocent people," she said.

"All right." Devlin closed his notebook, looking annoyed. "Mia. Go inside. I need to talk to Hattie alone."

We both grinned. "I like having Mia here," Hattie said. "She can be my witness in case you try to entrap me."

"I'm not trying to entrap you." He looked like he was wishing he was home in bed sleeping all of this off. "What was your relationship with Rutherford?"

Oh… I said nothing. Messing with Devlin was one thing. Outright lying to police in a murder investigation when they would probably find out was another.

Hattie, however, looked right at him and lied. "I didn't know him personally. I knew *of* him, because everyone does. I met him a few times, but that's it."

Oh…Hattie. Why had she lied? If they found out the truth, she would look so guilty. But at the same time, it didn't serve anyone to have them going after an innocent person.

I used to lie to the police all the time. The fact I was now trying to be a law-abiding citizen who didn't lie to the police didn't mean I couldn't understand how helpful it could be at times for making sure justice actually prevailed. And by justice, I meant that good people didn't get arrested. Not necessarily people who were innocent of everything under the sun, but good people who weren't guilty of the specific incident in question.

Hattie definitely fit that bill.

But at the same time, if they figured out she modeled for Rutherford and had a torrid affair that had left him heartbroken, the fact she'd lied about it would look really bad for her.

Devlin's eyes narrowed. "Is that so? You never spent any time with Rutherford alone? You had no relationship with him at all?"

Did they already know? Or was he just pushing at her?

Hattie didn't even blink. "He did offer to have sex with me, but he wasn't my type."

"Too young?" I asked.

"Too haunted."

Devlin and I both looked at her. "Haunted?" Devlin asked.

"Absolutely. You could see it in his eyes. He was a tormented artist, not a happy, inspired one. I don't take other people's burdens into my bed. I like myself more than that." She paused, then snapped her fingers as if she'd just had a brilliant idea. "But ask Glory Starr. When we pulled him out of the water last night, I could have sworn she said something about posing for him."

Oh, that was nicely done. I was impressed.

"Glory Starr?" He wrote the name down. "Who is that?"

"She was in the boat with Bootsy and the others last night, but she took off when we got back to shore. She was supposed to summon Jack the Ripper's ghost, but surprisingly, failed to. She's going to be entertaining at the pre-wedding party at the Yacht Club today."

Devlin grunted. "Anyone else you know of who knew him?"

Hattie sighed. "Pretty much everyone knew him, but no, I don't know anyone else who has had an up close and personal relationship with him. Find the person who took my anchor, and you'll find the murderer."

I wanted to show Devlin the photograph of the naked woman with the butt tattoo, but then I would have to explain how I got the photo, and I had a feeling that wouldn't go over well for us.

"Maybe." Devlin closed his notebook. "I'll be back with some more questions, I'm sure. Have a nice day, ladies." He paused to look at me. "Remember what I said."

I wasn't sure which part he was referring to, but I nodded. "Okay."

He made a noise of exasperation. "Stay with Hattie or Lucy tonight, until we're sure you're not in danger."

Oh, that. Right. I'd already forgotten about that. "Sure."

"In danger?" Hattie's gaze grew sharp. "What kind of danger?"

Devlin kept his attention on me. "Call me if you notice anything."

"I will if you'll call the mayor for me."

He raised his brows. "You're going to barter keeping yourself alive to get me to make a call? That makes no sense."

"Of course it does. Griselda will hunt you down if I get murdered, and you'll be haunted your entire life by the guilt of knowing that one simple phone call could have saved my life. It will totally work. I'm much too adorable for you to get over if I die."

He narrowed his eyes at me.

I smiled.

Finally he grunted. "I'll see what I can do."

"Perfect. Thank you."

He shoved his notebook in his pocket. "I'll be back."

"Can't wait," Hattie said.

"You sound like the Terminator," I observed. "'*I'll be back.*' Is that a threat or advance notice of a warm hug?"

The corner of his mouth quirked up, but he shook his head as he turned away. "I'm going to shoot Hawk for getting me to agree to watch out for you." He muttered it under his breath, but definitely loud enough to make sure we heard it before he disappeared around the corner in the direction of the docks.

I grinned. "He adores me," I said to Hattie. "It's pretty clear I'm winning him over."

"What kind of danger?" she asked, uncharacteristically ignoring a chance to talk about my dating life.

Which was fine. I wasn't going to date him, so there was really nothing to discuss. "The deck was bugged. Devlin thinks an assassin might be hunting me."

She cocked an eyebrow at me. "Really?"

I shrugged. "It's happened before."

"Which part?"

"Both of them, but my house was tapped by the feds and I knew about it. The assassin thing was a rogue murderer sent by my ex's family. And my ex-mother-in-law also tried to kill me, but they were together so I combine them into the same event. It's easier to keep track of that way."

She frowned. "I'm pretty spectacular, but I'm not really equipped to take on a professional killer. I think you should sleep at Devlin's house, not mine."

Ah…there she was. I'd missed her dating interference so much for these last thirty seconds. "I'm celibate. Forever."

She raised her brows. "So you say, but I'm not sure I believe you. I think you should make him jealous with Beau. He'll come after you so fast."

I grinned. "Devlin is a thirty-something, hot, sexy cop who could probably scale a building after running a marathon. Beau is old enough to be my dad, plus he's cranky. I don't think Devlin will be threatened."

"Rich old men love to date young hotties," Hattie said. "It's not impossible."

I was pretty sure Beau would shoot me himself if I tried to flirt with him. "I don't want Devlin to want me. And Beau has a crush on my mom. So we're good."

I heard a loud crash from the front of the marina, and I grimaced. "I need to go check and make sure my painter didn't just fall off a ladder. I'll see you at the Yacht Club around one." I paused. "Is it a dress-up event?"

"No. It's like a beach day." Hattie headed back into the kitchen. "Remember, when we walk in there, we're going to be poking at a murderer and trying to expose him. They don't usually like that."

I thought of the assorted guns that had been pointed at my face lately and grimaced. "Let's not poke at him. Let's just expose him."

"Same thing, babycakes. Try not to die. I like you."

CHAPTER 11

I was excited.

I was nervous.

And I felt like I was perched on the tippy top edge of a cliff that had a straight drop off that either would land me on a trampoline or a valley of nails pointing upwards.

Why? Because I was literally standing on the precipice of my old life. Going to the parties of the rich and famous had been my mom's shtick. We'd done it countless times, all with the goal of conning something out of someone, usually a luxurious vacation stay.

We'd sleep in our car the night before. Then in the morning, we'd go to a rest stop to shower and change into designer brands, real jewels (obtained under not quite fully honest circumstances, of course), with makeup and hairstyling that rivaled even the most professional artistic creations.

Then we'd call a car service and show up to the party in a Rolls Royce.

By the time the party was over, we'd either be on the run, or else we'd be sitting pretty with an invite to a summer at the Hamptons.

And when that invite ran out, we'd do it again.

An adventurous, no-holds-barred way of life that I'd both adored, and been hugely embarrassed and horrified to be a part of. So, I'd left. For good. Until today.

Until I was standing on the dock at five minutes before one, waiting for Beau to show up and get me into a fancy party that I hadn't been invited to, so I could work my way through the crowd and get what I wanted.

Sending myself into that party was kind of like handing an addict the keys to my ex-husband's basement.

All morning, I'd been watching the preparations at the Yacht Club, which I could see from my marina. Balloons. Banners. Tents in the parking lot. Flowers lining the docks. Bouquets anchored in the lake.

Two hours ago, I'd seen the bride and her party arrive in a pontoon boat covered in white roses, trailing vines of water lilies, and a white lace canopy, escorted by six small motorboats covered in more white flowers, silver bells, and white twinkly lights, carrying what I assumed was the wedding party.

It was gorgeous. Magical. And told me exactly the level of money I was dealing with for this party. Top of the line.

But, as I'd done during the first seventeen years of my life, I was going anyway. With ten years of rust on my party skills. Without my mom to show me the way. With murder, Hattie's freedom, my reputation, and my first-ever real home at stake.

The pressure was on.

I took a deep breath and shook out my shoulders as Beau cruised up to my dock, driving a gorgeous speedboat that looked like it could make it from one end of the lake to the other in less than a minute. He raised his brows. "I'm stunned by your metamorphosis."

I grinned. "Designer labels and jewels make a girl, right?"

"Did you steal the jewelry?" He slowed the boat, but didn't pull into the slip.

I grabbed the edge of the boat and hopped in, showing off my newly acquired lakeside prowess. "That's so rude to ask me."

"I'm rich and famous. I can be rude. Did you steal them?"

"I bought the clothes this morning, and I haven't stolen jewelry since I lived with my mom." I settled back in the co-pilot's seat, stretching my arms back as he hit the gas and spun away from my dock.

"Still not an answer."

I touched the necklace that had been my sweet sixteen gift from my mom, which I hadn't worn since I'd left her. It was the first time I'd worn any of my jewelry since then. I'd expected to feel guilt when I put it on, but I'd just felt like she was with me. "My mom would never have put me at risk by giving me stolen jewelry." I was pretty sure of that last bit, but my mom was tricky that way. Did jewelry obtained from willing victims count as stolen if they offered it while under sneaky and manipulative influence? Such a dodgy line.

Beau smiled. "Ah…the lovely Tatum. You really believe that about her?"

I watched the Yacht Club as we got closer. "She loved me. Still does."

"More than the thrill of the con?"

"Yes." I didn't want to talk about my mom anymore. I might have left her, but I still missed her every day. She'd been literally my entire world. "Nice T-shirt," I said, changing the subject. "Good to see you dressed up for the occasion."

Beau was wearing a sport jacket and pressed khaki pants, which were accented by monogrammed rainbow flip-flops and a white tee shirt with a bloody dagger on it.

He grinned as he hit the gas and peeled out. "It's the cover for my upcoming release. If I'm going to this, I'm going to milk the hell out of it. If the bloody knife freaks people out, then all the better."

Okay, so now I had to be jealous of him. That would be amazing to have the freedom to not care about what anyone thought about me. "And the flip-flops?"

"I have great feet."

I laughed as I settled in the co-pilot's seat. I might not have my mom by my side, but I had Beau and his bloody knife. "You should date Hattie. She's equally enamored of herself."

"We tried that. Didn't work."

I raised my brows. "You and Hattie dated?"

He shot me a glance. "The woman is like a siren call. No man can say no."

"I can see that." My heart began to hammer as we approached the docks for the Yacht Club. The last, and only, time I'd been here, there'd been an incident. Or two. I couldn't afford to screw it up again.

But having an actual invitation was magical, and within moments, the boat was docked, and we were on our way up the ramp in search of a murderer.

Fun times.

Seriously. I was really looking forward to it. Except the murderer part, of course.

———

"BEAU! *BEAU HAMMERLY!* YOU CAME!" A fiftyish woman in a gorgeous, light blue silk dress was standing at the top of the ramp. Her hair was shoulder length, light brown with perfect blond streaks in it. There wasn't a single hair out of place, and her makeup was perfect. She literally looked like a caricature of every stereotype of the rich, country club sort. She fluttered her hand at us at just the right angle to force our gazes onto the massive diamond sparkling on her left hand.

It was almost as big as my head. But not nearly as gorgeous, of course.

Behind me, Beau made a sound like someone had just stabbed him in the throat, and I grinned. "Beau is so delighted to be here," I said. "He just loves being out with the regular people."

I heard him cough behind me, but the woman didn't even appear to notice me. She held out her hand to him as he reached the top of the ramp. "I'm Kate Callahan. We are *so* thrilled you're joining us."

Oh…she was bride-to-be (aka estranged half-sister of the dead guy)! This was getting fun really quickly. She looked optimistically chipper for a woman who'd just had her brother found murdered. But I got that. Who wants their wedding derailed by a rude brother who dares to get murdered on her weekend?

Beau shook her hand, and I saw her gaze go to his T-shirt. Her eyes widened, and I grinned, waiting for her shock.

But to my surprise, she simply fluttered her hand in front of her face, like she was overheated. "Is that from one of your books?"

Beau grunted. "It's the cover of my upcoming release, *The Dangling Knife.*"

"It's so dangerous." She beamed at him. "Everyone will love it. A bloody knife." She winked. "It's perfect for this wedding. We're going to premier Vic's newest show after lunch." She suddenly got a thoughtful look on her face. "Have you sold the movie rights to *The Dangling Knife* yet?"

Beau looked like he wanted to throw himself over the railing and end the torture of having to be social. "No."

"Well, I know we, my fiancé and I, would love to produce the movie. I heard it stars a woman as the lead protagonist. Is that true?"

Beau got a look on his face like he was about to turn and walk out, so I decided to jump in and rescue him with some delightful social banter. "I'm so sorry to hear about Rutherford," I said. "He was a very talented artist."

My comment got her to notice me in a hurry. She looked me up and down, and I could tell her smooth forehead would have totally frowned at me if it had still been able to move. "Thank you," she said stiffly. "And who are you?"

Wow. There was significant disdain hidden in that question. I was impressed. It took talent to be that judgmental and still have the question sound friendly. That kind of skill wasn't easy to master.

"Let me introduce my lovely date," Beau said, suddenly much more sociable. He tucked his hand around my elbow. "Mia, this Kate Callahan. Kate, this is Mia Murphy, the daughter of the woman I've loved for more than a decade."

And just like that, he sealed my welcome.

"Welcome." Kate beamed at me, apparently forgetting that we'd just been talking about her dead half-brother, before turning back to the man with the bestselling novels. "Beau, I'm so sorry. There must have been a mix-up. We had you down as not attending. Just give us a moment to rearrange the seating to get you and Ms. Murphy a spot. We'll find you an excellent table."

Beau nodded. "If you will have one of your staff retrieve the boxes from my boat, I have signed copies of some of my books as favors for the guests. Just a few, of course."

Her eyes lit up with genuine delight. "That's fabulous. Will you sign one to me?"

"As long as you post it on your social media accounts." He said it with such deadpan that I wasn't sure if he was kidding.

Kate blinked, and I could tell she wasn't sure either. "Um, okay, then." She did a graceful gesture with her hand. "Festivities are that way."

Beau took my arm. "Thanks so much. We'll head inside." He moved us out of range of Kate.

"What do you think?" I whispered.

"I'm not selling her the rights to my book. She's a terrible actress, her fiancé skewered the last mystery he directed, and they have no artistic appreciation for life."

"Well, I'm glad to know that." I elbowed him. "But I meant about the fact her half-brother is dead. Kate didn't seem all that upset. Do you think she killed him?"

Beau levered a condescending sigh in my direction. "If she did kill him, she would be trying to make it seem like she was devastated by the loss. The fact she isn't even trying to pretend she cares means that it hasn't even crossed her mind that she could be a suspect, let alone have actually done it."

"Oh." That was a good point. Mystery writers were so handy to have around when trying to solve a mystery. I looked back over my shoulder at Kate, and then blinked when I saw her talking to Agnes Higgleston, president of the Founder's Society and my potential ticket into a life of local legitimacy. Agnes was waving her hands and chatting very enthusiastically while Kate tried to inch away and talk to someone else. "Is Kate an OG?"

Beau pushed me to the right around a pillar wrapped with about six tons of breathtakingly beautiful white roses as someone shouted his name and came at him from the left. "An OG what?"

"An OG. Original Gal, in this case. One of the lucky people with an ancestor in the town cemetery."

Beau glanced over his shoulder at Kate, then understanding illuminated his face. "No, Agnes is here because her daughter Avery is engaged to Kate's son, Joel. Agnes gets invited to all the Callahan events as a future family member."

I couldn't hide my surprise. "Really?"

"Yeah." He grinned. "I get a lot of joy out of watching Kate try to pretend she doesn't wish for a watery grave for both Agnes and Avery."

"Both of them? She doesn't like Avery?" Agnes I could understand. Her enthusiasm for small town life might be a little overwhelming for someone trying to claw her way back into the world of flash, glam, and red carpets.

"Kate wants Joel to marry into the Hollywood elite, not toss his fortune off to a local, gold-digging girl with no career-helping connections. But Joel has never been a particularly affable fellow, so it's no surprise he doesn't care what his mom wants." He nodded to his right. "That's Joel and Avery over there."

I turned and saw the soon-to-be married next gen holding court in the corner. Joel was tall, athletic, and attractive, dripping in designer labels and class. Avery was tall, athletic, and attractive, but she looked more like she was drowning in her labels. She wasn't wearing nearly as much jewelry as everyone else, and her hair actually looked like it would move if a breeze came up. A local girl marrying up. I was all for that. *You go, girl.* "What do you think of Avery?"

Beau shrugged. "Don't know much about her. Not enough to know her inner motivations in marrying Joel."

"Huh." I watched the interplay between Joel and Avery. They were leaning in toward each other. He looked a little tense, but she had her hand on his arm, and he kept touching her back and looking at her as she chatted with the guests. Solid body language between them. I was going for true love for the win, at least until life interfered and ripped their happy little bubble apart.

No, wait. That was me that happened to. They would probably be fine.

We'd gotten only a few yards when someone grabbed my arm. "Mia!"

I spun around and saw Hattie and Esther standing behind us. I almost started laughing when I saw them. Hattie was wearing a turquoise "Hattie's Café" hat and T-shirt, along with hot pink pants, matching sandals, and sunglasses. "You look like a billboard for the café."

"Exactly! Successful marketing requires constant vigilance!" She gestured to Esther, who was wearing a lavender jumpsuit and bejeweled sneakers that I knew for a fact cost several thousand dollars. She was also sporting about half a million dollars of jewelry, mostly funded by the tremendous diamond hoops in her ears, and the emerald and diamond butterfly pendant, and the stacked rings on her index finger. "You remember Esther?"

"Rogue," Esther corrected. "You find the murderer yet?"

"Ssh!" Hattie waved her. "Top secret."

Esther grinned. "I've never been involved in a murder situation. It's fun."

"Fun" wasn't a word I typically associated with murderers, but I appreciated the positive attitude. The world could use more of that. "What's the deal with Kate?" I asked, as Beau got drawn away by a group of polite, raving fans wearing expensive country club gear. Really rich people were kind of difficult to impress, so I was impressed that Beau was that sought after. "She said that a bloody knife was perfect for this wedding."

"She hates Avery," Hattie whispered. "She thinks Avery is a gold-digger who wants her hands on the family fortune. She probably wants to use a bloody knife to stab Avery repeatedly until she agrees not to marry Joel."

I stared at her. "That's a little aggressive."

"Maybe." Hattie nodded.

"Did you see how much weight she lost?" Esther added. "She's gearing up for that wedding."

I glanced over at Kate again. She was pretty lean, but no more than I associated with a lot of the celebrities trying to convince the world that they had negative percentage body fat.

I watched Kate laugh as she leaned in to chat with a little group of well-groomed women. She looked radiant. Truly happy. Which was great, because everyone deserved to be happy, but I really didn't get how she could be all-in on the happiness train when her brother had just been murdered. "She and Rutherford must really have hated each other."

Hattie shrugged. "You know those Hollywood types. Oh! There's Olympia! I want her to sign my breasts. Let's go."

Olympia? I spun around, and my breath caught when I saw the singer standing in the middle of the room, chatting. She was wearing silver pants, a silver tank top that had tiny mirrors sewn all over it, and a pair of hot pink platform boots. Her silver hair was in a tight knot on top of her head, and several diamond rods were stuck through it.

I was so impressed. She looked like a complete idiot, and not only didn't she care, but she carried it with so much attitude that it would only enhance her fame, fortune, and diva status. I greatly admired that level of self-confidence.

She glanced over at me, and I met her gaze. Her gaze slipped right past me, but I was pretty sure there'd been a moment of subconscious recognition. As soon as I introduced myself, she'd remember.

What she'd remember was up in the air. Would she remember her childhood pal from the Hamptons? Or the fact that I was part of a mother-daughter pairing that had bilked people out of treasures? I was pretty sure the party I'd met her at was one of the one's we'd had to bolt from after almost getting caught.

She had been one of my most inspiring memories as a kid, and I was glad she had found success.

My heart actually pounding a little bit, I started to follow Hattie and Esther across the floor toward Olympia, when someone grabbed my arm. My well-honed (aka Stanley PTSD) fight-or-flight kicked in and I ripped my arm free, spun away, and whirled to face my assailant with my hands up in karate-chop position.

Agnes squawked and jumped back, looking rightfully alarmed.

Yikes. "Sorry." I immediately lowered not-so-lethal hands and clasped them behind my back. "Hi Agnes. It's great to see you again."

"You, too." She had a Gucci bag slung across her body, which I was guessing was a birthday gift from her future son-in-law. "What did Wanda mean when she called you a drug dealer?"

I'd been hoping she hadn't actually overheard that little nugget. But since she had, I needed to reframe this, and fast. I paused for a moment to think, then leaned in. "I used to be an undercover agent for the FBI. Taking down drug kingpins was my specialty. But it's top secret. If word gets out, someone might come and assassinate me. I've made a lot of enemies taking them down."

Her mouth dropped open. "No way."

"Yeah." I grinned. "No one suspected me. Everyone overlooks cute women, don't they Agnes? You would know. You're adorable." Compliments were powerful, and honestly, there was something about Agnes that was kind of adorable. Maybe it was her passion for the town?

She stared at me, then a smile widened her face. "I do know that." She lightly fist-bumped me. "Girl power everywhere," she whispered. "Your secret is safe with me."

"Awesome." I smiled, feeling relieved that I'd pegged her correctly as a woman who believed in gossip above all else. "Congratulations on Avery being engaged to Joel. You must be so proud."

Her face lit up with absolute, unconditional joy. "She's so happy. That's all a mother wants, is for her daughter to be happy and secure. I love her so much. I'd do anything for her."

Jealousy hit with a sudden, fierce gut punch. Her absolute love for Avery was so complete. So evident. I'd never seen that look on my mom's face when she talked about me. Not once. Not even a little. My throat suddenly clogged up, and I had to clear it before I spoke. "She's very lucky to have you," I said honestly. "Not every mom is like that."

"I know that." Her smile faded, replaced by a fierce protectiveness. "Joel's mother Kate doesn't like Avery. She wants to break up Joel and Avery. She doesn't even care what Joel or Avery want."

We both looked over at Kate, who was now standing beside a very fit and attractive silver fox with about six decades under his belt, and an impressive ability to carry off a very expensive suit. She had her hand on his arm, and was leaning into him, in much the same way that Avery had been leaning into Joel. "Her fiancé?"

"Yep. Victor Ramos." Agnes looked more cheerful again. "At least Victor adores Avery. I think he can be the dad that Avery never had. I don't know what he sees in Kate, but I'm glad he'll be a part of Avery's life."

Avery didn't have a dad either? I had no idea who mine was, or if he knew I even existed. "I'm glad things are working out for her." I didn't even know Avery, but I felt a bond with any girl who grew up without a dad.

Like Olympia, for example. I peeked across the room and saw

that Hattie was holding a Sharpie out to her and talking animatedly. Olympia looked like she wasn't sure the money she was getting for this performance was enough to keep her talking to the crazy lady with the turquoise hat and matching hair.

Just past Olympia, sitting beneath a truly beautiful display of draped, iridescent fabrics was a red-haired fortune teller whose artfully painted nipples I had seen recently. I needed to go talk to her, but before I did, I decided to plant a little seed with Agnes.

I was willing to bet Agnes was very connected with the local scene. She was the type who would make it her business to know everything of note about anyone she deemed important. Plus, if she wanted to win Best Lake Town, then solving murders quickly would make her happy.

I wanted to make her happy, because then she would appreciate me and want to help me. Team win.

I was going to go for it. "Hattie's being accused of killing Rutherford—"

"What?" Agnes sounded shocked. "I've known Hattie for years. She'd never do that."

"I know, but the evidence is pointing in her direction."

"Evidence? What evidence?"

"The anchor Rutherford was chained to was Hattie's. And some other stuff." No way was I going to admit anything that the cops hadn't already figured out "I'm not going to let her go to prison, but that means I need to figure out what really happened. Do you know anything about Rutherford that might be helpful?"

Agnes frowned "Like what?"

"Like, who he was sleeping with? A jilted lover? A jealous husband?" I didn't want to lead her by mentioning Glory, so I mentally crossed my fingers, hoping for confirmation.

But Agnes shook her head pretty quickly. "No, sorry. I don't."

I sighed. "Bummer." If Agnes didn't know, it probably meant no one else knew either, because I had a feeling that if there was gossip to be known, Agnes would have her hands deep in it. "I need to figure it out before Hattie gets arrested for it. So, if you can think of anything that might be helpful, will you let me know?"

"Yes, of course." She watched Hattie chatting with Olympia. "She could be in the Founder's Society, you know. Hattie's one of us."

I knew that, but I decided to see what info I could get out of her. "Really? Why hasn't she joined?"

"Yet. She hasn't joined, *yet.* I'm working on her. I think she's coming around." Agnes took a breath. "Look, I know Hattie's innocent, so please let me know if there's anything I can do to help."

The more help I could get, the better. "Just keep an ear out for anything significant. Someone in town knows who killed him, which means there is information to find."

"Absolutely. I'll ask the Sisters in the Founder's Society to keep an ear out as well. We have a lot of connections in this town."

"I'll bet you do." I wondered if Agnes actually ran this town, instead of the mayor. "Thanks for your help."

She pulled out her phone. "You got it. I'm on it. I'm going to make some calls right now."

She hurried away, and I headed off to chat with a red-haired possible murderer.

CHAPTER 12

As Agnes wandered off, already chatting on her phone, I sauntered over to Glory and took a seat at her table, channeling my goal of getting an instant confession out of her.

She had a crystal ball in front of her, and she was wearing drapey, bright clothing. Flowers cascaded around her, beautiful shades of yellow and pale pink. The expensive, famous wedding planner was a genius. Maybe I needed to try to get her to donate her services for the fundraiser. Seriously. Or I could just steal all the flowers after the party.

Wait, no. I wasn't a thief anymore. Darn it. That was so inconvenient.

I settled comfortably in the lush, velvet seat and smiled warmly. "Hi, Glory."

"Mia. It's great to see you again." She smiled at me, but the smile didn't go quite to her eyes. Obviously. Because we both knew that she'd bailed on the scene last night. "What spirit would you like to talk to tonight?"

We were going to pretend we hadn't bonded over pulling a dead body out of a lake thirteen hours ago? Sure. I could go with that. "Rutherford's. I thought I'd ask him who killed him. Does it work like that?"

Her face paled ever so slightly, and her eyes blinked rapidly for a couple times. "It's too recent to contact him. It takes time for a spirit to be willing to revisit. Anyone else?"

That was shockingly convenient. The spirits were so unhelpful. "How about the Jack the Ripper ghost? He might have seen who dumped Rutherford in Dead Man's Pond. Give him a try."

She cleared her throat. "I've been trying to reach him. I had the same thought. He's not communicating."

"Well, that's frustrating, isn't it?"

"It is," she agreed. "I am happy to contact someone else, though."

"How about the people who stole your portrait from Rutherford's Church Island studio and then torched the place? I'd like to talk to them." I paused at her shocked face. "Oh, wait, I already am, right? That was easy." I propped my elbows on the table and rested my chin on my palms. "Burning up a beautiful, old chapel? Really? Wasn't that overkill?"

"It wasn't on purpose. It was an accident—" She stopped suddenly, and clapped her lips together, looking horrified that she'd just blurted that out.

Wow. She was a terrible criminal. "It wasn't an accident. I know that. You know that. What's going on?"

"It was! We must have accidentally kicked over a can and—" She stopped again.

I really need to remember not to hire Glory to run any significant crimes with me. They had not accidentally kicked over a can. I knew that, because I'd almost died witnessing it. I leaned forward and lowered my voice. "Did you kill Rutherford, Glory?"

"What?" Her eyes widened. "No!"

"Then why were you there?" Yes, I knew that we'd been there, too, and we hadn't murdered him, but it was still a pressure-filled question that could evoke a telling response.

She looked around then leaned in toward me, her voice a panicked whisper. "If the police saw the painting, they'd know I was intimate with Rutherford, and that's all the motivation they'd need. I had to get it out of there."

I wondered how many women had the same motivation. "Why did you kill him?" See? I could ask the same question a bunch of times just like the police.

She frowned at me. "I just said I didn't kill him."

"Right. I forgot. If you had killed him, why would you have killed him?"

"Because he loved *her*—" Her eyes narrowed and she sat back suddenly, folding her arms across her chest as if she'd just realized I was winning the conversation lottery. "Go away."

Her? Her who? Wasn't that interesting? And then, suddenly, I knew exactly who Glory was talking about. "The woman with the tattoo? That he'd been painting?" It had taken only one look to know that Rutherford had loved her. If Glory had seen the painting, she'd have known, too.

She stared at me. "How did you see that painting?"

Um…oops. See? Glory wasn't the only one who had room to develop some better skills with interrogations. "This isn't about me," I retorted. "It's about you. You'd kill him because he loved someone else?"

"No." She appeared genuinely worried, but I couldn't tell whether she was hiding her guilt or not. Which I guess made sense. The woman lied about seeing ghosts for a living, so she was clearly very good at lying. "I didn't kill him. I *loved* him."

Well, that certainly didn't preclude murder. Crimes of passion were a thing for a reason. "Where were you Monday night between midnight and three am?" I tossed out one of the times Devlin had asked Hattie about earlier.

She stared at me, and her face literally went white. I thought for a second she was going to throw up.

Excitement rushed through me, and I leaned in. "You were on the lake with Rutherford that night, weren't you? What happened?"

She shook her head. "I need to leave." She pushed back her chair to stand up, and I caught her wrist.

She froze, half out of the chair, staring at me with wide eyes.

"The cops want the easiest answer," I said softly. "They know he was on the lake on Monday night. It won't take much for them to figure out who was with him. If it was you, and you slept with him, you look like the obvious suspect. The cops won't look past you." Whether she was guilty or not, it was the truth. Except for Hattie being first in the potential suspect line, of course.

Silently, she eased herself back down into the chair. "So, what do you want?"

"I want to find out who really did it. So, tell me what you know, and I'll be on my merry way."

She bit her lip. "Why do you want to know?"

"Because I'm obsessed with puzzles, and getting attached to Rutherford for a while made it personal. Plus, I am morally opposed to police officers, and I delight in doing their work for them and making them look like incompetent fools." Okay, slight exaggeration, but I could play a part way better than Glory could.

She nodded, completely understanding my ridiculous point. "All right." She studied me for a moment, and I could see her thinking carefully over what she was going to tell me.

I decided to help her. "What did you and Rutherford fight about on Monday when you were on the lake?" It was a guess, but her panic had made me pretty sure she'd been on the lake with him. And if she'd had a happy little time, she wouldn't have looked so worried. So, I was guessing fight.

"He wanted to get married, but I wasn't ready." She didn't meet my gaze, and I knew instantly that she was lying.

Why would she lie? She was definitely covering up. "Why weren't you ready?"

She glanced at me. "He was a lot older than I am. I wasn't sure about the age difference. I needed time." Tears filled her eyes. "And now I'm out of time. I told him no, and now he's dead."

The tears looked real, but she was definitely not telling the truth. I knew enough about lying to recognize the flicker of her gaze and the way she was suddenly shifting in her chair and fiddling with her ear. "You're lying to me, Glory. What was really going on? The cops aren't stupid. They're going to find out, and you'll be in trouble. I can help."

She stared at me. "I did love him."

"But?"

She looked down at her ball. "He wasn't always a good guy."

Oh…yes. "Like what?"

She glanced up at me. "He leaked me info on his family, and I used that info when I did readings for them."

Hah! I knew she was a fraud! "Like what?"

"Like someone was having an affair." She shrugged. "That kind of stuff."

My jaw dropped. "Blackmail? You guys were doing *blackmail?*"

"No. It wasn't like that. It was for fun."

Was it? Holy cow. I didn't believe that for a minute. Glory might be innocent of blackmail, but Rutherford the manwhore? I wasn't going to be so quick to declare his innocence. "What about the woman in the painting? Was she in on it?"

Glory leaned forward. "You leave her out of it," she whispered. "She didn't do anything. Leave her *out* of it."

I leaned in, mimicking her pose. "Who is she? You know who it is, don't you?"

"No—"

"Glory, if you didn't do it, then it might have been her. Do you want to take the fall for her?"

Her eyes widened in horror. "She didn't—" But she stopped, and I could see her doubt.

Holy cow. This was so easy. "Who is she, Glory? Let me talk to her. If she didn't do it either, then we need to help her. I won't tell the police—"

"Tell the police what?" A hand came down on my shoulder,

and I looked up to see a ridiculously handsome police officer frowning down at me.

Panic flashed across Glory's face, and she looked like she was ready to bolt.

I scowled at him. "I'm a little busy." He needed to move on immediately. I was so close to getting the info I needed from Glory. Now was not the time for His Manliness to interrupt. "Glory's trying to contact my dead mother."

I saw Glory glance at me, and then relax slightly, realizing that I wasn't going to rat her out to the cops.

Devlin didn't smile. "Your mother's not dead."

"She might be. That would be just like her, to die without telling me first." I smiled encouragingly at Glory. "You were saying?"

Glory cleared her throat and made a pretense of studying her crystal ball. "I'm definitely getting a sense of her spirit, but it's unclear whether she's in this world or the next one."

"Right? She's a slippery wench that one."

Devlin's fingers tightened on my shoulder. "Mia. We need to chat. Come with me. Now."

I looked up at him. "Did I make a deal with you? I'm pretty sure I didn't. Which means that I actually don't have to go anywhere with you." Wow. It felt good to claim my space like that. After being indentured to the FBI for two years, I was never going back to owing anyone anything ever.

Devlin narrowed his eyes. He didn't look at all amused by my witty, self-empowering banter. Weirdly, I was still attracted to him when he was being grouchy. "Mia. I'm asking you to accompany me for a moment."

I didn't move. "Why?"

Glory leaned forward, looking very intently at her magic orb. "I'm seeing a bed, lots of naked skin, and the two of you. A pink bedspread. Heart-shaped pillows. And handcuffs."

I tried really hard not to picture me, Devlin, and kinky playthings, but it was a little difficult. So I tried to fake it. "You have a pink bedspread with heart-shaped pillows?" I frowned at Devlin. "Because you don't seem the type. And hello? Why are you trying to seduce me? I thought we were just friends."

"We're not friends." He looked pained. "And I don't have a pink bedspread."

I sighed. "You law enforcement types never do."

"He didn't deny trying to seduce you," Glory pointed out.

"Good point." I eyed him. "Seriously, Devlin. You're supposed to be my protector. Why would you muddy that with nakedness?"

He swore under his breath, slid his hand under my arm, and basically manhandled me to my feet, which, again, was both annoyingly attractive and attractively irritating. "She'll be back in a minute," he said to Glory, just before propelling me out of the luncheon and into the kitchen, of all places.

I had a split second to admire the sheer size and efficiency of the culinary operation before Devlin cornered me and blocked my view with his muscular torso and broad shoulders. "What are you doing here?"

I frowned up at him. "I'm accompanying my friend Beau, who needed a date."

"No, you're not." He leaned in, just close enough that I caught a scent of something very delicious that wasn't coming from the kitchen. "Listen. Stay out of this investigation."

I put my hands on my hips. "Why?"

I expected him to give me some speech about police business, but he didn't. "Because I don't want you hurt."

"I won't get hurt." Well, I was hoping I wouldn't. "And if I do, I'll make sure Griselda doesn't blame you." This was always about the bottom line, and that was police business. Le sigh.

He swore and ran his hand over his hair. "It's not about Hawk." He cursed again. "Look. I'm trying to keep my distance because Hawk warned me off you. You're trouble. You're important to a federal case. And it's only a matter of time until someone tries to murder you."

My heart sank a little. "He actually warned you off me?"

"Yeah." Devlin's dark eyes settled on my face. "But you know what they say about things like that?"

"No. What?"

"It just makes a guy want a girl more."

CHAPTER 13

MY STOMACH SUDDENLY DID FLIPS. "What? Are you *actually* trying to seduce me?" Because that took everything to a whole different level, and fast. "For the record, you need to know that I only sleep with men who have pink bedspreads, and since you already admitted you don't, well, it's really a lost cause for you." Awesome. I was completely in control here. #girlpower

Devlin studied me, looking all smoldering and hot, instead of amused at my wittiness. "If I decide to seduce you, you'll know it. You won't need to ask me."

My stomach did another little flip, but I raised my chin. "You're that handy, are you?"

"*Handy?* You make it sound like I'll fix your fence."

I definitely enjoyed his reaction to my word choice. "I don't have a fence, but are you? Handy?"

He met my gaze without flinching, with that absolute confidence that was way too attractive in a man. "I'm extremely *handy* when it comes to seduction, but in the meantime, your marina is bugged, you're already up to your eyeballs in murder, and now you're running around asking questions, as if you don't already have a target on your back." He brushed his fingers over my cheek. "Please go to Lucy's, Mia. Get off the grid until I get this sorted out."

Okay, so the way he said it was super sweet. Almost enough to get me to hurl myself right over the railing and into the water so I could swim straight to Lucy's.

Except I didn't like swimming that much, and I definitely didn't like hiding. Or taking orders from men for that matter. So, that was an oh-for-three for Dev. "My mom would disown me if I hid from danger."

"You haven't spoken to her in a decade."

"Right? And that's us getting along. So imagine how long it would be between visits if she actually disowned me? No one wants to see that." I put my hands on my hips. "If you don't want me dead, then find out who killed Rutherford and bugged my marina before they find me. I'm not going to sit around while you or Chief Stone throw Hattie in prison for murder."

"Mia—"

I met his gaze. "Don't try to control me, Devlin. It'll never work, and if you do, you'll have no chance of ever seducing me, no matter how insanely hot you are. I literally *hate* being controlled."

He grinned. "You think I'm insanely hot?"

"Did you not hear anything else I said?"

"I'm a guy. Of course not. My brain shut down after you said I was 'insanely hot.'"

"I didn't say that. You're imagining things." I ignored the flash of amusement in his eyes. "Is there anything else? Or can I go back to communing with my mom?"

He paused. "Yeah. One thing."

"What?"

"Will you go to dinner with me?"

My heart turned over, and then started racing. "I took a life-long celibacy vow after I got divorced."

"I'm not remotely attracted to you, so that's perfect. How about seven o'clock on Tuesday evening? I'll pick you up."

"What? No—"

"Gotta go." He pressed a kiss to my knuckle, then strode out the door, leaving me standing in the corner of the kitchen, trying to decide whether or not I had won that round. What had just happened?

I looked over at the pastry chef, who was staring at me, his tray of fruit tarty things apparently forgotten. "Were you listening to that?"

He nodded.

"Does it sound like I have a date for Tuesday?"

"It does."

"Dammit. I'm going to have to fix that." I let out a breath. "Do you work here on a regular basis?" Maybe he had some inside scoop.

He shook his head. "Just special events." He paused. "Did I hear you correctly that Hattie is going to prison for murder?"

"No. They just want to put her there. She'll be fine. Did you know Rutherford? Do you know anyone who would want him killed? Or blame Hattie for it? Or did you do it?" I threw in that last one because nothing ventured, nothing gained, right?

He stared at me for so long I thought maybe he'd frozen his brain with sugar. "Rutherford?" he asked. "Rutherford Callahan? Someone killed him?"

Oh…um…oops. I'd assumed word was already getting around, but it hadn't gotten to the dessert chef. Maybe that was why the people at the party were so chipper. Maybe people didn't know yet.

If I was Kate, and I was all about my wedding, I definitely might try to sit on the news that my estranged half-brother had been murdered, at least until I got that ring on my finger. Of course, I wasn't Kate, and if I were lucky enough to have a brother, I'd definitely care if he were murdered, but different strokes and all that.

The pastry chef was still waiting for an answer, staring at me expectantly.

It wasn't my place to spread that news. "What? Look at the time. I need to go." I darted out of the kitchen and nearly ran straight into Lucy, who was wearing a cute little white jacket, black pants, and a name tag.

The tray she'd been carrying went flying, and it clattered to the floor in a pile of broken dishes and very loud, clanging silverware. "You're going to get me fired," she muttered as we both lunged for the scattered dishes.

"Your date is the caterer?" I asked, as I picked up pieces and dropped them on the tray.

"The pastry chef," Lucy said. "He's on my route. He got me in," she kept her voice low as we quickly picked up stuff. "They needed help."

The pastry chef whose bubble of joy I'd just burst? "He might be in a bad mood on the way home. He didn't know about Rutherford's murder until I blurted it out."

"I drove myself, so that's fine."

Yay. Lucy had an exit plan that didn't depend on anyone else. That was awesome. "That's great you're on the staff. You can get the inside scoop. That's pretty brilliant." I was impressed. Lucy hadn't been all that dialed in on that kind of con artist strategy and execution a few days ago. That was awesome she was rising to the challenge.

"Right? I thought it was a good call. Besides, I like to keep busy at these things. I'm not that great with socialization."

That I could believe. "Great job." I stacked the broken plates on her tray, then paused when music started to drift out of the main ballroom.

A split second later, Olympia's gorgeous voice burst through the speakers, and the few folks who had been in the hall went running toward the ballroom, leaving Lucy and me alone with the broken platter.

I really wanted to go into the ballroom and join the private concert, but I knew I couldn't. Not yet. I'd had plenty of these experiences as a kid, but I still got goosebumps. I quickly helped load the scattered food onto Lucy's tray, keeping half my attention on the singing. "Have you heard anything interesting?"

"The head chef, Felix Verbeck, is having a fit at the kitchen staff," she whispered. "He's freaking out that the wedding's going to be canceled. Jake was in there trying to calm him down, and then he got Jake all riled. It's crazy in there. Oh, and Joel is totally pissed at his mom for having the wedding."

"His mom, the bride? Joel wants her to cancel the wedding?"

"Yeah. Apparently Joel and Rutherford were close. He's the only one who cares that Rutherford is dead. He's trying to talk his mom into delaying the wedding, which is sending Felix, Jake, and Kate into fits. Apparently, Joel even talked to Vic to try to get *him* to pressure his mom into postponing the wedding, so that didn't go over well with Kate at all."

Well, at least there was one decent human being in the family. But it didn't really illuminate the Rutherford situation...unless Joel didn't want his mom to get married. But that seemed rather extreme to murder his favorite uncle to keep his mom from tying the knot. I was going to move on past that theory. "Does anyone seem unnaturally happy that Rutherford's dead?" I thought of Beau's comment. "Or over-dramatically sad?"

"No, but there was drama." She looked around to make sure we were alone, then leaned in. "When I arrived, I saw Glory and Avery arguing in the women's bathroom." She paused. "It's a really nice bathroom. Have you been in there? They even had roses all over the sink, and each stall is its own room—"

"I've been in places like that." I gestured impatiently, trying not to get caught up in the awe of the super rich. "What were they arguing about?"

"Right." She grinned. "I heard Avery say Rutherford's name, but when I walked in, they both shut up. Glory was crying, and she ran out. Avery looked mad, and she hurried after her, calling to her. I ran out after them, but they were already down the hall, and Agnes and Kate were in hot pursuit, so I couldn't follow."

I grabbed a napkin and started rubbing a grease stain off the carpet, trying to figure out how the pieces went together. "I talked to Glory. She said she loved Rutherford, and she didn't kill him. I could tell she was lying, but I'm not sure which part she was lying about."

Lucy put the broken pieces of a coffee cup on the tray. "What if Avery knew Glory killed Rutherford and called her out on it?"

I sat back on my heels and stared at her. "That would mean Avery knows the truth."

Lucy nodded. "She definitely knows something, if not the whole truth. I just couldn't hear enough to know."

I tossed the wadded napkin onto the tray. "I need to talk to her—"

"Talk to who?" Hattie crouched beside us. "What's going on?"

"Avery," I said. "She and Glory were in a fight earlier about Rutherford. Glory already admitted to me that she loved Rutherford—"

"I knew it." Hattie snapped her fingers. "Every woman who models for him falls in love with him." Hattie made no move to help us pick up the dropped plates, which wasn't totally surprising.

"Glory said she didn't kill him." I set a plate fragment on the tray. "But before I talk to Avery, I want to circle back with Glory with this new info. I feel like I can get to her, but Devlin interrupted me—"

There was a sudden commotion from down the hall. We all turned to see Kate and Glory talking in the corner. Glory was crying, and Kate was doing that super-quiet yelling thing where her voice never went above a whisper, but the shouting was evident.

I tried to hear what they were saying, but they were too far away. It was a minute, maybe two, but the body language between them was high-octane tension.

Then, just as quickly as they'd started, Glory spun around and stormed back into the ballroom. Kate took a moment to pull her shoulders back, take a breath, and then she followed Glory back into the ballroom.

I shoved the last dish back onto Lucy's platter. "I need to find out what that was all about."

"Oh, me, too!" Hattie jumped to her feet, but I didn't wait for her. I just raced into the ballroom. I threw the door open and stepped inside, scanning for Glory and Kate.

I'd planned to head straight for Glory's booth to finish our chat, but she wasn't there. Frowning, I scanned the room. Even though food was being served, many people weren't in their seats. There were simply too many notable people that needed chatting up, so folks were roaming in their expensive outfits, making the rounds with that delightful laughter that no one actually believes is genuine.

"Where are they?" Hattie asked as she came up beside me.

"I don't know." As I spoke, I saw Kate. She was circulating with her fiancé. She looked like a radiant bride. Maybe too radiant? How did she turn it on like that, with her brother dead, only moments after what had clearly been an upsetting discussion with Glory?

I narrowed my eyes. I'd come in here to talk to Glory, but the longer I watched Kate, the more I felt like she was the one I needed to talk to.

As I watched, Kate made her way over to the deck doors, where Olympia was arguing with Devlin. His arms were folded over his chest, and he looked like an unimpressed, immovable force. Devlin was so adorable when he was being stubborn and intractable. Except, of course, when he was in my way. Then, not so cute.

Kate walked up, and she started arguing with Devlin as well.

I needed to be a part of that conversation. "I think I'm going to go chat with Devlin, Olympia, and Kate—"

As I said it, I saw Glory darting past the glass doors, heading toward the patio. "There's Glory. It looks like she's leaving." Crud. I really wanted to get in that conversation with Kate and Devlin.

"I'll follow her," Hattie said. "You deal with Kate. I'll text you and let you know where Glory goes."

I grinned. "Perfect. Thanks."

"You got it." She blew me a kiss, then bolted through the crowd, not even trying to be subtle as she hurried toward the patio in pursuit of the fortune teller who had already disappeared from sight.

Devlin saw me staring at Kate and shot me a glare, so I quickly ducked my head and hurried across the ballroom to my table. I slid into the seat beside Beau, who had his arms folded and a very cranky look on his face.

He glared at me. "I thought you were going to entertain me. Where have you been?"

"Listening to Kate and Glory argue." I nodded at the happy trio by the doors. "I need to break up that conversation and find out what Kate knows. She must know more than she's letting on. Her brother was *murdered.* There's no way that she's simply ignoring that. I need to talk to her."

His face brightening, Beau raised his brows. "Really? Kate is an angry bride. Devlin is a cop on murder duty. And Olympia is supposed to be quite the diva, and she looks a little strung out. She might kill you for daring to speak with her. She has quite a reputation."

"I'm very difficult to kill." I leaned back in my chair, watching. "And Devlin wants to date me."

"Kate didn't seem impressed by you," Beau observed.

"She definitely wasn't," I agreed. "But I need to be in that conversation."

Beau didn't watch them. He was watching me. "How are you going to handle this?"

"I'm thinking." I drummed my fingers on the table, watching the trio. "Olympia is my best chance to get into the conversation," I said. "She's the weak link. She has no skin in this game, and probably just wants to leave."

Beau grinned. "She's a tough cookie."

"I know. So am I." I watched the celebrity, trying to decide the best way to handle her. I could assume that she'd have some level of recognition of me, pretend we're besties, and make it awkward for her to admit she can't place me? Or introduce myself as her childhood pal? Or just pretend we're strangers?

Honestly, I suspected she didn't remember me at all. I was probably one of thousands of people she'd met over the years at the Hamptons.

But Beau was right. She did have a reputation. But I also knew how people worked.

Yeah, I knew what to do. "Want to help me?"

Beau's face lit up with pure delight. "Quite possibly. What do you need me to do?"

"I'm going to steal something from her, and then give it back. Then she'll owe me and she'll trust me. Instant bonding."

He grinned. "You're going to pickpocket her?"

"I'm going to take something. I need to figure out what. And you're the distraction."

"This is fantastic."

"Good. Let's go." I stood up, refusing to let myself think about the fact that I was officially setting up a con right now. A plan that would use my skills to manipulate someone into trusting me so I could get something from them. I was literally about to do exactly what I'd promised I would never do again.

Okay, so apparently, I *was* going to let myself think about it.

Which was fine. Because that meant I could justify it because this was to save an innocent person from prison and find a murderer. It wasn't for my own entertainment. It was for the greater good. So, it was fine. It wasn't like I was becoming the person I'd left behind.

Beau trotted after me and I strode across the room. "What are we doing?" he asked.

I had a flash of regret for getting a nice, old mystery writer involved in Murphy shenanigans, but I quickly ditched it. The con was in play, which meant total focus and total commitment.

"We're going to pretend to chat as I circle around her." I could feel my adrenaline rushing as I quickly eased through the crowd, keeping Beau on my right so that I could pretend to be looking at him when I was really looking past him.

Olympia's snug-fitting outfit didn't leave space for a wallet or a phone. I couldn't see an outline for either of them. I swore under my breath. Her earrings were big, but they didn't look like real jewels. She wouldn't care if I gave them back to her. I needed something big, something significant, something that she would be incredibly grateful to me for returning. Her level of gratitude and emotion was critical.

"What are you going to take?" Beau asked as we weaved through people.

"I don't know." Frustration rippled through me. I didn't know how long the trio would keep talking. I needed to gain an entry fast. But I couldn't see anything on Olympia I could take. Normally, I could do a drive-by test run where I felt her pockets to see if anything was in there, but time was too tight. I needed to strike on the first run.

"Mia?"

Ignoring Beau, I switched to Kate, scanning her. My gaze fell on her massive diamond ring. Kate was gesturing as she spoke, and I could see the ring sliding around on her finger as her hand moved, which meant the ring was loose. I remembered that Hattie and Esther had mentioned that Kate had recently lost weight.

Rings were risky. They could get caught on a knuckle, or tweak the person's hand. But this ring was loose. It might work. I wiggled my shoulders, trying to relax them. It had been a long time since I'd tried a ring.

"Mia?" Beau tapped my arm. "What's the plan?"

It was the only thing I could find. I had to go for her ring, and I had to get it the first time past. I pulled Beau behind a pillar. As I did so, I saw Lucy rushing past with a tray. "Lucy!" I grabbed her arm, and she almost dropped the tray as she veered over.

Lucy knew about my past.

Beau knew about my past.

I could trust them. I had to trust them, because I had no other choice.

"I need your help." I paused as they both looked at me expectantly. "I need to take Kate's ring off her finger, and I need a strong distraction." Bumping her as I walked past wasn't going to be enough, especially with Devlin there. I literally needed to steal a massive diamond ring off her finger while she was standing in front of a very good cop.

Beau and Lucy both looked over at Kate, then back at me, their eyes wide. "That is so cool," Lucy said. "I didn't know you could do that."

I took a deep breath, committing to leaving behind my fear. I had to go all-in on confidence now. There was no other way. "I can do rings," I said easily. "But I need you guys to distract. It's very specific what I need from you. Are you in?"

They both nodded eagerly.

And just like that, the old Mia was back.

CHAPTER 14

I FELT A RUSH, a massive, exhilarating, alarming rush.

It was like the old days with my mom, when we were plotting. I could tell both of my pals were absolutely pumped to help, riding on the thrill of the con. Their excitement was contagious, chasing away the last of my resistance.

I bounced on my toes and flexed my fingers as I gave them very quick instructions, which was all I had time for. Neither of them was an expert, but they were fearless and enthusiastic, which would hopefully give me enough wiggle room to get what I needed from them. "Got it?"

They both nodded.

"Okay, go."

"Now?" Lucy exclaimed.

"Right now. Before they stop talking to Devlin." I flipped my hands at them to shoo them away. "Go, go, go."

"Right!" They fist bumped each other and then hurried off, Lucy with her tray, and Beau with a shit-eating grin.

I let out my breath as I circled back to the left behind Devlin. He couldn't see me. Lucy's job was Devlin and Olympia. Beau's was Kate. Mine was to steal.

I bounced on my tiptoes as I positioned myself about five feet behind Devlin, lurking behind a small group of guests.

As I waited, Lucy hurried up to the trio with her tray of champagne glasses. "Good afternoon," she trilled. "May I offer you some champagne?" As the three heads turned toward her, I stepped out from behind the guests that I'd been using as a shield.

I headed straight for Kate as Beau came in from the left.

The timing had to be precise. I had to be in place at the exact moment Beau struck.

Lucy was annoying them by describing the type of champagne and nearly shoving glasses in their hands, ignoring Devlin who was telling her to go away.

I was about six inches behind Devlin's right shoulder when Beau stumbled across my path. He literally launched himself right into Kate, hitting her so hard that she fell flat on her butt.

I tried not to laugh as Beau gasped and apologized. Lucy squawked and leaned over to help, and managed to tip her tray and all the champagne on Devlin and Olympia's feet. Chaos broke out, as Beau apologized and took Kate's hand to pull her to her feet.

He extended his hand to help her up, but as she reached for his hand, he grabbed the back of her wrist, which put her hand below his, facing the floor, her fingers loose. As Beau locked his hand around Kate's wrist, I ducked past Devlin, slipped my hand beneath Beau's forearm, and put my index finger and thumb on her engagement ring.

I wiggled it, and like the adorably sweet munchkin that it was, it slid right off her finger into the palm of my hand. Barely stifling a victory cheer, I had it in my fist and I was across the room by the time Kate made it to her feet.

I could feel the warm metal in my palm, and for a split second, I was transported back to my youth, to the absolute thrill of victory. I looked down and peeked at my hand, grinning when I saw the diamond winking up at me.

So easy, even with newbies helping me. Yay, me! *I still have it, Mom!*

I could almost imagine my mom standing beside me, giggling triumphantly as she debated whether to keep it, or to use it to get us an entry into the world we wanted access to that night. I could almost feel my nefarious past urging me to slip it into my pocket and sashay into the sunset on my way to a pawn shop.

But that me didn't exist anymore, on any level.

So I immediately spun around and practically sprinted back over to the little group. "Kate! Kate!"

As I shouted her name, I saw Devlin's gaze flick to me in surprise, then his eyes narrowed as he watched me approach. Suspicion was etched all over his handsome face, which of course, made no sense, because what did I ever do to arouse his suspicion?

As I approached, Lucy veered away with her tray and empty glasses, and Beau grinned just a little too big. I tried to scowl at him to turn it down a notch, but I had to keep my focus on Kate as I held up the ring. "Kate! I found this by one of the tables. Isn't this yours?" I waved it right in front of her face.

Kate's mouth dropped open and she looked down at her hand. Then she looked up at me, shock etched on her face as I held out the massive ring.

"Yes," she gasped, as I dropped it into her hand. "Where did you find it?"

I waved generally behind me. "By the table."

She clutched it to her chest, tears suddenly filling her eyes. "I didn't even realize I'd lost it. I knew it was loose, but I had no idea." She met my gaze. "Thank you." Her sincerity was so emotional that I felt a flash of guilt, but I quickly reminded myself that it was for a good cause. I had to stay the course.

"You're welcome," I said.

Olympia studied me. "Not everyone would return a ring."

I shrugged. "Then I'm glad I'm the one who saw it," I said, as I turned to Kate. "I'd noticed it on your hand when I arrived with Beau, so you were the first person I asked."

Beau nodded, confirming that yes, I was with Beau, so yes, I was worthy. Establishing social proof of my acceptability: check.

Kate beamed at me. "Thank you so much. I'm so indebted to you for getting this back to me."

To my right, I could see Devlin frowning, watching the discussion, but not interrupting. Good man. Never mess with a bride and her engagement ring.

Olympia frowned at me. "You're with Beau?"

She knew Beau, too? Mystery writers were so handy. "I am."

She narrowed her eyes. "Do I know you?"

I decided to go all in. Hattie and Lucy were teaching me about girl bonding, and I was going to unleash my inner bestie. I pretended to study her. "You look familiar," I agreed.

Kate leaned in. "You two know each other?"

"Maybe." I cocked my head. "Did you go to the Hamptons as a teenager?"

Olympia nodded. "For a few summers."

I snapped my fingers as if I suddenly remembered what we'd done together. "I know! The Wallenschmidts! Didn't we team up for that crazy scavenger hunt and almost get run over by the killer pig?"

She stared at me. "That was you?"

I was going to send that killer pig a thank you note. Who can forget a killer pig? "Yes! Didn't it bite you in the butt?"

"Yeah, it did." Olympia nodded slowly, but I could tell she still couldn't place me. The pig, yes? A sketchy kid with a criminal mom? Apparently not.

"And then we escaped it by climbing that trellis, and we broke into their bedroom," I prodded.

Olympia narrowed her eyes. "Climbing the trellis?"

Okay, so she was sadly a lost cause. I couldn't help but feel a little bummed. I'd held onto that memory for years. It was tough to be reminded that you didn't matter. "Yes, but anyway, Kate," I turned back to her, and got back to business. "I saw you arguing with Glory. Is she being a problem? I know her a little bit. I could talk to her if you want."

Devlin opened his mouth, probably to tell me to shut up, when Beau stepped in front of him and began yammering about a death threat or something. Did he get death threats? We were like twins. Devlin was trying to get Beau out of his way, but Beau was delightedly stubborn.

No wonder he had a crush on my mom. She was also incredibly immovable when she was on a mission.

"I can handle Glory." Kate was restless. "I need to get back to my party." She fluttered her hand. "This whole murder thing needs to go away."

I knew right then that Kate hadn't killed Rutherford. Nothing was more important to her than her party and getting married, and a bunch of murders weren't going to help with the wedding plans. "I hear you."

I could tell by Devlin's body language that he was about to toss Beau over the railing. I had maybe a minute left before he took over the conversation. "What were you and Glory talking about? It was Rutherford, I bet. She loved him, you know."

Kate blinked. "She loved him?"

"Yes, she did." I was pretty sure Kate's surprise was fake. "Do you think she killed him?" I watched her face closely, searching for any lies or tells that could tell me what she wasn't going to tell me.

"Glory?" She looked startled. "She's not a killer."

She believed it. I was sure of it. "Who do you think did it?"

Kate pressed her lips together. "This is my party. We're not discussing my brother—"

"Right, I know. Sorry. What did you say Glory was saying?" I lowered my voice. "She admitted to me that she and Rutherford were blackmailing people. Was she trying to continue that with you?"

Her eyes widened with absolute shock. "Blackmail?" she echoed, her voice the slightest bit squeaky.

Holy crap. Glory and Rutherford had been blackmailing *Kate*. About what? Was she the one having an affair? That was such a great reason to kill Rutherford.

And Glory, I suddenly realized. It also would be a great reason to kill *Glory*.

Fear suddenly hit me. If Glory wasn't the one who'd killed Rutherford, she could very well be the next one on the metaphorical chopping block. And if Hattie was near her, she could be caught in the crossfire.

I was nearly having a panic attack with the need to text Hattie and tell her to watch out, but I knew I needed to stay focused. Another minute, another thirty seconds. I had Kate on the retreat, and I needed to finish it.

"Kate," I said quietly. "Someone killed Rutherford. Whether you want to admit it or not, he was killed, and that brings a murder right to your doorstep." I paused as she stared at me. "Tell me about the blackmail—"

"Why you? Why would I tell you anything?"

"Because the cops want to put Hattie in jail for it, and I won't let that happen."

"Hattie? *Hattie?* That old lady who runs the café?"

Oh, Hattie would not like that description. I nodded. "Talk to me, Kate. I'm not a cop. I don't care what you've done. I just want Hattie to stay out of jail. Tell me what you know." I let her see that it mattered to me. Kate was hard and cold, but inside her was a girl who'd been rejected by her dad.

I got that. Of course, I didn't know whether my dad actually knew I existed or not, but the impact was the same. I'd grown up without a dad, and so had Kate, in a way. That meant that somewhere inside her was a heart that had been battered and shriveled, but it was still there. "Hattie's my friend," I said quietly. "I need to help her."

Kate glanced at Devlin, then back at me. "Glory," she said equally quietly. "She told me she knows who killed my brother."

I stared at her in shock. "She *knows*?"

"Yes." Kate cleared her throat. "She wanted money in exchange for telling me. I won't be blackmailed. *I won't.*"

"I remember you," Olympia said suddenly. "Mia Murphy, right?"

I had totally forgotten that Olympia existed, and it took me a minute to refocus. I looked at her, trying not to shout at her to stay quiet for one more millisecond. "Yeah, that's me."

At that moment, Devlin stepped around Beau.

"You and your mom stole my grandmother's earrings." Olympia's face darkened. "You and your mother were little thieves, working your way through the party."

Oh…*crud.*

Kate stared at me. "What? You're a thief?"

Devlin chose that moment to walk over. "Sorry for the inter-ruption, ladies—"

"I'll bet she stole your ring and gave it back to you," Olympia said to Kate. "So you'd like her and answer her questions."

Mother of pearl. She was so suspicious. "I didn't—"

"Is that true?" Kate put her hands on her hips. "Did you steal my ring?"

I felt my soul sinking into the beautiful carpet, but I raised my chin. "I am so offended by that," I said haughtily. "If I had stolen your ring, I would have kept it, not given it back."

"Liar," Olympia said. "Your mom did that same thing to my grandma with her earrings, but the Wallenschmidts saw her take them. So you two snuck out in the middle of the night. I was invited to that party to perform, and you almost blew my chance because they blamed the earring theft on me."

Kate's eyes widened. "You little—"

"Excuse me," Devlin cleared his throat. "Mia, I think it's time for you to go."

I spun toward him, desperation strangling me. "Tell them,

Devlin. Tell them that I worked for the FBI for the last two years. Tell them that I'm one of the good guys." I stared at him, begging him. I knew this was more than I could fix alone, because everything Olympia said was probably true. I didn't specifically recall whether my mom had hit up her grandmother, but I knew that my mom had done a lot of things, and I'd helped her. "Devlin. Tell them."

Kate and Olympia both looked at Devlin, with his uniform, his strong jaw, and his melt-worthy brown eyes.

He could save me right here if he wanted to. Or at least, lessen the damage.

But I saw his gaze go to the ring, and then to me, and I realized he knew I'd taken it. *He knew.*

He was a cop who was surgically attached to playing by the rules. He'd never lie for me. Not ever.

"Did you know Rutherford was blackmailing people?" I was desperate to get him to put me on the same side of the law that Griselda had put me on: believing that I was doing the right thing, even if I did it a little illegally.

He looked at me long and hard, then turned to Kate. "I didn't see Mia take your ring, but I did witness her handing it to you," he said. "And she's telling the truth that she has been extremely helpful for the FBI. She has an instinct for details, and she made tremendous personal sacrifices to help the FBI."

My throat tightened with sudden emotion. He hadn't lied to them. But what he'd said might help. A public vote of confidence.

Olympia didn't look convinced, but Kate sighed. "I'm sorry for jumping on you, Mia. For blaming you for stealing my ring." To her credit, she looked embarrassed. "It's just been a stressful few days, and I don't even know who to trust anymore." She looked at Devlin. "Make this go away, Officer Hunt. This is my party, and I don't want it derailed by a murder."

And then she spun away, and strode back across the room, waving at her guests, her voice raised in greeting.

I turned back and found Olympia and Devlin staring at me.

159

Devlin was watching me thoughtfully, and Olympia still looked annoyed. My life, the one I'd tried to rise above, followed me everywhere. My past. My present. The choices I was still making today, even if it was for the right cause.

Suddenly, I felt tired. The battle I'd been fighting my whole life seemed like it was unwinnable.

I sighed. "Look, Olympia, I don't know what my mom did at that party. It's very possible she did steal earrings and try to manipulate your grandmother. She did that a lot. But she was my whole world, and all I had. I loved her then, and I still do, even though I haven't seen her since I walked out on her and that life when I was seventeen. I can't change the past. But I'll be straight up with you that I've done everything I can to not live that life since I left her."

It was a great speech that would have been the truth twenty minutes ago. But since I'd just stolen Kate's ring, it felt like a big, ugly lie to myself as much as to her.

Olympia's face was expressionless, which I guess wasn't surprising. In her life, people probably lied to her a lot.

"Hattie is my friend," I said. "I don't believe she killed anyone, which is why I'm trying to find out who really did it. I just want the truth." I slanted a glance at Devlin. "And I don't necessarily trust the police to do it right, no offense, Devlin."

He raised his brows. "I'm very good at my job."

"Not good enough, I think." I shrugged. "I always remembered that summer with you. You were one of the few people who was nice to me when I was a teenager. I was always glad that you made it professionally, even with an absentee dad and a lot of other challenges. You were my inspiration, and for that, I thank you."

I managed a smile, then turned and walked away, feeling weirdly emotional and deflated, especially when she didn't run after me, saying she forgave me and saw that I was a good person. Because she clearly didn't think I was.

Seeing Olympia, reliving the impact my mom and my childhood had had on others, and then having her see me for who I was, a pickpocket who was still choosing that way to solve her problems...it had been crushing.

I'd been flat-out busted today.

Devlin had salvaged my reputation with Kate, maybe, but not with Olympia. And I had no defense, because I'd done exactly what Olympia had accused me of doing. What if Kate told Agnes, the mayor, or Gladys that I might have stolen her ring? People I was trying to win over who were already suspicious of me? How many chances would I get before I could never earn their trust?

Did it make a difference that I was doing it to save an innocent person from prison, and to make sure a real murderer got caught?

I wasn't sure I knew anymore... And unlike when I was a kid, I couldn't run away in the middle of the night to another party, another mark.

Every single choice I made to repeat the past I was trying to rise above was a choice that would put down roots in this life I was trying to build.

How much was I willing to sacrifice of my own integrity, my future, and my dreams to help someone else?

Maybe it was time to stop.

Stop what? Keeping an innocent person who was my friend out of prison?

I couldn't stop that.

So, maybe it was time to find another way...if there was one.

And if there wasn't...then what?

I'd made it only a few yards of self-pity, when Lucy grabbed my arm and yanked me into the corner, her face radiating. "Holy cow. That was awesome. You're incredible."

Beau appeared over her shoulder, his wrinkled face stretched in a huge smile. "That was fantastic. I had no idea how fun that could be. You have to teach me how to do that."

"Me, too!" Lucy said. "The way you took that ring right off her finger. I mean, I was looking for it, and I still couldn't see the moment you did it—"

I took a breath, my emotions still raw. "It's a slippery slope," I said. "It's like drug addiction. You have to be careful opening that door."

"I want to open that door," Lucy explained. "Let's open it!"

Beau's smile faded as he studied my face. "You haven't done that for a while, I take it."

"I've done it for fun, but not for real. Not since I left my mom." I shifted restlessly. "It was fun. Too fun. But I saw the damage and I broke trust—" I bit my lip, suddenly not wanting to talk about it anymore. "I'm pretty sure that Rutherford and Glory were blackmailing Kate—"

Glory. Fear suddenly gripped me again, and I pulled out my phone and texted. *Hattie. Where are you?*

No reply.

Hattie. Glory might be in danger. Or you might be. She might know who the murderer is.

No reply.

Sweat trickled down my neck, and I looked up. "Have you guys seen Hattie or Glory?"

Lucy frowned. "No. We've been with you."

At that moment, someone screamed. We both spun toward the patio, which Jake had left open. "What the he—"

"There's a body in the water!" someone shouted. "Off the back deck!"

Hattie.

My gut dropped, and we all sprinted for the door.

CHAPTER 15

EVERYONE WAS RUNNING for the patio, but I managed to duck around people and get to the railing. I grabbed the iron rail and leaned over, peering down at the water. The blue striped awnings covered most of the view, and for a minute, it was all I could see.

Then movement at the end caught my eye. I looked closer and saw two people in the water. One with red hair floating face down. And one with turquoise hair, a turquoise shirt, and pink pants, who looked like she was sinking as I watched. My stomach dropped. "Hattie!"

Lucy grabbed the railing beside me. "Oh, *no*."

I ducked around the guests gawking over the railing and sprinted for the ramp.

"Stay back!" Devlin raced past me. "Keep everyone back!"

Jake leapt into action and blocked the ramp with his body. "Everyone return to the dining room," he shouted. "Go back inside."

"No!" Lucy shoved at him, and I ducked under his arm. "Our friend is down there!"

I scooted past Jake and ran down the ramp, my heart thundering with every breath as Devlin dove off the dock, right where the two figures in the water were.

STEPHANIE ROWE

"Hattie!" Lucy shouted behind me, and I heard her feet on the ramp as she got by Jake.

"Hey!" Jake yelled. "Get back here!"

There was no chance I was going to listen to him. Panic clutched at me as I ran. Kate was shouting. I heard her yell something about Hattie, and fear gripped me. It *was* Hattie in the water. "No!"

I ran harder, gasping as I made it to the end of the dock. Devlin reached Glory and flipped her over, locking his arm around her chest as he began to swim back to the dock with her. "Call 9-1-1," he shouted. "Mia! Call 9-1-1!"

I grabbed my phone and pulled it out, frantically dialing 9-1-1 as I scanned the bottom of the lake for Hattie. The water was clear enough that I would be able to see her if she were on the bottom, but she wasn't there. I'd seen her in the water. But where was she?

"9-1-1. What's your emergency?"

"Possible drowning at Diamond Lake Yacht Club in Bass Derby—" I suddenly saw a shadow under the dock, between the boards. "Hattie!" I threw my phone at Lucy and jumped in. The cold water hit me with a shock, but I plunged under the dock anyway. "Hattie!"

It took a split second for my eyes to adjust, and then I saw her bright blue hair disappear beneath the surface. "Hattie!" I plunged through the water, panic closing around my chest as she sank out of sight.

There was a splash behind me, and then Lucy shouted. "Where is she?"

"Under the dock! Hattie!" I could see her under the water, a hot pink figure on the bottom. Not moving. *Dear God.* I sloshed through the water, but it felt like it was taking forever to get there.

And she didn't move. She was just on the bottom. Not moving.

I finally reached for her and—

She shot up out of the water. "Mia!"

I screamed and stumbled back. "I thought you were dead!"

Lucy reached us. "Hattie? You're okay?"

Hattie's hair was plastered to her head, and water was streaming down her cheeks turning her makeup into runny black rivulets. "I can't find it. You have to help me find it."

"Find what?" I was trying to regroup from the terror of thinking Hattie was dead. "What happened?"

"A note! Glory had a note in her hand! It was one of those cardboard RSVP cards from today's party, with big black letters scrawled on it. I could see that it said 'meet,' 'dock,' and 'now,' but her hand was covering the rest. She asked me if I sent her the note, and then she was killed. I checked her body. It's not on her. She must have dropped it. We need to find that note! It was definitely sent by her attacker to get her outside!" She ducked under the water again, and started swimming along the bottom.

Lucy and I looked at each other, then we both dove under the water. I swam along the bottom, scanning for the cardboard. It was thick and laminated, so I was pretty sure it would survive an immersion.

But my mind was reeling. Someone had sent Glory a note? Had they lured her to the dock to kill her?

The thought was chilling. I'd held out hope that Rutherford was a crime of passion, that maybe there wasn't intent. More like an accident.

But this changed everything. This was planned, premeditated and terrifying.

We did have to find that note. What was written on it? And could we trace the handwriting?

I sifted through the sandy bottom, but it was soft. Nothing. I ran out of air and surfaced. Hattie was still under, but Lucy was up. She held up her empty hands.

Hattie came up. "A murderer who kills in the middle of a party! Do you realize how bold that is? No one is safe! We need to find that note!"

"We'll find it." I dove back under again, swimming along the bottom. So much sand. How would we find the note? There was a dead woman that said I needed to keep looking. *Glory was dead.*

Maybe Hattie was wrong. Maybe Glory was all right. Just unconscious.

But either way, she'd been attacked and left for dead.

I came up for air, and saw Devlin wading toward us. "Where's Hattie?" His voice was taut.

I pointed at the pink blob under the water. "She thinks Glory dropped a note from the murderer in the lake. We're looking for it."

Lucy popped up. "I can't find anything. Devlin! Is Glory all right?"

Devlin ignored her and slogged through the water to where Hattie was. He reached down and tapped her shoulder.

She came up, breathless. "Devlin! Did anyone see what happened?"

"Yes." He glanced at me. "Kate saw who attacked Glory."

"Kate did?" She must have bolted for the patio as soon as we'd parted ways.

Hattie's eyes widened. "Who was it?"

Devlin hesitated, and that slight hesitation scared the bejeebers out of me. I grabbed Lucy's forearm a split second before he answered.

"You," he said. "Hattie, she saw you."

CHAPTER 16

HATTIE'S EYES WIDENED, then she snorted with annoyances. "Me? Well of course I was there. That doesn't mean I did it. I didn't."

"What happened?" Devlin asked.

We were all standing in the water under the dock while chaos raged above us. It was quiet where we were, a surreal sense of peace.

The last time I'd been hiding under a dock, a murderer had a gun in my face, so maybe not all that peaceful, actually.

"I came out on the deck to look for Glory, but she wasn't there. I looked over the railing to see if she'd gone down to the water. She was on the docks." Hattie wiped a stream of water off her forehead. "I thought she was leaving, so I sprinted after her. I reached her and she grabbed my arms. She asked if I sent her the note."

The note we hadn't found.

Devlin frowned. "What note?"

Hattie shrugged. "She had it in her hand and waved it at me. She looked terrified, guys. Like she thought I was going to kill her."

"You?" Lucy shook her head. "No way would anyone believe you were going to kill them."

"Well, she did. I asked her what note. She said the note that said to meet on the dock about Rutherford. Then she looked over my shoulder. Her eyes got wide, and then, before I could turn. Boom!" Hattie smacked her hands together.

"Boom?" I shook my head. "What's 'boom?' What happened?"

"I don't know. I woke up in the water, and Glory was gone. I was so pissed, right? I thought she'd shoved me in. But then I got out and guess what!"

"What?" I could hear the ambulance screaming in the distance now.

"I saw her on the bottom of the lake." Hattie's eyes were wide. "I jumped in and dragged her to the surface, but it wasn't good. By the time I got her close to the dock, Devlin was there and he took over."

Devlin raised his brows. "So you didn't see anyone else? No one?"

"No. I just told you that. I was trying to keep Glory from getting in the boat and—"

"Don't say anything else, Hattie," I interrupted quickly. I knew she was innocent, but admitting she'd been wrestling with Glory right before someone had killed her wasn't going to help her.

Hattie looked over at me, and her brows went up. "I have nothing to hide. I'm trying to help them find out who attacked both of us."

I gave her a look, and I saw the moment she realized the situation she was in.

She swore and pointed to her temple. "I have a lump. I'm sure it matches Glory's."

Devlin ignored her comment. "I'm going to have to ask you to come out of the water. Now."

Lucy and I exchanged glances, and I spoke up. "Devlin, you know it wasn't Hattie. She's eighty years old—"

"I am not eighty!" Hattie glared at me. "I'm so offended by that."

Devlin slid a glance in my direction, and I saw the regret on his face. He didn't want to arrest Hattie, but right now, he had no choice. He had an eyewitness that said she'd attacked Glory, and Hattie had already admitted she'd been there and had no other explanation. "Hattie. You need to come with me now."

She met his gaze, and something in her body language shifted. Alarm flickered across her face at whatever expression she saw on his face. "All right." She lifted her chin and began to slosh through the water.

As she passed by, she looked over at us. "Keep looking," she hissed.

Devlin also looked over at us. "This is a murder scene. Both of you, out of the water." He pointed to the ladder. "Out. Now."

Murder scene. That meant Glory really was dead. Granted, it all needed to be official and announced, but dead was dead.

Glory had been murdered, and her killer had had a chance at Hattie.

This wasn't like Dead Man's Pond.

This was different. I could see it in the stiff lines of Devlin's body.

Hattie was in real trouble right now. She needed me to step up. "Look," I said. "Glory asked Hattie if she'd sent the note. Hattie saw the note in her hand. If we can find the note and maybe match the handwriting—"

"My team will search. Get out. Now. Or I *will* arrest you." Devlin glared at me.

I blinked. "That's so hostile. There's no way I'm going on a date with you. I don't date hostile people."

"He asked you on a date?" Hattie's brows shot up. "What did you say?"

"I said no, of course. I'm celibate."

Devlin ignored me and began to usher Hattie out from under the dock. "Get out. Now."

I looked at Lucy and raised my brows.

She grinned and nodded her agreement.

"We're going to look anyway." I dove under the water before he could argue, and Lucy followed me down.

Devlin would have to choose whether to abandon Hattie and drag us out of the water, or to continue to escort his favorite murder suspect onto the dock and leave me and Lucy alone.

I had a feeling he wasn't going to choose us.

Under the water, I could barely hear the sirens and the shouts. It was quieter. Almost peaceful. It gave my brain space to think as I ran my hands through the sand.

We had a major situation pending.

Was it a fluke that Hattie had been on the scene again? Or was someone targeting her? Had the murderer tried to kill Hattie and failed? The thought was chilling. Or maybe he'd just hit her hard enough to leave her at the scene with all the evidence pointing to her.

And now we had *two* dead people. Who was next on the killer's hit list?

I surfaced and Lucy popped up next to me.

I could hear people shouting on the dock, and Devlin was still in the water, waiting for Hattie to climb out first. I looked over at Hattie, and she peered at me through the ladder as she climbed out. Her blue eyes were wide and more than a little worried.

I gave her a thumbs up, and Lucy gave a fist pump. "We got this," I told Hattie. "Don't worry. We'll come bail you out."

"No," she said. "I can handle Chief Stone. You stay here and find whoever did this. You find him, and fast."

I nodded. "We will."

"No." Devlin shook his head at me over Hattie's shoulder as she climbed up the ladder. "Don't even think about it, Mia."

"Think about what?"

Devlin glared at us as he started to climb. "Get out of the water. Both of you."

"We still have a minute," I retorted, and then dove again.

Beside me, Lucy also went under.

I stayed under as long as I could, and when I came up, I was on the far side of the dock. Lucy came up beside me, and we both looked toward the ladder.

Devlin had already gotten out of the lake. I smiled. Choice made. I wanted to think it was because he implicitly trusted me to find that note, and he was deputizing me to step up and help, but that was a total lie. He trusted me with nothing when it came to murder.

It made me realize that I missed Griselda, who had always trusted me to take action, often at extreme risk to myself, but he'd depended on me for help, and I'd liked that.

Devlin definitely wasn't relying on me for help. Le sigh. No date for him if he couldn't agree to let me flourish. I should have dated Griselda while I had the chance. Oh, well. Single forever, just how I liked it.

Lucy and I looked at each other, and then, without speaking, we both dove again.

There was literally no chance I was getting out of that water until I was forced to. If there was a chance to clear Hattie's name right now, I was going to find it.

CHAPTER 17

WE DIDN'T FIND IT.

Then we got locked down in the Yacht Club for hours while Devlin and his pals interviewed everyone.

Olympia escaped to her private jet.

We didn't escape until hours later, when we were finally back in Beau's boat and heading toward the Eagle's Nest, having accomplished absolutely nothing toward the goal of discovering the true murderer. We did get to eat some great food, though, so that was a sparkling light on the events, right?

"It's time for Mia to blow Devlin's mind with all-night sex," Esther announced. "It's our only chance." She was sitting in the co-pilot's seat as Beau chauffeured me and my posse back to the Eagle's Nest. Esther's boat had been on the wrong side of the murder scene, so she couldn't get it out. Lucy just wanted to ride with us.

Beau had been in such a good mood from witnessing a real-time murder and participating in a pickpocketing scheme, that he forgot that he hated people in time to stop Esther and Lucy from vaulting into his boat as we began to pull away from the dock.

Even now, he was grinning, despite the fact that Esther had just launched a sex talk in his presence.

"I'm not sleeping with Devlin," I announced. My feet were on the railing, and I'd ditched my country club boat shoes. My sneakers were still damp from our fruitless under-the-dock search, and the breeze felt good on my bare toes.

"I agree with Mia." Lucy had taken over the bow seat with me. Her feet were also up on the rail, showing off sparkly neon green toenail polish that was very fitting for a former baton twirler. "Devlin has arrested her two best friends. That definitely bans him from being lucky enough to be manipulated with sex."

"Right? He's not worthy." And...hello? Lucy had just called herself one of my best friends. Yay!

Esther raised her brows. "That man spent four hours interviewing every guest. You need to find out what he learned. If you're not going to fry his brain with sex, then how are you going to manipulate him?"

I grinned and waved my phone. "Angelina Stefanopoulos works in the police station. She's Hattie's bestie. She'll report in anything that I need to know." I'd already chatted with Angelina twice since Hattie had been arrested.

To no one's surprise, Hattie had already managed to procure someone to order her a pizza and beer, take a run to her house for her fluffy slippers and sweatpants, and set up an air mattress with flannel sheets so she could be comfortable.

Hattie might soon become my idol.

"So, what next, then?" Beau asked as he slowed the boat to cruise into a slip at the Eagle's Nest.

I glanced back at him. "You're in?"

He had the wherewithal to look horrified, and he even made a choking sound. "No. I'm not in. I'm simply curious."

I glanced at Lucy, and she grinned. Beau was definitely in. He'd caught the bug.

I had as well. With one caveat. "No more pickpockets or cons," I said. "But other than that, we're good." As Beau pulled in, I noticed that the green canoe that belonged to Cargo, my only employee, was tied up at my dock. I'd never met him, but I'd seen his boat a fair amount.

Maybe today was my lucky day.

This time, it was Beau's turn to shoot me a skeptical look. "No more cons, eh? Even for a good cause?"

I glared at him. "No more criminal activity." I hadn't had time to process the whole pickpocketing thing, because of the sudden murder and all, but it didn't take much to show me that I couldn't afford to go down that road again. "But I'm all in for interfering with Devlin's goal of arresting one of my friends. Who wants to raid Hattie's kitchen for some snacks while we figure out what to do next?"

"I'm in!" Lucy leapt out to the boat before Beau had even reached the dock.

"Me, too!" Esther sounded thrilled. "Hattie's the best chef in the entire state. Even my money has never been able to buy me access to her kitchen. If I'd realized her being in jail would give me free rein in there, I would have arranged for it long ago."

I narrowed my eyes, not quite sure if she was kidding, but alarmingly certain that she was dead serious. Note to self: do not ever become a great chef idolized by Esther.

To my surprise, Beau tossed one of the dock lines around a piling and secured his boat. "I'll consider observing your planning discussions as part of the interviews you owe me," he said. "I want to take notes, videos, and photographs as I see fit."

I grinned. "Of course." I was genuinely happy as I helped Beau tie the boat and then followed the trio up the ramp. I might not have my mom at my back, but I'd created my own team, all of whom were in it for the right reasons...or at least, not for the wrong reasons.

Either way, they were with me, and it felt good. It felt empowering. I wasn't on my own to help Hattie. I had a baton-twirling mail carrier, a cranky mystery writer, and quite possibly one of the richest women in the entire state. And, of course, my cat.

I stopped. My cat?

I realized suddenly that he hadn't come down to the boat to greet me.

We'd been family for only a short time, but his need for my well-being had already become apparent. Where was he?

Frowning, I looked around as the others traipsed across the dirt parking lot toward the marina building where Hattie's Café was. The painters and landscapers were gone, and the marina looked pretty amazing, but I couldn't focus on that. All I could think about was where King Tut was.

What if someone had come after him?

What if it was like one of those movies, where they silence the dog so that he won't alert anyone that an assassin was approaching— "No. Stop." Those were terrible thoughts. Why was I doing that to myself? "King Tut?" I called out as I stepped out into the parking lot.

I checked his spot under the tree where he liked to eat his latest catch, but he wasn't there. He wasn't on the roof. He wasn't sitting in the window of the apartment.

The front door of the marina store was open, so he wasn't trapped in there. "King Tut?"

Panic was just setting in when I heard a meow. I looked up ahead, and I saw him sitting on the roof of my car. Relief rushed through me, and my heart sort of melted a bit.

I had it bad for him, apparently. "I'll meet you guys inside!"

I needed to give my two-thousand-pound cranky beast a snuggle.

As the others headed into Hattie's Café, which she'd apparently left unlocked, I veered off to greet King Tut. I held out my arms as I reached the car. "Hug time!"

He didn't leap into my arms with delight and glee.

He simply sat there, staring at me, the tip of his tail twisting ever so slowly. One twitch. Two twitches.

I dropped my arms as I stared at him.

It was his angry pose. "What are you mad about?"

He continued to stare and flick his tail.

I knew he wasn't mad that I'd gone to the party without him. He wasn't that social. Plus, he was a cat, right? Maybe he was hungry. "Do you want to eat?"

He stared at me, and a low growl emanated from his chest.

The alarm that had disappeared at the sight of him returned with a vengeance.

I looked around to see what had upset him. I didn't see anything amiss, but I knew better than to believe that.

Two people had been murdered, and a bug had been discovered under my porch. Things were afoot, and if my cat felt that something was wrong, then it was.

Lucy came back to the porch. "Um…Mia? We've got a situation—"

"Hang on." I walked over to the car and stared at King Tut. "What's going on?"

He said nothing.

But he continued to sit on my car.

The car. He never sat on my car. Which meant he was on it for a reason.

"Mia? Seriously. You need to come inside—"

"Hang on." My mom had taught me to rely on my instincts, and I'd never forgotten that lesson. I peered in the windows at the front seat, but I didn't see anything. I glanced at King Tut, and he continued to flick and stare.

"Mia. Hattie's kitchen—"

I held up my hand and peered in the back window. Most of my clothes were still in my car because I hadn't moved into the marina yet since it was due to be fumigated tomorrow. I'd grown up living in a car many nights, so I knew how to make the most of the space. I was neat and organized.

My clothes had been moved. "What the heck?"

"Mia. You need to come inside—"

"Someone's been in my car." I opened the hatchback and studied the clothes as Lucy came up beside me.

"Someone's been in the café as well. Hattie's kitchen has been trashed. Esther can barely find anything to eat."

I looked sharply at Lucy. "Really?"

"Yep. They vandalized it, too." She glanced at my car. "What happened here? Did they steal something?"

I shook my head. "It's just clothes in here. Nothing to take." But one pile was higher than it should be. Frowning, I moved a stack of sweatshirts, and then swore under my breath when I saw a large metal lockbox. "That's not mine."

Lucy whistled softly. "Someone stashed it in there?"

"Apparently." My heart started to pound. There was a bright and shiny padlock on it. "We need to get this out of my car." If someone wanted it in my car, then I definitely wanted it out.

I grabbed it and tried to pull it, but it was too heavy to move. "Lucy?"

She grabbed a side and tried to pull, but it was useless. "It must weight several hundred pounds. It's like a safe."

"Well, then, let's see what's in it." Whatever it was, I could handle it. I'd handled a lot more when I was undercover for the FBI, right? How bad could it be?

After nearly being incinerated in the Church Island arson incident, I'd gotten in the habit of keeping my lockpicks with me, so I quickly went to work on the padlock.

It took only a moment. I handed Lucy the lock, then pulled the lid up.

Inside were rows of white powder wrapped in clear plastic bags.

Holy cow.

Shock ripped through me, and I fell to my knees. Not again. *Not again.* This couldn't be happening again. I suddenly couldn't breathe. I was back in that moment when I'd found the drugs before, when I'd had to make the decision that would wreck my life. And how difficult it had been to wipe its taint off me, and now…now…it was in my car. *Mine.* No one to blame but me.

177

"Mia? What's in there? You look like it's a severed hand." Lucy leaned over to peer in the box. "Oh, my God."

I still couldn't breathe. I bent over, bracing my hands on the dirt. My hands were shaking. I was sweating. *No. I didn't have time for a panic attack.*

I closed my eyes and tried to slow my breathing. *I could handle this. It would be fine.*

"What's going on out here?"

I looked over my shoulder, and my gut congealed when I saw Beau and Esther standing beside Lucy, both of their jaws hanging open.

I had no words. No excuses. I just stared at them, wanting to crumble. Everything I'd fought for was lost. There was no way they'd believe me that it wasn't mine. God, maybe even Griselda wouldn't believe me. Maybe he'd think I'd been involved the whole time after all.

There was so much powder in that box.

Enough for me to be the drug dealer I'd claimed I wasn't.

CHAPTER 18

LUCY WAS the first to recover. "Is that what it looks like?"

I staggered to my feet, shrugged noncommittally, trying desperately to hide my rising panic. "I'm guessing it is. Yeah."

"Holy crap." Esther's jaw was still down. "That is worth so much money. How much? Millions?"

"Probably." Dear God. Tens (or hundreds?) of millions of dollars of drugs were in my car. It was bad enough that it made me look guilty, but the even bigger concern was the fact that it had come from somewhere. We could all be gunned down in a split second if we stood in the way of whoever wanted it back.

Frantically, I looked around, scanning our surroundings for any cute little assassins racing toward us with assorted guns.

There were none, for the moment at least.

I looked at my cat. King Tut was giving me a baleful look, clearly not impressed that I'd managed to get us tangled up in this. "Who did it?" I asked him. I was sure he knew.

He ignored me and began to clean the parts of him that no one wanted to see him clean, which I was pretty sure was pretty much like flipping me off for being so pathetic.

I took a breath and pulled my shoulders back. I was not going to be the loser that my cat thought I was.

Esther pulled her gaze off the plastic bags and studied me thoughtfully. "You're really a drug dealer?"

"No." I cleared my throat. "I'm not. I don't know how this got here."

Beau said nothing, but he was watching me intently. Not taking notes. Not recording a video. Simply watching silently, like he was some creepy stalker.

Or like he was a very perceptive mystery writer who was trying to decide exactly how guilty I was and what I was guilty of. I shot him a desperate look. "It's not mine. You have to believe me."

"You did have the key to the padlocks." Esther pointed to the lock in Lucy's hand. "That does seem to incriminate you."

"I picked the lock." I frantically grabbed the lock and jammed it back on the lockbox, then wiped my prints with the nearest pair of sweatpants. "Someone planted it here. You guys, we need to get this out of here. Whoever it belongs to will probably be heavily armed when he comes to get it back."

Everyone stared at me, and no one moved.

"You guys need to leave. I'll handle this." I was already reaching in my pocket for my car keys. "I'll drive it into the woods and dump it or something—"

"Since it's in your car," Beau said thoughtfully, "I think it's safe to assume that dumping it in the woods isn't going to solve your problem."

I stared at him. "What are you talking about?"

He folded his arms over his chest and leaned against the car. "Assuming you're telling the truth that it's not yours, then someone put it there for a reason. You need to find out what that reason is, or you might make a choice that's exactly what they want you to do."

Fear prickled down my neck, but Lucy hit him in the shoulder. "You're so creepy!"

Oh, man. "Look, whatever it is, I'm getting it away from the marina. I don't want to endanger you guys."

"I like danger." Esther folded her arms resolutely. "I'm not leaving. Let's set a trap for them."

"We are not going to trap them." I shoved my clothes back over the box and then closed the door. "People like that have machine guns. Very sharp knives. And an absence of basic human morals. So, they would be happy to kill us. I need to call the FBI." Griselda might blame me, but he was my best chance. I didn't want to be in the middle of whatever was happening. I pulled my phone out of my pocket, but my hands were shaking so much that it slipped out of my fingers. It hit the ground and bounced under my car. *Crap!*

I dropped down to my knees to peer under. It had bounced all the way to the middle of the undercarriage, just out of reach.

At that moment, we heard a siren in the distance.

I jumped up, and we all turned as flashing blue and white lights blinked through the branches of the road that approached the marina. I could see enough of the vehicle to know who was driving it. "It's Chief Stone."

"And my aunt's car is behind his," Lucy said. "Why would the mayor and the police chief be here, and not at the Yacht Club?"

Understanding shot through me. "They were tipped off. They're coming for this. For me." Oh, man. I dropped to the ground and started to wiggle under my car for my phone. "I need to call the FBI. They'll stop them."

"How? Aunt Eloise and Clyde are here *now*," Lucy said.

"The FBI is magic. Stall them. Don't let them come over here." The gravel from the parking lot was grinding into my belly as I wriggled forward. My head hit the undercarriage, and I grimaced as I reached for the phone. Still three inches short.

"I'll handle them!" Lucy took off running, with Esther right behind her.

Beau continued to stand there. I knew, because I could see his feet to my right. "I'm not a drug dealer, Beau. I swear it. We need to win this battle. Please go stall them."

"I'm observer status only. I already told you that."

Damn. I'd totally thought he was lying about that. Just goes to show, you should never trust a rich, cranky mystery writer with a crush on your mom, right?

I lunged for my phone and my fingers closed around it. As I grabbed it, King Tut landed beside the front tire, scaring the bejeebers out of me. I glared at him as I unlocked my phone. "That was rude."

He walked under the car and tapped my forehead gently, a low purr emanating from his chest.

It wasn't much, but the tiny bit of affection suddenly made my throat tighten. I couldn't lose my new life just because someone wanted me to go to jail. Resolution flooded me and I immediately texted 911 to the Keep Mia Alive chat that consisted of me, Griselda, and Devlin. I'd created it shortly a recent murder attempt on me, not really thinking I'd need it. Just more to annoy them.

Who knew, right?

No response, but I could hear Lucy and Esther chatting loudly and frantically about the drama at the Yacht Club while Chief Stone kept telling them to get out of his way.

I didn't have much time.

I texted 911 to the chat again as I began to wriggle out from under the car.

No response.

I texted 911 again.

And again.

And again.

And again.

I could hear footsteps, and Lucy and Esther's raised voices trying to stop them.

Beau crouched down, peering at me under the car. "No luck with the FBI?"

"If Griselda's phone is off, he won't get messages." But Devlin's phone should be on, right? Guess who didn't get to ignore me right now? Yep, that's right. Bass Derby's hottest cop didn't get the choice about whether to cater to my every whim and need right now.

So, I texted again.

911.

911.

911.

911.

911.

I had to be annoying the hell out of him by now. No matter what he was doing, he'd have to look at his phone to shut it up.

911.

911.

911.

911.

911.

What was he doing? This was ridiculous. I could have had my head severed from my body by now.

Beau raised his brows. "Your so-called close and personal relationship with the FBI seems a little sketchy."

"They'll come." With King Tut strolling along beside me, I finally got out from under the car, my heart pounding. Esther and Lucy had created a human wall, which was one of the sweetest things I'd ever seen.

My phone suddenly rang. Devlin's name flashed across my screen! I grabbed my phone and ducked behind my car, listening to Lucy argue with her aunt and cousin.

I answered the phone without preamble. "I just found massive amounts of white powder in a lockbox in my car," I whispered before he could say anything. "Chief Stone and the mayor just showed up here. I think someone tipped them off. They're in the parking lot. Griselda isn't answering."

Devlin swore. "Stall them." Then he hung up.

Stall them. *Stall them?* My team was already trying to stall them, and it wasn't working. I didn't think it would be appropriate to tackle the police chief and the mayor and hurl them off the dock into the lake, but maybe that was what Devlin had meant.

Men were tricky to understand sometimes.

At that moment, the mayor and Chief Stone practically sprinted around the bumper of my car, followed by Esther and Lucy, who were all still protesting.

Beau had backed up slightly, making it clear he wasn't a part of the situation.

I both respected that and was highly irritated by it.

Mayor Eloise Stone stopped when she saw me. "You're Mia Murphy?"

The only time we'd met had been at the police station, when I'd pretended I was an advance scout from a movie production company. Since I'd also been covered in beer and flour at the time, I was a little surprised she recognized me in proper Yacht Club clothes. Of course, I'd gone swimming in them and then crawled under a car, so maybe the vibe was the same.

Plus, she was a political heavyweight, right? It was her job to remember everyone she met.

Chief Stone giggled with what could only be called an alarming level of glee. He'd tried to arrest me within seconds of me driving over the border into Bass Derby, and our relationship hadn't really improved over the six days I'd been in town. "You."

I smiled and stood up. "Yes, it's me." I smiled at the mayor. "We've never officially met. I've heard great things about you. Did you notice the painting and the landscaping? I'm rehabbing the Eagle's Nest Marina to make it worthy of Bass Derby's charm. What can I do for you?"

Maybe a little bit too speechy, but I was desperate to get my bonus points in where I could.

Apparently unimpressed with my great declarations, Chief Stone pointed at my car. "That's the one. Right where they said it would be."

Yeah, they were totally tipped off...but why the tipoff? Did this have something to do with Hattie? Or were we in an entirely new, and equally fun and enjoyable game? So many options. All of them fantastic.

"Please open that." Eloise nodded at the rear door of my car, making me wish I'd been a little more heads-up in speedily relocating my car in this particular crisis. Clearly, I needed to up my game.

"My car? Why?" I put my hands on my hips, suddenly not sure whether I'd actually locked my car or not.

I didn't remember locking it. I'd gotten out my keys to drive it away, not lock it.

Crap. It would be so obvious if I locked it now.

"Because we want to search it." Chief Stone pulled out a pair of bolt cutters. "Open it up."

What? What was he, a boy scout? That was much too prepared. I immediately moved to stand between him and my tailgate. "Do you have a search warrant?" I hated going on the offensive, because it always created more resistance, but he was waving bolt cutters at a possible drug stash.

There weren't any ways in which that worked out well for me.

He paused. "A search warrant?"

Dear God. Did the man not pay any attention when he was in the police academy? "Yes. It's private property."

"We got a tip—"

The mayor interrupted her son. "We don't need a search warrant if you give us permission to search. Innocent people don't mind."

"What kind of accusatory statement is that?" Esther jumped in to defend me. She even put her hands on her hips and glared at the mayor, because being old and rich in a small town gave you the ability to get away with antagonizing the town's autocracy. When I was old and rich, I was totally going to do that, too. "I have nothing to hide," she continued, "but I'd never let anyone run through my house looking for things unless I was forced to by law. Why on earth does the fact Mia treasures her privacy make her guilty?"

"Yeah." Lucy added her agreement. "That's so true."

It might be true, but Eloise had a point. Protesting a search made me look guilty. And since I was protesting because there was actually something I didn't want them to find, it was difficult to argue the point.

And since Eloise was the one who was trying to keep me from having the fundraiser at the marina, I didn't just need to stop them from opening the lockbox. I needed to do it in a way that won her love and loyalty forever.

I was good at people. But that was incredibly tricky, I wasn't going to lie.

I took a breath. "What kind of tip?" Giving myself time to figure out how the blazes to handle this. Where the heck was Devlin?

"Drugs." Chief Stone looked positively thrilled. "You've been working on your ex's business the whole time. I knew it!"

"Drugs?" I frowned, trying to look distraught, which wasn't all that much of a stretch for me right now. "You mean the kind that I gave up my entire life, marriage, family, and friends to stop when I lived in Boston?" Ouch. That reminder felt good.

"Yes!" He almost shouted his glee at getting the chance to become involved in something so exciting. "There are drugs in your car!"

"There are?" I sat down on the bumper, as if my legs had given out. "Oh, God." I pressed my face to my hands. "They said to go into Witness Protection. They told me that Stanley would be able to reach me even from prison. I didn't believe them." I looked up. "I wanted a life. Is that so much to ask? I wanted a life that I chose, I wanted this life, in this town."

Chief Stone ignored me and headed right toward my car, but Lucy subtly tripped him, and he faceplanted right into the side of my car.

I looked at Eloise, ignoring Clyde's screech of agony and outrage. I knew I had only seconds to get her on my side. I had to appeal to what mattered to her, and that was this town. "Do you know that during the trial, I looked at the listing for this marina every single day? I read every article I could find about Bass Derby. This beautiful town was what kept me going every day when I was in that tiny safe house, waiting for the nightmare to be over. I turned down Witness Protection because I wanted to be *here*." All true. Every little bit of it. Except that I would have turned down Witness Protection even if I hadn't found Bass Derby.

No one was controlling my life again. Ever. I'd rather live in a gutter than have someone control my life again.

"Did you?" Eloise raised her brows, but I could tell my words had struck a chord. The woman spent more time marketing Bass Derby than running it, from what I could see.

"This—" I spread out my arms. "This was my dream. To belong to a community where people are good and kind, not running around with machine guns and hurting innocent people. And now…" I sighed. "You're telling me that it has followed me here?" I leaned back, banging my head against the back window. "You're telling me that there are *drugs* in *my* car?"

"You're a drug dealer," Chief Stone said. "Everyone knows it."

I looked at Eloise. "I'm not a drug dealer," I said. "I'm just a woman who's trying to rebuild her life after finding out her husband was a drug kingpin, and then giving up any chance at a normal life to put him in prison."

Empathy flickered in her eyes. Lucy had told me that Eloise had had her dreams of Hollywood fame destroyed. She'd slunk back to town pregnant and alone, only to discover that the true love she'd left behind had married her sister, Lucy's mom, in her absence.

It meant that Eloise and her son, the warm and fuzzy police chief, held deep and lasting bitterness and resentment toward Lucy. But it also meant she might understand about broken dreams and bad exes.

"Open the car, Mia." Her voice was hard, refusing to revisit the past I'd tried to unlock. "Sob stories don't work on me."

Crap. If I said no, I could keep them from finding the drugs, but my reputation would be shot in this town. Forever.

None of my friends said anything. They'd already tried everything, and I knew they already considered me the expert at this kind of thing.

And they were right. It was up to me. I knew what I had to do. I knew I had to say no and refuse to allow the search of my car. My reputation wasn't as important as not going to jail. But the moment I said no, it would be over. My dreams. My reputation in this town. I would be blackballed, and in a town this size, that would be all it would take. But my mom had always said that staying out of prison was the number one goal, and I had to go with that right now.

But the cost made me want to cry. "I'm sorry, but—"

My phone rang. I looked down, and relief nearly brought tears to my eyes when I saw Griselda's name flash across my screen. "Hang on. It's the FBI." I held up my hand to ask for a moment, then answered it. "Hello, Agent Straus." I used his real name.

I hoped he didn't think I was turning over a new leaf or anything ridiculous like that. Calling him Griselda was back on the table as soon as I didn't have people I was trying to impress listening to my conversation.

He wasted no time. "What's going on?"

"The mayor of Bass Derby and the chief of police are here now." My voice was shaky, on the edge of emotion. I hated that. I hated looking vulnerable. I cleared my throat, and tried to sound like I had everything under control. "Apparently, they got a tip that there are drugs in my car."

"Are there drugs?"

I knew the volume was too low for Clyde and Eloise to hear his question, but I still shot a nervous glance toward the mayor and the chief. "It looks like it," I said neutrally.

"How much?"

"A lot."

He swore. "Who's in charge there?"

"The mayor." I didn't hesitate. She was Chief Stone's mom, and I'd already seen evidence she ran the town and the police department.

"Put her on the phone."

"Okay." I held out my phone. "Agent Strauss from the FBI would like to speak with you."

The mayor's eyes widened, but she took my phone. "This is Eloise Stone, Mayor of Bass Derby. To whom am I speaking?"

Of course she wouldn't trust a sweet little drug dealer like me with the truth.

There was silence while she listened to whatever Griselda was telling her.

I looked at Lucy and Esther, who were standing shoulder to shoulder by my side, which sort of made me get a little emotional. What a show of solidarity, right? I would really miss them if I got sent to prison.

Wait. No. No prison. Definitely no prison.

"Yes, I understand." The mayor gave me a strange look as she nodded in response to whatever Griselda was saying.

I hoped he came through for me. I knew that his number one, and only, agenda was his work. Protecting me only came into play when it furthered his work goals. Most of the time that meant that he threw me out in front of the proverbial speeding bus, but I had no other choice but to hope that today his goals and my well-being aligned.

I felt so helpless, standing there, my fate in Griselda's hands.

This was why I'd turned down witness protection. So that my fate would never be controlled by anyone else. And yet here I was, in the same situation. Again.

I needed to get better control over my life.

Eloise handed the phone to Chief Stone. "He would like to speak with you."

Chief Stone glared at me, and took the phone. "Chief Stone here." He was silent for a moment. "But—" He stopped, then tried again. "But, I—" Again, Griselda apparently cut him off, which made me grin.

I knew that side of Griselda.

After another moment, Chief Stone handed my phone back to me.

I put it to my ear. "What's up?"

"Chief Stone is now working for me. Do as he says."

I gritted my teeth. "You know I don't like orders—"

"And you know I don't care. I'll be there by tonight."

"Tonight? You're coming?" But he'd already hung up.

I shoved my phone in my pocket, trying to ignore the sudden anxiety hitting me at the thought of Griselda bringing the FBI back into my life. I couldn't go through that again. *I couldn't.* But I didn't have time to freak out. "What did he say?" I asked Eloise.

The mayor raised her brows. "He said you're a hero."

My throat suddenly tightened, and my eyes filled with sudden, unexpected tears. "He did?"

"Yes." She was looking at me differently, thoughtfully. "He used that actual word."

I pressed my lips together, trying to contain the emotion threatening to overtake me. I'd given so much to take down my ex, but I'd never thought of myself that way. "He's never said that to me."

"Well, he clearly thinks it." Her gaze went to my car. "He said not to touch that until he gets here. It's part of an important federal investigation."

Chief Stone nodded. "I'm to keep watch. Not let anyone near it." He sounded like he thought he was pretty important, which I was all right with right now. "All of you, I will have to ask you to leave."

I raised my brows. "It's my marina."

Lucy elbowed me. "Oh, for heaven's sake, Mia. Let it go."

I wanted to let it go. I really did. I was definitely of the opinion that I needed to stay as far away from the sordid world of white powder and plastic bags, but I didn't want to go.

First, I wasn't sure I trusted Chief Stone not to decide to open my car anyway and mess everything up.

Plus...this situation didn't feel right. It felt like I was missing something. Because this wasn't just a random event of finding white powder in my car. There were so many things at play. How did this relate to Hattie? Or did it?

Something wasn't adding up. How did the drugs connect back to Hattie being arrested? Or were there two different situations happening?

It looked like there were two different situations.

Which meant that there probably wasn't.

Distract and redirect. I'd learned that lesson well from my mom, which meant I could see that we were probably dealing with that right now.

But what was going on? Hattie's freedom was at stake, and now, I was on their radar as well.

What the hell was going on?

Chief Stone glared at me. "Leave. Now. I need to secure the premises."

I didn't want to leave him there with my car, but—

At that moment a worn-out pickup truck I recognized from our evening at Dead Man's Pond peeled around the corner and practically shot into the parking lot. I could see Bootsy at the wheel as she hit the brakes, skidding to a stop only inches from Chief Stone, who immediately squawked and dove to the side.

Before he had time to recover his dignity, all four doors to the truck opened up, and out poured the Seam Rippers. "Margarita time!" Shirley shouted as she nearly leapt out of the passenger seat.

I grinned as another truck pulled up behind Bootsy's, and Seam Rippers were unleashed into my marina. In less than two minutes, there were ten folding chairs, two card tables, two coolers, a portable grill, and, of course, several blenders set up in a semi-circle. The posse of seventy-something quilters parked their butts in the chairs, put their feet up and started gossiping.

We all stared at them in shock, but then I noticed Esther grinning.

I looked over at her and raised my brows.

She held up her phone and gave me a thumbs up, and suddenly tears filled my eyes.

All these women, who I'd met only once or twice, had chosen to stand behind me. Mostly because I was Hattie's friend, but still.

Chief Stone immediately started protesting and trying to get them to leave, but I knew that would never happen. The Seam Rippers were going to stay there and safeguard my car until Griselda arrived. Chief Stone would never get through all of them. A few of them, maybe, but all of them?

No chance. These were women who summoned the ghost of a serial killer. A cop wasn't going to intimidate them into backing down.

Eloise had a small grin pulling at the corner of her mouth. "Looks like Mia is already popular in this town."

"Mia's the greatest," Bootsy said as she began to unroll an industrial-length outdoor extension cord. "Did you see how great the marina looks? And she's saving the fundraiser after Jake gave away their spot."

"Oh, no, she's not," Shirley said as she began setting up the blender. "The mayor believed the rumors that Mia's a drug dealer, and she banned Wanda and Gladys from putting the fundraiser on here."

"What?" Bootsy stopped unrolling the extension cord to stare at Eloise. "Tell me that's not true."

"Yeah," Esther said. "The FBI just told her that Mia's a hero. Mayor Stone, isn't it time to take advantage of Mia and let her host the fundraiser? She's good for the town, not bad."

The other Seam Rippers all started protesting on my behalf. This was amazing. I'd never experienced anything like this before.

Eloise met my gaze as the Seam Rippers closed in around her, protesting as they unpacked their plastic margarita glasses.

"Will you call Gladys and Wanda and tell them they can host it here?" I asked.

She gave me a long look. "I'll see what happens after the FBI looks in your car."

"It might be too late at that point," I said. "I'm good for the town, not bad for it. And the fundraiser will do so much better if it's actually on the lake. Jake shut them down." Dammit. My voice had cracked a little bit.

Too much at stake. Too much of my past coming back for me. I needed to pull myself together.

Eloise gave me a long look. "I'll consider it."

"All right. Thanks." That was better than an outright rejection, right? So, there was still a window…a window that would open or close depending on how I handled the next few hours. Or however long it took to find a murderer, a blackmailer, and whatever else was involved.

I looked over at Lucy and Beau, who were waiting for me to follow them into the café to see what was up with Hattie's kitchen, and I smiled.

I had a team. We could do this.

We could definitely do this.

Or die trying…right?

CHAPTER 19

L<small>UCY HADN'T BEEN EXAGGERATING.</small>

Hattie's kitchen was trashed.

Food everywhere. Someone had spray painted *murderer* above the stove. Pots and pans were tossed on the floor. A sharp knife was sticking straight up out of a wooden cutting board. A milk carton had been stabbed and leaked all over the carnage. "Wow. This is really hostile."

"Right?" Lucy said. "Who would do this? No one even cares that Rutherford and Glory are dead. And who would even believe Hattie did it? This makes no sense."

Her last words stuck in my head. *This makes no sense.*

She was right. It didn't make any sense.

I didn't move from the door. I continued studying the chaos. "It looks very intentional, doesn't it?"

Lucy looked over at me, her eyes glistening with interest. "What does that mean?"

"A basic tenet of pickpocketing is to distract people, usually by bumping them. Their attention goes to the distraction, and then they don't even feel it when I lift their wallet."

She nodded. "How does that relate to the kitchen?"

"It means, give a person something to pay attention to, and

they won't notice the thing you don't want them to notice." I looked around. "So, what is it that they don't want us to notice?"

"Oh…" Lucy rubbed her jaw. "Like, they stole something?"

"Or planted something, like in my car." I grimaced as I looked at the amount of carnage that had been left behind. "This would take us forever to figure out what was missing or added." If we even could. "Would you be able to tell?"

She shrugged. "I'd notice something major, like if they stole the stove or the dishwasher, but something small? No." She glanced over. "I'm assuming that telling Chief Stone is a bad idea? If they planted evidence to incriminate Hattie, I'm not about to let the cops find it."

I grinned. "You're learning fast. Your mind is turning criminal. I'm so impressed."

She laughed. "I always wanted to be a criminal. I just didn't realize it. So what do we do? Search it?"

I shook my head. "We need to find out what happened here." I ran back to the front door of the café, quickly pulled down the shade, and locked the door. "We need to deal with this ourselves," I said as I hurried back to the kitchen, where Esther was already locking the back door.

"You know the cops will search Hattie's café," Lucy said. "If they haven't already. We don't have much time."

"Keep an eye out and make sure Chief Stone isn't coming in here. I'm going to call Hattie."

"Okay." Lucy hurried to the window and peered out while I pulled out my phone and dialed Angelina, who was the grandma of the Greek twins who worked for Hattie.

She also worked at the police station and had been very helpful when Lucy had been in trouble earlier in the week.

It took her seven rings to answer, a split second before voice mail would have picked up. "Sorry, Mia," she said cheerfully. "I was running a payment for a speeding ticket."

I knew about those tickets. "How's Hattie?"

"Sassy and worried," she said. "I've never seen her worried like this before."

I swore under my breath. "Is Devlin there?"

"No, he's still at the Yacht Club, I think."

I knew Chief Stone was guarding possible cocaine at the moment. "Are there any police officers there?"

"Officer Stevens. He's retired, and they hire him for the summer season when things get busier with all the tourists. Why? You want to talk to him? He's napping in Devlin's office, but I can wake him up for you."

Perfect. "No, don't wake him. Can you get your phone in to Hattie? I need to talk to her." I knew it was probably not allowed, but Angelina seemed like her loyalties were more with the girls than the badges.

Angelina didn't even hesitate. "Hang on. Let me make sure he's really asleep."

"No problem." I heard the sound of bumping, scratching, and her breathing, and a few clicks and noises, then suddenly, I heard a voice that made emotion clog my throat.

"Tell me you found the murder note," Hattie said, her voice strong and confident.

Lucy turned away from the window and ran over to me. "Hattie! Are you okay?"

"Of course I'm okay. They're afraid to do anything but serve my greatest need. And Officer Stevens has a crush on me." This time, I heard a little bit of weariness in her voice, and I remembered that Hattie was tough, but she was also in her seventies and human.

"We didn't find the note," I said. "But we're working on things."

Hattie swore. "What's going on?"

I knew we didn't have much time. "We're standing in your kitchen right now. It was trashed."

"My sanctuary was invaded?" She suddenly sounded much more alert. "We need to hunt down those little fu—"

"I don't know who did it," I interrupted, before she could start declaring her intent to murder while she was in a jail cell for murder. "But I'm guessing someone trashed it to hide stealing something or stashing something."

"I'm still morally offended. You need to clean that up before I get out of prison."

"Me? Why?"

"Because you own the building and failed to provide adequate security. Obviously. I might have to sue you for back rent."

"You haven't paid me any rent." I raised my brows at Lucy, who was grinning. How worried could Hattie be if she was plotting to put the burden of the invasion on me? I relaxed slightly.

"Details, schmetails. What's the plan, then? I assume you have a plan, since I'm trapped in this little cage awaiting my demise and unable to fend for myself in any way."

I grinned. "You will never convince me you're helpless and pathetic. Do you have a safe?"

"Nope. I need to get in there to see what's been moved."

"What if we Facetime? Can you do that?"

She paused, and I heard her talking to Angelina. "I'm covered. Let's do it."

I quickly switched over to video, and my throat tightened when I saw her face, and the gray cement wall behind her. Her turquoise hair was matted from her swim, and she was wearing a dull gray sweatshirt that looked like it had come from the lost and found.

She gave me a hard glare. "Don't look at me like that, Mia. I'm fine. Let's get to business. Start walking."

I nodded, swallowing hard as I began the tour of her kitchen. Hattie already felt like family. She was closer to my mom's age than mine, but she felt more like a friend than my mom. But I'd had so little in my life when it came to people who mattered that Hattie and Lucy and everyone I'd met here already meant so much to me.

It made the stakes so high.

As I walked, Hattie whistled softly. "Someone was really mad," she said.

"Right? It feels personal. Who would want to go after you?"

"I don't know. Everyone loves me."

"Someone clearly doesn't."

"That was rude."

I walked the phone along the side of the kitchen with the prep counters. "But true. Think on it. See what you can come up with? What about someone whose heart you broke?"

"That's a very long list—Wait! Go back!"

I moved the phone back.

"My recipe box is moved. Open it."

I saw a large metal lockbox very similar to the drug-filled one in my car. I quickly pulled it down. "It's locked."

"Really? You actually said that?"

"Right. I got that." I quickly pulled out the lockpicks and popped the lock. I pointed the camera in there. "See anything?"

"Yes. What's that envelope in the back there?"

I saw a ratty legal-sized envelope in the back. I quickly grabbed it and opened it. My gut sank. "Oh, Hattie." I held it up so she could see it.

It was a series of notes that were to Rutherford, telling him to meet out at Dead Man's Pond. There were a number of them, as if she'd practiced writing the note several times.

Lucy whistled under her breath. "That doesn't look good."

"That's the same writing that was on Glory's note! I'm really being set up?" Hattie sounded stunned. "I can't believe it. I'm adorable and loved. No one hates me that much."

"Holy cow." Lucy leaned over my shoulder. "This is bad. What if they've stashed things like this elsewhere, like at Hattie's house? You know the police will search there—" We stared at each other in sudden realization.

"My portrait!" Hattie exclaimed. "We need to hide that!"

Oh, *man.* "I'll get on it. Who knows you keep recipes in there?"

"Anyone who has been in my kitchen." She paused suddenly. "Wait a second. Go back in the box."

I pointed the phone into the recipe box. "What is it?"

"Is there a blue card in there? There's one recipe that's on a blue card. I don't see it. It's bigger than the others."

I quickly thumbed through the contents. "No. Nothing."

"That's my cinnamon bun recipe. Best in the state. Whoever was in there stole it. Whoever put that note in there knew about that recipe. They knew which one to take."

I blinked. "This is about *recipes?* You've got to be kidding."

"Hey." Hattie's voice was low. "My recipes are definitely worth murdering over."

"They are," agreed Lucy. "Especially that cinnamon bun one."

Okay, so I'd been stunned about a number of things since I'd arrived, especially when I'd found out so recently what would drive people to murder in this charming small town. I didn't think there was much left to shock me, but I'd been wrong. "You think that all this murder is over *cinnamon buns?*" I couldn't keep the doubt out of my voice, and I almost tried hard to do it.

Lucy put her hands on her hips. "Don't mock her buns until you've tried them."

"I'm not mocking her buns. I'm sure her buns are great. But murder? For buns?"

Hattie raised her brows. "Really? You're this worldly spy girl, pickpocketing thief, and you can't imagine the amount of money involved in food? Really? What about Ben & Jerry's ice cream? You think they don't make any money off their recipes for ice cream?"

I blinked. "Well, that's different—"

"Only because they decided to make money off their fantastic recipes," Hattie said. "My recipes are that good. I've been offered over a million dollars for that recipe alone."

This time, I didn't have to fake my shock. "You're kidding."

"Nope."

"Then why do you have them in a metal box that someone could just pick up and carry out of here?"

Hattie stared at me, and then Lucy started laughing. "She has you there, Hattie."

"It's Bass Derby," Hattie said. "No one steals recipes in Bass Derby."

"Except when they do," I pointed out. "Like when they trash your kitchen, call you a murderer, and then steal the recipe. Then it happens."

Hattie's eyes narrowed. "You're not attractive when you sass old ladies."

"Well, you're not old, so I'm safe."

Hattie grinned and winked at me. "Nice catch, Mia. I was testing you there."

"I'm too afraid of you to ever call you old. I'd never make that mistake."

"Awesome. I love ruling by fear." Hattie glanced over her shoulder. "Angelina is stalling Officer Stevens, but she's losing the battle. I gotta go."

"Wait! Who would want to steal your recipe?"

"Anyone who has ever tried them."

"Could you possibly narrow it down a little? That would be helpful."

"Hide my recipe box. Get the portrait out of my garage. Don't let the cops in my kitchen. I'll figure out how to get out of here soon." Then she hung up, leaving me staring at a Hattie-less phone.

Lucy put her hands on her hips. "She's not wrong, you know. Her buns are really good. Anyone who's had them would be likely to steal the recipe. The buns are like crack."

I didn't want to think about drugs right now. "Well, the better question is: who would murder for them?"

Lucy raised her brows. "Oh, well. That's probably a much smaller pool, then."

"One would hope, right?" I looked around the trashed kitchen.

"Assuming that the mess was supposed to distract us from the missing recipe and incriminating notes, then there's nothing else to find in here. We need to go hunt a murderer."

Lucy's eyes widened. "You know who it is?"

"No, but I know two people involved in food who were at the Yacht Club today."

She paused then nodded slowly. "Chef Felix and Chef Zoltan."

"Is Chef Zoltan the dessert chef?" I remembered that the cranky head chef had been named Felix.

Lucy nodded. "He dated Hattie for a while. So did Felix. She ditched them both."

"And that's how it became personal." Hattie really needed to stop dating people. It made things so much more complicated. "Who was more upset when she broke up with them?"

"Zoltan still loves her, but in a good way. He might murder *for* her, but he'd never murder someone and get her in trouble for it." Lucy paused. "Felix was really mad. He still hates her."

"So, Felix is where we start, then." Felix, the angry chef. "Time to figure out why he was so desperate to make that wedding party happen even though the bride's brother had just gotten murdered."

"Maybe he's just a jerk with no sense of humanity."

"Or maybe he's a murderer."

Lucy grinned. "I hope he's the murderer."

I grinned. "You're so bloodthirsty."

"Right? It's so fun."

I looked at Beau, who was leaning against the wall, arms folded across his chest. He'd been listening avidly the whole time. He hadn't been participating, but I'd been aware of his gaze on us intently, listening, taking mental notes. I knew that he could hold out participating only for so long. "Beau? Can you go over to Hattie's house and hide the painting that's in her garage?"

He stared at me. "You want me to do work?"

"Yes. There's a massive portrait of her in her garage that Rutherford painted. It gives her motive. Plus, you need to search her house to make sure that they haven't planted more evidence against her."

He didn't even pretend to consider my request. "No."

"Please?" I had no time for Mr. Antisocial to be pulling his I-hate-the-world attitude. "It's for Hattie."

"No."

At that moment, Esther slipped inside, undeterred by the locked doors. Either she had a set of keys, or she and I had some skills in common. "Bootsy is plying Chief Shone with margaritas. He'll be passed out in an hour. What's the plan?"

Damn. I was glad the Seam Rippers weren't my enemy. They looked so harmless, like cute little quilters, and that was soooo wrong. "Well, I asked Beau to go to Hattie's to relocate an incriminating portrait that's in her garage and then search her house for evidence that the murderer might have planted there, but he refuses. Would you do it?"

"Oh, goody! Yay! That's awesome! Of course I will." Esther clapped her hands. "Do you have a gun I can take? Maybe I'll disturb the murderer in the act? That would be so fun."

"A gun?" Oh… I didn't like the idea of that. "Never mind. Don't do that. I don't want you endangered." Or, more likely, I didn't want her to kill anyone. I had enough to do trying to keep Hattie out of prison. I didn't need to add to that.

"Too late! I'm on it! You can't stop me! Beau, I'm taking your boat!" She turned and ran out of the café before any of us could move.

Beau looked at me. "I will find a way to hold you responsible if anything happens to my boat as a result of this."

At that moment, we heard his boat engine start up.

He cursed and then took off, moving at an impressive pace. He burst out the door, shouting. Lucy and I ran to the window in time to see him race down the dock, yelling and waving his arms while Esther began backing his boat out of the slip.

Lucy grinned. "This is what happens when you leave your keys in your boat. Rich old ladies steal them."

Beau reached the end of the dock and didn't slow down. He literally ran right off the end of the dock and vaulted onto the bow of his boat.

"You know," I said, "He definitely misrepresented himself. I thought the only exercise he ever got was being grumpy."

"Right? You can't trust rich people. I think that's the lesson of the day."

"Rich people. Celebrities. People with cinnamon bun addictions. They're all untrustworthy."

"I know. The only people you can trust are pickpockets, mail carriers, and café owners."

"Exactly."

Beau started gesturing to Esther, who cupped her ear, as if to say she was too deaf to hear him (which was definitely a lie). Then she hit the gas. The boat shot forward, and Beau pitched backward to the floor of the boat, disappearing from sight.

"He reminds me of you," Lucy said sweetly. "I can't think of why."

"Because he is pure grace and agility when it comes to boating." I grinned as Esther opened up the motor and the boat shot down the lake toward Hattie's. "Thank heavens the Seam Rippers are on our team, right?"

"Amen, sistah."

We both peered to the right to check on the safety of the drug stash in my car. Chief Stone was sitting in one of the Seam Ripper's chairs, and he did indeed have a pink, slushy drink in his hand. He wasn't smiling, though. "Has he ever been in a good mood?"

"Only when he arrests people. He really enjoys that. I think he's angry and bitter because you keep interfering with that joy."

I grinned. "Well, hopefully we can give him someone to arrest, and then we'll all be happy." I pulled back from the window. "You want to help me with something?"

Lucy's face lit up. "Oh, I'm sure I would. What do you have in mind?"

"We need to break into Felix's house and see if he's been making cinnamon buns lately, or practicing his penmanship on note paper like the ones in Hattie's recipe box." Had it really been only a few days since I'd resisted breaking into Lucy's boyfriend's house? How quickly things could change. For the better. Right? Definitely it was better that I was now embracing breaking and entering, right?

I grimaced. It was so difficult to lie to myself convincingly. I'd have to work on that.

Lucy grinned. "Fun! Where does he live?"

"I don't know." I pulled out my phone and tried searching for him, but no luck. I then called Angelina, at the police station. My new favorite police station employee was very helpful, and in less than five minutes, we had the address we needed. We needed Felix's address, but Lucy obviously knew where our dessert chef lived, since he was on her mail route, so yay for handy mail carriers, right?

I hung up. "Want to go check out the house of a potential murderer?"

"I do." Lucy frowned. "But how do we know he's not there? I mean, it's one thing to break into his house, but it's something else to get murdered by him, you know? In theory, it sounds like a great story, but in reality? Not so much."

"Good point. We need to make sure he's not there and not coming back." I paused for a second, then grimaced. "I have an idea."

Lucy grinned. "From the look on your face, I bet I'm going to like it. You have a plan, don't you? Are you going to pickpocket someone?"

I sighed. "No."

"Then what?"

I let out my breath. A couple days ago, I'd roped Hattie and Lucy into a Double Twist, one of the cons my mom and I used to run. One con. That was it. For a good cause. Then no more.

Until today.

Until I had to call in the Top Notch.

I grinned. *Top Notch.* This was going to be fun. I did enjoy this one.

But first, we needed the right wheels. I pulled out my phone and dialed the only super rich person I knew who wasn't going to be in a cranky mood.

Esther answered on the first ring. "We're almost there."

"Is that Mia?" Beau asked in the background. "Tell her I'm going to shoot her next time I see her."

I grimaced. "Esther, do you have a nice car?"

"I do. Lots of them."

"Can I borrow one?"

"No. Absolutely not. If you want a nice car, earn some money and buy it yourself."

"In the next ten minutes?"

"Powerful women don't need help creating money. Right, Beau?"

"She's not borrowing my car," Beau said.

"It's to save Hattie," I pointed out. "I need a nice car." Top Notch would never work without all the details perfect. "And some of your clothes. How do I get into your house? Do you leave a key around?"

"Absolutely not," Esther said. "Beau agrees. Acquire your own wealth, Mia. It makes life so much easier."

"But—"

"No. Absolutely, unequivocally not. End of story. We're at Hattie's. Gotta focus. Stay out of my wealth, Mia. And Beau says he'll hunt you down and kill you himself if you touch any of his cars. So don't try it."

CHAPTER 20

THIRTY MINUTES LATER, Lucy and I were cruising down Main Street in a bright red Lamborghini SUV, with a weapons stash in the backseat that included my hairdryer and my infamous electric pencil sharpener. Lucy had wanted to go back to her house for guns, but there was no way I was going down that route.

Corded projectiles, only. They were my specialty, so why not, right?

While I drove, Lucy was on her phone pulling up random facts designed to stress me out. "So, as far as I can find on the internet, this car probably costs more than a quarter of a million dollars."

It still had that new-car smell. "It's a nice car." Understatement of the millennia. It drove like a zillion horsepower angel. I literally felt like the most powerful woman in the universe behind the wheel. The car maketh the woman, right?

Esther hadn't been kidding when she extolled the virtues of being a rich woman.

I'd driven nice cars before, but this was the first time I'd driven one where I didn't have to worry that someone was going to send the cops after me. It was so much less stressful.

But at the same time, it was more stressful, because I was

personally invested in making sure I didn't crash it and upset someone I cared about.

Lucy wasn't finished. "It looks like there are probably less than five thousand ever made of this particular Lamborghini SUV. You're literally driving a collector's item. What if you crash it? Or sneeze on it?"

"It'll be fine. Enjoy it. I doubt I'll be able to talk Esther into letting us borrow it again. This is probably our only chance."

Lucy put down her phone as I put on the blinker to turn into the Yacht Club parking lot. "Speaking of that, you're awe-inspiring."

I grinned. "Why thank you, my darling. Smooches to you, as well."

"No, I mean it. You literally talked Esther into handing over her brand-new Lamborghini to hunt murderers. I've never seen anything so magical. She had no chance against you."

For a moment, I contemplated being upset with myself for channeling the old Mia, and then I decided that was just silly. I was getting tired of all the drama about trying to hate myself. I was a great influencer. That was handy. Sure, I could use it for evil, but I could also use it for great good...and getting the chance to drive a nice car. Instead of going all pouty on myself, I decided to own it. "My mom was always good at influencing people. I might have learned a bit from her." Old Mia wasn't entirely bad, right? Old Mia could come in handy with New Mia, who had friends, a home, and a law-abiding life. I just had to make sure that Old Mia never got to cross that invisible line, of course.

I could do that.

"Oh, no." Lucy shook her head. "That was more than influencing. You could talk a mom out of her newborn baby. Who *are* you, Mia? You're more than a pickpocket."

How astute my mail-carrying friend was, eh?

I parked the car right in front of the staff door of the Yacht Club kitchen and turned to Lucy. How much longer could I hide the truth of who I was from the people who I was afraid to lose if they found out the truth? At least another few minutes, and that was all I had time to think about. "We need to focus here, Lucy. You know what to do, right?"

Lucy grinned. "My darling, I know everything."

"All right, then." I opened the door and got out. As Lucy got out on her side, I adjusted my outfit. With Esther's grudging consent, we'd raided her massive, well-stocked closet. I'd helped myself to the most over-the-top, expensive items I'd been able to find, including a pair of massive diamond studs that would be giving me a neckache within the hour.

I was wearing *so much money* right now, and none of it was mine.

I felt like I was a teenager again, dressing up with my mom to pretend to be something we weren't, and never would be: rich, respectable, and worthy. It felt familiar and right...and at the same time, I kind of wanted to run home and shower until I was me again. Not the old me. The new me. The one who didn't have to put on a façade ever, ever again.

But Hattie was in jail, which meant that I had to do whatever it took to help her.

Including wearing leather pants so tight that sitting down had been risky. Esther was smaller than I was, but wore her clothes with some actual breathing room, so it worked. My silk tank top cupped my breasts with enough attitude that no man could fail to pant over them. Dark Cherry Fire lipstick and my own, old, scuffed Chuck Taylor sneakers completed the outfit. It was expensive, eccentric, and perfect.

Lucy was wearing a white collared shirt, black pants, and black flats, which she'd accented with a pair of reading glasses. She was so much bigger than Esther that we'd had to buy her clothes. Not the same level of money that I was wearing, but that was okay. Her job was different than mine was right now.

Her braids were now in a bun, and she was carrying her phone and an iPad. "You really think this will fly?" she asked.

"It's up to you. It's like a twirling competition. You're just putting on a show." Lucy wasn't the best at the con, but she'd been a state champ at twirling, so she had to have some performing chops, right? "You got this."

She took a breath. "All right."

I strode up to the back door of the kitchen, and paused. I took a breath, steadying myself, channeling my focus. I was no longer Mia Murphy. I was Elena Vanderveer, of the fictional Vanderveer family. Rich. Celebrity. Haughty. Entitled.

So entitled.

I looked over at Lucy, and gave her a disdainful glare. "Well. Are you going to open the door for me or do you expect the knob to turn itself?"

Her eyes widened. "God, you're an elitist, entitled diva. I hate you already."

I had to stifle a grin. "I'm very hateable," I agreed cheerfully.

"Right?" She grinned, then opened the door. "Miss Vanderveer," she said with an impressive amount of hero worship and deference. "Chef Felix is this way."

I stalked through the door then stopped, waiting for her to get inside and lead the way. When I'd been in the kitchen earlier, I'd been too distracted by Devlin to notice much, but this time, I did. The kitchen was gorgeous. I was pretty sure it was about fifty times the size of Hattie's. On Hattie's behalf, I had a little bit of kitchen envy.

There were stacks of plates everywhere, set up, waiting for the wedding tomorrow. The kitchen was quiet, and the staff was gone. Crap. What if Felix had already left? How had they gotten the place cleaned up so quickly? It had still been in full swing when I'd left, because they'd been feeding people and trying to continue the party when they'd been trapped there by the police.

I looked at Lucy, and she shrugged. "Maybe we're too late?"

No. I needed him to still be there. I didn't want to risk running into Felix when we searched his house. But as I stood there in the empty, dimly lit kitchen, suddenly, I realized that maybe showing up at the kitchen of a potential murderer hadn't been the most well-thought-out plan either.

If he were here, he could shoot us and cart us off, and no one would know.

So…yeah… "Maybe we should leave—"

At that moment, the man we'd come to see came striding around the corner, talking on his phone. He was larger than I'd remembered, and moving like a man on a mission. He stopped dead when he saw us, and he lowered the phone from his ear. "Who the hell are you?"

I had no choice but to go full-on Top Notch, regardless of the danger to our lives. We were committed. I flipped my silk scarf over my head and raised my chin. "Rude man. I'm leaving."

I whirled around and headed for the door, hoping that Lucy would figure out how to handle this. *Come on, Lucy.*

I stalked to the door and stood beside it. "Open it. I will not be spoken to that way."

The corner of Lucy's mouth twitched, but she nodded. "Of course, Ms. Vanderveer." She gave a little wave to Chef Felix, then hurried after me.

She reached the door and glanced at me, her eyebrows asking questions.

I folded my arms over my chest. "I don't like waiting."

"Right. Sorry." She pushed the door open, and we both stood to the side just enough that Chef Felix could see my nifty Lamborghini, parked right up by the door with its pretty little hood ornament glistening in the light from the kitchen.

"Wait!"

Lucy spun around. "Elena Vanderveer waits for no one. Never speak to her like that."

Oh, Lucy was good! I was so proud of my con-artist protégé.

"Elena Vanderveer?" Chef Felix gave me that slow inspection that only smarmy, elitist men have truly perfected. His gaze went from my massive, diamond earrings, to the label on my scarf, to my breasts, down my painted-on leather pants, and ending with my sneakers.

I really wanted to hit him in the head with a rolling pin and grab his wallet, but violence wasn't my thing. So, instead, I lifted my chin, cocked my hip, and set my hand on it, looking bored, entitled, and bitchy.

His eyebrows went up, and he looked back at Lucy. It was at that moment that recognition occurred, as I knew it might. I'd told her how to play it, but I didn't know if she would be able to pull it off. *Come on, Lucy.*

"You're one of my servers."

"I don't actually work for you. I was testing you." Lucy sounded equally entitled in a servant-of-the-powerful kind of way. "Ms. Elena Vanderveer would like a word with you."

"I don't anymore. He's rude. I'm leaving." I gestured to the screen door. "Open it." I could practically feel the air conditioning on my nipples. Had the tank top slipped a millimeter and exposed the girls?

Ah, well, if they had, it would only work in my favor.

Felix had biceps that were too large for him not to care about my breasts. He had that vibe.

Sure enough, he immediately ditched the rude face and came striding across the kitchen, all gazillion pounds of testosterone and asshat. "I'm so sorry for the misunderstanding. It's been a taxing day. How may I be of service to you?"

I turned my head to look at him, but I didn't answer right away. I pulled my sunglasses down just enough to see over the rim, and gave him a low, slow, head-to-toe inspection, then put my sunglasses back on and looked at him. "I don't know. *Can* you help me?"

God, I sounded like a diva. I usually hated playing the diva role, but I had a feeling that Felix deserved it.

He raised his brows and stood a little taller. Yeah, just as I thought. He responded to hot women in power. Not that I was hot, but showing my cleavage was pretty much all it took to fit into that category, as long as you had the right attitude.

"I can." There was absolute confidence in his voice, which I did admire. "Tell me what you need."

"What I need is a…" I paused and gave him another once over. "…chef."

His expression grew shrewd, not quite hiding his interest. "For what?"

"To cook." I let disdain ferment through my voice. "Obviously."

Lucy coughed and turned her head.

Felix narrowed his eyes. "A party?"

"No. My house. I fired my last personal chef." I fluttered my hand toward the ballroom we'd been eating in earlier. "I was not expecting to find my new chef in this little town, but lunch was delicious."

He blinked. "You want to hire me to be your personal chef?"

I pulled my glasses down to peer at him again. "I live in L.A. Is that a problem?"

I could practically see him salivating. "No, it isn't."

"Good. I will have you prepare sample meals of course. Cook me three meals. I will return in two hours to try them. If I approve, next week, you'll fly out and cook for a week. We will see."

"Tonight?"

"Yes. Why? Is that a problem? You have other plans?"

He stood taller. "I'll fit it in. What kind of food do you like?"

I fluttered my hand at Lucy. "She'll take care of this. Speak with her. I don't care to linger in the staff area." I held up my hand as he started to speak. "Wait!"

He stopped and waited.

Holy cow. This was actually kind of fun. He was like a bratty Rottweiler that I could control. "I also want four desserts."

Felix blinked. "Desserts?"

I knew that Zoltan was the dessert guy. Felix would have to summon Zoltan back to the kitchen, which meant both houses would be empty for searching. "Yes. Four different desserts, all of them with chocolate." Because chocolate was royalty. "You will have this for me in two hours?"

He glanced at his watch. "Yeah, sure. I'll do it."

"Wonderful." I had a sudden inspiration and I held up my hand, palm down, fingers down, a pure diva handshake. "My name is Elena Vanderveer. And you are?"

He strode up to me, frowned at my fingers, and then grasped my index finger and shook it. "Felix Verbeck. I used to be a private chef in LA, so I'm sure I can handle your work."

He was so close, close enough that I could see his phone sticking out of his front pocket, where he'd stashed it upon seeing us. Oh...temptation galore. "For whom?" *Don't do it, Mia. Don't do it.*

He cleared his throat. "I'll have to check with them and make sure it's okay to share their name. Celebrities like their privacy."

"Oh, I do know that. I appreciate that you recognize our need for discretion." *Don't do it, Mia.* But what if there was good info on his phone? Maybe it would be helpful? No. I shouldn't do it. I nodded stiffly to him, then whirled around in a very diva-ish move...but immediately tripped on my laces. I fell into him, and when I felt his hands grab my butt to keep me upright...well, all guilt fled. I snatched his phone and handed it to Lucy before I'd even regained my balance.

She dropped it down the front of her shirt as I stood back up.

I shot him a quelling glare, as if it were his fault that I'd fallen, then I spun around and walked up to the screen door, so my face was inches from the screen. "This needs to be open."

Lucy hurried over and pushed it open for me.

I winked at her and then strode out to the car, leaving Lucy to give him a list of things I wanted for dinner.

A couple minutes later, she came running out and swung into the passenger seat. "If he's not the murderer, I'm going to feel really bad making him cook all that food."

"Isn't he rude and unpleasant, and abusive to his kitchen

staff?" I backed out of the parking spot and hit the gas, the clock now ticking. How long did we have until he figured out we'd played him and headed home?

"Yes, he is." She bit her lip.

"So?"

She looked over at me. "Karmic justice?"

"Karmic justice, baby." But even as I said it, a little bit of guilt gnawed at my belly.

I prided myself on being a good person. I'd sacrificed every-thing to be able to look at myself in the mirror and be proud of the face that looked back at me.

How much leeway did a former criminal get before the relapse was called complete?

When Lucy pulled his phone out of her shirt and held it up with a grin, I realized that I maybe, just maybe, had pushed it too far. I opened my mouth to tell her to toss it out the window so he'd find it… but instead, I said, "Is there anything relevant on his lock screen?"

Damn. I really had no self-control, did I?

Lucy shook her head. "No, but maybe someone will call or text him." She set it on the dashboard. "I'll watch it." She grinned at me. "Great move, Mia."

"Thanks." I hoped it paid off, and led us right to the murderer. At least then, I'd know it had been the right thing to do. Because otherwise, I might have to conclude that I'd done it just because the phone had been there and I wanted to.

I wasn't like that. Really I wasn't. Was I?

CHAPTER 21

BARELY TEN MINUTES into our rush to get to Felix's place, Lucy and I had just made it out of the town center when I saw Devlin's SUV heading right toward us.

We didn't have time to get bogged down by police chitchat. "Don't make eye contact," I said, gripping the wheel as he drove toward us.

He was driving fast, hopefully too fast to notice the car driving toward him. The sun was starting to set behind us, which I knew would make the identity of the driver just a little bit more difficult to discern.

Lucy snorted. "He's a decent cop, and he has the hots for you. There's literally no chance he's not going to notice you're driving this car."

"Men can be very unobservant," I countered. "Right now, he's got his cop brain turned on, and he's heading to the Eagle's Nest with cocaine and murder on his mind. He'll see a Lamborghini, go all gaga over it for a moment, then focus on corpses. He's definitely not going to notice us."

He shot past us, and I grinned at Lucy as he rounded the bend and disappeared from sight. "See?"

She folded her arms over her chest and leaned back. "Right

now, he's just realized that you were driving the car he just hurtled past. He's looking for a spot to pull a U-Turn. Any second now, we're going to hear sirens."

"You're overestimating him—" At that moment, I heard the sound of a police siren. "Crap!"

Lucy grinned. "I clearly overestimated him. My apologies."

"Apology not accepted. You summoned him to us." I saw a dirt road up ahead, and I hit the gas, trying to make it to the road before Devlin got us back in sight. "It's fine. I can fix it."

Lucy raised her brows. "You're going to try to outrun a cop trying to pull you over? I'm pretty sure that's illegal."

"I have no idea what you're talking about. I would never do that." The Lamborghini SUV was humming, and I was really tempted to unleash its full potential on the windy, dirt road I was heading toward.

"Obviously you would never do that." Lucy twisted around in her seat, watching behind us. "He can't see us yet. If you care."

"Why would I care?" I reached the dirt road and hauled the luxurious steering wheel to the right just as Devlin's blue lights came into view.

I shot down the road, going deliciously fast as I sped around the corner. Who knew it was possible to make an SUV that handled like a sports car? Apparently, Lamborghini did. All I could say was…I felt like royalty zipping along in it.

But I was on a mission, so the moment I was out of sight, I pulled off the road and turned off the lights. "Ssh."

"You really think he won't realize we're down here in a bright red Lamborghini?" Lucy was literally laughing out loud. "You're such an idiot. How did you not wind up in jail about a dozen times?"

"Because I'm good at this—" As I said it, Devlin drove around the corner and pulled up behind me, his lights still flashing. I sighed. "Well, I used to be."

"I'm not sure you ever were good at it. Maybe you're just delusional." Lucy sounded amused. "You have to get rid of him quickly."

"I will." I watched him open his door, Lucy's words rattling around in my brain. *Maybe you're just delusional.* That would certainly explain a lot, but it was also a little disheartening. Being a criminal was literally my only life skill. What if I had rejected it so completely that I wasn't even good at the one thing I didn't want to be good at?

I mean, yeah, I didn't *want* to be a criminal, but everyone had to have something that they were great at, right? I needed to be great at the thing I didn't want to be, because it was all I had. I know it didn't make sense, but it did, at least to me.

Without my childhood skills, I was… I didn't know. What was left?

Devlin stepped out of his SUV, muscular and way too attractive, like he always was. Why did he get to me? I didn't like cops, I didn't trust them, and I really didn't want to date one.

But there was something about him. Which was why I definitely wasn't going to go on the date with him.

Lucy suddenly squawked, and hit my arm. "You're wearing Esther's clothes and jewels. He'll be suspicious. We'll never get out of here if he gets suspicious."

Yikes. She was right. Lucy and I both leaned over the back seat, frantically searching the clothes we'd worn to Esther's.

Lucy found my sweatshirt first. "A hoodie!"

"Awesome." I yanked it over my head and pulled the hood up, while she held the sunglasses and then shoved them back on my face.

Devlin was leaning against the car, arms folded across his chest, watching us scramble.

Damn him for being so sneaky.

The corner of his mouth was not quirked in a smile. In fact, he looked downright annoyed.

Probably not at me, though. I mean, there were murders galore and cocaine parties happening right? That would make any cop annoyed.

I punched the ignition button to get power, and then rolled down the window. "Good afternoon, Officer," I said, plastering a cheerful smile on my face. "Was I speeding?"

Lucy snorted in apparent disgust, clearly having no faith in my ability to distract Devlin from anything we didn't want him thinking about. In retrospect, I totally should have stayed with the very tight silk tank top to distract him.

Except I didn't want to use that with him. He was too dangerous to my sweet, little emotional self.

Sadly, Devlin proved Lucy right yet again. "What the hell is going on? Where did you go? Why aren't you at the Eagle's Nest? I was on my way there to see you."

Right. Um. "Funny thing—"

He gave me a look that was thoroughly unamused. "I don't have time for this game, Mia. I've got two dead bodies, and the FBI only about an hour away to check on the cocaine in your car."

"Is it cocaine?" That was such an easy topic to distract him with. He'd handed it right to me. What an agreeable chap he was. "I was hoping it was just baby powder or something."

Devlin inclined his head. "I haven't been there yet, but I'd guess that it's highly likely. What else would it be, given your life?"

Well, that wasn't the best news I'd heard all day. Large amounts of drugs tended to attract unsavory sorts, and I had no need for unsavory sorts in my life. "If it is, where do you think it came from?"

A valid question that I didn't have the answer to.

"I don't know." He paused, giving me a look I couldn't quite decipher. "It's in your car. If it's cocaine, it's not a good situation for you."

I stared at him in sudden comprehension. "You think Griselda will think it's *mine*?"

"No. I don't. But he's not the only one who works for the FBI."

I leaned my head back against the seat while I digested that fact. "It's not mine."

"Last time, it was your husband's, but he's in prison. If it's not yours, whose is it? It needs to belong to someone, and it's your car that it's in."

I bit my lip. "I don't know where it came from, so I don't know whose it is."

"Exactly. There's no one to point the finger at, so yeah, if it's cocaine, it's a problem for you."

I swore under my breath and slid down in the seat, suddenly feeling overwhelmed. And maybe a little terrified. "What do I do?" My voice was a little shaky and weak, which I hated.

I could handle this. *I could handle this.* I made myself sit up taller, refusing to collapse in abject terror.

"Griselda—I mean Hawk—will be here soon. We'll talk then."

I let out a long breath, trying to stay calm, too close to the edge of panic to appreciate that Devlin was now defaulting to the name Griselda. "That's really not comforting."

How much did I trust Griselda to believe me? He'd believed in me all along, but how long would that last in the face of serious evidence to incriminate me? I'd been married to a drug dealer, and the feds had believed I was completely uninvolved and unaware of what Stanley had been doing.

But would they still believe it now? I had far too much experience with cops following the path of most obvious clues. It was bad enough when it meant they were chasing down my new besties for murder, but when it meant I was going to prison for major drug possession and even dealing?

That was so bad on so many levels.

Lucy leaned over. "I'll testify on Mia's behalf."

My throat got tight with emotion. How sweet was that? "It's okay, Lucy—"

"No, I will. Seriously. Character matters. Mia is an awesome person, and she's willing to do whatever it takes to protect innocent people—"

"Like Hattie?" Devlin interrupted, his gaze becoming shrewd. "Where did you get this Lamborghini?"

Right back to the topic I'd been trying to avoid. Which was probably good. Defending Hattie felt like something I could handle. Going to prison for drugs did not. I paused for a moment, trying to figure out how much was safe to tell him. "It's Esther's car."

"Why are *you* driving it?"

"Because my car might have cocaine in it?" Oops. That drug reference was totally on me. I needed to get my mind to a new place.

Devlin narrowed his eyes at me.

I smiled at him, and I could see Lucy out of the corner of my eye doing the same thing. She looked very innocent. I was impressed. I hoped I looked as innocent as she did.

"What are you up to?" It wasn't a friendly, curious question. Not that he was ever friendly and curious, but this felt a little more attacky than usual. What had I ever done to make him doubt my good intentions? Nothing. Ever.

"What's going on with Hattie?" I asked instead. "Have you figured out any other suspects?"

He ground his jaw. "I can't talk about it—"

"Oh for heaven's sake!" I threw up my arms in irritation. "Two people are dead, and Hattie's in jail—"

"Not anymore. Officer Stevens got confused and released her. Do you know where she is, by the way?" As he spoke, his gaze slithered sneakily to the back seat, as if Hattie would ever be relegated to the back seat of any vehicle.

I blinked. "Hattie tricked him into letting her go? I'm so impressed by her." Where was she? We needed to grab her and bring her with us!

Beside me, I heard Lucy try to suppress a snort of laughter as she pulled out her phone, no doubt to text Hattie and congratulate her.

"She tricked a police officer." Devlin didn't sound nearly as amused as we were. "It's not funny."

"Au contraire, it is very funny." I raised my brows at his cranky look. "You literally grew up as a teenage gang member. How can you possibly fail to admire that kind of fortitude? You should be asking her for an autograph."

The corner of his mouth twitched the tiniest bit. "She needs to be back in jail."

"Why? She's innocent."

He met my gaze then. "Because if someone else gets killed while she's in jail, then she has a rock-solid alibi. As long as she's out of jail and running around, then if someone else gets killed, she could be in trouble for it. If she's innocent, the best place for her to be right now is in jail."

I blinked. Well, damn. I hadn't thought of that. Another murder? Like Esther and Beau at Hattie's house right now? Now that Hattie was out of jail, the murderer could wave his wand of death freely and add to the list of corpses she was responsible for.

Suddenly, I felt overwhelmed. Two dead bodies. The drugs. Hattie in danger again. Lucy and I on our way to break into the home of a possible murderer. What was I doing? I had no business trying to solve a flipping murder! What if I made it worse? What if I unearthed evidence that implicated Hattie even more? Or got Lucy killed? Or Beau? Or Esther?

Devlin, mercifully, interrupted my destructive train of thought. "So, tell me again, where are you going?"

I stared at him, suddenly feeling like I was drowning. I didn't know what to do.

I could tell him that we were going to Felix's, but I didn't know what Devlin would find if he decided to search the house. Cocaine with my name on the shipping label? A signed double-murder confession from Hattie? I had to find out before I sent Devlin after him.

But at the same time, I was scared that the people I loved were going to get tangled up in more murder. Drugs. Assassins.

I had to deal with this, and fast. I couldn't trust the cops. I'd learned that long ago, and my brief stint with Griselda hadn't convinced me otherwise, despite the fact that I trusted *him* on some levels.

So, I raised my chin and hoped I was making the right call. "We're going to get some fresh donuts. Do you want some? It's hard work hanging out at the marina trying to keep Chief Stone from stealing my cocaine."

Devlin stared at me in disbelief. "Donuts?"

"Donuts. You know the kind with the cream filling?"

"I like the chocolate ones," Lucy said. "Can't beat chocolate."

Devlin groaned. "Mia, I swear I'll arrest you right now if you don't—" At that moment, his phone rang. He looked down at it and swore. "It's Hawk." He pulled back and stepped away from the car as he answered it. "Hunt, here," he said.

As soon as he stepped away, Lucy grabbed my arm. "I texted Hattie. She's on foot, so she's meeting us at the town cemetery in five minutes. We need to get her before the cops find her."

Dear heavens. We had a senior citizen on the lam. "We need to ditch Devlin." But he was so persistent in his quest for attention, a trait that was only good in a Labrador Retriever puppy.

Lucy nodded. "Can you take advantage of the fact he has unresolved attraction and interest in you?"

I bit my lip. "He *is* supposed to be my bodyguard." He was pacing now, running his hand over his hair as he argued with Griselda. His shoulders were tense, and his body was taut. Whatever they were talking about was ramping up his tension.

He didn't have time to deal with me, and we both knew it.

I leaned out the window. "Devlin! Lucy and I need to go. We'll meet you back at the marina."

He held his hand to tell me to wait. I could tell that Griselda was giving him an earful.

I heard Griselda say something, and Devlin scowled. "I don't have to let her do anything—"

I grinned, pretty sure that Griselda was telling Devlin what a pain in the butt I was, and how difficult it was to stop me when I got stubborn. "Remember what else Griselda said? That I was smart and I was worth listening to when I had an idea?"

Devlin looked over at me. "Yes."

"Well, this is one of those moments. I need to go do this, and I need you to do what you do. I need you to trust me." I paused. "Please."

Hawk said something, and this time, Devlin handed me the phone.

I reluctantly took it. "Hey, bestie."

Griselda did not return the warm and fuzzy salutation. "You have drugs."

Well, that felt a little prickly. "I don't have drugs. My car has white powder that looks like it could be drugs. There's a difference."

"And your marina is bugged with high-tech devices."

"Devices? Plural?" I shot an accusing look at Devlin. "You didn't tell me there were more."

"I've been busy."

"You're my bodyguard. Too busy for that? What if I die and then Griselda doesn't have a witness for the appeal?"

He stared at me.

I tried to look vulnerable and pathetic.

Lucy coughed and pretended to be looking at her phone.

Griselda interrupted the staring contest. "I'm going to be there in an hour. I need you to meet me at your marina. I have a lot of questions for you."

"Great. I'll be back by then-ish."

"Where are you going?"

"It's a girl thing. You wouldn't understand."

"Mia—"

"No." I was getting mad now. I think it was the PTSD from the drugs coming back into my life. "You don't own me anymore. And Devlin never did. I'm not a suspect, so you don't get to control me. Either of you. So back off. You're lucky I called you about the drugs. I could have just driven it into the woods and dumped it.

So back off, and I'll see you in an hour." If we survived our venture into murder-land, of course.

Devlin raised his brows, but Griselda apparently knew when to back off. "Fine. But don't be late."

"Fine." I handed Devlin the phone. "Bye."

He took the phone. "Before you go, remember that anyone who has murdered will do it again." He searched my face. "I hate sitting at dinner alone. If you die, and I have to go on the date by myself, I'll feel awkward. Don't make me feel awkward."

I shot him a skeptical look. "I thought you said you were never awkward."

He didn't smile. "Remember how dangerous it was dealing with your ex?"

I lifted my chin. "I do."

"Well, pretend this situation is that dangerous. Because it could be."

Two dead people were proof he was right. "I'll be fine." I put the car into drive. "I'll meet you at the marina in a bit."

He scowled, but didn't stop me as I executed a perfect three-point turn and started driving down the dirt road, back to the main road.

As I glanced in my rear-view mirror, I could see that Devlin was back on the phone now, talking to Griselda, but watching me. I knew he didn't want to let me go, but I also knew that he was trapped. By Griselda, by cocaine, by death.

All good things to be trapped by.

We reached the main road. "Which way to the cemetery?"

When Lucy pointed to the left, I pulled out.

The irony of Hattie hiding in a graveyard when she was an escaped murder suspect was not lost on me.

I hoped she was still there when we got there.

CHAPTER 22

THE CEMETERY WAS ABANDONED WHEN I pulled into the dirt parking lot on the east side of it. The sun was starting to set, so long shadows were drifting across the gravestones, which was a tiny bit creepy. Or maybe the shadows were creepy because I was now thinking about drug lord assassins again. Because that was fun.

The cemetery, with all its great hiding places for assassins, was actually quite extensive, far more gravestones than I would have expected in this small town. So many headstones and crypts for evildoers to hide behind with assault weapons and butcher knives.

Wow. Um. Yeah. I needed to think about something else. Like sweet senior citizens who outsmart cops. "Do you see Hattie?"

Lucy leaned forward, scanning the cemetery. "No. Do you?"

"No." A part of me didn't want to get out of the SUV, which made me realize that I had to get out immediately. Fear was like a freight-train if you let it take control. I'd long ago learned that fear had to be stopped dead or it would leave me strewn across the highway like carnage.

So I hopped right out of my nifty car into the assassins' playground known as the Bass Derby town cemetery.

But I did retain enough sense to leave the engine running for a quick getaway as I got out of the car. Because I might be stubborn, but I was far from stupid.

"Hattie?" I stage-whispered her name. Yes, I know, what difference did that make? We'd driven up in a bright red Lamborghini, so it's not as if we were being subtle, but it still felt prudent to whisper. Why? Because murderers, death, cocaine, high-tech listening devices, and other fun stuff were lurking behind every shadow in my mind.

There was no response from Hattie. I looked back at Lucy. "You're sure she's coming?"

Lucy nodded. "She should be here any second."

"Okay. Stay with the car in case she arrives from the street. I'll check the cemetery." The idea of assassins whispered through my mind, but I shoved it aside and focused on my mission, which was retrieving Hattie.

Some of the gravestones were more like family crypts, and I could easily imagine Hattie (not hit men) hanging out in them with her feet up and a margarita in her hand.

If Agnes and her pals were anything like the Seam Rippers, I was pretty sure that plenty of parties had happened in the cemetery.

Which was a little weird.

As weird as partying in a thunderstorm on a lake while trying to communicate with a serial killer's ghost? Yep, probably.

I climbed over the old, crumbling stone wall that bordered the cemetery. As I walked through the rows of granite, I couldn't help but peek at the names. Some were so worn that they were difficult to read, but others were still crisp. I saw several from the 1600s, but there were also some from the late 1980s.

Up front was a row of Parker headstones.

Then a cluster of Carson.

There was a massive display near the middle that was for the Dutch family. Where had I heard that name? I know I'd heard that since I'd been in town.

I found one Higgleston headstone, and I crouched down to

read the script of Agnes's ancestor. Clara Higgleston, born in 1845, died in 1906. That was it. No additional relatives or information, but apparently one, lone Higgleston was enough to give Agnes the presidency.

I glanced around. What if I found a Murphy headstone? It was a common name. I could claim it. It wasn't as if my mom or dad were around to contest it. Maybe that would win me over with Agnes once and for all? Hmm…the idea had merit.

I heard a scratching sound behind me, and I spun around, scanning the graveyard in sudden panic. Movement to the right caught my attention, and I sucked in my breath before I saw it was a bunny.

I let out my breath, trying not to panic. A bunny. It was a bunny. Not an assassin.

Dammit. I refused to have a panic attack. So what if there were cocaine and bugs in my marina? *So what*? They didn't get to control my life, and make me panic in fear just because a little bunny ran across my path.

Bunnies were *cute*.

I refused to start living a life where I couldn't appreciate bunnies.

"Mia!"

I spun around and then my heart leapt when I saw Hattie at the edge of the woods, still wearing her hot pink pants from when she'd arrived at the party, though she also had on the gray sweatshirt that the police station had apparently loaned her. Her hair was a mess, her makeup gone, but yay! "Hattie!" I sprinted across the cemetery and flung my arms around her.

She laughed as I hugged her. "You're totally overreacting," she said, but she hugged me back, clinging just a little bit more tightly than I think she wanted me to notice.

Hattie. So tough. So badass. But in her heart, she was as vulnerable as the rest of us.

I pulled back. "Devlin's looking for you. We need to get out of here."

"I had to make a run through the woods," she said as we hurried across the cemetery. Hattie was moving a little stiffer than normal, but still with far more energy than most twenty-year-olds. "I couldn't risk being picked up off the sidewalk."

I glanced around to make sure no cars were passing by who would notice a turquoise-haired senior heading toward Esther's not-so-subtle car. "You literally ran through the woods like an escaped convict. I'm so impressed."

"Hey, a girl has to do what a girl has to do." She raised her brows as her gaze finally fell upon the Lamborghini. "Nice wheels."

"Thanks. I didn't steal them."

Hattie shot me a curious look. "Why would you think I'd assume you stole them?"

Her question made me realize that I was still a little worried about my reputation. Dang it. I did not have time to be wallowing in emotional baggage right now!

"Hattie!" Lucy leapt out of the Lamborghini, threw her arms around Hattie, and hugged her tightly. My throat got a little tight when I saw Hattie hug her back. I was so glad she was safe.

"From now on, you stay with us. You need an alibi if the cops find another body," I said.

Hattie looked over at me as she climbed into the passenger seat. "More bodies?"

"That's what Devlin thinks." I jumped into the driver's seat while Lucy sat in the back.

I loved that Lucy moved to the back instead of having Hattie sit back there. There was something about Hattie that deserved special treatment, and we both knew it. Hattie was a treasure, for the town, for the café, and for us. I looked back at Lucy, and she grinned at me.

Everything felt right now that we were back together.

Hattie settled back into the seat with a sigh of delight. "This is the kind of car I deserve."

"We all deserve this car," Lucy said.

"Right?" My panic and fear that had been tightening its grip on me after my conversation with Devlin was gone now. Seeing Hattie again had revitalized me. I needed to help her. I needed to make sure she was okay. I had a mission, and I wasn't going to let her down.

Hattie frowned as I turned right. "We're not going to the marina to check my kitchen?"

"No. Chief Stone is there guarding the cocaine in my car. If the Seam Rippers haven't gotten him passed out, he's not blind enough to miss us driving up in this nifty red Lamborghini SUV." Because it was pretty nifty.

Hattie raised her brows. "You have cocaine in your car?"

"Looks that way."

She grinned. "Well, damn. That sounds like a good story. Are Lucy and I the dealers for that as well?"

I let out a breath, feeling better by the minute. "Definitely. I want us all to go to prison together, so it's the best way."

"Awesome." She peered at the GPS. "What's at 18 Bitter Street in Peculiar? Another meth lab that's not actually a meth lab?"

"Chef Felix's place."

Hattie stared at me. "Felix? Why?" Her eyes widened. "Ooh… you think he's the murderer?"

"He had reason to steal your recipe and he's threatened by your success, so yeah. Why? Do you disagree with me?"

Hattie bit her lip, staring out the window for a long moment. "No," she said finally. "I wish I did, but I could see it. He has that mysterious air of danger to him."

I glanced over at her. "Was that longing I heard? Did you literally just find Chef Felix more attractive because he might be a murderer?"

She lifted her chin. "I would never."

I glanced at Lucy, and she grinned. "Dull men bore Hattie. She couldn't date Felix because she was better than him at baking. But if he managed to get her arrested for a murder she didn't commit, then that's well-done. It makes him interesting."

Hattie looked over at me. "Don't even tell me you don't get it. You're not even close to being ordinary. I don't believe for a second that an average man would interest you."

"Which is why you married the drug dealer," Lucy said.

Hey. That was a low blow. "I didn't know he was a drug dealer."

"No," Hattie agreed, "but the fact he was a drug dealer meant he was a certain kind of guy that attracted you. I get it, because I'm that way."

"And me, too," Lucy said.

Hattie grinned. "See? We're all sisters of the heart." She leaned over the center console toward me as I drove. "Tell us your secrets, Mia. No more hiding. We know you can pickpocket. You were attracted to a drug kingpin. You survived two years undercover against him. Who *are* you?"

I tightened my grip on the steering wheel and kept my gaze on the road. "Mia Murphy. Owner of the Eagle's Nest and a swimming cat."

"But what *else?*" Lucy leaned forward between the seats. "Felix might be at his house when we arrive. He might kidnap us, chop us up, and kill us all. This might be the last chance we have to be together."

I looked over at her. "Really? That's your pep talk? That we might all be part of a group murder in a few minutes so we should bond?"

She grinned. "Yeah. I think it was a good one, personally. Nothing bonds people like death."

"And my cinnamon buns. They bond people, too." Hattie added. "If Felix really stole my recipe, I'm going to have to take him out, so then I'll deserve to be in prison, so we won't be together in that case either."

I raised my brows. "You'd have to kill him for stealing your recipe?" I couldn't keep the amusement out of my voice. Bass Derby residents and their drama. Seriously.

But Hattie nodded. "I have to make an example of him, or my

recipe box will start being raided left and right. I can't have that, can I?"

"You could get a safe to store them in, instead of murdering people," I pointed out, helpfully.

She paused for a moment, and I could see realization dawning about that easy solution. But did she admit my brilliance? No, she didn't. "I could," she said instead. "But this isn't about me. It's about you."

Nice conversation pivot.

"It is," Lucy agreed. "Talk to us, Mia."

I ignored them. "Hey, look at that. We're only a few minutes away. Does everyone have their weapons ready?"

Hattie folded her arms across her chest, leaned back and studied me. "This is my guess. You're the daughter of a famous serial killer. You have that same need for a thrill, but you've got this massive heart, so you get your rush out of dancing close to dangerous people and then taking them down. Am I right?"

I couldn't help but laugh. "Honestly, I don't know who my dad is, but my mom would definitely have been attracted to a dangerous man, so it's entirely possible my dad was someone nefarious. But I don't like being near dangerous people. I just want to run a marina in a lakeside town."

Hattie snorted. "Hah. You're lying to yourself if you believe that's all you want." She patted my arm. "You have the thrill of the hunt running through your veins, girl. You know it. I know it. Devlin knows it."

Griselda had said the same thing when I'd told him I was moving to Bass Derby. My amusement faded. "I'm not a hunter."

"I know!" Lucy bounced on the seat. "You were a homeless kid living on the street, and you stole in order to survive. You probably collected other homeless kids, supported them, and risked your life on a regular basis to protect them, like that Hart billionaire family from Oregon."

I started laughing. "You're such a dork." But I was also touched. Lucy and Hattie both saw that edge to me, but they both still thought I was a good person. The edge didn't make them hate me.

Suddenly, I wanted to tell them. I wanted to have friends who knew the real me, the secret me, the me that I was trying so hard to leave behind.

But the real me was ugly. A criminal. An adrenaline junkie who got off on pickpocketing and cons.

"Tell us, Mia," Hattie said. "You can trust us."

"Well, maybe not Hattie, but definitely me," Lucy said. "As a postal carrier, I have very high ethics."

"Okay, so you can't trust me with a lot of things," Hattie agreed, "but I do promise not to turn you in to the cops if you're really an escaped criminal on the run."

"I'm not on the run."

"But you are a criminal?"

Dammit. She was too good. She was going to get it out of me, one way or the other. And heck, if I was going to risk my life to keep Hattie out of prison, then shouldn't I at least know whether she was going to reject me as soon as she figured out who I really was?

I took a breath as I turned right. "Fine. I'll tell you, but you have to make me a promise. Both of you."

Hattie nodded. "Of course. What's up?"

I looked in the rearview mirror at Lucy, who also nodded. "You bet."

I flexed my fingers around the steering wheel. My hands were literally shaking. I'd lost my mom. My husband. His family. My home. I couldn't handle losing more. But I had to tell them, because I had to know now if I needed to protect myself from their rejection. "Once you find out the truth about me, you have to promise that if you can't handle it, you'll tell me right away. I need to know."

Hattie and Lucy looked at each other.

"That sounds so promising," Hattie said. "I knew you were interesting. The more likely a person would be to run away from you screaming, the more likely I am to think you're fantastic and a woman worth admiring. So yeah, I'm in."

"Me, too," Lucy said. "You're the most interesting thing to happen to Bass Derby since the Fourth of July fiasco when I was seven."

Oh…that sounded interesting. "What Fourth of July fiasco?"

They both looked at me.

"Right. My turn to talk." I took a breath, surprised to realize that my hands weren't shaking any more. "I was raised by a single mom," I started.

Hattie nodded. "Girl power. Of course. That makes sense."

"My mom's name is Tatum Murphy," I continued. "She's a very successful and somewhat famous con artist who has bilked celebrities out of millions of dollars, both in actual money and items of value. I spent the first seventeen years of my life at her side, learning how to steal, lie, con and run away in the middle of the night to avoid being arrested." I kept my attention on the road. "I left home when I was seventeen because I didn't want to live that life or be that person anymore. And then I married a drug kingpin, which showed me that I can never leave it behind, no matter how much I try, no matter how much I want to."

They were silent, so I kept going.

"I've never had real friends. I never had a home. Just me and my mom, lying and tricking our way through every single day." I took a breath, and then added the one thing that I'd been trying to deny for so long. "And I miss it," I whispered. "I miss that life, at the same time that I want to stay as far away from it as I can. It was the worst life ever, but at the same time, it was the best." I swallowed. "I want my new life in Bass Derby. Friends. Roots. A business. A home. But stealing Kate's ring today… I loved it with all my heart and soul."

God, it hurt to admit that. I was so crushed that I was still that girl. But at the same time, it also felt liberating. The truth had been eating away at me all day, and now it didn't have to, because it had been heard.

I let out my breath and waited for a reply from my friends.

But there was silence.

I looked over at them. "Well?"

"That's it?" Hattie asked. "Are you done? I didn't want to interrupt."

"That's it for now. I mean, there's a lot more, but that's the gist of it." I was so nervous. "So? What do you think?"

Hattie broke into a huge smile. "You're absolutely brilliant, Mia."

"Totally," Lucy said.

"What?" They were okay with it? My hands started to shake again, but I fought to stay focused as I turned on my blinker.

"Not enough women in this world are taught to be strong, capable, and creative survivors," Hattie said. "You are unstoppable, brave as all hell, and you have the hugest heart of anyone I've ever met. I would be honored to call you my friend, every single day."

Sudden tears filled my eyes, and I couldn't even see the road anymore.

"Me, too," Lucy said. "You saved me from prison, Mia. You didn't even know me, but you were willing to risk everything to help me. Plus, you're funny. Every girl on the planet would be lucky to have a friend like you."

I stopped the car and looked over at them, unable to stop the tears from streaming down my cheeks. "You guys mean that." My voice was hoarse.

Hattie grinned. "Mia, you're looking at two women who became friends because neither of us like rules, being told what to do, or living a boring life. You fit right in, baby. If you'll take us, we'll take you."

I laughed through my tears. "I'll definitely take you."

"Yay!" Lucy leaned over the seat and hugged me. I held onto her fiercely, emotions rushing through me at a rate I could barely process. Hattie leaned in and hugged us both, and for a moment, I was wrapped up in a hug with the two most amazing and trouble-making women I'd ever met, with the exception of my mom, of course. "You guys know that I'm not that tough, right? I really do want a quiet life at the marina."

Hattie raised her brows. "Sure. You can go ahead and think that."

"It's pretty cute that you're so delusional," Lucy added.

"I'm serious! I love the marina, and my cat, and sitting out on my deck!"

They stared at me, and I saw Hattie's eyes widen as she finally heard me. "Really?"

"Yes!"

Lucy and Hattie exchanged glances, then Hattie shrugged. "Well, you can do both then."

"I don't want to do both—"

"I think you do," Lucy said.

The way she said it caught my attention, and I looked over at her.

She shrugged. "You can be more than one thing, Mia. We're all more than one thing. It's okay to be both."

"I really don't like murderers."

"But you like the thrill, don't you?" Hattie grinned. "We all like the thrill, Mia."

"I do," Lucy said. "I didn't realize I did until I met you, but I'm all in. Thank you for bringing that into my life." She grinned. "Admit it, Mia. You love the thrill."

Before I had to decide whether to admit that to myself or them, my phone rang. Habit made me check who was calling, and my gut sank when I saw it was Griselda.

"Oh, yummy! The FBI," Hattie said. "Can I talk to him?"

"No." I silenced my phone. "He's going to tell me to get back to the marina, or ask me to turn myself in for drug dealing." I tossed my phone on the dashboard. "We don't have time for that. We need to hunt a murderer."

Wow. That did not sound good to say out loud at all.

"And find a cinnamon bun recipe," I added.

Much better.

Murder? No thanks.

Sticky buns? Yes.

As I pulled out onto the street again, Lucy patted my shoulder. "Ladies, I just want to say that if I was going to get triple murdered with anyone, I'd choose you two."

I burst out laughing. "Definitely the feel-good optimism we were all hoping for."

"Positivity is everything," Hattie agreed. "Here's to triple murders with the girls."

"How about we just find out who killed Rutherford and Glory, find the recipe, and turn it over to Devlin? No close encounters with murderers needed." I felt like that was a much better plan.

Hattie snorted. "You have no sense of adventure. I'm going to have to work on you."

"Or not. You could let me live in my little dream world of no murderers."

"Could I?"

I glanced at Hattie, then laughed at the skeptical expression on her face. "No?"

"Definitely not. I'm a much better friend than that." She leaned back in her seat. "Onward, driver. Let's go do a little breaking and entering."

"I've changed my mind," I said. "I don't think I want to be friends with you."

Hattie grinned. "Liar. You love me."

What could I say? She was right. Which meant the murderer needed to watch out, because we were on our way.

CHAPTER 23

B<small>Y THE TIME</small> we turned onto Bitter Street in Peculiar, I was pumped, focused, and ready.

Lucy leaned forward. "I bet people get shivved here at night."

"Only at night?" I inspected the trash strewn on the broken sidewalks, the overflowing dumpsters in the alleys, and the boarded-up windows on some of the row houses. "We're good then, since it's not completely dark yet."

"I wish we'd gone back to my house for some guns," Lucy said.

"The hairdryer is excellent. We'll be fine." But my heart was racing as I eased to a stop in front of 18 Bitter Street. We all looked up at the building. "On the plus side, none of the windows are boarded up."

"Well, no wonder I didn't want to date Felix," Hattie said. "I must have sensed this abject poverty and dead-end life on a psychic level."

I raised my brows. "Are you psychic?" I asked.

"Everyone is psychic. We're just not tapped into our greater powers. I'm working on it, though, and clearly having success, right?" She pointed at the building as proof of her psychic powers.

"Obviously," I agreed.

A few potential hoodlums were standing on the front steps of a nearby building, but they were the only people on the street. They were definitely the kind of loiterers who could take out mafia leaders in a dark alley. But not the three of us. Because we were tougher than that.

Other than the miscreants who were juggling hunting knives (well, just kidding, mostly), it was creepily silent.

"You really think Felix lives here?" Lucy asked.

"Well, we'll find out." I really, *really* wished I'd passed his address on to Devlin and let the local hot cop deal with this situation, but apparently I wasn't that kind of girl. "Ready?"

"Maybe I should stay here and protect the car," Lucy said.

I looked over at her. "Seriously?"

She put on a hopeful face. "No?"

"No. I'm not going in there alone. Did I mention that pickpockets and con artists are non-violent, non-confrontational pacifists?"

"Oh, come on," Hattie said. "Life is meant to be an adventure. Better to go suddenly at the end of a knife than slowly in a hospital bed."

We both stared at her, not quite sure if she was wrong.

"I could charge big bucks for my fantastic life wisdom. You two are lucky to get it free." Hattie patted the seat beside her. "Let's do this. What did you bring?"

With a resigned sigh, Lucy dropped our arsenal over the seat.

Hattie stared at the assortment. "A hairdryer, a nail gun, and an electric pencil sharpener? It's like we're a joke in a bad movie or something."

Lucy rolled her eyes. "Mia wouldn't let me bring my rifles. She's like a weirdo pacifist or something."

I'd literally just claimed that I was. "The nail gun is a gun," I pointed out.

Hattie picked it up. "Are there nails in it?"

Oh...I'd forgotten to check. "I don't know. I hope not."

Hattie checked the contents, and then grinned. "I'll take the nail gun."

Oh, boy. "No shooting people."

Hattie handed me the hairdryer. "You focus on messing up Felix's hair, and I'll focus on the rest."

"Awesome. I want the pencil sharpener. That worked so well the other day." Lucy grabbed it and wrapped the cord around her wrist, then let it swing. "I bet I could kill someone with this."

I picked up the hairdryer. "We don't kill people. We just defend ourselves as necessary."

"You're so boring, but fine." Hattie winked at me as she reached for the door. "Let's go, ladies—"

My phone rang suddenly, making us all jump.

Lucy leaned back, her hand on her chest. "I honestly think my life just got a decade shorter. How did you do this for the first two decades of your life?"

"I was more resilient back then, not rusty, and we always focused on rich people who wouldn't want to sully their reputations by making a stink about anything or killing anyone." My phone rang again, and I pulled it out of my pocket and looked down. "It's Devlin."

Lucy settled back in her seat. "Put him on speaker."

"Yes, let's chat with our favorite hot cop," Hattie agreed.

I knew we were avoiding going inside 18 Bitter Street, but I'd promised Devlin I'd stay in touch, so there we go. "Hattie, be quiet or he'll know you're with us." At her nod, I answered the phone on speaker. "What's up?"

Devlin didn't waste time with compliments and assurances of my safety and well-being. Which was fine. "Where are you?" he asked, sounding a little put out.

"Almost to the front of the line. Why? Did you decide you wanted a donut? Cops do love donuts, don't they?"

"How long until you're back at the marina?" he asked, clearly in some kind of a mood.

I glanced at 18 Bitter Street. "If we don't get shivved in the parking lot, not too long. Why? New developments?"

He completely ignored my shivving comment, probably

assuming I was joking. I wasn't. "I'm at the Eagle's Nest. Griselda is here, but your cat is refusing to allow anyone near your car."

Oh…now I knew why he was cranky. I started laughing. I couldn't help it. King Tut was the best. "What's he doing?"

"I think he's part demon. Chief Stone is going to need stitches."

Hattie snorted, and Lucy started giggling.

"I thought King Tut had a crush on you," I said. "Can't you chat with him about this?"

"Chat with a demon cat?"

"If you keep calling him a demon, he's not going to like you anymore." I was trying not to laugh, but I couldn't help it. I could envision King Tut sitting on the roof of my car, puffed up, growling, hissing, and pinning his yellow glare on anyone who came near. He was terrifying when he was a mere fifty percent committed to raising hell. If he was all in? I was sure everyone present would have nightmares for years. "Did he leap off the car at Chief Stone?"

"Something like that."

Lucy, who had almost been King Tut's victim herself, burst out laughing, and Hattie was grinning. "God, I wish I could have seen that," Lucy gasped. "That's so beautiful."

"Was Chief Stone hopped up on margaritas at the time?" I asked.

"He might have been."

"Oh, God." I couldn't stop the laughter, and even Hattie struggled to stay silent. Poor Chief Stone. Tricked into margaritas, attacked by King Tut, power usurped by the feds. "That's brilliant."

"Mia." I could hear the quirk in Devlin's voice, and suddenly I realized that he was as amused as we were. Of course he was. He worked with the guy. "You need to get home and get your cat off the car."

Home. I had a home! That sounded so great. "Right. I'm on my way. I'll be there in a few minutes. But just so you know, King Tut goes on all dates with me, so if he hates you, there will be no hanky-panky."

"I already told you. I'm not attracted to you, so that's fine. Hurry up." He hung up.

"God, I love that cat," Hattie said, gasping as she finally was able to laugh. "I have to confess that it's possible I'm friends with you only so I can get close to him."

"It's possible that I'm friends with myself only so I can get close to him," I agreed.

"That cat is terrifying," Lucy said. "I'm delighted to pawn him off onto my cousin and anyone else standing in my way. But I want to be clear that I'm friends with you *despite* that prehistoric beast."

I grinned back at her. "Once you get to know him, you'll love him."

"I treasure my life too much to get to know him," Lucy said, her eyes still sparkling with delight over the idea of King Tut humbling Chief Stone. "But I will love him forever for terrorizing my cousin. Can we get this over with quickly so we can get back to the marina and witness that poetic brilliance in person?"

"Yes. I agree," Hattie said. "I think the fun's at the marina, not here." She opened her door and got out. "Everyone has to stay alive so we can watch King Tut in action and taunt Mia about her soon-to-be torrid affair with Devlin."

"I'm not having a torrid affair with him—"

Hattie slammed the door shut right in the middle of my protest.

Lucy grinned. "You know he's wildly attracted to you, right? His playing it cool is a total fail."

I didn't want to think about dating. Not now. Not ever. So I ignored her comment, shoved my phone in my pocket, and picked up the hairdryer. "You ready?"

Her amusement faded. "To go hunt a murderer? No. You?"

"Not even remotely."

"Great. So, we should leave it to the cops and go home instead?"

"Of course we should." I put my hand on the door handle. "Are we going to?"

She grinned. "Not a chance. It's go time, babe."

"Let's do this." I opened my door and got out before I could talk myself out of it.

Two lock-picking minutes later, we were inside the building.

CHAPTER 24

THE LOBBY of the building smelled like neglect, amorality, and hopelessness. Or maybe that's what I felt when I stepped onto the broken tile that had once been nice and saw the pillars that had once framed a lobby that might have been grand.

"It's like money and wealth dried up and became haunted shadows of death and crime," Lucy whispered.

I slanted a glance at her. "Do you do that intentionally?"

"Do what?"

"Set a creepy mood so we freak out and can't focus."

"You know what?" Hattie set her hands on her hips. "I think that Lucy made a good point about that Lamborghini. Those deviants were definitely eyeing it. I'll guard it while you guys check out Felix's place." She held out her hand. "Key, please."

I raised my brows. "You're wimping out?"

"No, but three of us is overkill. If you two die, someone needs to alert the authorities and arrange for your funeral. And if you guys come running out of there with an axe murderer on your tail, you need me to have the engine running." She wiggled her fingers. "Keys."

"Hey." Lucy put her hands on her hips. "I'm the one who

suggested staying in the car. I think it's a good idea, but I feel like I should get to do it since I thought of it."

"Do you?" Hattie raised her brows. "You're forty years younger than I am. Don't you think it makes sense for the old lady to be in the car, not engaged in combat?"

"You said you're not old."

"I'm old when it's convenient for me. Keys or not?"

I glanced at Lucy, and she shrugged. Honestly, I'd feel better with someone guarding the car and with Hattie off the front lines. With a sigh, I handed the keys to Hattie. "I didn't realize you had the capacity to be scared."

She grabbed the keys. "I don't. I just really wanted to drive that car." She pressed her lips to the keys. "A freaking Lamborghini, guys! For real!" She spun around and jogged toward the door, literally chortling with glee. "You go, girls! I have faith in you!"

The glass lobby door shut behind her, and I could see her sprinting down the steps. She leapt into the car and the engine roared to life. I narrowed my eyes. "How long until she can't resist the temptation, and she takes it for a spin around the block?"

"Thirty seconds?"

It took ten.

Lucy and I looked at each other. "It's fine," Lucy said. "She'll be back by the time we need her."

"Of course she will. This is going to work out great. Let's go have fun, shall we?" I started walking toward the elevators.

"Fun? In this creepy horror movie set?" Lucy followed me, both of us scanning the lobby for any sign of human, or zombie, life. We saw none. I think we were both happy about that.

I glanced over at her. "Is it possible to have a more positive attitude?"

"No. I was embracing my raw, unbridled terror. Suppressing your emotions isn't healthy."

"It is in this case." I pressed the dirty white button for the elevator, then stepped back to wait for it. "Attitude is everything. Let's have some positive affirmations here, Lucy."

She raised her brows. "Positive affirmations? Seriously?"

"Yes. Mindset matters." I swung the hairdryer in a circle, as if I were winding up to hit someone, which maybe I was. "This is going to work out great," I said. "We're totally capable of handling this." The elevator began descending from the seventh floor down toward us. Unfortunately. I kind of wished the elevator didn't work, but you don't always get what you want, right? "I feel great about this."

Lucy stood next to me, staring up at the numbers above the elevator. "Felix is going to be passed out drunk on the floor, with a signed confession in his hand."

"Nice. I like that." The elevator was on the fifth floor now. "The powder in my car isn't drugs. It was a funny joke."

"Totally funny. Griselda and Devlin are going to have a duel at dawn for your heart. We'll post a video online, rake in the ad fees, and retire rich as Croesus in a month."

I looked over at her as the elevator hit the second floor. "That's quite a plan. Who survives the duel and gets me?"

"No one *gets* you. The survivor will receive the honor of being allowed to treat you like a queen and worship the ground you walk on for years and years, filling your life with adoration, love, great sex, and all the freedom you want."

I grinned as the elevator reached the ground floor. "That's brilliant. I love that."

"Me, too." She started swinging the pencil sharpener, timing it with the arc of my hairdryer. "You're right. Positive affirmations work. I feel so much better."

"Right? I do, too." The door slid open, and my heart jumped as a tall, muscular dude in jeans and a sideways baseball hat glared at us. The bulge in his jacket looked like a gun, and his eyes were dark and ruthless as he assessed us, cataloging us with well-practiced efficiency.

He reminded me of Stanley's enforcers. Huge. Dangerous. Merciless.

The hairdryer drooped to a stop by my ankle as panic started to close in around me. Was he going to kill us right here? Right now? After all I'd escaped, now was going to be my moment, at the hands of some random guy I didn't even know—

He walked past us, into the lobby, and out of the building, without even looking back.

We were completely irrelevant to him.

Relief rushed through me so fiercely that my knees almost gave out. Lucy caught my arm, keeping me upright as I stumbled into the elevator. I closed my eyes and sank down to the floor, bending my head between my knees as the elevator started to rise, trying to catch my breath.

"What's happening?" Lucy crouched in front of me. "Are you okay?"

I shook my head, trying to catch my breath. "I had a flashback to my old life. I thought he was going to kill us. He reminded me of Stanley's hit men."

"Oh…" Lucy sat down next to me and leaned against the wall of the elevator. "Panic attack, then?"

I fisted my hands and banged knuckles against my forehead. "I want all that out of my brain. I don't want it to live there anymore. Not the memories, or the fear, or any of it. I just want it gone."

Lucy sighed. "I have things like that in my head, too. My mom used to call them land mines. You think you're doing alright, and then you run into something that sends you catapulting back into some trauma that you thought you'd gotten a handle on."

Land mines. "That makes sense."

"Yeah." She leaned her head on my shoulder. "But here's the thing, Mia. I've been around you a lot in the last week. I know you're a complete badass, and you can handle anything. Screw the land mine. Let it blow up. It can't actually hurt you."

I took a breath and looked over at her. She was grinning at me, her dark brown eyes filled with warmth and understanding. "I used to be a lot more resilient. Before the Stanley thing."

"Well," she said briskly. "The first time almost getting shot over drugs is always the worst. I'm sure it gets easier."

I raised my brows. "You think?"

"Probably. Most things do. Either that or they compound until they break you forever."

I stared at her. "I vote for option one."

"Then let that sucker go, girlfriend." The elevator came to a stop on the fourth floor. The doors slid open to reveal an empty hall with maroon carpeting that had probably once been luxurious and brilliant. Now? Old and stale. "You ready? Time to get off your victim butt and get to work."

I laughed. "My victim butt?"

"Yeah. You're not a victim. You literally took down a drug king's empire, stayed alive, and started a new life. You win. So, yeah, not a victim." She stood up and stepped between the doors, using her body to keep them from closing.

Resolution flooded me. She was right. I *had* won. So, yeah, I was a winner, and I had this. I summoned my teenage "I'm unstoppable" mentality and stood up, dusting the carpet yuck off my winner-not-a-victim butt. "Let's go."

Lucy grinned and gestured to the hallway. "Ex-FBI spies first. Former baton twirlers last."

I swallowed my habitual protest that I hadn't been an FBI spy. It sounded badass, and I was tired of the trauma following me around. It was time to channel my inner asskicker, in whatever incremental steps I could. Step one? Own it. "Good plan," I said, walking past her. "FBI spies are way tougher than baton twirlers."

"Hey. Baton twirlers are beasts." She stepped out after me. "Underestimate us at your own peril, babe."

"Then I guess we're pretty much unstoppable together."

"Pretty much," she agreed, tightening her grip on her cord.

The elevator doors started to slide shut, and I jumped back inside and pulled out the stop button to keep the elevator on the floor we were on. "Just in case we're running for our lives when we leave."

"Good call. It would suck to die because the elevator was slow."

"Among other reasons." I scanned the hallway, made note of where the stairwell was, checked to see if anyone else was around, and then started down the hall toward apartment 44.

We fell silent as we walked, our sneakers quiet on the old carpet. I was trying to listen for the sounds of murderers sneaking around behind the doors we were passing, but my heart was thundering so loudly that I was pretty sure that a herd of buffalo could be charging up behind me and I wouldn't hear it.

So, I looked back over my shoulder. Then in front. Then back.

Lucy was doing the same.

Nothing visible was stalking us. So why didn't I feel safe? "We should have sent Esther over to the Yacht Club to see if Felix was still there."

"You already sent her to Hattie's to hide the portrait and search for planted evidence. We can handle this. If Felix is living like this, there's no way he's passing up on the chance to become Elena Vanderveer's personal chef. He's sweating his way around that kitchen right now."

I took a breath. "You're right. He was desperate. We're good." But desperate people often made stupid decisions, so I knew we weren't one-hundred-percent safe. "Let's make it fast."

We finally reached the door that had a "44" on it. I chewed my lip as I stood there.

"Do we knock or just break in?" Lucy asked.

"Knock."

"What if someone answers? What if *he* answers?"

I shook out my hair so that it was falling forward over my face, then pulled up my hoodie. "I'll be a drug addict, and he'll shut the door on me before he takes the time to recognize me."

"You think that'll work?"

"Yep." Context was everything when it came to being recognized. "He'll never expect Elena Vanderveer to be at his door, looking like an addict. It'll be almost impossible for him to match me to her."

"Almost?"

"Almost." I waved her off. "Go around the corner."

"Fine, but I'm going to rescue you if he tries to murder you." Lucy stepped back, swinging her pencil sharpener like she knew how to use it. It probably wasn't unlike wielding a baton or a sledgehammer, both of which she was highly skilled at. So, yeah, she was a little terrifying.

"Don't kill anyone with that."

She grinned. "You're such a buzzkill."

Oy. I'd created a monster. "Go away."

She blew me a kiss, then ducked around the corner.

I cleared my throat, hid the hairdryer behind my back, knocked on the door, and waited, my heart pounding.

No one answered.

I knocked again, hitting the door harder.

Again, no answer.

"I don't think anyone's there," Lucy said, leaning around the corner.

I pressed my ear against the door and listened for the sound of anyone moving.

Lucy watched me while I knocked again and yelled.

Finally, I looked back at her. "He's either not home, or he's dead."

"Not funny."

"Right. I forgot. Murder is real." I pulled out my lockpicks and quickly went to work on the lock. It clicked and I eased the door open. "Hello?"

No one replied.

I looked back at Lucy. "It's clear. Let's go."

"Want me to wait outside in case he comes back?"

Dammit. That was a good idea. I didn't want to go in alone, but she was right. "Yeah."

She nodded. "Leave the door open, though, in case you need me."

"Right. Caw Caw if you see him coming."

"Or I could text you."

"Right. That's probably more subtle." I summoned the same courage I'd used to get through my FBI stint and eased into Felix's apartment.

The setting sun made it just dark enough for long shadows to hide in the corners, which wasn't the feel-good experience I'd been hoping for. I knew time was short, so I decided to take a chance, and I turned on the lights.

Brightness flooded, revealing chaos and disarray. I was standing in a common room that was the living room, dining room, and kitchen all together. A short hallway on the right looked like it led to two bedrooms and a bathroom.

I quickly walked into the common area, picking my way over the chaos, looking quickly around. It smelled faintly of turpentine, reminding me of Rutherford's chapel and all the paints. Hattie's spare anchor wasn't there, and there were no lists of blackmail victims or signed confessions visible, so I headed toward the bedrooms.

Following the scent of turpentine, I found the source of it in the first bedroom.

Glory's painting was leaning up against the wall, and a laundry basket in the corner held jeans that smelled of turpentine and smoke.

Glory's painting was *here?* Felix was the one who'd torched the chapel?

"Holy cow," Lucy spoke from behind me, startling me.

I spun around. "You're supposed to be guarding the hall."

"It was too stressful being alone out there. I was afraid you were getting murdered in here, but wow. He was one of the ones who helped Glory steal the painting?"

"Apparently." I realized suddenly that we'd forgotten about the two people who had been with Glory. Felix, apparently, had been one, but there was still another at large. "Let's look around." It was then that I noticed the closet. It was full of clothes like I'd seen on Glory. I suddenly looked around, and I realized we were in a woman's bedroom.

We weren't in Felix's room. We were in *Glory's*. The breath rushed out of me in startled shock. We were in the bedroom of a woman who'd been murdered only hours ago. "This is Glory's stuff. It's her room."

Lucy sucked in her breath as she looked around. "You're right. How does a twentyish woman wind up roommates with a middle-aged chef?"

"I have no idea. But we'll find out."

"What if she was murdered by her own roommate? That's so concerning."

"Yeah, it is. But convenient, since we're here now and can look around." It was creepy to be in Glory's room, but we had to pull ourselves together. The cops would probably be there soon to check out her stuff, once they figured out she lived there. I was glad we were there first, especially since no one had called or texted Felix an incriminating or helpful message, but I had the phone in my pocket, and I was holding out hope. "Maybe black-mail stuff is in here." I ran over to the desk and began pulling out drawers. "Look for a computer, or notes or anything."

"I'm on it."

It took about thirty seconds before I understood why criminals who were tossing a house made such a mess. It was just so much faster to hurl things out of my way, and with Felix potentially on his way home and the cops soon arriving, time mattered. I yanked open a drawer, then frowned when I saw a framed photograph of two girls and a boy in their late teens. Maybe eighteen or so. They were in swimsuits, frozen in midair as they leapt off a dock into the lake side by side.

The girl on the right had flaming red hair and a huge smile. Her arms were wrapped around her knees as she cannonballed into the water. Pure joy. *Glory*. In the middle was a guy with brown hair doing a jackknife. He was wearing goggles, so I couldn't see his face well, but he didn't look familiar. He had a large birthmark on his left forearm, and I hadn't seen anyone with that in town.

The girl on the left was doing a flip, so her face wasn't visible. She was upside down, her knees tucked to her chest, her back to the camera. But on her lower back was a mark that looked alarmingly familiar.

No way.

I pulled out my phone, turned the camera on the picture, and then zoomed in on the picture. *Holy cow.* My heart started racing. "Lucy. Come see this."

She hurried over and leaned over my shoulder. "What?"

"Look at the mark on her back." I zoomed in again for her, waiting for her to recognize it.

She sucked in her breath. "That's the same tattoo as the woman Rutherford painted."

I nodded. "The woman he loved." I pointed to Glory. "She and Glory were friends, or at least they've known each other since they were teenagers. Glory knew who the woman was, and she must have known that Rutherford loved her. One look at the portrait, and she would have known, just like I did."

"So, you think it was a lover's spat? That Glory got jealous of Rutherford, and killed him, and then this woman killed Glory?"

"Maybe." I'd suspected that Glory had known who the tattooed woman was, but now I had confirmation. If only I hadn't been dragged away by Devlin, I might have gotten it out of her. *Glory! You can tell me now!* My heart pounding, I quickly began searching the other drawers. "See if you can find a photograph where we can see her face. Or the guy. Because the guy clearly knew them both, too."

We went silent as we frantically searched the rest of the drawers. We found several duplicates of that same picture, but no others.

Frustrated, we looked at each other. "What does this have to do with Hattie and her recipes?" Lucy asked. "Three teenagers going swimming, and a hot and heavy romance with Rutherford doesn't connect to putting the blame on Hattie and stealing her recipes. This doesn't make any sense."

"It must make sense. We just haven't figured it out yet. If that woman murdered Glory, then she's out there somewhere, trying to pin it on Hattie."

"Why Hattie?"

"If we figure that out, maybe we'll figure out who it is." I took a picture of the three teenagers, shoved one of the copies in my pocket, then set another on the desk. "Maybe the cops will follow up on that photograph."

Lucy put her hands on her hips, looking as frustrated as I felt. We kept getting more clues and more details, but no more clarity. "What now? Check the kitchen for the recipe? Maybe Felix and Glory had a plan to open a new café or something."

"Maybe." I looked around the tossed room, frustrated that we hadn't found more. "Yes, check the kitchen. I'll check the other bedroom."

"Right. On it." Lucy nodded. "Let's make it fast. I'm getting creeped out being here."

I took another glance around the room, didn't see anything helpful, then grabbed my hairdryer and headed out to the hall. The front door was closed now. "Lucy? Did you close the front door?"

"Yeah, and I locked it."

"Okay." I paused to listen, but I heard nothing. My heart racing, I turned away from our exit and hurried down the hall toward the second bedroom while she ran into the kitchen. I glanced in the bathroom as I went by, noticing the closed shower curtain, which reminded me of my recent assassin incident when I was hiding in the bathroom with King Tut, hoping to avoid being shot.

What if someone was hiding behind the shower curtain?

I snorted at the thought. Who would be hiding behind the shower curtain? That literally made no sense. If Felix was here, he would have already come out for a friendly visit.

The shower was fine. I wasn't about to let one near-death experience transform all bathrooms into death traps.

253

Ignoring the bathroom, I headed toward Felix's bedroom. But as I put my hand on the knob, I looked back at the bathroom again. The apartment was a mess. It wasn't inhabited by the kind of people who took the time to close the shower curtain neatly after getting out.

The shower curtain should be partially open. Askew.

It wasn't. It was pulled shut nice and tight.

Dammit. I was going to have to check that out, wasn't I?

CHAPTER 25

"HOLY CRAP, MIA!" Lucy shouted from the kitchen. "Felix has been baking cinnamon buns!"

Victory shot through me. "That's awesome! Did you find the actual recipe?" As I spoke, I eased back toward the bathroom.

"No, not yet. But he's not stupid enough to leave such a valuable item out on the counter."

"While you're searching for it, see if you can find a reason why he'd murder Rutherford and Glory." We had pieces, but nothing was coming together. We had to figure out how everything was connected.

Lucy slammed a cabinet door. "Like what?"

"A signed confession would be nice."

"I'll work on it."

"Perfect." At the threshold of the bathroom, I wrapped the cord of my hairdryer around my hand, and raised my hand, ready to swing it. Lucy was making noise in the kitchen, but the floor creaked as I stepped into the bathroom.

I froze, waiting.

No movement from the bathtub, but I could see a faint shadow where there shouldn't be a shadow. A shadow about the size of a person crouched down in the tub. Fear shot through me, but I caught myself before I ran for the front door, screaming in terror.

It wasn't Felix in there, because he would have come out.

Anyone who was aggressive and wanted to harm us wouldn't be hiding.

So, it was someone who didn't want us to know they were there. More scared than we were? At least, less skilled with corded implements, hopefully.

Awesome. I'd control the situation. It was all good.

While Lucy continued to shout things from the kitchen, I bit my lip, gripped the hairdryer, then yanked the curtain back and leapt backward at the same time as I came face to face with Joel's mom, Kate.

Yes, the very same Kate whose engagement ring I'd stolen and returned only a few short hours ago.

We stared at each other in shocked horror. She was hunched down in the tub in her party outfit, including high heels that had no business climbing into tubs.

After a long moment, she stood up, lifted her chin, and put her hands on her hips. "What are you doing here?" She sounded impressively haughty, as if this was her turf and I was the intruder.

Too bad for her, I knew more than she did. "You're trying to find the blackmail evidence, so you can destroy it, aren't you?"

Her eyes widened in doe-eyed innocence. "What?"

"The evidence of your affair. Now that Glory and Rutherford are dead, you want to get rid of the evidence—" I stopped suddenly as the pieces fell into place. *She* was the murderer. She was being blackmailed, so she'd shut them down.

How obvious was that? I was such an idiot! She was literally the most obvious suspect we had, and I'd totally ruled her out.

Not that I was going to admit it right now.

Being highly averse to telling a murderer I knew they were a murderer when we were alone together, I did a quick pivot. "We're looking for the blackmail evidence, too. They were blackmailing me and Lucy as well for taking over my ex's drug empire." Again with the drug empire claim. I seriously had to find another cover story. "I don't know who killed Rutherford and Glory, but I'm so grateful. Aren't you grateful? Best day ever when those two died." I raised my voice. "Lucy! Kate's here! She's looking for the stuff, too!" I beamed at her. "Let's all work together, and maybe we can find it sooner."

She stared at me.

I upped the wattage on my smile as her hand slid behind her back. Did she have a gun? I was so tired of people aiming guns at me. But if it was a gun, wouldn't she have pointed it at me already? She would.

So not a gun.

Probably.

But not definitely.

"So, I'm totally thinking we can pin this on Felix," I said, silently calculating how long it would take me to dive out of the bathroom if she did pull a gun out from behind her back. Could I make it? I was near the door. "I mean, I love Hattie, so she can't go down for it, but Felix?" I shrugged. "He stole her recipes, so clearly a bad guy. It's an easy set up. We'll just leave some evidence to—"

"Mia." Lucy spoke from behind me, her voice a little high-pitched.

Kate's gaze went behind me, and her eyes widened again.

I didn't want to spook Kate into shooting us. "It's fine, Lucy," I said, not taking my gaze off Kate. "She's with us. It's all good—"

"Put the hairdryer down." Felix's low command sent fear shooting down my spine.

I quickly turned, and then my mouth went dry when I saw Lucy standing behind me. Felix was beside her, a gun pressed to her temple.

So many guns. Was everyone in this town armed?

She made a face at me and mouthed "Sorry."

I shrugged. "Perfect job getting him right where we want him. Excellent work, Lucy."

Felix narrowed his eyes, clearly unsure whether to believe me. Obviously, he was still trapped in the thrall of how Elena Vanderveer had fooled him before.

Or maybe not such a successful fooling, seeing as he was home and not feverishly cooking. Clearly, I was a little rusty, which was very disappointing. I didn't want to be the old me, except when I did, and then I wanted to be as good as I ever was. Naturally.

"Get into the bathroom." He shoved Lucy, and she stumbled across the tile.

I caught her arm, and she moved beside me, both of us squishing against the sink so that we weren't between Felix and Kate, because who wanted to be between them if they decided to take each other out?

Keeping his body in the doorway to block the exit, he aimed at the three of us. "You do realize that I can do Find My iPhone from my computer, right? And track you guys here?"

Lucy elbowed me. "You should've turned that sucker off."

I sighed. See? This was what happened when you try to straddle the line between thief and law-abiding citizen. You make stupid errors. "Yep, I should have, but in my defense, I thought he was going to get a phone call that would lead to all our answers. I felt like that was a good plan."

"I like the idea, but the execution wasn't so stellar."

"I'm not going to argue with that one." As I spoke, I glanced back at Kate, who looked both alarmed and annoyed. Was she working with Felix or not?

I couldn't tell.

Either way, we were trapped, and Felix was too far away to get the gun from him.

There was no window in the bathroom.

He could literally shoot us right then, and there was nothing we could do.

No, there was something we could do. I just didn't know what it was yet.

He raised his brows at me. "You were saying something about planting evidence that I killed Rutherford and Glory? Do continue."

I thought fast. "I made that up because Kate killed them, and I didn't want her to shoot me. Did you know they were black-mailing her for having an affair?"

His gaze slanted to Kate.

"I'm not having an affair," she announced. "That's ridiculous. And I didn't kill my own brother or that ghost person." She pulled her hand out from behind her back, and Lucy and I ducked before she waved her wallet. "I do have a proposition for you, however. I can pay well."

I raised my brows. "I love propositions. What's your plan?"

She glared at me. "Not you. Him."

"Him? Why were you hiding if you wanted to talk to him?"

"Because you weren't him. Obviously." Kate waved her wallet. "Shall we go in the other room and chat?"

Felix studied her. "Toss me the wallet."

She did, and he picked it up and opened it. I could see a thick wad of bills in there.

Money might not buy happiness, but it sure helped when dealing with potential murderers. I needed to get a wad of it to carry around with me.

"I can get more," she said. "I'm extremely wealthy."

"I know who you are." He flicked the gun. "You can come out."

I knew he didn't mean us, but I bounced out in front of her anyway. "Awesome. I have some great ideas—"

He put the gun against my forehead. "Shut up. Back up. Sit down."

The metal was cold. Stressful. My fingers itched to grab the gun from him, but I knew that often went badly for the person who was smaller, not accustomed to guns, and increasingly terrified. The odds didn't feel great, not when he had a gun *and* he looked ready to use it. "Look—"

"Now."

There was an edge to his voice that sent chills down my spine. The kind of chills that warned me to back off. I didn't want to let him lock us in the bathroom, but it was better than being killed, so I did as he said.

I mean, let's be honest. Getting locked in the bathroom wasn't really a big problem for me, right?

"Toss your phones to me," he commanded. "And give me mine."

That was so inconvenient that he'd learned his lesson about leaving me with his phone. Reluctantly, we both unloaded our devices, tossing them at his feet.

He kicked them out in the hall. "You," he said to Kate. "Tie them up."

"What?" I shot to my feet in alarm. Getting incapacitated was such a bad idea. "I have money, too—"

"I don't care."

And he didn't. Five minutes and a roll of duct tape later, Lucy and I were in a bit of a difficult situation. Lucy already had a strip of duct tape across her mouth, and now it was my turn.

Kate walked over to me and ripped off a piece of tape. "Have a nice day."

She was so heartless. "You're very heartless," I commented.

"Men are called strong, powerful, and alpha. Strong women are called heartless, bitchy, and caustic. Where's your support for women?"

I blinked. "I'd be more supportive if you hadn't tied me up."

"I did it in the name of girl power everywhere." She crouched in front of me, her dark eyes blazing. The strip of duct tape for my mouth was on the tips of her fingers, a shiny silver threat of silence. "Do you know where I'd be if I listened to my dad and believed him that I was worth nothing? Nowhere. You know that."

Felix was no longer in the doorway. I didn't know where he'd gone, but this was my chance. "I do know that, Kate," I said urgently. "I admire your strength. I really do. I was raised by a single mom who fought hard for every meal we managed to get."

She raised her brows. "Single moms are incredible."

"I know, right?" Beside me, Lucy's eyes were wide and frantic. She was moving slightly, and I knew she was trying to work her hands free. "Look, Kate, we need to work together. Take down these men who are trying to destroy us. I'm on your side, not theirs."

She stared at me, then shook her head. "You don't understand."

"Help me understand," I said urgently, trying desperately to girl-bond with her.

She glanced back over her shoulder at the empty door, then leaned in. "I'm sorry," she said quietly. "But everything is at stake. I have to finish this."

"I'll help you finish it! So will Lucy. Right Luce?" Lucy nodded frantically, and I did the same. "Whatever it is, we can help. My dad ditched me, and my husband tried to murder me, so I'm all about desperate measures in desperate times. I'm with you."

Anguish passed over Kate's face, but she shook her head. "It's too late. I wish you hadn't seen me here, but since you did, you leave me no choice."

Oh, I was not taking responsibility for whatever dastardly things she had planned. "Look, it's fine that you had an affair. I honestly don't care. I just don't want Hattie to go to jail for it. Let's pin it on someone else, like one of those men who has tried to crush you."

She raised her brows. "Of course the woman who betrayed her husband wouldn't be able to figure this one out. You don't get it."

I was so confused right now. I felt like she was dropping clues like hot coals, and all I was doing was letting them burn me. "What don't I get?"

She slapped the duct tape over my mouth. "Love, Mia. Love."

Love? She was talking about *love*?

As Lucy and I sat there like helpless toads, Kate walked out. She shut the door behind her, and I heard the click of a lock. Uh, hello? What bathroom door locked from the outside? That was just weird.

Normally, a locked door was the opportunity to amuse myself.

Right now? With my wrists duct taped behind my back? It was just a tease.

Love. She said it was about *love*. Whose love for whom? Love betrayed? In the name of love? Motherly love? Romantic love? Scorned love? There were simply far too many options when it came to love.

I looked over at Lucy as I heard the scrape of something heavy, like a dresser, being dragged across the floor. They'd blockaded us in. Which was fine. I could get the lock open, and Lucy could shove the item away. Girl power, right there, baby.

Once we got ourselves un-duct-taped, of course.

Lucy raised her brows at me and tried to say something.

I mumbled something equally unintelligible back, and she rolled her eyes at me, somehow knowing that I was mocking her. I tried to grin, but the duct tape made that a fail. Instead, I head-gestured to tell her to lie down.

She stared at me.

I jerked my head again, being as clear as I possibly could.

She gave me a look that said I was an idiot.

I was definitely not an idiot. I was a quick-thinking former criminal, and I was going to use every skill I had right now to keep us safe.

So, I laid down on the floor and nodded my head at her to do the same.

It took a few more minutes of very poorly played charades before she finally did. The whole time, I could hear movement and low voices from the apartment. I didn't know what they were doing, but I had a bad feeling it wasn't going to go well for us if we didn't take control of the situation very soon.

Once Lucy was on her side, I sat up, and wiggled backward

until my fingers touched her face. I tried to find the edge of the duct tape, but all I did was get my finger up her nose.

I heard her start to laugh, which then made me start to laugh, which was a little bit more difficult than one might think with a duct-taped face.

Lucy did figure out what I was trying to do, and with both of us moving and laughing, I managed to get my fingertips on the corner of her duct-tape gag. It took a number of tries, and then we both finally moved at the same time, and the duct tape ripped off her face.

"Good God!" Lucy whispered. "That was brilliant. I'm definitely choosing you to get abducted with every time it happens."

I raised my brows at her, because my duct tape made it impossible for me to wow her with my wit and charm.

"Right. Your turn." We swapped positions, and, due to our extensive experience, we managed to rip that duct tape off my face with much more grace and aplomb than we had only moments ago. Quick learners lived better lives. Or longer ones, at least. Hopefully.

The moment the tape was off my face, I sat up. "Did you see anything we can use to cut our wrists free?" I whispered it, in case Kate and Felix could hear us over all the ruckus they were making out in the apartment.

"No, but there has to be nail clippers, right? It's a bathroom."

"Glory did have nice nails," I said.

"Right? I was thinking the same thing."

"You check the medicine cabinet. I'll check the vanity." I rolled onto my knees and wiggled over to the drawers that I'd had open only moments ago. While Lucy worked on getting the medicine cabinet open in a fun hands-free challenge, I pulled the top drawer open with my teeth. Right there on top was a manicure kit. "Got it!"

"Perfect! We'll be out of here in no time."

No time ended up being more time than either of us thought. It actually wasn't that easy to get a manicure kit out of a drawer, open it, remove a set of clippers, flip them open, and then start snipping micro cuts through several layers of duct tape, all while your hands are taped behind your back.

We were about ten minutes in with Lucy only about a centimeter through my duct tape when I caught the scent of something a wee bit acrid. Alarm shot through me. "Do you smell that?"

Lucy paused and sniffed the air. "Is that smoke?"

We both lay there on the floor, making big, obnoxious sniffing sounds as we tried to figure out what we were smelling. It took only a moment before the scent became stronger, and I knew for sure it was smoke. I swallowed. "Um, Lucy? I don't want to alarm you, but I'm pretty sure that he just torched the place. He's going to burn us up." I used "he" but I had a bad feeling that it was a "they" situation.

I doubted Kate had left the apartment before the torching had occurred. So much hostility in that bride-to-be, right?

"No way. That's completely not on my daily plan for today." Lucy started working on my duct tape again, little, tiny snips. "I got this."

I tensed as I watched tendrils of smoke drift under the door. "I think you need to hurry."

"No problem. The higher the stakes, the better. Baton twirlers are competitors. We thrive on pressure." But there was an edge to her voice that wasn't the most reassuring tone I'd ever heard.

"How far through it are you?" I couldn't help but think of how fast Rutherford's chapel had ignited, and how there had been clothes that smelled of turpentine in Glory's room.

"Making progress. Crap. I just dropped the clippers." At my sharp intake of breath, she laughed. "Hah. Just kidding. Tension relief."

"You almost made my heart stop completely."

"Good. The human body gets stronger when challenged."

"Or it shatters into a thousand sobbing pieces." I felt the pressure on my wrists as she worked on the tape. My eyes were starting to sting now, hopefully from invisible tears and not from invisible smoke, but I wasn't all that optimistic about my delusions. "Lucy." I tried to keep my voice calm. "You're going to have to rip it."

"No one rips through several layers of duct tape."

"You made a cut. That has to be enough. We don't have time." Sweat was starting to drip into my eyes. I wasn't sure if it was from the heat of the fire coming through the closed door, or from my rising sense of panic. "You're freakishly strong. Use it!"

At that moment, the fire alarms went off, shrieking violently.

"Lucy," I shouted. "The fire department won't get here in time. We gotta go!"

"Fine. I'll try." She moved closer to me, and I felt her fingers fluttering over mine as she tried to find the cut in the duct tape.

My heart started racing, and the urge to leap to my feet and run was almost uncontrollable. Except I couldn't run, because I was taped up. I took a breath, and tried to control the panic trying to take me. *We got this.* "Lucy. Do it now."

"I can't get a grip—"

"You can. Right now." I used the arrogant, unyielding tone that Griselda had used on me so many times whenever I called him in a panic, telling him I couldn't spy on Stanley anymore. It was incredibly irritating, but at the same time, it had always worked on me. "Lucy. It has to be now. Do it."

"God, you're obnoxious as hell with that tone."

I felt the tape tightening on my wrists, and then there was a tearing sound as my wrists came free. "You did it!"

I shot to my feet and then fell face-first into the towel rack.

"Your ankles are still tied," Lucy said dryly.

"Yep. I realize that." I grabbed the clippers and clipped a few millimeters through her wrists. I got far enough to rip the tape, and then her hands were free. "Do my ankles."

I stood up more carefully this time, and turned on the shower as she went to work on my ankles. As the cold water poured into the tub, I dumped the bath towels into the water.

The tape fell away from my ankles, and I stumbled.

My eyes were definitely stinging from the smoke under the door now, and I grabbed towels and packed them along the bottom edge of the door. But how much time was that going to buy us? There was no window. If there were flames in the apartment, no one was going to get through there to save us.

I turned on the faucet and threw hand towels in the sink, drenching them.

Lucy got herself un-taped, then grabbed the towels. "Unlock the door. I'll take over the towels."

"Okay." I still had my lockpicks in my back pocket, so I went down on my knees to get to work on the door. The doorknob was still cool, which was a good sign. Hot doorknobs meant fire was much too up close and personal.

Lucy draped a wet towel over my shoulders. "This isn't how I dreamed of dying. I had much bigger plans. More dramatic, so you better get us out."

"I agree." I kneeled on the wet towels as I began to work my magic. "Death is a person's finale, right? The finale always has to be really good, or everything up to it is a disappointment."

Lucy pulled her shirt over her face as she coughed. "Right? It's like a movie. No matter how good it is, if the ending disappoints, then the movie is a fail."

"Total fail."

Her gaze met mine, and I saw the worry in them.

Which made sense.

We were kinda close to being murdered and all.

CHAPTER 26

UNLESS WE DECIDED today wasn't our day to be knocked off.

Which I felt like a good decision.

"No," I announced. "I'm not dying today." At that moment, the lock clicked, and triumph rushed through me. "We're clear!" I grabbed the doorknob, turned it, pulled the door open, and ran right into a massive piece of furniture "I knew they were up to something." I shoved at it, but I didn't have even close to enough leverage to get it to budge.

Lucy shouldered it, but it didn't move for her either. She hammered it with her fists. "No, no, no!"

"Come on!" We both leaned into it, pushing as hard as we could, but it didn't budge. We were both coughing now. Lucy looked at me with desperation in her eyes, but I shook my head. "We're not giving up."

I grabbed her arm and pulled her back toward the bathtub. "Let's get a running start and hit it with everything we have."

"We'll break our shoulders. I like my shoulders."

"You have great shoulders," I agreed. "But I feel like it's worth the sacrifice."

"Not really, but fine." She took a breath as she stood beside me. "On three?"

I nodded. "One."

"Two."

"Three!" We both charged the monstrosity. I turned my shoulder, bracing against the pain of impact, but as we launched ourselves through the air—

The piece of furniture shot to the left and disappeared from sight.

With a shriek of alarm, we shot through the smoky air, and I crashed into the wall on the other side of the hallway. "Lucy?" I scrambled to my feet and spun around.

Lucy had been snatched out of the air by the potential assassin that had given me the panic attack in the elevator.

I blinked in surprise. "What—"

Hattie jumped out of the kitchen, a wet kitchen towel wrapped around her face to cover her mouth and nose. "I found my recipe! That lowlife really stole it! What the heck, right? Learn to make your own buns!"

"Hattie! What are you doing here?" I held a towel to my face as I scrambled to my feet. "Did you move that furniture?" I knew Hattie was a badass, but moving that blockade? How was that possible.

"I saw the smoke, so Vinnie and I came running up to save you." She beamed at Vinnie, the potential assassin, as he set a startled Lucy down. "He was admiring the Lamborghini. I was admiring the Lamborghini. He thought about stealing it, but I corrected that idea. And then he realized I was the Hattie of Hattie's café." She beamed at him. "Instant bonding."

Leave it to Hattie to convert a thief into a hero.

Oh, wait… Moment of self-awareness there. Maybe I was just one of many in a long line of Hattie redemption savior initiatives…

At that moment, there was an explosion from Glory's room, and we all ducked. "Let's get out of here!" I shouted. The sprinkler system finally triggered, and water started pouring down on all of us, but the smoke was still thick, and there were flames coming out of Glory's room.

"Let's go, Vinnie!" Hattie jumped onto his back and the massive dude piggy-backed the spritely senior out the door in a speedy sprint. Lucy was hot on their heels, and I brought up the rear. I paused for a moment in the doorway, looking back at the apartment. Smoke was thick everywhere, but the flames were eating their way through Glory's room. Nowhere else. Just Glory's room.

Which meant Felix was trying to hide something in there. It hadn't been simply to burn *us*, although that had probably been a fun bonus. What had we missed? The painting? The picture? Something else?

Frowning, I pulled the towel over my face and stepped back into the apartment. What had he been trying to hide? I eyed the flames. I could probably make it in there—

Lucy grabbed my arm and yanked me backward. "This isn't your moment to be a hero, Mia! Let's go!"

At that moment, I saw a notepad on the kitchen counter with writing on it. People always left their most recent notes on their pads. What if there was a magic clue on there? "Wait!" I twisted free of Lucy and ran into the apartment. I grabbed the notepad off the counter, and then ducked as there was another explosion from Glory's room, most likely from all the turpentine clothes we'd seen in there. I yelped and sprinted for the door, where Lucy had stopped to wait for me. Was that friendship or what? Yay for saving her from a murder rap!

Lucy and I burst out into the hall as smoke poured out around us. The alarms were even louder in the hall, and the sprinklers were drenching us and everything in sight.

"The stairs are around to the right." We sprinted down the hall, then charged out onto the landing. Below us, I could hear Hattie shouting for Vinnie to stop and wait for us. Again, how sweet was that? "We're right behind you, Hattie!" I yelled as we ran down the stairs. "Keep going!"

Tenants were pouring out of the doors into the stairwell, slowing our exit. I was surprised how many people lived there. The building had seemed abandoned, but it appeared that it was actually inhabited by a lot of people who hadn't felt social.

Up ahead, I could see Vinnie and Hattie literally plowing past people, shouting at everyone to get out of their way. "I think he's a perfect match," I said as we scooted after them.

"Cars, aggression, and a big heart? Yep." Lucy nodded. "The thirty-year age difference would be perfect for her."

"Not for Hattie. For you."

"Me?" Lucy sounded shocked as we sprinted down the stairs. "I'm never dating again."

"He befriends old ladies and rescues her friends from a fire. I think that's a good start."

"Not enough. I'm out of the game." Lucy was much fitter than I was, but she was staying with me, which was nice. I mean, we were out of the flames, so it wasn't life or death, but still. This much exercise was kind of life or death for me. If I passed out and fell, I could die.

It was so great to have friends. I was definitely not giving them back. "He is attractive, though, in a tall, muscled, bad-boy kind of way, right?"

"Who likes tall, muscled bad-boys who rescue old ladies and their friends from burning buildings?" Lucy said. "No one ever."

"Ever," I agreed. "Definitely no appealing characteristics there at all that could help a gal get over a bad relationship."

"Exactly."

We burst out the emergency exit, and the Lamborghini was parked right there, engine running. In the driver's seat was one of the sketchy potential muggers that we'd seen when we drove up. I stumbled to a stop, but Hattie and Vinnie charged right up to the still-intact Lamborghini.

Vinnie carefully set Hattie down, and she yanked open the door. "Thanks for watching it! Come by the café anytime to collect your free dessert!"

Free dessert? That was how she bribed scary gang members? With *dessert?*

I needed to try her dessert.

"Awesome!" The six-foot-six street urchin unfolded his body from the front seat, and I was pretty sure I saw the bulge of a gun beneath his arm. "I'll be by with some friends."

Some friends? Really? His friends were kind of terrifying...

"They have to pay. No free dessert for them. Just you." Hattie leapt into the driver's seat. "Let's go, ladies!"

Lucy dove into the backseat, but I paused. "Esther entrusted me with the car. I don't think I should let you drive—"

Hattie hit the gas and shot forward twenty feet, then screeched to a stop.

Vinnie grinned at me from across the alley, where he was flanked by his pals. "I think you better get in or she's leaving without you."

"You think?" Honestly. Give a woman seven decades under her belt, and she thinks she can get away with anything. I ran up to the car, opened the passenger door, but then a sudden thought occurred to me.

I spun around and waved to the gang members. "Did you guys see a rich lady leave here?"

They grinned. "Yep."

"Where did she go?" I ignored Hattie revving the engine impatiently.

"Well, she had a little trouble leaving. Her car wasn't where she'd left it."

Of course it wasn't. It suddenly made me very glad that Hattie had gone back out to protect our very tempting vehicle. "So, how did she get home? Did she call for a ride?"

One of them shook his head. "That guy who lives in the building gave her a ride."

Felix. Kate had left with Felix. "Did you overhear them say where they were going?"

They all looked at each other, and then shrugged. "What's it to you?"

"Bribery? You want me to bribe you?"

They shrugged again.

Hattie rolled down the window and leaned out. "Lunch. Whoever offers info, gets lunch at my café."

They all started talking over each other immediately, making it impossible to sort out who was saying what. Hattie and Lucy got out of the SUV, and Vinnie came over, and between the four of us, we started to piece together what had happened.

Kate had come sprinting out the front door, looking panicked. She'd freaked out when her car hadn't been in front (apparently already relocated by the time we'd arrived, which was why we hadn't seen it). She'd called someone for a ride, getting more and more panicked when Vinnie's friends had approached her for some "friendly chatting."

Apparently, she had offered her engagement ring and the contents of her purse if they wouldn't kill her, which all of Vinnie's friends had been very offended by. They weren't murderers, apparently. Who knew?

Then Felix had come running out after her, heading toward his truck, which was parked safely on a side street.

Kate had begged for a ride. He'd resisted, then she'd won him over, and they raced off, driving off at a high speed.

Vinnie's pal, who claimed to be named Francis, said that Felix had said he had to make a stop before taking Kate back to her house. "Where was the stop?" I asked.

No one knew.

"Where is her car?"

No one knew that either.

I wanted to search her car. "Hattie will give lunch for a week to anyone who brings her the car, with all the contents intact."

"A week?" Hattie put her hands on her hips. "No way. That devalues my brand so much. Seven lunches for one car?"

"Hattie. You're going to go to prison for *murder*. I think that's worth lunch."

"Murder?" Vinnie looked horrified. "Who would accuse you of murder?"

"The police." Hattie rolled her eyes.

"Want us to take them out?"

"What?" I stepped in between them. "No one goes after the police. Honestly. Just free lunches for a week for whoever brings the car to her café. Hattie's Café—"

"No. Bring it to my house. Less visibility there." She rattled off her address—

"That's where Felix said he was going," Francis said. "I remember that address."

We all stared at him. "He's going to *my house*?" Hattie asked.

"Esther and Beau are there," I said, alarm rising fast and furious.

"We gotta go!" I blew kisses to the gang. "Thank you!"

We all raced for the SUV, and Hattie gave me a murderous glare when I reached for the driver's door. Did I want to risk her wrath or Esther's? Um…I decided to head for the passenger door. Hattie scared me more.

I hadn't even gotten the door shut before Hattie hit the gas and took off, almost sideswiping the gang of hoodlums who'd been so helpful.

Instead of pulling out their guns, they all cheered and raised their fists in support of her.

I looked over at her as she hit the road. "You're like a siren call when it comes to men."

"I know. It's a blessing and a curse." She grinned. "Just kidding. It's not a curse. Call Esther and Beau. Tell them that Felix is on the way."

I reached for my phone, and then swore. "Felix took our phones."

"Oh, for heaven's sake. That's so pathetic. Use mine." She

tossed me her phone and I tried them both, but they didn't answer.

I texted them both, but no reply. "How long did it take us to get free? Do you think they had time to get to your house already?"

Fear was mounting fast and furious. Not for me. For the two feisty seniors who I'd sent into danger. If anything happened to them…

At that moment, Hattie's phone rang. It was Beau. Relieved, I answered it. "Beau! It's Mia! Did you get my text—"

"Listen to me. Do as I say."

I froze, my gut going cold at the tension in his voice. "What's wrong?"

"We found something at Hattie's. Meet us here."

"But Felix and Kate—"

"Come straight here. Don't call the cops."

I frowned. Beau's tone was definitely off. "What's going on? Can you talk?" Was someone already there with them?

"Make sure to use the back door by the paint. The same one you picked the lock on the other day. Don't be late." He hung up abruptly, and I sat back, tapping the phone against my chin.

"What did he say?"

I filled them in, and Hattie frowned. "When did you pick the lock on my backdoor?"

"I didn't. The only back door I've picked the lock on is the chapel on Church Island—" I stopped, staring at them. "He's not at your house. He's on Church Island, and he's in trouble."

"Church Island?"

"He mentioned the paints. He has to be talking about the chapel." The fact that his words told us to go to Hattie's meant that we definitely didn't want to go there. Whatever was happening there wasn't what we wanted to deal with. "We're going to Church Island."

"How?" Lucy said. "I don't have a boat, and Hattie's is at her house."

I didn't want to say this. I really didn't. But if Beau and Esther were in danger... "Hattie? Tell me you know a boat we can borrow."

She grinned. "I know a boat we can borrow."

Ten minutes later, I discovered the boat in question was Devlin's Lake Police boat, sitting happily by itself at the town dock. We stood on the dock staring at it. "You want us to steal a police boat?"

"I do," Hattie said cheerfully. "Don't you?"

"I do," Lucy said. "Definitely. Don't you, Mia?"

"Absolutely, unequivocally not."

Two minutes later, we were heading out onto the lake in a stolen police boat to rescue two senior citizens from the site of a recent arson incident.

I was pretty sure that nothing could go wrong.

Especially since we still didn't know who the murderer was. Felix? Likely. Could he have already made it to Hattie's and kidnapped Esther and Beau? Unlikely. But not impossible.

But someone had Beau, and maybe Esther.

And that same someone wanted us to go to Hattie's.

Which meant we definitely weren't.

CHAPTER 27

THE SHADOWS WERE long and heavy as we approached the island. The lake was still, like a mirror, reflecting the glorious pinks and oranges of the setting sun, and the pine trees that lined the lake.

It might be the most beautiful sunset I'd ever seen.

But the minute I saw a boat tied to the main dock, it didn't matter. "Whose boat is that?" I scanned the dock, desperate to see Beau and Esther kicking back in Adirondack chairs with margaritas.

But the dock was empty.

There were no body parts, though, so that gave me hope.

"I don't know," Hattie said. "It's a nice boat, though. I'd steal it."

"I don't know who it belongs to either," Lucy said. "If it was a street address in town, I could tell you who lives there, but I don't know the boats."

I bit my lip as Hattie gave the island a wide berth, scanning the woods to see if I could see anything. "Can you get closer?"

"If I do, they'll realize Devlin's not driving." Hattie opened the glove box and handed out binoculars. "See what you can see."

Lucy and I both raised the binoculars and scanned the shadowing island as Hattie stayed far enough away for us not to be identifiable. "I feel like a creepy neighbor," I said as I scanned the trees.

"Definitely. What if it's a skinny-dipping party of old men?"

I looked over at Lucy. "Really? That's where your mind goes?"

"Old men are sexy beasts," Hattie said. "Don't knock it till you've tried it."

"You date men thirty years younger than you."

"And older ones. It's about their soul, not their body. Do you see anything?"

I was just about to say no, when I saw a flipflop on the dock. I zoomed in on it, and my gut sank when I saw a rainbow-striped flipflop with a monogram on the side. "Guys. One of Beau's flipflops is on the dock." That man was smart. No wonder he was a mystery writer. "He left it there to tell us that's where he is."

"Well, then. We gotta go save them." Hattie hit the gas, swinging wide around the island. "I'll go through the back entrance. Since they're docked in front, it's probably safe to assume they don't know about the model's access channel."

I listened to the low chugging of our engine. "They'll still hear the boat. The lake is completely still." There was no storm to hide our approach this time. I was getting so worried for Beau and Esther that I could barely handle it. "Can you pull up close to shore? I'll jump off. You drive the boat away. They'll think they're in the clear."

Hattie raised her brows. "There are no car thieves to win over here. We'll all go—"

"They need to hear the boat leave," I said.

"So, we'll set it free." Hattie began to drive closer to shore.

"You're going to set Devlin's boat loose on the lake? He'll kill us."

"And then we'll be stranded," Lucy said.

"They have a boat. We'll get off." Hattie pulled up to shore. "Get out, ladies. My friend is on that island, and we're going to go get her."

I shook my head. "After I get out, I need you to circle around on the front of the lake. Make noise. They'll be paying attention to lake police, and not the women tromping through their bushes."

Hattie folded her arms over her chest. "No. I'm coming."

I raised my brows. "Hattie. One of the basic tenets of pickpocketing and con artistry is distraction. Give them something else to pay attention to, and they won't notice what you don't want them to see. We need you to do this."

"I'll do it." Lucy moved over to take the wheel. "I'll anchor in front and then swim in. You guys get started."

"Awesome." Hattie slung her nail gun over her shoulder, vaulted out of the boat and landed thigh deep in water. "Let's go." She didn't even wait for me. She simply scrambled up the rock and then disappeared through the bushes.

I swore under my breath and quickly jumped out of the boat. "Lucy—"

"Go! I got this!" She gave me a quick wave, then eased away from shore, keeping the engine slow enough that it was difficult to hear.

I didn't have time to wonder about the wisdom of chasing a reckless senior into vegetation to possibly confront a murderer. There was no way I was letting Hattie get killed. So, I followed her up the rock and sprinted into the bushes.

I caught up to her within a few yards. Just as I touched her shoulder, we heard the roar of Devlin's boat, and I knew Lucy had hit the gas as a distraction.

"This way," Hattie said. "The chapel might be burned, but the only place with a clearing is where the pews are. We'll go in the front—"

"No." I thought about Beau's call. "We're going in the back of the chapel. Through that door I exited."

Hattie frowned. "The chapel burned down."

"It's stone. It didn't burn down. We're starting where Beau sent us." I wrapped the cord of my hairdryer around my hand.

Hattie frowned at me, clearly trying to intimidate me into being her mindless servant.

Too bad for her I'd stared into the jaws of death enough times that her glare didn't bother me.

Instead of crumbling in terror, I gave her my best Griselda stare, though I had little hope of convincing Hattie to do anything.

But to my surprise, she grinned. "That was an admirable glare. You win, but only because I admire that chutzpa of refusing to do my bidding. Women stepping into their power is always cause for celebration." She patted me on the shoulder. "Nice work, little protégé."

I grinned. "So, we're going in the back?"

"Nope. But I'm not going to kill you, so take that as a win. Let's go." She started off again, but I didn't move.

"Beau used code to get us here, and then left his flipflop on the dock," I pointed out. "He has made bazillions of dollars masterminding mysteries. He might be good at it."

She paused to look at me. "The flipflop was clever," she acknowledged. "I'll give him that."

"So?"

She narrowed her eyes at me.

I narrowed them right back at her.

"What do *you* think?" she finally asked. "Not, what did Beau tell you to do. You have a lifetime of experience in breaking and entering, sneaking around, and thinking like a criminal. So, what does your gut tell you?"

Being called a criminal usually felt slightly judgy and offensive, but the way Hattie had framed it actually made me feel proud of who I was. I would love her forever for that.

She gestured impatiently. "Well?"

The back door. The answer popped into my head immediately, and I knew it was right. My mom had trained me to trust my gut, so I did. "The back door."

Hattie sighed. "You're sure?"

"Absolutely."

Her eyes lit up. "I love that confidence. Let's do it." She held up her hand. "Silence from here on out."

I nodded, and readied my hairdryer.

She wrapped the cord of her nail gun around her hand again, gave me a wink, and headed off in a different direction.

It took us fifteen minutes of trekking in the dimming light before Hattie finally held up her hand. She pointed ahead. I scooted up next to her and peered through the bushes.

She'd brought us directly behind the chapel. The stone walls were still standing, and they completely blocked our sight line to the area in front. The door I'd exited was only a few feet away, also still intact.

I bit my lip. A good thief always knew their surroundings. I should take a moment to sneak around, but my gut was telling me to go straight in that door. "Wait here," I whispered as I stepped out into the clearing.

"No chance of that." Hattie was right behind me, so close I could feel her breath on the back of my neck. "Let's take these sumbitches down, girl."

Trying not to laugh, I waved my hand to tell her to zip it, then I tried the door.

It was locked.

Yay for me!

I pulled out my tools, and quickly got to work while Hattie stood guard. Since I'd done the door before, it was much easier. In less than two seconds, I heard a click. Triumph rushed through me, and I eased the door open, peering through the crack to make sure there was no one aiming a gun at my pretty little face.

It was dark in the chapel, and it smelled of ashes and carnage. I eased the door open and slipped inside. It was a charred disaster zone, but the stone walls and the metal roof were still intact. Most of the stained-glass windows had blown out, and almost everything inside was burned up.

What I didn't see was a famous mystery writer and a rich eccentric senior citizen, or anyone else. "Hattie—"

The door behind me slammed shut, putting me into dim, creepy darkness.

I immediately stepped to the door to open it back up, but it had locked again. "Hat—" I cut myself off when I heard a man's voice outside the door.

Fear shot through me, and I leaned against the door, listening. I could hear Hattie's voice and the man's, but I couldn't hear what they were saying. Was Hattie in trouble? Had she kicked the door shut so he wouldn't know I was inside?

My heart started racing. Should I unlock the door and jump out to rescue her? Or had Hattie kicked it shut for a reason? The wrong decision could get her killed, but I had no idea what to do.

I heard their voices moving away, and I ran along the inside wall of the chapel, trying to track them. They went by the shattered window, and I heard her call the guy an idiot and delusional, neither of which gave me helpful info on how to handle the situation—

I tripped on something, and fell on my face, making a loud clatter.

Hattie started yelling about abducting senior citizens, clearly trying to drown out my clumsiness as I scrambled to my feet. He told her to shut up. She yelled louder and then suddenly, there was a thud, and silence.

Oh, dear God. Had he killed her? There was no way Hattie would have gone silent if she'd been able to talk, not when she was trying to protect me.

Fear gripped my throat as the silence stretched on.

Somehow, he'd silenced Hattie, and he was waiting to hear me move.

I pressed my back against the wall, my heart pounding so freaking loudly that I wouldn't have been able to hear him if he were sneaking up to the wall—

A light suddenly flashed above me.

A man was leaning in the window, shining a flashlight around the interior of the chapel. It was dark, but the light reflected just enough illumination onto him that his face glowed faintly.

Enough that I recognized him.

It was Victor, Kate's movie-making fiancé.

Holy crap. What was he doing here? Frantically, my mind went over everything that had happened, trying to figure out how he played into things, but then his flashlight brushed over the metal pail I'd tripped on, and I pressed myself tighter against the wall.

I was literally right below him. All I had to do was reach up and I could grab his flashlight…which would leave me trapped in the chapel with a possible murderer on the outside with three people I cared about.

I tightened my grip on the cord of the hairdryer, but I didn't have the room or the angle to swing it.

All I could do was hope he didn't look straight down. People usually didn't. But people also didn't usually murder celebrity portrait artists and ghost whisperers, so predictability wasn't necessarily my friend at this moment.

He took his time, and during the entire, arduous wait, there was no sound from outside indicating Hattie was alive. Sudden emotion tried to clog my throat, but I fought it off. I didn't have time to worry if she was okay. I had to focus. I had to figure out how to turn this around.

The light went off and he retreated from the window, but I didn't hear footsteps.

He was certain I was in there, and he was waiting for me to make a move. God, was he like the world's most patient murderer? This was so freaking annoying!

I leaned my head against the wall and tried to think.

There was a lot I didn't know, but what info *did* I have?

I knew Victor was hiding outside, instead of vaulting through the window to hunt me down. So, he was a little wimpy or non-confrontational. I also knew he was willing to do something to Hattie to shut her up. So, a wimpy, abhorrent human being with no ethical boundaries.

I quickly glanced around, searching for what I could use. There was a paint can by my foot, so I slowly slid down the wall and picked it up, gripping tightly to keep it from dropping.

Then I inched myself to the right until I was no longer directly below the window.

Holding my breath, I slid my back upward along the wall until I was standing up, the paint can in my left hand, and the hairdryer in my right. My shoulders were just above the sill, so I would be almost even with him if he leaned in again.

I itched to look out the window and see what I was dealing with, but I couldn't risk being spotted.

So, instead, I wrapped the cord of the hairdryer tightly around my hand, checked the length of the cord to make sure it was what it needed to be, swung it to make sure it was solid, then positioned my body and arm for maximum rotation.

Was I an idiot for thinking this could possibly work twice?

Probably, but I refused to think negatively.

This was going to go swimmingly well.

Right? Of course right.

But my heart was still pounding as I raised the paint can, gave it a good luck kiss, then hurled it across the chapel. It landed with a clatter.

Instantly, Victor popped up with a cackle of glee, pointing his flashlight into the chapel.

At that moment, I uncorked my body and swung that hairdryer as hard as I could.

To my delight, I got him right in the face. He swore and dropped the flashlight. I immediately launched myself at the window, scrambling up the wall as he staggered away from the building, holding his face and cursing.

I leapt off the ledge and tackled him.

I wasn't big, but he was already off balance and too pretty for battle, so he hit the dirt when I landed on him.

I yanked his hands behind his back, tied his wrists and ankles with some nearby nautical ropes, and then leapt to my feet. Hattie was face-down on the ground, not moving.

My heart dropped. "Hattie!" I lunged for her, and dropped to my knees beside her, and touched her shoulder. "Hattie?"

CHAPTER 28

"Mɪᴀ!" Hattie shot to her feet, and I screamed, stumbling backward. "Nice work!"

I stared at her, fear clogging my throat. "You're okay?"

"Well, yes." As she spoke, I saw a trickle of blood on her forehead. "I mean, he did knock me out for a second, but I stayed down until it was safe. Nice work!"

"He *hit* you?" What a turd! Suddenly, I didn't feel at all bad about messing up his pretty face.

"I'll be fine." Behind her, Victor was groaning, which was quite satisfying, given the trickle of blood on Hattie's forehead. "Did you find Esther and Beau yet?"

I shook my head, holding up one finger to indicate we needed to be quiet. We treated Victor to a gag to keep him quiet, then I led the way around the corner of the chapel. I peered around the corner, and my heart nearly stopped when I saw Beau and Esther tied up in the front pew.

Kate was standing in front of them, aiming a gun at them.

Anger tore through me, but before I could race out there screaming, Hattie grabbed my wrist and yanked me back. I spun to face her, and then saw the fear in her eyes.

At the sight of Hattie being worried, all my fear vanished,

replaced by that awesome feeling that I was in complete control. It was the best state of mind to be in when running a con, so I was all in on the confidence train right now.

I glanced back at Victor, who was still down.

"I need an outlet," Hattie whispered, holding up her nail gun. "I need to plug into his generator and turn it on."

I blinked. "You are not shooting Kate with nails."

"Well, you wouldn't let me bring a gun, so nails are all I have."

"It's not all we have." I bit my lip, frantically thinking. "We have our brains."

"Brains? *Brains?* I love you, Mia, but there is a time for brains, and there is a time for shooting nails at brides, and this is the time for the latter."

"No, it's not." I frantically thought through everything I knew, everything I'd found out, every clue I must have missed. Why had they burned the chapel? To hide evidence? Of what? *Blackmail.* I suddenly remembered the filing cabinet that I hadn't taken the time to unlock.

That was why Beau had told me to go into the chapel. "We gotta go!"

I whirled around and sprinted down the side of the chapel, Hattie right behind me, which showed me exactly how fast of a runner I was (not). I needed to work on that. Later.

Hattie boosted me in the window, and I jumped down, shining Victor's flashlight around. There! I saw the filing cabinet in the corner.

I ran across the chapel, dodging carnage, and then went down on my knees in front of the filing cabinet. The metal was fairly untouched by the fire, in an area of the chapel that hadn't been hit too hard. I made quick work of the lock and opened the drawer as Hattie came up behind me.

Inside were file folders, lined up neatly.

The top one had Hattie's name on it. "Oh! Me!" She grabbed it and opened it.

I averted my gaze, figuring that it was more naked

photographs of her that I didn't need to see, but her surprised gasp got me looking at her in a hurry. "What?"

"My recipes." She held out the file. "Rutherford has all sorts of notes about them. I remember him asking me about them, but I didn't realize…" She went quiet as she read through the files. "What a pig," she said. "He wrote down everything we talked about while he was painting me. Even—" She suddenly closed the folder and stuck it down the front of her shirt. "Never mind."

"What?"

She glanced at me. "Let's just say that if the cops found that folder and believed he was blackmailing me for what's in there, they might believe I'd killed him."

I stared at her. "What did you do?"

"You don't get to know, but what you do get to know is that I didn't kill him, so let's look at the other folders." She grabbed another one, but I sorted more methodically through them, looking for Kate and Victor's.

I found one for Felix and one for Victor.

I opened Victor's and scanned it. I was expecting to see evidence of the affair that we'd been hearing about, but that wasn't it. That wasn't it at all. "Oh, wow."

"What?"

I showed Hattie and her eyes widened, then she started laughing. "No way. Victor's broke from investing in Felix's cupcake business? Kate is literally marrying him for his money. And he has none? Because of cupcakes? Oh, God. That's so funny. This is why women need to be empowered. Earn your own money, Mia. Never count on a guy." She grabbed the folder and started reading it.

"Already learned that one, thanks." I opened the folder with Felix's name on it and scanned it. "Check this out. Felix used to be a celebrity chef in LA, and he was fired for stealing from his clients." I paused. "He was renting a room from her. That's why they were living together."

"He was subletting from her?"

"Yep. He used to live here, so he moved back to get a fresh start. She needed help with rent and he needed a place to stay. Rutherford was blackmailing him because someone died while Felix was out there, and Rutherford had evidence that Felix was involved—" I looked up at Hattie sharply. "He's murdered before!"

"Gotta watch those kinds of folks. One death, then another, and it just becomes too much fun to stop." Hattie flipped a page in Victor's file. "Oh…it looks like Felix and Victor knew each other. He was stealing scripts for Victor." She looked up. "This Hollywood biz is so cutthroat. Why can't people just create their own stuff?"

"Right?" I handed her Felix's file. "Take pictures of all the pages and text them to Devlin."

She took the folder. "What are you doing to do?"

"I'm going to go keep Kate from shooting Beau and Esther."

She scowled. "That sounds fun. I want to come."

"You need to get the files to Devlin. Without them, we have nothing. Come out when you're done."

"Fine, but I still think you get all the fun."

"You got to drive the Lamborghini home and make friends with gang members."

She brightened. "Right. I did. Okay, fine, you can go throw yourself in front of a bullet to save them." She began laying the sheets out on the floor. "Bye."

I blinked. Throw myself in front of a bullet? I sincerely hoped that was not the only option.

She waved her hand at me. "Go sacrifice yourself. Best of luck."

"I'm not going to sacrifice myself. I'm going to be a hero."

She raised her brows. "I thought you didn't want to be a hero."

"It's better than being shot."

"Good point. Now go."

Leaving Hattie with the flashlight, I made my way across the chapel, and let myself out the locked door, so that Victor wouldn't see me come out. I left the door open for Hattie so she wouldn't have to climb out the window. This time, I went around the other side, so I came up behind Kate. She would have to turn to face me, turning her back on Esther and Beau.

I took a breath to steady myself. I was about to get a crazy woman to point a gun at me. This was everything I'd dreamed of. Two crazy women aiming guns at me in less than a month. A girl's life goals right there.

I saw Beau's gaze flick toward me, but he immediately looked away, which I appreciated.

Esther, on the other hand, noticed me, and her eyebrows shot up. Relief rushed over her face, and she beamed at me.

Kate, of course, immediately started to turn around to see what had made Esther so happy, so I quickly leaned against a nearby tree and folded my arm across my chest, trying to look as chill and unconcerned as was humanly possible.

Kate saw me, and she spun around to point the gun at me. "You're here? You're supposed to be at Hattie's house."

Behind her, I saw Beau immediately jump to his feet and head for the woods.

Esther's eyes widened, and then she jumped up and began to hop after him. Who duct tapes the ankles of senior citizens? Honestly, that was such overkill.

"I'm notoriously unhelpful when it comes to things like that," I told Kate. "Who was waiting for me at the house?" I'd spent my childhood learning how to evaluate people, and I was pretty sure Kate wasn't a killer. She wouldn't pull that trigger.

On purpose.

By accident? A definite possibility.

Plus, where was Felix? I needed to get Kate on my side, and fast, in case he showed up.

Her eyes narrowed and she blatantly ignored my question. "Get over to the pew."

She started to turn toward the bench Beau and Esther had vacated. They were still in sight, hopping toward the main dock, so I quickly moved away from the tree and pulled out my hairdryer, getting her attention to snap back to me. "Why did you want me to go to Hattie's?"

"Why do you have a hairdryer?" she retorted, apparently trying to prove she could be as unhelpful as me. It was like a contest of the gods.

"It's not a hairdryer. It's a gun that shoots poison bullets. The FBI gave it to me when I was undercover, in case my drug lord hubs tried to kill me." I swung it back and forth, grinning as her gaze kept flicking toward it.

People were attracted to motion, and I was giving it to her.

"That's a hairdryer." But she sounded about one or two percent unsure if she was right.

Time to sow her seeds of doubt. I caught it mid-swing and pointed it at her. "It worked on an assassin who broke into my safe house. They carried him out on a stretcher. But who knows? Maybe it doesn't work anymore. Should we try?" As always, I kept with enough truth that my words resonated with honesty and believability.

She looked torn between mocking me and running for her life. "Victor!" she shouted.

I smiled. "He's not available to help you." Fear-based sweat was dripping down my back, but I kept my voice calm.

Alarm shot across her face. "What did you do to him? Victor!"

Again, her chap didn't respond. God, that was handy. "I used my hairdryer on him," I said truthfully.

"Victor!" She pretty much screeched his name, but again, there was no reply. I imagined him worm-crawling across the dirt, trying to rush to the aid of his lovely bride. Such a romantic fellow. She was so lucky.

"You're about to marry a bad man," I said conversationally. "You know that, don't you?"

Her face paled. "He didn't do anything—"

"I married a bad man. It didn't work out well for any of us.

They drag you down into their hell and leave you there to burn for their crimes."

She stared at me. "Victor is innocent. He didn't do anything."

I grinned cheerfully. "Here's the thing, Kate. You're already up for attempted murder for leaving me and Lucy tied up and setting the place on fire—"

"On fire?" She blinked. "I didn't set anything on fire."

"Did you notice the flames?"

Her gaze shifted. "Maybe."

"You left me and Lucy duct-taped in a burning apartment. That's attempted murder, and you were a part of it." I shrugged. "The only way to get out of the charge of attempted murder is to actively attempt to reverse the crime." That was true, but didn't quite apply here, since the attempted murder was already over, but I was going for the bigger picture of quality human beings living past today.

Her mouth dropped open. "I didn't—"

"I saw Rutherford's files. I know Victor is broke and paid Felix to steal scripts for him in L.A. You needed the money, so you killed your own dear brother to get the inheritance."

She blinked. "I didn't kill him."

"No? Did Felix then? The three of you working together?" Behind her, I saw Lucy emerge from the woods. She was dripping wet as she started helping Beau and Esther get the duct tape off.

"No. We didn't kill him." The gun lowered slightly. "Victor's a good man. He didn't ask Felix to steal scripts. That would never work. Felix just—"

"Felix did what, sweetheart?"

We both spun around to see Felix walking through the pews, aiming a gun at us. Yep, so it probably had been Felix waiting for us at Hattie's. I was glad we'd missed out on his trap.

His ruthless gaze suggested that, unlike Kate, he was fully prepared to shoot us both. Lucy, Esther, and Beau were out of sight, which was fantastic, but that gun in his hand was definitely not good news.

He nodded at me. "Thanks for taking care of Victor. Well done."

Kate glared at me. "You're such a rude woman. What did he ever do to you?"

"You're yelling at *me?* There's literally a man standing here aiming a gun at us!"

"He's not going to shoot me. He needs money from me. Money always wins, Mia. It can buy you anything. You don't have money, so guess what? He'll shoot you and set you up for Rutherford and Glory's death."

"Me? Why would I do it?"

"Hey!" Felix shouted. "I didn't kill Rutherford. He was working for me. He was collecting the recipes from Hattie so I could up my game and get hired back to L.A. I needed him alive."

Yeah, I'd already figured out that one. "He didn't try to blackmail you back?"

"No. He wanted my money. I wanted the recipes. We were a good team."

If that was the case, then who the heck killed Rutherford? I had seen all the recipes in Rutherford's file, and at Felix's house, so I knew that much was true. I waved my hand at Kate and the burned-out chapel. "This is just about food?"

"People have to eat every single day, and they want food that tastes good. Food is all about money," he said. "All about money."

"Victor and I were investing in Felix's business," Kate said. "He's right. Food is money."

That's what Hattie had said. "Cinnamon bun recipes?"

Felix nodded. "Worth millions right there."

Well, damn. My mom and I had been stealing the wrong things all these years. Who knew we were supposed to kneecap the caterers, not swipe the guests' jewelry? All that wasted time. If I ever spoke to my mom again, we could have a good laugh over that one. "So, neither of you murdered Rutherford?" I watched them closely as they answered, trying to look for truth and lies.

"I needed his help," Felix said. "I came here to search the chapel for the recipes. He said he'd collected a lot already."

I put my hands on my hips. "Kate?"

She shrugged. "I'm not mourning his death, but he was giving me money, so alive was better. He was going in on the restaurant as well. We needed his money." She looked annoyed. "It was pretty rude of him to die, honestly."

Yes, very rude. Murder victims were so thoughtless sometimes. Unfortunately, I believed them both. I could be wrong, but I was a great liar, and I could tell when people were lying. But that didn't mean I was giving up. "What about the attempted murder of me and Lucy when you burned down the apartment?"

Kate held up her hands. "That wasn't me. The apartment was fine when I walked out. Nothing was on fire."

Felix frowned at me. "On fire?"

Honestly. Did no one look up at the building they'd just been in once they got outside to see if the people they'd locked in a bathroom were about to be incinerated? I felt like that should be protocol from here on out. "The apartment. It was on fire when Lucy and I were trapped in the bathroom. Attempted murder."

"Murder?" He stared at me in alarm, then suddenly dropped the gun. "I didn't try to kill you." He put his hands in the air. "I'm not a murderer. Kate, drop the gun."

She immediately did the same and held up her hands. "We didn't try to kill you," she repeated. "Swear."

Huh. Okay. So apparently, I'd completely misjudged the situation when I'd decided he was ready to shoot me. The PTSD might be having its wooly way with me, interfering with my excellent people-reading skills when a gun was pointed at me.

I needed to work on that.

They both looked ridiculous with their hands in the air while I was holding them at gunpoint with a hairdryer, but I decided to take advantage of their apparent panic over being called murderers. "What about the fire on this island?" I took a chance. "Felix, I know you were with Glory that night. She admitted it." Well, not really, but I figured I was good with that guess.

Felix shook his head. "I was with her, but we didn't set it. I swear. It blew up after we were out."

I frowned. "Who else was with you?"

He shook his head. "No one. We did hear some movement in the corner behind a wrapped-up painting, though. We thought it was a raccoon, but after the church blew up when we left, we figured maybe it had been an arsonist," he said. "If you find who was behind that painting, you'll find the arsonist."

Yeah, okay, moving on from that quickly. "Maybe the third person wasn't behind the painting. Why did you steal Glory's painting?"

"To protect her," Felix said. "She texted me in a panic when they found his body. I met her on shore, and we took off for the island. She didn't want to get accused of murdering Rutherford." He sighed. "She was a good kid. I can't believe she got killed."

He wasn't exactly devastated over Glory's death, but his regret was real.

Kate waved her arms. "Look, we just wanted to open a celebrity restaurant in LA. We were going to call it Kate's."

This had to be about more than food. It didn't make sense. People were *dead*. I stared at the two of them with their guns on the ground and their hands in the air. "Why did you want us to go to Hattie's? You weren't going to kill us?"

"Kill you?" Felix looked horrified. "We were going to make Hattie hand over all her recipes if she wanted to see Beau and Esther again. I couldn't find a bunch of them at her kitchen, so I knew she had them at the house."

"Her kitchen?" I suddenly noticed the bandage on his forearm. "Wait a sec. What happened to your arm?"

He got a guilty look on his face. "A bob cat attacked me."

"When you were hiding under my deck on Friday night? Stealing recipes?"

His gaze shifted. "I don't know what you're talking about."

King Tut had definitely attacked him under the deck. It hadn't been an assassin. It had been Felix trying to steal Hattie's recipes. Honestly, this felt like such overkill. Recipes? Really? "Did you trash her kitchen to hide that you'd stolen the recipes when you went back a second time?"

He frowned. "I didn't go back a second time. I got what I wanted the first time. Wasn't going to go take on that cat again."

I frowned. "You didn't write murderer all over the wall? That was pretty aggressive."

He looked slightly appalled. "I'd never deface a kitchen. Kitchens are sacred."

"Why did you decide to set her up for murder?"

He brightened. "I didn't do that, but that was really great. To have her in jail meant free access to her recipes. I think it was a sign from the universe that it wants me to be a successful chef."

"No one wants you to be a successful chef!" Hattie strode up behind him. "You can't steal your way to success! Get a little bit of skill and you could do it." She was holding her nail gun like she knew how to use it.

"Hattie, don't—"

She swung the nail gun, and Felix ducked just in time to avoid having his face smashed in. "Hey!" He held up his hands. "Look, I'm sorry, but you wouldn't share them—"

She swung again, and this time, she clipped his shoulder. "You're such a rude, little man! How dare you steal from a sweet, old lady like me!"

He ducked and spun around, only to get hit in the face by Esther with her tiny little fist.

He dropped instantly and didn't move.

I stared at Esther. "So much aggression in that little body, Esther."

She put her hands on her hips. "I clearly recall asking you to call me Rogue."

"Rogue it is." Yeesh. I wasn't taking the chance of having that fist aimed in my direction.

Beau and Lucy came running out of the bushes. "Esther got away," Lucy said. "I tried to get her in the boat, but she wanted to save you."

Beau started grinning at the sight of Felix on the ground. "I always found that man to be rude."

"And not talented," Hattie said.

At that moment, Kate took off running for the main dock. Lucy and I looked at each other, then we both sprinted after her.

Ten minutes later, we had all three of them tied up, the folders laid out, and Officer Stevens on his way to book them for such fun things as robbery and assault.

But not for murder. But if they hadn't done it, who had?

CHAPTER 29

"WHAT DID WE MISS?" I was sitting in the bow of Devlin's purloined boat, my feet up on the rail as we headed back to the Eagle's Nest.

Lucy, Hattie, and I had decided to leave before Officer Stevens showed up. We'd left him enough evidence, and Devlin was getting antsy about King Tut. Beau and Esther had agreed to stay and wait for Officer Stevens, since they were the ones who'd been abducted. Happily, Lucy and I had repossessed our phones from Felix, so we could now call for help the next time we were duct taped and locked in a bathroom.

"Well, one thing we missed out on, was that we forgot to cut off Felix's hands so he can never cook again," Hattie said as she drove the boat. "Total missed opportunity right there."

I looked back at her. "You're very cutthroat."

She grinned at me. "You gotta make an example of people who try to mess with you."

I knew she was kidding, but that struck too close to home with my ex, so I decided to pivot to a new and more cheerful topic. "I was talking about murder."

She shook her head. "I appreciate the sentiment, but I think murdering Felix is overkill."

"Really?" Lucy was rifling through Devlin's emergency gear, looking for a towel, since she was wet and cold from her swim. "That surprises me. I would have thought you'd be okay with killing over cinnamon buns."

"It does have its merits," Hattie agreed.

I turned around so I could face them. "You guys. This is serious. There's still a murderer running around town, and we don't know who it is."

"Yep," Hattie said. "But you'll figure it out."

"It's not like any of us are being murdered right now, so we have time." Lucy pulled out a blanket. "Perfect." She wrapped it around herself and sat down next to me. "I can't believe they kidnapped Esther and Beau to hold them hostage for all of Hattie's recipes."

"I would have sacrificed them both to save my recipes," Hattie said. "It was a dumb plan."

I'd seen the way Hattie had clung to Esther, and I knew she was lying. And the way she and Beau had looked at each other… "I think there's still a little flame with Beau," I said.

Hattie snorted. "Absolutely not. He's too cranky for me."

"He's not that cranky. He just likes to pretend he's cranky."

"Hattie and Beau?" Lucy shook her head. "Never."

"They dated once."

Lucy stared at me. "No way."

"He told me."

"That little shit," Hattie muttered. "I can't believe he told you."

Lucy and I grinned at each other. "She did give him a look once he was free," Lucy admitted.

"I saw that look too. He did the same thing to her."

Hattie growled. "There was no look."

"There were definitely looks—"

Hattie cut the engine, the boat settled to a sudden stop, and we both flew forward. I almost went over the bow and into the water, but caught the rail just in time. "Hey!"

Hattie smiled innocently. "Just helping you develop your

boating safety skills. You always have to be ready if the driver hits a rock. You don't want to be the one who flies over the bow, gets run over, and loses a leg, do you?"

I stared at her. "You're very alarming sometimes."

She brightened. "Thank you. That's the best compliment I've received all day." She leaned on the steering wheel. "What's the plan, ladies?" She nodded up ahead. "Lots of grumpy law enforcement testosterone up ahead."

I turned and saw that my marina had come into sight. The lights were on, and I could see Devlin's silhouette standing by my car. And even from here, I could see a large, feline silhouette on top of my car. The Seam Ripper chairs were still there, but they were empty now. I guess once Devlin and Griselda showed up, the Seam Rippers felt their duty was done.

"I don't think you should go, Hattie," Lucy said. "They'll arrest you again."

"No, they won't. I was released."

Lucy snorted. "Devlin made it sound like Officer Stevens wasn't supposed to release you. Mia and I will swim in."

"No, Hattie should turn herself in," I said. "If Hattie's in jail, then she has an alibi if there's another murder."

They both looked at me. "Another one? Who else is going to get killed?"

"I don't know, because I don't know what's going on." I hated that I had no idea what was up. I needed to know.

"We'll stay together," Lucy said. "We'll be your alibi about the drugs, and you and I will alibi Hattie."

"I agree," Hattie said. "We're in it to win it together."

I looked at my marina. As I watched, Devlin turned to look at the lake, then started down the ramp toward the dock. There was no way I was risking Hattie and Lucy just so they could be character witnesses in the event of me being arrested. "He sees his boat. You guys go to Hattie's."

Lucy raised her brows. "Are you sure?"

"Yes, get Hattie home. I'll deal with this, and meet you there as soon as I can. The cocaine in my car has nothing to do with Hattie, so I'll take care of it." I stood up and took off my sneakers. "Take the hairdryer with you. I don't want to swim with it."

Devlin shouted and gestured for us to come in.

"I gotta go." I sat on the edge of the boat, then glanced back at my friends. "Stay out of trouble, guys. Just for a little bit."

"You bet." Hattie blew me a kiss. "Thanks for everything."

"Any time." I waved at them both, then launched myself off the boat. The water was shockingly cold when I hit, but since I wasn't strapped to a dead guy or wearing heavy boots, it was a definite step up from my last dive into the water. Hattie tossed me a life jacket, then hit the gas and the boat shot away across the lake, leaving me swimming gracefully through the water.

Life jacket? I didn't need a life jacket.

But in case I had a sudden, deathly cramp, I looped my arm through the strap and swam briskly back toward shore.

For about three minutes, at which point I realized that swimming was actually a lot of work, and Esther's too-tight leather pants were definitely not meant for water.

Devlin folded his arms across his chest and glared at me as I did my best not to drown.

He did not offer to save me.

He just stood there watching me, with a long, red, four-clawed cat scratch on his forearm. *Good kitty.*

There was no way I was going to put on a life jacket to swim in a quiet lake with Devlin watching me, so I stubbornly kept swimming. I was still about twenty yards out when another man joined Devlin on the dock.

I recognized that overly confident, irritatingly controlling silhouette immediately, and a thin wiggle of fear shot through my belly. I paused, treading water. "Griselda."

"Mia." His voice was low and contained, showing me just how annoyed he was.

I wanted to be sassy and irreverent, but seeing Griselda

standing on my dock brought back all sorts of PTSD from my Stanley undercover time.

The two men were of similar height and build. Both of them muscled, fit, and had that relentless law-enforcement attitude. Griselda was wearing his suit, as usual, and Devlin was in his police uniform. They were standing shoulder to shoulder in almost identical stances, both of them looking annoyed with me.

"You guys look like clones." Oh, good. I still had the sass. Sounding rude and sassy was so much better than sounding alarmed and traumatized. What if it was cocaine in my car? Would I be in prison by the end of the day? Fear hammered at me, but I raised my chin, refusing to give in.

"You stole the cat," Griselda said. "I told you he wasn't your cat."

Now, that got me mad, which felt so much better than fear. You could mess with me, but my cat? My mama bear came to life with alarming ferocity. "Hey," I snapped, as I began to breaststroke toward them, keeping my head above water. "That cat chose me. He deserves to choose his own life, so don't even think about trying to take him."

Griselda's eyebrows shot up. "He's a demon."

"He's a sweetheart who has good taste." I tested to see if my feet could touch, and relaxed when my toes landed in the sandy bottom of the lake. Yay for not drowning! "If he doesn't like you, it's on you, and not him." I eyed Devlin as I began to wade toward the dock. "He used to like you. What did you do to him? Do I need to hunt you down for hurting an innocent cat?"

As I spoke, I looked over toward my car. Relief rushed through me when I saw King Tut sitting like a Roman statue on top of my car. He was watching me intently, his ear pricked as if he were basking in every word that fell from my lips. I waved at him. "Hey, sweetheart!"

He let out a yowl, then shot off the roof of the car so fast that Chief Stone screamed and dove out of the way.

King Tut sprinted down the ramp, darted right between my

stalkers, and shot out into the air, legs and claws extended as he soared toward me.

Oh, dear God. I was going to get ripped apart!

I shrieked and dove under water. King Tut landed with a splash right where I'd been. He dove straight down toward me. His paws were flared out as he swam. His ears were pinned tight against his head. Weirdly, his lips were pulled back slightly, making him look like he was a deranged lunatic grinning at me with his sharp teeth. His thick fur undulated around his head as he swam. He was terrifying, and at the same time, he was breathtaking beauty and grace. I held out my arms to him, and he swam right into them.

I hugged him and stood up, taking us about shoulder height out of the water. King Tut had his paws around my neck. He was kneading furiously, purring like a maniac. My throat literally tightened with emotion as I hugged his soggy, warm body to my chest. Total love and acceptance felt so good. I couldn't believe I'd gone my whole life until now without a King Tut.

Armed with feline love, I felt so much better, almost like my normal, confident self. I grinned at Devlin and Griselda. "Yes, clearly he is a demon. You're so right."

I kissed his adorably pink nose just to prove that I was in King Tut's inner circle. To my relief, he didn't decide to smack me down for being so bold. In fact, he actually lifted his face to mine and pressed his little nose against mine. It was the sweetest, most trusting little gesture he'd ever done, and suddenly, I knew I would give my life to keep him safe.

He was my baby, now and forever.

"I'm on it," Chief Stone yelled. "Keep the cat occupied!"

We all turned to see Chief Stone with his crowbar, heading for my car.

Griselda swore and took off in a sprint, shouting at Chief Stone to drop the crowbar. I watched him go. "It's amazing how agile Griselda is in those dress shoes," I commented. "I have to think it's not easy to navigate a wet boat ramp in those things."

"They have good soles." Devlin crouched down on the dock, so he was closer to eye level. "Did you steal my boat?" His voice was low and not all that affectionate. In fact, he sounded a little tense.

I waded over to the dock and smiled up at him. "I did not steal your boat."

"Did Hattie steal it?"

"Hattie? Who's Hattie?"

He swore under his breath. "Mia, I swear—"

"Did Officer Stevens call you?"

He blinked. "About what?"

"Wow. He decided to handle it on his own? That's a little worrying." That was the truth.

Devlin's eyes narrowed. "Handle *what*?"

"Abduction. Kidnapping. Blackmail. And possibly attempted murder of me and Lucy, but I'm thinking there was someone else involved."

He stared at me, then swore under his breath again. "You're not kidding."

"No, I'm not. Did you happen to call the mayor for me? The fundraiser is tomorrow."

The look of stunned disbelief on his face at my gall was almost comical. "The fundraiser? Really? Are you serious? I'm dealing with murders. What happened with Officer Stevens? What exactly is he handling?"

"That's a no, you didn't call the mayor? I'm so disappointed in you. This matters to me. You want to date me, but you won't even handle something that matters that much to me. Imagine what you'd be like once you already had the date? I can tell I would be deeply appreciated and pampered. You're every girl's dream, Dev." I was sure there were many girls who'd dream of a date with Devlin, because he was irritatingly attractive. But I'd already tried out the relationship where I wasn't treated well, so you know, been there, done that, time to try something else.

Like being single forever.

Still holding King Tut, I headed toward shore, trying to make it look like I was just copping an attitude, not avoiding showcasing my total lack of upper body strength by trying to pull myself up on the dock.

"Mia!" Devlin called after me. "What happened with Officer Stevens?"

"Nothing happened *with* him," I said as I waded through the water. "But three people kidnapped Esther and Beau and held them at gunpoint on Church Island. Lucy and I rescued them, and called it in. Officer Stevens is headed there now."

Devlin dropped an f-bomb, which was alarmingly attractive on him, and pulled out his phone as he sprinted down the boat ramp, clearly intending to corner me when I got to shore.

No way. I wasn't getting trapped by law enforcement, especially when my future was being discovered in the back of my car at this very moment. Just because Devlin was more concerned with local crimes than federal drug charges didn't mean I was going to miss out on the moment of discovery of the white powder.

I started running…well…sloshing awkwardly, because the water was still knee high. You know that awkward flail when trying to run through water? When you're lurching around, your feet are swinging out, and you're not even getting anywhere because it's freaking hard to run in water?

That was me. Princess Grace all the way.

Chief Stone and Griselda got my car door open. I needed to be there when they opened that metal box. I needed to know what I was dealing with. "King Tut! Guard the car!"

My feline beast leapt from my arms, landed in the water, and bounded toward shore with far more agility than I had, his tail flicking with pure delight as he sprinted up the shore with a terrifying yowl.

Chief Stone whipped around, screamed, and ran for his car.

Griselda put his hands on his hips and glared at King Tut.

Oh…I knew that stare. There was no way King Tut was going to withstand that—

But to my surprise, he blew right past Griselda, jumped into the back of my car, and sat down on the lockbox that they'd just uncovered. He crouched down, and let out a low, aggressive growl.

God, I loved that cat. He'd never let anyone arrest me. Why had I been so worried? We'd make a break for the Canadian border together. Feeling much more chipper, I reached shore and slowed to a walk as Devlin reached me.

I kept moving, and he fell in beside me. "Mia—"

I was actually a little mad at him for ignoring my fundraiser need. And arresting Hattie. And still being attractive. So, I ignored his attempt to engage me in discussion. "Griselda. I need you to call the mayor now and tell her to give me the fundraiser."

He turned to look at me as I approached. "When I spoke to her earlier, I asked her to let you host the fundraiser as a personal favor to me, because I owed you. She agreed."

I blinked. "Really? She didn't tell me that." Did that mean he now owed her a favor? He'd indebted himself to *her* on my behalf? Wow. I never would have expected that from him. Mr. Tough Guy actually had a heart?

He shrugged. "She said she'd call whoever she needed to call. It's done."

I suddenly felt like a huge weight had fallen from my shoulders. "Thank you," I said, meaning it.

He nodded. "You're welcome."

Our gazes met, and something passed between us. I wasn't sure exactly what it was. A shared history of my trauma? A bonding over our awesomeness? I didn't know, but it felt more personal than it should be. Than it had been. Some of the tension that had been gripping me since I'd found the white powder released. This was Griselda. He believed in me. It would be okay.

"You could have told me you spoke to the mayor, Hawk," Devlin said.

Griselda glanced at him. "She stole your boat?" There was an undercurrent of amusement. "You can't handle three civilian women? Really?"

Devlin raised his brows. "How many times did Mia steal your phone?"

Griselda grinned. "Many. You?"

"Only once."

"So far," I said. There was a weird undercurrent happening between my boys. I wasn't sure what it was.

"Is the cat locked up?" Chief Stone shouted from his car.

The two law enforcement irritants turned to inspect my car. My cat growled. "No," I called back. "Not yet."

"Get the cat, Mia," Griselda said. "Or I'll shoot him."

"You won't shoot him, but that was rude to say, and now he'll never be nice to you."

"The cat likes *me*," Devlin said.

"He liked you when you came back to save me, but now? I'm not so sure." I folded my arms over my chest. "If that is cocaine, am I going to jail?"

Devlin and Griselda exchanged a meaningful look that sent chills down my spine. "Is it yours?" Griselda asked.

The question made the chills grip my gut. If he even had to ask it, that meant I wasn't as scot-free as I'd thought. "No." I met his gaze. "I don't know where it came from or why it's in there."

He studied me.

I let him.

"Whose is it, then?"

Oh, *crap*. He was totally treating me like a possible criminal. I threw my hands up in the air. "Oh, for God's sake, Griselda. Seriously? You know it's not mine. Don't be an idiot. I am so done with you men. Come here, King Tut." I held out my arms, and the cat leapt into them. "And Devlin, you can forget the date. There's no chance."

Devlin held up his hands. "Hey, that discourse was all Hawk," he said. "Not me. I'm not taking the fall for him being an idiot."

"You're going on a date with her?" Griselda said. "I told you she was off limits."

I kept walking, but I totally turned my head just enough to be able to see what was going on with the boys.

Devlin shrugged. "I find her interesting."

"She *is* interesting. And she's off limits."

Wait, what? They both found me *interesting*? I wasn't sure if that was a compliment or not.

"Off limits for what, exactly?" Devlin asked.

I liked that question. Clever. Precise. Well done.

Griselda narrowed his eyes. "Off limits for anything personal."

"Romantic?" Devlin pushed. "Or personal in general? Like I can't talk to her unless it's about drugs? Or just that I can't ask her out on a date?"

Griselda stared at Devlin.

Devlin didn't look away.

Holy crap. They were having a stare down. Over me?

This was *awesome*.

"Mia is a key witness," Griselda said.

"Yep. I know that. But she's not *my* witness." Devlin's brows shot up. "Is that the problem? *You* want to date her, but it's against the rules?"

No. Freaking. Way. Griselda wanted to *date* me?

I didn't even pretend I wasn't listening anymore. I turned all the way around to watch them. I needed to see facial expressions and body language.

Griselda's facial expression went into complete lockdown. "Don't date her, Devlin."

"Do *you* want to date her?"

Did he? I leaned in. I'd never remotely thought of Griselda in romantic terms. I could, of course, see that from an objective standpoint, he was attractive. And we were sort of friends. But *romantic?*

Griselda's eyes narrowed. "Do *you*?" he shot back at Devlin.

Devlin's gaze flickered toward me, and I realized he'd been aware the whole time that I was listening. Of course he was aware. Griselda probably was, too. They were trained for that sort of hyper vigilance.

Without taking his gaze off me, Devlin answered Griselda's question. "I do want to date Mia," he said. "She's riveting."

Riveting. *Riveting.* I wasn't going to lie. That felt good, especially since Devlin knew about my past.

Griselda's stoic expression faltered. For a split second, I saw a hint of vulnerability on his face. Vulnerability? What the heck? He stared at Devlin for a long moment, then turned toward me.

"Mia."

I stood taller. "What?"

"Don't date Devlin."

When Devlin's eyes narrowed, I couldn't help but grin. "Why not?"

"Because I trust him with your life, but I don't trust him with your heart." Griselda's gaze was unyielding as he focused on me, ignoring Devlin's sudden scowl. "Dev and I go way back. We know each other and owe each other our lives. But don't date him. Just don't."

My gaze went to Devlin, who was strangely silent. He looked annoyed, but he didn't protest.

What the heck? Was Devlin not a good guy?

I lifted my chin. "What about you, Griselda? Is Devlin right? Do you want to date me? Because if you do, I have to take that into account in evaluating your orders not to date Devlin."

Griselda stared at me for a long time. I could see the muscle ticking in his jaw. Finally, without answering, he turned away. "Let's find out if this is cocaine."

Cocaine? He'd completely avoided my question. Which could only mean that the answer was yes, but he was too much of a rules boy to even admit it.

I was stunned. Both of them? Interested in me? I didn't even know how to respond.

Then a soul-deep chill of fear settled in my belly, and I knew exactly how to respond.

As they turned back to the car, I cleared my throat. "Gentlemen?"

They looked at each other, then both turned to face me. "What?" Griselda asked.

"Neither of you need to worry. I'm not interested in dating anyone ever again." I paused, then added softly. "I think that part of me broke when Stanley pointed that gun at my head. I loved him. I thought he loved me. To have the man you love be willing to shoot you in the face without hesitation…" My voice caught with sudden, unexpected emotion.

Despite my terror that Stanley would kill me if he found out I was spying on him, I'd never really, *really* believed he'd do it. Love was love, right? I'd been tormented by guilt when I was spying on him, torn between my fragile heart and what I knew was the right thing to do.

But when he'd pointed that gun at my forehead, there had been no hesitation or remorse in those ice-cold eyes. Love or not, he would have shot me at point-blank range and walked away without remorse.

The experience had killed a part of me, the part that had once been a little girl, dreaming of a prince charming to sweep her away from a life of crime. The part of me who had been a woman who had, for a very brief time, finally believed she was worthy of being really and truly loved.

I realized that both men were watching me way too intently, probably dissecting every expression on my face.

I raised my chin and cleared the emotion from my throat. "So, yeah, I'm done with romantic entanglements of any kind. Let's all be friends and keep Mia out of prison and the morgue. Cool?"

They looked at each other, and I saw something pass between them. What it was, I wasn't sure, but it was definitely some unspoken male psychic communication.

Whatever it was, they didn't tell me.

"No morgue," was Griselda's only response.

"No prison," was Devlin's.

Good. We could all leave that other stuff behind. "Great." I mustered up a smile as I hugged King Tut. The cat loved me unconditionally, right? So, that was all I needed. Plus Lucy and Hattie and Beau and everyone else I'd met in Bass Derby. I had enough. I had more than enough.

But as I watched the only two attractive, age-appropriate men in my life turn back to the lockbox in my car, I couldn't suppress the wave of regret that I was so broken. They were both the kind of men that a less-screwed-up woman could definitely appreciate as a way to move beyond her checkered past.

Then I thought about how awful I felt that I couldn't bring myself to get naked with either of them. Maybe my regret that I didn't want to throw them down and have my wicked way with them was a sign that all was not completely broken inside me. If it was, I wouldn't feel regret, right? I'd feel nothing, right?

So maybe, just maybe, there was hope for me.

Then Griselda snapped the lock with the bolt cutters and opened the lockbox.

Sitting in neat little rows were bags and bags of white powder.

CHAPTER 30

CHIEF STONE LEAPT out of the car and raced over. "Drugs!" he shouted gleefully. "It's drugs." He turned toward me. "Mia Murphy, you're under arrest for possession of drugs."

"Someone shut him up," Griselda muttered as he leaned over the box, studying the plastic baggies. He didn't touch them. He just looked at them.

Devlin leaned in next to him, ignoring the request, which meant I had to deal with Chief Stone.

I held up King Tut. "If you touch me, my cat will kill you."

Chief Stone stopped. "Threatening a police officer is a crime."

"I didn't threaten you. I advised you of a potential threat to your well-being, because I'm kind, thoughtful, and a good citizen." I tried to peer past him to see what my prince charmings were up to, but Chief Stone's hefty build was surprisingly difficult to see through.

"Put the cat down, and put your arms behind your back."

I hugged my cat. "No."

His eyes narrowed, and I realized my mistake. Griselda could protect me from Chief Stone right now, but once he left town, I was on my own with Chief Stone. I couldn't afford to make him my enemy. "I meant—"

"Mia." Griselda interrupted us.

We both turned to see him sitting on the bumper of my car, a plastic bag in his hand. The bag was open, and I knew he'd tested it. His face was unreadable, and so was Devlin's.

My heart started pounding. "Is it cocaine?" It was. I knew it was. My past was coming back for me—

"No."

"No?" I stared at him. "*No?*"

Griselda shook his head. "It's powdered sugar."

"Sugar? It's *sugar?*" At his nod, my legs gave out. I went down to my knees, and bent over, trying to catch my breath as emotions flooded me. *I was safe. Dear God, I was safe.* "You're sure?"

"Yep."

King Tut hopped out of my arms, and I covered my face with my hands, which were suddenly shaking. Tears filled my eyes, and I couldn't breathe.

"Mia." Devlin crouched down in front of me. "Breathe. It's okay."

I nodded, trying to catch my breath. Devlin had seen me have another panic attack, so we were in second-time-around category. It was amazing he still wanted to date me, knowing that I could fall apart, but hey, who could even begin to understand men, right?

"Take a breath."

I nodded and sucked in a shaky breath. "I didn't realize how scared I was that it was cocaine," I whispered. I couldn't look at Griselda. He'd never seen me fall apart before. I'd always kept it together in front of him, mostly because when I'd been in the middle of it, I hadn't been able to afford falling apart. The panic attacks had started after Stanley had gone to jail.

Devlin gently squeezed my shoulder. "I know. You've been through a lot. It's okay. No drugs."

His touch felt surprisingly reassuring. I knew he was an attractive guy who wanted to date me, but his hand on my shoulder still felt good. I felt safe, like I had someone who would grab me if I shot off a cliff to plummet to my death.

The emotions inside me began to settle, and I was able to take in a deeper breath. And then another.

"What's wrong with her?" Chief Stone asked.

His question brought me fully back. I opened my eyes, and saw Devlin's face right in front of mine. We met gazes and I saw the humor in his eyes at Chief Stone. I grinned, and we both started laughing.

"What? What are you laughing about? Does this mean I can't arrest her?"

"You can arrest her for other things," Griselda said. "But not for drugs. Not today."

I looked up at Griselda. "Don't give him ideas. He desperately wants to arrest me."

Griselda looked over at Chief Stone, who appeared to be pouting. "Mia's a good one," Griselda said. "I'd recruit her if I were you—"

"No." I shot to my feet. "I'm not working with the police again." Panic started to close around my chest, but Devlin came and stood close beside me.

"Wrong thing to say, Hawk," Devlin said. "Let her go."

"Yes, let me go." I clasped my hands on my head. I wanted to slide sideways behind Devlin and use him as a shield to protect me from Chief Stone and Griselda and their ideas about recruiting.

But I couldn't be weak.

So, instead, I stepped away from Devlin and took up my own space. "I'm not working with the cops," I said. "So no one ask me. Ever." I levered a gaze at the three of them, who did that man thing and looked at each other, but no one argued.

Good.

Instead, Griselda tossed the bag of powdered sugar at me. "Whoever put this in here definitely wanted it to look like cocaine, which meant they knew your past and wanted to get you busted, or at least freak you out. Who would do that?"

"Who?" The question startled me as I caught the bag. I hadn't gone there yet with my thinking. I'd been worried about who put actual cocaine in my car. Once I'd learned it was sugar, I'd stopped caring about the who. "That's a good question." I turned the bag over, looking for a name on it, for some indication of where it had come from, but the bag was just a regular bag.

"It might be a joke," Chief Stone said.

I turned to him. "Did someone call you and tip you off?"

He looked like he didn't want to play the "help Mia" game, but one glance at Griselda got his tongue working. "Yeah. I got an anonymous text. The number wasn't one I had in my phone, so…" he shrugged. "I don't know who sent it."

Griselda looked pained. "You ran out here to arrest Mia without verifying the tip?"

"I was going to open the car and look for the cocaine first," Chief Stone snapped. "Until you feds came in and interfered."

Griselda held out his hand. "Give me your phone so I can get the text off it. We can probably trace the number."

"Well, aren't you fancy." Chief Stone looked super annoyed, but he trotted over to be Griselda's minion.

While Griselda and Chief Stone worked on plans to track down whoever had faked the cocaine, I stayed where I was, trying to sort it out. Someone had definitely set me up to get arrested. Or hated. Why?

To get me put in jail.

That's why. It's the only thing that made sense. If I hadn't had personal friends in Griselda and Devlin, Chief Stone would have hauled me off to jail and kept me there for at least a day or two. Why?

"What are you thinking?" Devlin interrupted my thoughts, watching me closely.

"Someone wanted me in jail," I said slowly, still processing.

"Chief Stone would have arrested me. Who would want me in jail?"

His eyes narrowed. "I'd want you in jail so you'd stop investigating the murder. Maybe I'm not the only one. What did you figure out, Mia? Who did you make nervous?"

Oh…that was an interesting theory. I was going to take it as a compliment. I was so excellent that someone wanted me in jail? Yep, I was excellent. I'd take that. "I thought it was Felix, Kate, and Victor, but it's not. They just kidnap old people and duct tape charming women in their late twenties."

He swore. "I forgot about them. I need to get over there. Can you call Hattie and tell her to get my boat over here, ASAP? And don't bother telling me she doesn't have it. I don't have time for that. Just get my boat."

Yay for cops who were too busy to deal with the shenanigans of senior citizens and their pals. I quickly texted Hattie, and she said she'd be over in a moment. When I looked up, Devlin was still watching me. "You rattled someone," he said. "Think on it."

I frowned, trying to replay everything I'd done. Everyone I'd spoken to. "The powder got in there earlier in the day, so someone I spoke to at the party maybe?"

Devlin pulled out his notepad. "Who did you speak with at the party?"

I let out my breath, trying to think. "Not that many people. Jake. The dessert chef. Olympia. Kate. Beau. You. Esther. Glory."

"Maybe Glory did it before she died."

"Maybe." I bit my lip. Someone had known I was trying to find out who really killed them. If I didn't speak to them directly, they at least knew I was looking. Who had I poked? *Who?*

Devlin asked me a few more questions, and I decided to let him in on the whole situation at Felix's house, including the stolen recipes, and Lucy and I being duct taped.

After I caught him up, he lowered the notebook and stared at me. "You were duct-taped, left in a locked bathroom, and then the apartment was set on fire? Leaving you to *die*?"

"Yeah." I rubbed my jaw. Thinking. Thinking. Thinking. What had I missed? Had someone been in Glory's room?

"Mia."

I walked away from him, thinking out loud. "If someone wanted me locked up, then they must have figured I knew something, but not something serious enough they needed to kill me for. Just put me off the scent for a few days. That doesn't make sense."

"Mia—"

"But let's think. When they found out Griselda was coming to check the cocaine, they'd know that I wouldn't get arrested. So then, they decided to kill me and Lucy. I feel like that's pretty extreme, don't you think?" I must be so close to the truth. "But maybe not for a murderer. Better to murder again and go free than to let a former FBI spy figure out that you're the killer, right?

"Mia!"

I turned. "What?"

"I'm banning you from working on this case."

"Really?" I rolled my eyes. "You can't ban me from thinking and making random trips around town. Sorry about that, Dev, but that's the way it is."

"You almost *died*—"

"When?" Griselda walked over. "When did Mia almost die?"

I smiled at Griselda. "Earlier today I was duct taped, locked in a bathroom, and then the apartment was set on fire. If I weren't so resourceful and clever, your star witness would now be dead because Devlin failed to keep me safe." What? Me throw Devlin under the bus as a distraction? I would never do that.

Devlin groaned. "Mia—"

Griselda looked like he was going to strangle Devlin. "Is this true?"

"Absolutely," I said. "It's completely Devlin's fault."

Devlin narrowed his eyes at me. "How is it my fault? I told you repeatedly to stay out of it."

"You kept wanting to arrest Hattie, and did, in fact, so I had no choice but to find out who really did it. So, it's on you." I eyed Griselda. "It's on both of you, actually, because you wouldn't help me either. See what happens when you arrest my friends and refuse to believe me?"

A muscle flicked in Griselda's cheek. "Mia—"

"Did you really expect that you could tell me to lay low, and I would?" I put my hands on my hips. "Honestly, guys—"

"Your job is to stay alive," Griselda snapped. "You have a responsibility to lay low. Do not get involved with murderers, Mia. For hell's sake. What's wrong with you?"

"What is wrong with me?" Suddenly all the warm and fuzzy feelings I'd started having toward him vanished magically into thin air. "I don't like you anymore."

Griselda swore. "Mia, wait."

I was definitely *not* going to wait. I'd had enough.

I turned on my heels and stalked off to my store. I jogged up the steps, held the door for King Tut, and then slammed the door behind me.

Then remembered all the listening devices that had been found in the marina.

I pulled the door back open, and yelled at the XY contingent huddled by my car. "Are the bugs you found also fake?"

Griselda looked back at me. "No. They're high tech. They're an issue."

"Great." I waved at him. "Good to know. Thanks." I slammed the door shut again, and then leaned back against the door, trying to calm down and focus.

All I wanted was for the real murderer to be found, and Hattie to be in the clear. I simply wasn't going to waste energy thinking about Griselda and Devlin, romantic entanglements, and being recruited by cops.

I looked down at King Tut, who was sitting at my feet, staring up at me. "You're literally a menace to anyone who shows up at my place. How did someone get my car open with you around?"

King Tut began to purr.

"You were off fishing instead of guarding the place, weren't you?"

He didn't answer me, but his tail flicked with delight as he basked in whatever memory was filling his kitty cat brain. Who knew? Maybe he'd been on an all-day underwater swimming bender when my car had been invaded. But he'd warned me about it, so I supposed he was forgiven. But it still didn't give me any answers.

"Argh!" I hit my palm against the door and strode across the store. I rifled under the register and found a blank piece of paper and a pen. I started listing everyone I could remember talking to since we'd found Rutherford in the lake.

Wanda and Faith were the sixth and seventh names I wrote down.

I paused. The dynamic duo who were putting on the fundraiser? That didn't feel right.

I wrote down the mayor's name.

She was pretty cutthroat. She'd definitely set me up to save her town. But why would she care about me? Unless she thought her son had murdered Rutherford... I chewed the end of my pen, thinking about that one. I recalled that the chief had vomited at the sight of the last dead body he'd seen recently, so I scratched him off the list of potential murderers.

But would he have put the cocaine in there simply to have the fun of arresting me? Texting the tip to himself?

I didn't know him well, but I'd venture a guess that he'd definitely have done it...if he'd thought of it. Was he clever enough to have thought of it? I wasn't sure. But if he had done it, then it would mean that the cocaine scare had nothing to do with Rutherford's murder at all.

At that moment, my front door opened. Hattie and Lucy rushed in, cheeks flushed, looking delighted.

"Is that Griselda out there?" Lucy asked as she slammed the door shut.

"Yep." I nodded. "It wasn't cocaine. It was powdered sugar."

"That's great news!" Hattie said as she set my hairdryer on the counter.

"Griselda's so attractive," Lucy said as she flopped down on the pile of life jackets I was using for a bed. "I can't believe you never told us that."

Hattie leaned against the counter and folded her arms. "I agree with Lucy. You totally withheld info on him."

I literally didn't have time to deal with romantic leanings and Griselda. "Lucy! Would your cousin have set up the fake cocaine in my car himself?"

"No." She shook her head. "Absolutely not. First of all, that's way too clever for him. Second, he'd never intentionally do anything that illegal. He's a bit of an idiot, but he does believe in the law. So no."

"Good. That means whoever did it might relate to the murder." I told them how Devlin and I both thought that it might have been to get me arrested and stop investigating the murder, and then I showed them the list of names. Fortunately, murder was more interesting than Griselda's hotness, so that was good.

We'd just started to go over my list when there was a knock at the door.

I tensed. "Who is it?"

"Devlin."

I relaxed. "Come in."

The door opened, and he popped his head in. He saw Hattie and Lucy and then gestured at me. "Can I talk to you for a sec?"

"No, I'm good."

He ground his jaw. "I just wanted to say that I'm sorry that you almost got killed, and for trying to control you. I just like you and I don't want to be investigating your murder. That's it."

A little warm feeling settled in my heart. "Thanks," I said, meaning it. "I appreciate that."

He nodded. "Dinner still on for Tuesday?"

"It was never on."

"I'll be here at seven." He nodded at my pals, then left.

Lucy whispered. "That was super sweet—"

The door opened again, and Griselda leaned in. "Mia."

Hattie and Lucy both went silent, staring at him.

I stiffened. "What?"

"I need to speak with you."

Something about the edge in his voice made me nod. "Okay." I handed Lucy the paper. "Keep going over the names. I'll be right back."

She silently took the paper, still gawking at Griselda, which was almost funny. I mean, he was moderately attractive, but not gawk-worthy.

I stepped onto the porch. "What's up?" I left the door open so that Lucy and Hattie could eavesdrop more easily. No need for them to get hurt in the effort of listening.

Griselda frowned at me. "Devlin said you've had panic attacks before."

I sighed. "I thought you were going to talk about the bugs."

He rubbed his jaw. "Look," he said. "I need to say this. I'm sorry."

My gaze snapped to his. "That you dragged me into the under-cover thing?"

"No. I'd do that again every time." He searched my face. "But I'm sorry that it got to you. You're an incredible person, Mia. Don't let it beat you. The world needs you exactly as you are, shiny, bright, and stealing people's phones."

My throat tightened. Griselda and I didn't have the kind of relationship where he said things like that. I was sassy. He was stodgy. No personal details shared. I didn't know what to say, so I shrugged. "Okay."

Something flickered across his face. "I'm concerned about your safety, Mia. You're important to this case. I'd like you to reconsider Witness Protection, at least until the appeal is over."

"The appeal will take years."

He inclined his head. "Yes. But I can put in a word to get you somewhere you'd like. Another lake town, but a nicer marina. No murders." His face softened. "I'll make sure you're safe, Mia. It might help with the panic attacks to know that no one is going to find you."

There was absolute silence behind me, but I knew they were listening.

"No assassins," Griselda said. "No cocaine. No murders. A nicer marina. What do you say?"

I let out a breath. After being out here in the real world for a week, the idea of Witness Protection had far more appeal than it had a few days ago, especially with the bugs, the panic attacks, and the abundance of corpses.

Then I looked back over my shoulder at Hattie and Lucy. They were standing in the middle of the store, not even pretending not to listen. They were both watching me with wide eyes, and as I looked at them, Hattie shook her head once, and mouthed the word, "No."

My heart tightened. I now had friends, and those could never be replaced.

I turned back to Griselda. "I'm all set. Thanks."

Behind me, Lucy and Hattie let out cheers, and I grinned.

Griselda sighed. "If you change your mind, you know where to find me. I can arrange it within hours."

"I won't change my mind, but it would be great if you'd figure out who put the bugs there, and encourage Devlin to find the actual murderer instead of focusing on Hattie."

He grinned. "I can do that. In the meantime, stick around. I might have some questions for you."

"Will do." I held up my hand for a fist bump, and barely hid my surprise when the stodgy old goat fist-bumped me back.

He turned and jogged back down the stairs, heading toward my car. I shut the door and turned back to see Lucy and Hattie beaming at me. "What?"

Lucy clapped her hands. "They're fighting over you! That's so sweet."

"Right?" Hattie said. "A love triangle of badge-wielding hotness. It's every woman's dream."

"It's not my dream, and there's no love triangle." I could feel my cheeks heating up. "Look, did you check out the list? Who might have set it up?"

"I have no idea," Hattie said. "But I do know that there's definitely a little competition going on with the two of them and you. It's pretty adorable. I'm happy to give you free coaching on how to manage the adoration of multiple men. I've made an art of it, and I really do need a legacy to pass my wisdom on to."

Lucy grinned. "I want in on that, too. I'll be your legacy."

"Perfect. We'll start training after I'm cleared of murder."

"No!" I waved my hands. "I'm never dating again, and I definitely don't want to deal with multiple men, especially cops."

"I do hear you about cops," Hattie said. "They can be pretty obsessed with rules, and you're not really the rule type. But yours are so yummy—"

"Stop. You have to stop." I held up my hands. "We need to figure this out—" I noticed that King Tut was chewing on something. Frowning, I walked over and picked it up. It was the picture we'd snatched from Felix's house of the three teenagers jumping off the float into the water.

My gaze went to the tattoo on the middle girl's lower back. "Maybe this is why they burned Glory's room," I said. "To hide all evidence of the tattoo girl. Maybe there were more pictures than what we found." I held it up. "We all saw her portrait in the studio, but you two were gone. Maybe the arsonist saw me there. Maybe he knows I've seen the tattoo."

Hattie grabbed the picture and studied it. "We need to know who she is—"

As she spoke, someone knocked on the front door again. I looked up to see Agnes standing in the doorway. "Yoohoo," she said. "I know it's late, but I saw your lights on as I was going by." She held up a notebook. "I was making some sketches about my idea for the tattoo shop, like you suggested. I wanted to drop it off—"

"The tattoo shop?" My heart started racing at her reference to the abandoned storefront at my marina. How had I not thought of that? "How long has that been a tattoo parlor?"

Hattie's eyes widened. "At least fifteen years. It's been empty for the last few, but—"

"How many other tattoo parlors are in town?"

We stared at each other. "None," Lucy said. "that's it."

Holy crap! "We need to check it!" I raced for the door. "We gotta go, Agnes! We'll talk later!" I sprinted down the deck with Hattie and Lucy right behind me.

The door to the tattoo parlor was locked, and I didn't have a key, but I had the door open in less than thirty seconds anyway. I flung it open, flipped the switch on by the door, and raced inside.

CHAPTER 31

THERE WAS a thick layer of dust on everything, and I sneezed as I looked around. There was a black reclining chair and a massage table. Beside each one was a black metal cabinet with many drawers, which I assumed held all the supplies for inking. There was a sink, a front register, a couch, and the remains of some plants that had once been alive.

King Tut hopped up on the reclining chair and claimed it as one of his many thrones.

And all along the walls were dozens, maybe hundreds, of framed sketches of completed tattoo art. "I can't believe we didn't think of this." We all walked into the shop, gazing at the walls. Each framed image had the original tattoo sketch, and a photograph of the finished tattoo.

"Look for the butterfly tattoo!" My heart pounding, I went for the back wall, walking slowly as I inspected each photograph. I couldn't believe we hadn't thought to look at my own shop! Hattie and Lucy went to other walls, and we all started walking along, scanning.

"What are you guys looking for?" Agnes asked from the door, a frown on her face.

I glanced over at her. I suddenly recalled chatting with her at the party as well. I stiffened slightly. What if she were the murderer? She'd said she'd help clear Hattie's name and I'd left her making calls ostensibly on Hattie's behalf. But what if—?

Hattie looked over at me and raised her brows, and I saw Lucy glance over as well, both of them noticing my hesitation.

Well, if Agnes were the murderer, there was only one thing to do, and that was bring her into our little bubble. I took a breath. "We think that the murderer may have a butterfly tattoo." I walked over and handed her the photograph of the teenagers. "We think it might be the girl in the middle."

Agnes glanced at the picture. I watched her face very closely, and I saw her eyes widen ever so slightly, and her lips tightened for a split second.

Holy crap. She knew something. I was sure of it. But what did she know?

I pointed to the tattoo on the middle girl's lower back. "That's the tattoo we're looking for. Do you want to help us look? It would go faster with your help."

"Yes, sure." Agnes tucked the notebook into her purse and glanced around. "I'll take this wall."

She hurried over to the wall I'd been checking and began to scan it, moving very quickly, as if she knew exactly what she was looking for.

My hairdryer was on my store counter, not available for self-defense, so I quickly looked around for a substitute. I saw a small desk lamp, so I unplugged it, wrapped the cord around my hand, and picked it up. I pretended to be focused on another wall, but I watched Agnes in the reflections of all the framed art before me.

Hattie looked over at me, then she glanced at Agnes. She raised her brows and shook her head, but I shook mine right back at her.

"You cannot hit that woman in the face," Lucy whispered over my shoulder, startling me.

I glanced over my shoulder at her. "If she tries to murder me, I'm definitely hitting her in the face with this lamp."

Lucy's eyes widened. "You think—"

"I don't know. Let's give her space."

Lucy went back to her wall, but I saw her pick up another desk lamp. Hattie grabbed a small towel, which was very alarming. Hattie was badass enough to take down a murderer with a dishtowel?

Silently, the four of us looked at walls. Well, Agnes looked at the wall. The rest of us watched her and pretended to look at walls.

I heard a car outside, and Lucy ran to look out the front window. "Chief Stone and Griselda just left."

Oh…crap.

We were now alone with a possible murderer.

Sweat began beading on my forehead. How much longer did we wait? I took a breath. "I'm pretty sure that Rutherford was in love with the woman with that tattoo," I mused, as I eased my way along the wall. "Glory knew who the woman was, which is why I think she got killed."

Agnes didn't look over at me.

"You think Glory was going to rat her out?" Lucy asked.

"Maybe. Remember how Glory and Avery were arguing about the affair? What if they both knew about it?" I looked over at Agnes as a sudden idea shot through me. "What if Avery knew, too? What if she's next to be killed?"

Agnes stiffened. "My daughter is not involved." She looked out the window. "What's that?"

I glanced at Hattie and we all obligingly pretended to look out the front window. But in the reflection, I saw Agnes snatch a photo off the wall and slide it into her purse.

My heart started to pound. What if Agnes had a gun in that purse? It was a really large purse.

Agnes cleared her throat. "I just remembered I have some-where I need to be. I'll stop by tomorrow."

Hattie rolled her eyes as Agnes headed for the door, which Lucy was standing in front of, and I grinned. Honestly, did she really think we were that stupid? I began to ease toward Lucy. "Remember the champagne, Lucy? The champagne at the party?"

She stared blankly at me for a moment, then her face lit up as she remembered her role with the champagne-engagement-ring-stealing-incident: be a distraction. "That was the best champagne!" As she spoke, Agnes reached her. Lucy stepped into her path, beaming at her. "Agnes, I just wanted to say that I think it's so great that Avery is marrying Joel. He's such a nice guy—"

I was right behind Agnes, so I gave Lucy a nod.

She beamed at her. "I'm so happy for you!" She reached out and pulled Agnes into a big hug, knocking the woman off balance.

I immediately snatched the framed sketch from Agnes' purse. I jumped back as Agnes twisted free and ducked away. "I'll see you guys later—" She booked it toward the door as I flipped the frame over.

It was a closeup of the butterfly tattoo. The sketch and the finished tattoo.

Hattie and Lucy hurried over and they peered over my shoulder. We all looked at each other. Did we call Agnes back, or let her go, and hand the image over to the police? We'd have to admit our involvement, but with Griselda in town, I felt comfortable admitting my involvement. Griselda would believe me, and Devlin could interview Agnes and find out what she knew. Or what she'd done—

"I wish you hadn't done that."

We all looked up to see Agnes standing in the doorway, aiming a gun at us. Lucy and I immediately put our hands up.

Hattie, however, put her hands on her hips and glared at me. "Seriously, Mia? You couldn't have grabbed the gun from her purse when you got the picture? I feel like that was really missing the boat there."

"Pickpocketing is about being quick," I retorted. "I didn't have time to search it." But she had a point. I really needed to get a gun radar. There were way too many of them around.

"I could have hugged her for longer," Lucy said. "I'm way stronger than she is."

"That was well done, by the way," I said. "You totally picked up on my cue to distract her."

Lucy beamed at me. "Right? I could be your apprentice. After you die, I could carry on your mom's legacy."

"Me, die? Why do I have to die?"

"Because you're the one who always gets us in trouble."

"Plus, you have assassins after you," Hattie said. "Eventually, you're going to lose that battle—"

"Hey!" Agnes waved her gun. "I have a gun."

I sighed. "I know."

"We all know that," Lucy clarified. "You're not exactly being subtle about it."

I put my hands on my hips. "Agnes. Why do you have a gun?"

"Because I'm going to shoot you."

I narrowed my eyes, listening to her intonations. Watching her body language. The shift of her eyes. "Nope." I shook my head. "No, you're not going to shoot us." I threw up my hands. "You're not the murderer, are you? Why isn't anyone the murderer?"

"She's not the murderer?" Lucy asked. "Are you sure?"

"Yep. You can see the way her eyes are shifting. She doesn't want to shoot us." I put my hands down.

"I might shoot you anyway," Agnes shouted. "Put your hands back up!"

There was an edge to her voice that got my hands back up in a hurry. She definitely didn't want to shoot us, but she was willing to if she had to. Her hands were shaking, but there was a desperation in her eyes that I recognized.

It was the same expression I'd seen on the face of my ex-mother-in-law right before she'd almost shot me, when she'd been protecting her son.

Holy cow. That was a mama bear expression on her face. Which meant…"Avery," I whispered. "*Avery's* the one with the tattoo."

Agnes's face became cold. "I really wish you hadn't realized that," she said. "You leave me no choice." She looked around. "Hattie, you would have been great in the Founder's Society, but I'm going to have to put this on you as well. You're just so convenient."

Threatening Avery had flipped the switch in Agnes. I could see in her eyes now that she was ready to do it. One, two, three and we'll all be gone. *Crap.* "Agnes," I said urgently. "My marina is bugged. The FBI is recording everything. They'll know—"

"You lie. I know you lie." She gestured with the gun. "All of you down on the ground. Lie down."

Holy cow. She was going to execute us one by one? That was incredibly sociopathic, but also super sweet from Avery's perspective. Would my mom go on a murder spree to keep me out of prison? No. But whatever. That was irrelevant because we're about to die.

Frantically, I looked around for a way out. My gaze landed on King Tut, who had crouched down in the recliner. His yellow eyes were fastened on Agnes. He was utterly still, except the very tip of his tail was twitching.

He was going to attack her.

Which was admirable and fantastic, except that Agnes was completely unhinged with a loaded gun.

I knew how people reacted to King Tut attacking them, and I knew that she might shoot him as he exploded through the air to take her out.

The image of my sweet kitty being snatched out of the air by a bullet sent shards of terror and fury exploding through me.

Not.

My.

Cat.

I leapt forward, drawing Agnes's attention and the gun toward me. But this time, I didn't feel any fear. I didn't care about the gun. All I cared about was getting that instrument of death away from my cat. I didn't even have the wherewithal for some clever con artist repartee. I was all instinct, all protective mode, all cat mama.

"If you pull that trigger," I said in a low voice, "you will regret it on levels you can't even begin to imagine."

Her eyes widened. "Back up."

"No," I growled as I continued to walk right toward her. "You don't get to come in here and point the gun at those I love. You crossed the line, Agnes, and it's over now." My voice was alarmingly menacing, but I didn't care. I'd spent my life channeling the adorable, non-threatening persona of a charming con artist, but that wasn't remotely accessible to me right now.

On his chair, King Tut uttered a low growl that was ten times more menacing than my voice. Agnes's eyes flicked toward the cat, and the gun started to swing toward him.

"No!" The scream erupted from my throat, and I launched myself at her.

Her gaze snapped to me as I shot through the air. She raised the gun, and I swung my lamp. It knocked the gun out of her hand, and the gun ripped free. Lucy charged up behind me and tackled Agnes, throwing her to the ground as the gun skidded across the floor.

I whipped around, fear thick in my throat, just in time to see King Tut launch off the chair with a terrifying screech of murder. Lucy yelped and dove out of his way, and Agnes shrieked and covered her head. The vision of King Tut being carted off to Kitty Prison for murder flashed through my mind, and I dove on top of Agnes, covering her with my body.

King Tut landed on my back, his claws raking across my upper shoulders. He jabbed his claws past my head, trying to get to Agnes, who yelped and buried her face in my chest. I wrapped my arms around her, bracing myself as those daggered claws shot dangerously close to my face. "King Tut!" I shouted. "I've got this! Stop!"

He hissed and swung again, trying to get to Agnes, while Lucy shouted to call 911. Swearing, I took a breath, then let go of Agnes, rolled onto my back, and bear-hugged King Tut to my chest.

He fought me, his claws digging into me. "It's okay, sweetie," I crooned, wincing as his claws slashed. I could feel his little heart hammering, and I knew he was in panic mode. "It's safe, kitty cat. We're good. You don't need to save us anymore. Good kitty. Sweet kitty."

He suddenly stopped hissing, and his body went still.

I pulled my head back to look at him. His yellow eyes stared at me. I smiled. "It's really okay, sweetie. You were a rock star to save us, though. Truly."

His body suddenly softened, and he began to purr.

Thank heavens. I sagged to the floor and looked over to see that Lucy and Hattie were sitting on Agnes as she tried to get free. King Tut tensed, and I tightened my grip on him. "Agnes," I said. "It's over."

"It's not over—"

"Mom! I saw your car here on my way to dinner with Joel, and I wanted to ask you—" Avery appeared in the doorway, and her mouth dropped open. "What are you doing to my mom? Mom! Are you okay?"

"She tried to shoot us," I said, easing to my feet, trying to move King Tut back from Agnes.

"What?" Avery looked horrified, but not necessarily surprised. "Mom? Is this true? Why did you do that?"

"Avery, you need to leave," Agnes said. "Just pack a bag, get the cash from under my desk, and go."

"Go?" Avery looked back and forth. "Get off my mom!"

"Can't do that," Hattie said.

"Yes, not a wise move," Lucy agreed, settling more firmly on Agnes's backside.

I realized suddenly that Agnes's gun was too close to Avery's feet. Avery followed my glance and saw the gun. We both dove for it, but she got to it first. She held it up, pointing it at Hattie and Lucy. Honestly, that was probably better. I might have shot myself if I'd gotten my hands on it.

"Get off my mom," she ordered.

"No," Agnes shouted. "Don't shoot them, Avery! I'm protecting you! I'll take the blame. I murdered Rutherford and Glory," she shouted. "I did it. Put me in jail! My daughter is innocent!"

"Mom! Stop that! I'm taking the heat to save you!" Avery looked at me. "I killed Rutherford and Glory. Not my mom!"

"No! I did it," Agnes yelled. "It was me!"

"No, it was me!"

"Oh, for heaven's sake." I put my hands on my hips. "Who killed who? Let's share some truths, gang!"

"Mom!" Avery knelt down beside Agnes. "Let me protect you," she said. "I can handle prison much better than you can."

"Protect *me?*" Agnes frowned at her Avery. "I'm protecting *you.*"

"Me?" Avery frowned. "Protecting me from what?"

"From going to jail for Rutherford and Glory's murder!"

Avery paled. "Me? I thought you did it! I was protecting you!"

Mother and daughter stared at each other in shock. "Wait a sec," Agnes said. "You didn't kill them?"

"No!" Avery looked shocked. "Why would I kill them?"

"Because you had an affair with Rutherford and you were going to lose Joel because of it."

Avery sat down the rest of the way. "I didn't sleep with Rutherford. I had him paint the portrait as a wedding gift to Joel."

"But he loved you."

"I know. Glory was pissed about that, but it wasn't my fault."

I looked at Hattie and Lucy and raised my brows. I held up my hand. "Wait a second. You both thought the other one murdered Rutherford and Glory to protect Avery's marriage to Joel?"

They both nodded.

"But neither of you did?"

They both nodded again, then Avery's eyes filled with tears. "You really didn't kill them, Mom?"

"No. And you?"

Agnes shook her head, and then suddenly the mother and daughter were hugging and crying. Hattie got up and gestured to

Lucy to do the same. The moment they were off Agnes, the older woman sat up and pulled her daughter into her arms.

Lucy and Hattie came over beside me, but Lucy made sure to keep her distance from my cat. "So, Avery was the tattoo girl, but not a murderer," Lucy said with a sigh. "If it's not them, then who is it?"

"Hang on." It wasn't them, but it also wasn't over. The love that had gotten both of them to protect each other was real. I leaned forward. "Um, guys?"

The sobbing mother-daughter duo ignored me.

I cleared my throat. "If neither of you killed Rutherford, then the murderer is still out there, in this town, right now."

They both looked over at me.

I continued. "Someone set me up with fake cocaine to keep me from finding out the truth—"

"Oh, that was me," Agnes said. "Sorry about that. I was afraid you'd find out that Avery had done it."

I blinked. "That was you? I thought we were friends."

"We were friends, but then you were going to put my daughter in prison, so I needed to get you off the trail. Hattie was very convenient, so I appreciated that."

"Fake cocaine?" Avery interrupted. "What did you use?"

"Powdered sugar. I stole it from the kitchen at the Yacht Club. Felix had a lot of it."

Avery grinned. "That's so clever. Thanks for trying to protect me."

"Any time, baby. You know I'm there for you." Agnes frowned. "But why did you think I'd killed them?"

Avery's cheeks turned pink. "Well, because you knew that Rutherford and Kate were trying to break us up. Remember when you got all upset when I told you about the portrait, and you said that Rutherford could use that to make Joel think I'd slept with him? I kept replaying that conversation in my head, and I thought that you must have decided that you had to shut Rutherford up."

Agnes nodded. "I did think that, but that's why I figured you did it."

My mind was in overdrive, thinking and thinking, trying to put the pieces together. "Do you think that really was Rutherford's plan?" Rutherford was a blackmailer. He definitely could have set that up.

The mother and daughter looked at each other. "Maybe," Avery finally said. "He really didn't like me marrying Joel. He said I was a gold digger."

Agnes's eyes widened. "He knew you weren't. He loved you!"

I closed my eyes as the final pieces fell into place. Crap. I really hoped I wasn't right, but I had a feeling I was. Love made people do crazy things. "Avery," I said softly. "What if Rutherford loved you so much that he was willing to do whatever it took to stop you from marrying Joel?"

She stared at me. "Rutherford was murdered. I doubt he murdered himself and then came back to life to kill Glory."

Was she being intentionally obtuse? Probably. I didn't blame her. "He tried to threaten you out of it, and it didn't work." I kept my voice gentle. "So, what if he went to Joel and showed him the painting? If he told Joel that you two had an affair and that you guys were in love, it would have resonated with truth, because he did love you."

One of the fundamental tenets of being a con artist was to lace as much truth as possible into your lies. The most truth, the more believable.

"What are you saying?" Avery asked.

But I saw the look of stunned anguish on Agnes's face, and I knew she'd just came to the same conclusion I had. "If Joel had believed you slept with Rutherford, he would have called off the wedding, right? Rutherford would have had you."

She blinked. "Rutherford would never have had me. I didn't love him."

"You know that. I know that. But did Rutherford know that?"

She stared at me, her mouth in a surprised "O."

"Do you think," I said gently, "that Joel might have killed Rutherford for sleeping with you? And then killed Glory because she found out he'd done it?"

Avery stared at me, her face ashen. "Joel?" she whispered.

I saw the anguish on her face, and I felt like my own heart was being stabbed. I knew what it was like to have your forever guy turn out to be a sociopathic criminal. Devastating was a good word to describe it.

Hattie looked at me, then she pulled one of the notes from her recipe box out of her pocket. "Is this Joel's handwriting?"

Holy crap. Was it *Joel* who'd broken into Hattie's kitchen and stuffed the recipe box and scrawled murderer everywhere?

Avery snatched the note and scanned it. Then the paper fell out of her hand onto the floor. "No. He didn't do it. I'll go talk to him. He'll explain—"

Holy cow. It had been Joel. I couldn't believe I'd missed that one.

Agnes grabbed her daughter's ankle as Avery tried to spring for the door. "Aves, honey? Maybe you need to let the police talk to him first. Just in case."

"He's innocent. Let me go. I'll just talk to him. He's right outside—"

"Outside?" Alarm shot through me.

"Yeah, he was driving—"

"I'm not outside." Joel suddenly loomed in the doorway, all six-foot-something of athletic muscle mass and agile youth.

I sucked in my breath at the look on his face. Icy-blue ruthless-ness in his eyes. Absolute lack of remorse.

I'd seen that expression before, on my ex-husband's face when he pulled the gun out and pointed it at my head.

It was the face of a murderer.

And we were alone with him.

CHAPTER 32

HATTIE AND LUCY sucked in their breath, and I knew they'd gotten the same vibe off him.

Joel was our murderer.

And now that I was looking at him up close, I realized something else: he was the boy in the photograph we'd taken from Glory's house. I recognized the birthmark on his forearm, which hadn't been visible when he'd been in the suit at the party.

He'd been friends with Glory and Avery as teenagers.

And yet, he'd killed Glory anyway.

With friends like that…right?

"Avery," he said quietly. "Get up."

She quickly rose to her feet. "Joel. You didn't kill Rutherford, did you?"

The rest of the room stared at Joel, waiting for his answer. If he confessed, he'd definitely kill us. If he denied it, then he was lying. Either way, we had only moments. I thought hard and fast, trying to think of a plan.

As I struggled to come up with a way to avoid being murdered, I saw the headlight from a boat drift up to my dock, and then disappear. Who had just arrived?

No one else seemed to notice. Joel looked at Avery. "I didn't mean to kill Rutherford. He invited me out fishing, and told me that you'd had an affair and you loved each other."

She covered her mouth with her hand. "And you believed him? You believed I'd do that?"

"No, but I was mad. We fought, he hit his head and fell in. By the time I got him out…" Pain flashed across Joel's face. "He was dead."

I remembered then that Rutherford had been Joel's favorite uncle. That they'd been close. Bummer for him. If you believed the story. I wasn't sure how accidental it was, but I'd give him the benefit of the doubt. "What about Hattie's anchor?"

Joel's gaze flickered toward me. "It was in the boat. He said it was Hattie's boat."

Hattie narrowed her eyes. "He borrowed my boat?"

"Yeah."

He was lying. I closed my eyes as I finally figured it out. "You knew, didn't you? You already knew about the portrait, and you invited him out fishing that night. And you took Hattie's boat because you planned to set her up for it all along."

His gaze settled on me, and a cold chill slid down my spine. *Crap.* I should have known better than to tell him I'd figured it out. Dammit! I needed to pivot and fast. "Or not," I amended. "Rutherford used to borrow Hattie's boat all the time, didn't he, Hattie? That would make sense."

Hattie's gaze slid to me, and then she nodded. "He did used to borrow my boat," she agreed. "I'm sure he took it."

Yay for Hattie being quick on the uptake!

Avery chewed her lower lip. "And Glory?"

Joel sighed. "I couldn't go to prison, Avery. She wanted money. I said no. She wasn't going to give up." He shrugged. "I did what I had to do."

He said it without any remorse or guilt whatsoever.

Sociopath, anyone?

King Tut began to growl, a low, menacing sound that reverberated through my arms. I heard a low burst of laughter from outside, and I realized that Beau and Esther were the ones who had arrived, totally clueless as to what was going on inside.

I backed up slightly, and my movement caught Lucy's attention. I raised an invisible glass to her, as if I were toasting Joel, giving her the "be like a champagne distraction" silent code. She nodded once, and immediately dropped to the floor with a groan and didn't move.

Everyone turned to look at her, and I pulled out my phone as I began to inch my way around the side of the shop. *Beau. Joel's the murderer. He's in here with a gun. Call 911.*

Lucy began to moan. Hattie raced to her side and started shouting at Agnes to call for an ambulance.

Beau texted back after a moment. *That little shit. I hate rich people.*

Really? That was his response. *Beau! Did you call 911? And you're rich, too.*

I called. I know I'm rich. But I'm the good rich. There was a long delay, then... *This is Rogue. I have Beau's phone. We're coming in to rescue you. Everyone away from the front window.*

Oh, God. *Don't drive into my window! Just wait for the police!*

You risked your life to save us. That means we owe you the same.

No. No. No. I couldn't be responsible for anything happening to them. *You do NOT owe me the same. Get back in the boat and leave.*

Radio silence from here on out. You know what to do. May the Force be with you.

Rich people were so freaking entitled! Did they have no common sense? *Get. Back. In. The. Boat.*

There was no reply, but I heard a crash and a curse from the side of the building.

Fortunately, Lucy and Hattie were making such a ruckus that no one else noticed. Avery was shouting at Joel for murdering her best friend, and Agnes was also yelling at Joel, but I couldn't tell what her beef was. She actually sounded like she was still trying to get Avery to marry him, but I had to be wrong about that.

Joel looked like he was about to start taking people out one by one.

Either way, no one seemed to be noticing me, which I figured was going to last for another couple seconds at most.

My phone buzzed. *We can't drive through the front window. Can't get your marina truck up the deck stairs. It's too narrow.*

Thank heaven for that.

What should we do?

I glanced around, trying to think. Joel was too big and strong for any of us to take down. And he was armed, sociopathic, and already well-practiced in the art of murder. What was his weakness?

There was no physical limitation that was enough for us to beat him, so it had to be psychological. I was an expert in that from my childhood. Assessing and exploiting vulnerabilities of the elite.

Joel was elite. Which means he was the target I'd been trained for since birth.

My gaze went back to Avery. Love. That was his weakness. Just as it had been mine, when I'd been blind to the truth about Stanley.

"He loves you, Avery," I said.

Avery stopped yelling and looked at me.

They all looked at me.

"My husband tried to shoot me when I made a mistake." Not that it was a mistake, but close enough. "You're lucky to have someone who loves you enough to do whatever it takes to make it possible for you to marry him."

Avery's eyes widened. "What?"

But Joel was watching me. Listening.

Keeping King Tut in my arms, I began to walk toward him. "I was ditched by my dad, just like you, Avery. But I fell for a guy who chose his own safety over mine. Not like Joel. He sacrificed himself so that he could marry you and protect you forever."

Hattie cleared her throat. "I love guys like that," she said. "Such keepers."

Avery frowned at me. "You can have him. He's a killer. Did you not realize that?"

Seriously? Avery was going to get us all murdered. "That's why your mom was willing to sacrifice herself to save your marriage to Joel. Because she knows how lucky you are, right, Agnes?"

Agnes was frowning at me.

Did she realize what I was doing? I really hoped so.

I stopped in front of Joel, who was still aiming the gun at us. Me, specifically. "Joel," I said, keeping my voice as quiet as I could. "We all know that Rutherford's death was an accident. And Glory's can be, too. We'll all back you up. But if you shoot any of us now, it's over. You'll go to prison, and Avery will be alone. She needs you, so don't mess this up. Be the guy who will have her back forever."

My heart was pounding as I watched his gaze flick to Avery. Had I called it right that he'd listen to a story about love and protecting Avery? If not, I'd be the first to die.

"I love you, Avery. I know you didn't sleep with Rutherford."

She nodded. "I didn't."

He looked down at the gun, then back at me. "Glory was an accident."

"Absolutely. Right, guys?"

"You bet," Hattie called out.

Lucy sat up. "Tragic accident. That girl drinks too much."

Agnes spoke up. "Accident," she agreed, but I could hear the tension in her voice.

She was going to go after him if he threatened Avery.

Avery was still so close to him. He could turn on her in a heartbeat.

We all held our breath, waiting, hoping. "Avery needs you, Joel," I said. "If you shoot us, you'll go to prison, and you'll never have her." It was the same logic I'd tried on my mother-in-law when she'd been planning to assassinate me.

It hadn't worked with her.

But she'd been mama-bear insane.

Joel was simply jealous-murderer insane.

After a long moment, he lowered the gun.

"Give it to Hattie," I said. "Avery, give yours to Hattie, too." I didn't want to take control of the guns, but I had faith in Hattie.

Hattie stood up and walked over, holding out her hand for the guns. Joel looked down at his gun, and then, to my relief, he set it in Hattie's hand. She quickly took it and passed it back to Lucy as we all took a breath of relief.

But as she held out her hand to Avery for her pistol, the bride-to-be raised her gun and aimed it at Joel. "Glory was my best friend," she said, her voice thick with emotion and grief. "And you killed her to protect yourself? And you call that love?"

Oh…no. I totally underestimated the power of the girl bond.

"Avery!" Agnes gasped. "Don't—"

At that moment, the front door flew open. Rogue leapt inside, holding a waterski she'd apparently stolen from my store. She swung it hard, hitting Avery in the head on the backswing. As Avery fell backwards, Rogue swung it toward Joel's head.

He ducked and she went flying past him, crashing into Hattie.

Beau appeared in the doorway, caught my eye, and winked. Then he tossed me the hairdryer I'd left on my counter. I caught it, whipped the cord around my wrist, and then swung it as hard as I could. Joel was still looking at Rogue when the hairdryer caught him under the chin.

As they say, the bigger they are, the harder they fall.

CHAPTER 33

EIGHTEEN HOURS LATER, I was firmly in the middle of what might have been the best afternoon of my life. Why? Because I belonged.

True to her promise to Griselda, Mayor Stone had green-lighted the fundraiser at the marina. After Devlin and Chief Stone had finished dealing with Joel and sorting out who needed to be arrested and who didn't, Wanda and Gladys had come charging into the marina at five in the morning to prepare for the fundraiser.

Those two women were a force, and I'd recruited my pals to help. Because it wasn't simply for the good of the Lake Association. It was for the Eagle's Nest Marina as well.

And now, two hours into the fundraiser, my little marina was teeming with activity. The landscaping and painting had been finished twenty minutes before the first guest had arrived. The cleaning company had finished their successful fumigation of my apartment an hour earlier. I'd moved my personal gear upstairs and worked like a fiend to make the marina store look presentable. Balloons, Murphy's Oil Soap for the floor, and a few flowering plants had glossed over much of the age and neglect. The only thing missing was Cargo, my only employee, but he hadn't shown up for work today. I still had yet to meet him, but I had hope.

It wasn't perfect, but it was a real, legitimate start.

People were milling around, down on the dock, on the deck, under the tent that was in the parking lot. Laughing. Chatting. Having fun. Raising money for the lake I already loved.

I was standing under King Tut's tree, which was on the shoreline, just beyond the parking lot. He was perched on a lower branch, watching the crowd, but staying out of it.

"Well done, my friend." Hattie put her arm around me. "You did it."

"It's awesome!" Lucy slung her arm over my shoulders from the other side, sandwiching me in the middle.

Warmth filled me. "Pretty amazing, right?"

Hattie nodded. "You'll have business after today. People like the flowers." She slanted a glance at me. "They like *you*."

I grinned. "I think it helped that you told everyone I'm amazing."

"Of course it did. You're lucky I like you."

"I agree."

Lucy squeezed my shoulder. "Happy Anniversary, Mia."

I looked over at her. "For what?"

"One week ago today, I met you in the parking lot." She pointed to the spot in the parking lot where she'd been unloading my mail when I'd first arrived in Bass Derby. "Right over there."

Hattie whistled. "I can't believe it's only been a week. I feel like you've been haunting me for several lifetimes."

I laughed. "I think it's the other way around. I did tell you that I moved to Bass Derby to have a peaceful, law-abiding life, right?"

Hattie winked. "Sorry, I don't recall that at all."

"Me either," Lucy said. "I'm pretty sure you said you moved here to teach us how to be brilliant criminals who bend the law to protect the innocent."

I held up my hands. "No more. That's it. You've both been a murder suspect. That's it. There's no one else left."

Hattie grinned. "There are always more adventures coming. That's the way life is."

"Right? Kinda like the two delicious adventures stomping their testosterone-laden way over here right now," Lucy said.

At her words, I noticed Griselda and Devlin walking toward us. Griselda had switched to jeans and sneakers, and Devlin was wearing the same. They looked remarkably similar, both with that law enforcement vibe.

I glanced at Hattie. "Don't you have somewhere to go?"

"Nope."

"I don't either," Lucy declared.

I rolled my eyes at them, then pasted a smile on my face as the men approached. "Good afternoon, gentlemen."

Devlin shoved his hands in his pockets as he surveyed me. "You impressed me."

Happy warmth surged through me. "In what way?"

"You figured out a lot that I hadn't seen." He was studying me shrewdly. "You know people, don't you?"

I shrugged. "My mom taught me to be an observer of people."

"Next time, how about we work together?" He held up his hand when I started to shake my head. "I'm not recruiting you or trapping you. Just asking if you'd find it fun to solve more puzzles."

I narrowed my eyes at him, then glared at Griselda. "You told him to phrase it that way, didn't you?"

"Nope. I did."

I noticed then that Beau was standing off to the side. I hadn't seen him approach, but he was there. "You?"

He nodded. "You like puzzles. They light you up. You're more interesting when you're sparkling."

"Interesting?" That word had a distinctly more ominous tone when uttered by Beau than it had when Devlin and Griselda had been using it. I put my hands on my hips. "I'm not here to enter-tain you."

"Nope. You're not. But it works out that way." He nodded.

"Glad you're in town, Mia. We needed you." He gave me a little wink, and then ambled back toward the docks. He didn't pause to speak to the people who tried to chat him up. He just headed for his boat, which was tied up at the end slip. As he climbed in, he looked over at me. "Mia!" he shouted.

A few people looked over to see what the town's resident celebrity was bellowing about.

"What?" I yelled back.

"I'd like to rent a slip here for my boat. Got space for me?"

I grinned. "You keep your boat at your house."

"I know, but I like to come to Hattie's Café for breakfast. I want to rent a slip here. I like the vibe. This slip, in fact. I don't care what it costs. I want it."

People were listening to Beau Hammerly declare his loyalty to the Eagle's Nest Marina and Hattie's Café. "I love that man," I whispered. Then I raised my voice. "Payment due at the start of the month."

"Deal." He started his engine, the loud roar a beautiful sound. He didn't bother to wave. He just backed out of the docks and headed down the lake, without even looking back. But I waved anyway.

"That man has never been nice to anyone," Hattie mused.

"Except you?"

She shook her head. "He was never nice to me in the way he's nice to you."

Lucy put her arm over my shoulder. "Everyone loves Mia."

"Not everyone," Griselda said.

We all looked over at him, and I realized his face was grim. "What?"

"We tracked the listening devices to a house nearby. It was vacant, but the tech was impressive." Griselda frowned. "You're being watched by someone with financial and technical resources, Mia."

I let out my breath. "I'm not going into witness protection."

"I know. I'm going to send someone to you."

Devlin frowned. "A bodyguard? I'm watching her."

"Not twenty-four seven." Griselda nodded toward the tattoo parlor. "Your new tenant will be here in a few days. I'm having them set up shop there. They'll even pay rent. Be nice."

"I'm always nice." But seriously? Another law enforcement stalker? "Is there another option?"

"No." He glanced at his watch instead of flooding me with other, more palatable options. "I need to go. Stay in touch, Mia." He glanced at Devlin, giving him a hard look that very clearly warned the local cop not to get personally involved with me.

As he strode off, heading toward the nifty black SUV that nearly screamed federal agent, I tapped Devlin's arm. "So what happened? Who did you arrest?"

He raised his brows. "Agnes and Avery get to walk in exchange for sharing details about Joel. The Church Island crew are all facing charges."

Yes. "And Joel?"

"Once we knew to look at him, we found plenty of evidence." He looked over at Hattie. "We located your missing boat against the shore in Dead Man's Pond. No anchor in it. We found beers that match beers from Joel's fridge. We were able to lift prints from them, and we're expecting to match his prints. The bug picked up him muttering to himself while he trashed Hattie's kitchen, so we've got him on that as well."

"The bugs did?"

He grinned. "They came in handy."

"He didn't happen to mutter a confession, did he?"

Devlin shook his head. "He admitted he torched the chapel to burn up any evidence that Avery had modeled for Rutherford. He also set fire to Glory's apartment. He didn't know what evidence Glory had. It was just bad luck that you were there at the time."

I let out a breath. "So, no one actually tried to murder me?"

"Not yesterday, no."

It was amazing how good that felt. "What about the murders? Did he confess to those?"

Devlin shook his head. "He admitted that Rutherford and Glory both died at his hands, but claims they were both accidents. We're looking into it. I'm sure we'll find what we need."

I knew that was probably more info than he was supposed to give us, and I appreciated it very much. I put my arm around Hattie, and felt her shoulders sag with relief. "So, it's over?" I asked. "Hattie's in the clear?"

He nodded, meeting Hattie's gaze. "All clear."

She nodded, and I was pretty sure I saw her eyes tear up for a split second, making me realize that despite her bravado, she'd been aware of the very real threat against her. Lucy threw her arms around both of us, and we group-hugged fiercely.

By the time we finished, we were all a little misty-eyed.

"I think it's time to join Rogue for some champagne," Hattie announced. "She brought her own stash."

Rogue had picked the table with the best view and kicked everyone out of it, except for the Seam Rippers and us. They were all making a lot of noise and having fun, which I felt was a much better choice than doing that on a lake during a thunderstorm.

"I'm in." Lucy tucked her arm through mine and Hattie's. "Let's go."

Devlin caught my arm as I started to leave. "Mia. Do you have a sec?"

"No—"

"Yes she does!" Hattie and Lucy took off, giggling as they abandoned me.

Resigned, I turned to face Devlin. I put my hands on my hips and raised my chin, summoning my resistance to his attractive hotness. "What?"

"I know you went through a lot with your ex. I don't want to make you uncomfortable." His brown eyes searched mine with just a little too much understanding. It was as if he could see right through my façade of toughness. "I would still like to take you to dinner, but I get it if you want me to back off. Your call."

I bit my lip. "So, you're totally ignoring Griselda's warning not to date me?"

He grinned. "Absolutely. I hate rules. That's why I left."

"Left where?"

His smile faded, and he ignored my question. "What's the call, Mia? Do you want me to back off?"

I took a breath. Yes. No. I didn't know. "Why doesn't Griselda want me to date you?"

"A number of reasons, but the primary one is that he wants to date you."

I blinked. "He doesn't."

"He absolutely does."

"What did you tell him?"

"I told him he had to ask you out. If he didn't, I wasn't waiting for him to come around." He cocked an eyebrow. "Did he?"

"No." Did I want him to? No. I didn't. I didn't want either of them. Did I?

At that moment, King Tut meowed. I looked up just in time to see him let go of the branch and drop. I caught him instinctively, and cradled him against my chest as he levered a yellow stare at Devlin.

Devlin reached out and scratched King Tut on the head. My cat allowed it. Was that a sign?

It didn't matter.

Even if my cat liked Devlin, I wasn't going to date him. "I'm not going to date you."

He narrowed his eyes. "But—?"

How had he heard that silent, implied "but?" I thought I'd hidden it well. The man was much too capable for my liking. "But I do need to eat, and I hate cooking. So you can show me the local food scene. Pick a place I'll be happy to discover, and I'll meet you there to eat."

A small smile played at the corner of his mouth. "How about I pick you up?"

I cocked my head. "Maybe next time."

His smile widened. "There's going to be a next time?"

"You're very irritating."

He held up his hands in surrender, but he still looked pleased. "Right. I won't get too far ahead. I'll find a place and text you where and when. Good?"

"Good." I took a breath. "The girls are waiting. I'll see you later." I didn't wait for his nod. I just spun around and hustled back to the party.

But as I jogged, I couldn't keep from smiling. And when a table full of silver-haired Seam Rippers saw me coming, raised their glasses, and shouted my name, my smile got even bigger.

I was home.

———

WHAT TO READ NEXT?

If you loved *Top Notch*, I have good news! The next Mia book, *Gone Rogue,* is up for preorder! Go grab it now *right here*, so you don't forget to order it! In the meantime, if you're up for that same fun and you enjoy some magic with your humor, try my *Immortally Sexy* romantic comedy series (it has some hilarious sexy times in it, so be forewarned!) or the *Guardian of Magic* paranormal mystery (contains some clever profanity, so also be forewarned! No sexy times, though!).

If you love cowboys, try my deeply heartwarming, family-oriented (but with a little spice!) *Wyoming Rebels* series or the spinoff *Hart Ranch Billionaires* series. Preorder the newest book, *A Rogue Cowboy's Christmas Surprise* (Coming Late 2022) or start with the first first book in the *Wyoming Rebels* series, *A Real Cowboy Never Says No.*

If you want more small-town stories with heart-melting, emotional romances, you'd love my *Birch Crossing* series! Get started with *Unexpectedly Mine* today, in which a billionaire hero gets stranded in a small town and gets his world upturned by a sassy single mom and her daughter.

Is dark, steamy paranormal romance your jam? If so, definitely try my award-winning *Order of the Blade* series, starting with book one, *Darkness Awakened*. Jump into the world of soulmates, passion, danger, and immortal warriors who will do whatever it takes to save the woman who steals his heart, no matter what the cost. Don't we all want a guy like that?

A QUICK FAVOR

Hey there, my friend!

It's Mia! Tell me, tell me! What did you think of *Top Notch?*

I hope you loved it, and my suffering wasn't for naught.

Just kidding. No suffering here! I love my life. And my hairdryer. And my cat. And my friends. And… well… the list goes on and on. And just wait until my next book, *Gone Rogue,* comes out. More fun on the way!

I hope I gave you some feel-good entertainment in these pages! If I did, it would rock if you'd do me a favor and help get the word out, so that other folks can find their way here.

Tell a friend. Tell an enemy. Leave a note for your barista.

Reviews are also incredibly helpful to encourage new readers to make that leap and try a new book. It would be super fab if you'd consider taking a couple minutes and jotting one or two sentences on the *etailer* and/or Goodreads telling everyone how freaking amazing I am. Or King Tut. Because we all know that he's the best. Even the short reviews really make an impact!

Thank you again for reading my story! I can't wait for you to see what happens next!

Smooches,

Mia

BOOKS BY STEPHANIE ROWE

MYSTERY

MIA MURPHY SERIES
(COZY MYSTERY)
Double Twist
Top Notch
Gone Rogue

ROMANCE

PARANORMAL

ORDER OF THE BLADE SERIES
(PARANORMAL ROMANCE)
Darkness Awakened
Darkness Seduced
Darkness Surrendered
Forever in Darkness
Darkness Reborn
Darkness Arisen
Darkness Unleashed

Inferno of Darkness
Darkness Possessed
Shadows of Darkness
Hunt the Darkness
Darkness Awakened: Reimagined

IMMORTALLY SEXY SERIES
(FUNNY PARANORMAL ROMANCE)
To Date an Immortal
To Date a Dragon
Devilishly Dating
To Kiss a Demon

HEART OF THE SHIFTER SERIES
(PARANORMAL ROMANCE)
Dark Wolf Rising
Dark Wolf Unbound

SHADOW GUARDIANS SERIES
(PARANORMAL ROMANCE)
Leopard's Kiss

NIGHTHUNTER SERIES
(PARANORMAL ROMANCE)
Not Quite Dead

NOBLE AS HELL SERIES
(FUNNY URBAN FANTASY)
Guardian of Magic

THE MAGICAL ELITE SERIES
(FUNNY PARANORMAL ROMANCE)
The Demon You Trust

DEVILISHLY SEXY SERIES

BOOKS BY STEPHANIE ROWE

(FUNNY PARANORMAL ROMANCE)
Not Quite a Devil

CONTEMPORARY ROMANCE

WYOMING REBELS SERIES
(CONTEMPORARY WESTERN ROMANCE)
A Real Cowboy Never Says No
A Real Cowboy Knows How to Kiss
A Real Cowboy Rides a Motorcycle
A Real Cowboy Never Walks Away
A Real Cowboy Loves Forever
A Real Cowboy for Christmas
A Real Cowboy Always Trusts His Heart
A Real Cowboy Always Protects
A Real Cowboy for the Holidays
A Real Cowboy Always Comes Home
SERIES COMPLETE

THE HART RANCH BILLIONAIRES SERIES
(CONTEMPORARY WESTERN ROMANCE)
A Rogue Cowboy's Second Chance
A Rogue Cowboy's Christmas Surprise (Nov. 2022)

LINKED TO THE HART RANCH BILLIONAIRES SERIES
(CONTEMPORARY WESTERN ROMANCE)
Her Rebel Cowboy

BIRCH CROSSING SERIES
(SMALL-TOWN CONTEMPORARY ROMANCE)
Unexpectedly Mine
Accidentally Mine
Unintentionally Mine
Irresistibly Mine

MYSTIC ISLAND SERIES
(SMALL-TOWN CONTEMPORARY ROMANCE)
Wrapped Up in You (A Christmas novella)

CANINE CUPIDS SERIES
(ROMANTIC COMEDY)
Paws for a Kiss
Pawfectly in Love
Paws Up for Love

SINGLE TITLE
(CHICKLIT / ROMANTIC COMEDY)
One More Kiss

ROMANTIC SUSPENSE

ALASKA HEAT SERIES
(ROMANTIC SUSPENSE)
Ice
Chill
Ghost
Burn
Hunt (novella)

BOXED SETS

Order of the Blade (Books 1-3)
Protectors of the Heart (A Six-Book First-in-Series Collection)
Wyoming Rebels Boxed Set (Books 1-3)

For a complete list of Stephanie's books, click here.

ABOUT THE AUTHOR

New York Times and *USA Today* bestselling author Stephanie Rowe is the author of more than fifty published novels. Notably, she is a Vivian® Award nominee, and a RITA® Award winner and a five-time nominee. She loves her puppies, tennis, and her family. She's pretty sure dead bodies are better in fiction than real life, but hey, never say never, right?

www.stephanierowe.com

ACKNOWLEDGMENTS

Special thanks to my beta readers. You guys are the best!

There are so many to thank by name, more than I could count, but here are those who I want to called out specially for all they did to help this book come to life: Alyssa Bird, Ashlee Murphy, Bridget Koan, Britannia Hill, Deb Julienne, Denise Fluhr, Dottie Jones, Heidi Hoffman, Helen Loyal, Jackie Moore Kranz, Jean Bowden, Jeanne Stone, Jeanie Jackson, Jodi Moore, Judi Pflughoeft, Kasey Richardson, Linda Watson, Regina Thomas, Summer Steelman, Suzanne Mayer, Shell Bryce, and Trish Douglas. Special thanks to my family, who I love with every fiber of my heart and soul. And to AER, who is my world. Love you so much, baby girl! And to Joe, who keeps me believing myself. I love you all!

Thank you to Elizabeth Turner Stokes for the most AMAZING cover. I am in awe of your vision and your talent. Plus, you're the coolest chick ever.

Huge, mega thanks to Lee Conary, the owner of Kezar Lake Marina, for the inside scoop on marina life on a Maine lake. Thank you for all the hours you spent hanging out with me, filling my head with so much good info. Anything I got wrong about boats, boating, lakes etc is definitely on me, not him. You rock, Lee!

Printed in Great Britain
by Amazon

86640881R00210